SWIMMING IN THE DARK

Paddy
RICHARDSON

SWIMMING
IN THE DARK

upstart press

For Jim

A catalogue record for this book is available from the National Library of New Zealand

ISBN 978-1-927262-05-4

An Upstart Press Book
Published in 2014 by Upstart Press Ltd
B3, 72 Apollo Drive, Rosedale
Auckland, New Zealand

The author gratefully acknowledges the assistance of a Creative New Zealand grant in the writing of this novel.

Designed by CVdesign Ltd
Printed by Printlink, Wellington

I will go back to my homeland,
I will cease my wandering.
My heart is still; it stays for its chosen hour.
In spring, the earth flowers
And is green once more
Everywhere and forever; everywhere and forever
The horizon is lit with blue.

'Der Abscheid' from Mahler's *Das Lied von der Erde,*
text by Hans Bethge

Part One

1

It was the cold that made her fall. She was going home, cutting across the park and there was still frost on the ground, the grass solid and glistening from that morning and the previous days of icy mornings. Her breath hovered in the air in front of her.

It was nearly five, already getting dark and the fog which had drifted like powdery ash around the town for weeks was down again. She was on her way back from school; late because she'd been in the art room. Her class was making a mural they'd planned together to fill an empty wall of the assembly hall. The general theme was New Zealand, though they'd argued about that, some of the kids wanted it to be about Alexandra while others thought that was way too narrow and boring — not everyone comes from Alex, dickhead — but they'd sorted it and now they were working on what was to be a giant mosaic of paintings and prints and photographs.

Using the words was Serena's own idea. She could see it in her head; all the words coiling up and across, intersecting the images. She was the one who was putting together the slivers of poems, the fragments of news pulled out from the local paper, the words Miss called colloquialisms, all of them joined and jumbled together with the fonts mixed up so you had something like: 'sweet-as the something-special smell of you when the sun Big Frost Hurts Clyde Couple Marry cakes the steady drum-roll sound you make when the wind as House Burglary Bungled, Burns drops'.

Like that.

She was walking fast, hunched against the cold, her hands

shoved low into her pockets. The words were what she was thinking about: fitting what she already had together, figuring out what she still needed and where she would find it.

Big Frost Hurts. Clyde Couple Marry.

Shit, it was freezing. She already had a cold: her nose was running, her eyes watering. What if you fainted out here or twisted your ankle so you couldn't move? How long would it be before your snot froze and the tears on your eyelashes turned into little threads of ice? She needed a hat, a woolly knitted hat with stripes of cool colours. Maybe she'd pick one up at the op-shop.

Sweet as. Sweet as.

When the dog came hurtling up at her she was thinking about the words and the cold and the hat. She recognised the dog, just about everyone in the town knew that dog, and while her rational mind understood it had to be a good, well-trained dog that wouldn't hurt her, the way it careered out of the mist and darkness frightened her and she staggered backwards, slipping on the slithery grass and fell.

Then he was there, taking hold of her arm and helping her up. She didn't need him to do that. She felt stupid and embarrassed.

He picked her bag off the ground and handed it to her. 'You okay?'

'Uh, yeah. I just kind of skidded.'

He whistled for the dog and clipped the lead onto his collar. 'Sorry about this fellow. He gets a bit over-excited.'

'It's okay.'

He glanced at her as he was turning to go. She saw him hesitate and then he stopped and seemed to be looking at her more closely. 'Aren't you one of the Freemans?' he said.

'Yep, that's me,' she said, 'just another bloody Freeman.'

She didn't know why she'd said that. Only, she'd wanted to sound upbeat and confident, not like some little kid who'd been so scared by a dog she'd fallen right over. But now that word, bloody, that had spurted out of her mouth seemed to vibrate uncomfortably in the mist and quiet. He stared at her for a moment and then he grinned. Okay, okay, he understood it was a joke.

'You're Lynnie's sister?'

'Yeah. Except now we have to call her Lyn-nette.' She made her voice and face snooty, showing off a bit because he was still grinning like he thought she was funny.

'Lyn-nette, eh? Is that right? And you are?'

'Uh.' She was flustered, couldn't think what he meant for a minute. 'Oh. Serena. I'm Serena.'

He looked at his watch, 'You heading home from school? You're a bit late, aren't you?'

She wanted to say it wasn't against the law but that sounded too cheeky. 'I've been in the art room.'

'Yeah? What've you been doing in the art room?'

So she told him and his eyes didn't shift away, like he was thinking about something different. He listened like he was really interested.

'Well, good for you. Nice to meet you, Serena,' he said. He turned and walked with the dog towards the car with the blue and yellow squares. She hitched her bag up and kept on going.

That was the first time.

2

Just another bloody Freeman.

There was Lynnie and Darryl and Jesse and Todd, then there was Serena. She was the baby of the family. Good thing the bastard left when he did or there would've been more of them.

When you read books — novels, Miss always corrects her — where there are families who haven't got much money, nine times out of ten, they're special. They're honest and worthy and inventive and they laugh a lot and love each other and are all so clever that it makes up for them having nothing.

Well, the Freemans were special as well. All the boys had been up in court, driving without a licence, driving under the influence, pinching beer out of the neighbour's garage, drunk and disorderly. Darryl'd been in more trouble than all the others put together. It was never Darryl's fault, though, it was always someone picking on him, blaming him when he hadn't even been there. The cops had it in for him. Yeah, right. Dropkicks; that's what she called them. The dropkicks.

And just before she ran away, Lynnie'd been caught nicking nail polish at the chemist's but Mr Johnston who owned the shop had felt so sorry for her he said he wouldn't press charges. Lynnie said he'd even let her keep the nail polish because he could see she'd learned her lesson and was really sorry. Lynnie could always come up with a good story. She could even cry when she needed to.

All of the Freemans had been in trouble one way or another. All of them except her and she was going to keep it that way.

She'd tried so hard to keep it that way.

The other thing in those novels about poor families is that the mother is especially special. Like sometimes she's super-talented and writes books or paints amazing pictures or sometimes she's just really wise and kind. But she's always beautiful. Despite the lines on her forehead and the little threads of grey in her hair from all the worry, she's always beautiful.

The especially special thing about Serena's mum is that she's always either picking the wrong men or helping herself to the ones who are supposed to belong to other people. Serena's mum says when it comes to men she just can't help herself, she just can't do without her cuddles.

Hence, there are kids at school who don't talk to Serena because of their dads going around for little visits with her mum. Hence, from time to time, there's a fair bit of yelling and screaming at their place and the phone ringing with neighbours saying they're calling the cops. Hence, the occasion of the brick that Mrs Green, alias That Stupid Bitch, chucked through Serena's mum's bedroom window.

Hence. She loves that word. Hence, whilst, hitherto, afore-mentioned.

The Freemans were special, all right. They even got special treatment. Like on the first day, every year at primary school, Serena's new teacher would be up the front of the room calling out the names on the roll, glancing up and looking over each kid, marking off the name. Then they'd get to her. Serena Freeman? They'd skim their eyes over her, just like they did with all the others. Then it hit them. That name they'd just called out. Freeman, oh shit, a Freeman. Whack! The recognition would hit them and their eyes would start darting and sliding, checking her out as if she had horns growing out the top of her head.

Can this one write its own name yet? Does this one wet its pants in class? Does this one bite? Does this one steal?

You get used to it. Those 'oh fuck not one of them' or 'oh that poor little kiddie' expressions on teachers' faces followed by them keeping a close eye. High school was better. More kids. More teachers coming and going. More anonymity.

Tell you what, though, after all those 'oh fuck, oh that poor wee kiddie' faces, it was fairly amazing to come across a teacher like Miss who seemed to think she was on the same level as the others. Not only the same level, but someone who had good ideas, someone you might even like to have a chat with. Someone special.

Those afternoons she went to Miss's house. Three afternoons, only three, but they were special. Coffee and cinnamon smells, cups with pink flowers, a piano, shelves filled with books. And Miss sitting on the wooden chair with the red cushion, leaning forward, listening to her. Really listening. 'And so, Serena, what did you make of our Mr Pip?'

Don't get her wrong. She's not saying what happened was because of Miss, nothing like that. But if it hadn't been for her she'd have kept her distance. Because she understood he knew all about them, everything: the dropkicks and her mum and the brick and the men. She'd even seen him right outside their house, his car parked on the kerb, talking to Darryl. But the way it was with Miss talking to her and lending her the books, it made her think she was better than that, not just one more of those dodgy kids. Miss liked her, so the fact that she had another adult who seemed to like talking to her as well didn't seem all that surprising.

Which was why the next time she saw him when she was walking home she stopped and patted the dog. He asked about the mural and she told him about the newspaper headline she'd just found. Most Earthquake Damage Caused By Shaking.

'Hey,' he said, laughing. 'Good one.'

And, yeah, she'd liked talking to him. That time and the time after — that was in the park as well — he'd asked about school and the mural and stuff and they'd kind of chatted a bit with the dog running around, well, he was nice to her, wasn't he? Then there was the next time when it started to rain while she was walking home and he'd pulled over and said he was going her way, did she want a ride? He never talked much himself, but he listened and he laughed about what she said, like she was really, you know, funny and clever. 'You're a bright girl, Serena.'

She didn't see him all that often so she didn't think it was weird him taking notice of her. It was only occasionally, never more than once a week. She thought maybe he liked to talk to her so he could find out the kind of stuff that was happening around school.

That's the way it was. That went on for ages. She'd be walking home and he'd be there.

3

'**Y**ou're a bright girl, Serena.'

She thought — anyway, she hoped — that him turning up more often was a coincidence. Happenstance. That was a word she'd just found. It was happenstance.

It wasn't that. It couldn't be. Everyone in the whole town knew who he was. Knew what he was.

She'd had the talks from Lynnie: Guys think they can do anything to us and get away with it because we're rubbish, so you be careful who you talk to, eh. And don't you get in anyone's car, Serena, and if anyone tries to put his fucking hands on you, you yell. Yell hard as you can, right? And if that doesn't work, kick him in the balls. Don't trust anyone. Guys, they can't keep it in their pants.

He never did or said anything that felt wrong or scary. Okay, he was a man and yeah, she talked to him. A lot; she'd started talking to him a lot. And, okay, sometimes she got into his car. But how could she say no if he pulled up beside her and said he was going past her street, hop in? Saying no, well it would be kind of embarrassing and rude. Anyway, he was old and he was married. She'd seen his wife heaps of times when she was in the school library helping out with the other volunteers, putting plastic covering on the text books. She'd seen her hands smoothing down the tape, seen all the rings embedded with little diamonds which came right up to the knuckles of her fingers.

'You're a bright girl, Serena. Pretty too.'

He'd told her, being in the job he was in, he needed to watch out for kids. He was always at school for the sports days and the inter-school matches and prize-givings. She told herself that was what he was doing with her. He was watching out for kids. Maybe, though

14

she didn't like to think that way, he was watching out that the last of the Freemans didn't go the same way as the others.

Pretty too.

She thought about talking it over with Miss. Except they never talked about personal stuff, not ever. Miss seemed to Serena to be the kind of person who lived in her head, not that she was cold or unfriendly but she knew a lot and she liked talking about ideas and facts. She wanted Miss to keep on respecting her: Miss treated her as an equal so the thought of saying to her, 'There's this man who keeps turning up wherever I am, he's kind of pestering me', well, that felt so wrong because maybe Miss would start to see her as this needy kid who couldn't manage her messy, stupid life.

Guys, they can't keep it in their pants.

How could she ever talk to Miss about anything related to that? Worst of all, Miss might start asking her questions, might insist she told her who it was and then she'd think she was making it all up. Because how could Miss believe that he would be after her? How could anyone? At prize-giving he sat right up on the stage and he gave out some of the prizes, shaking kids' hands while Mr Jensen, the principal, stood beside him nodding and smiling. She'd ridden past his house on her bike. It was massive with a three-door garage and a spongy-looking lime-green lawn and his wife's SUV parked on the tiles outside.

She changed the way she walked home from school, ducking in and out of streets, zig-zagging across parks and tracks until she got there. She stopped going to the pool at night, stopped going to the movies.

Then, over the next week or two, she saw him only a couple of times. Her heart started thudding but he'd just give her a wave, kept on going as he drove past. She'd been crazy. It hadn't been anything. It had all been in her head.

It was over.

4

The days turned long and scorching, the Christmas decorations went up in the main street and then it was the final school break-up. The school choir sang 'All through the Night' and 'Blow, Blow Thou Winter Wind' then Mr Smithson conducted the school band. You could see the teachers up on the stage were trying to look positive even when they lost their way through 'Angels We Have Heard On High' and had to start all over again.

Then it was their turn. The whole class went up and Mr Jensen pulled the covering off and, shit, that mural looked so amazing. Lakes, rivers, cabbage trees, mountains, beaches, the Auckland Sky Tower, the Beehive, churches and railway stations; all those paintings and prints and photographs with the words criss-crossing, marching over everything. Everyone clapped so hard. Mr Black said he was bowled over by the quality and it was and would continue to be a treasured artwork within the school.

She felt good. So good. All of the kids from her class went down to the river afterwards. They put in money and bought a giant pack of fish and chips on the way and some of them got their older brothers and sisters to get them beer and cider. They sat around for ages talking and eating and swimming and drinking.

Afterwards, she walked home on her own in the dark. The air was thick with the heat and the scents from the gardens she was passing and she could see the lights from Christmas trees glimmering behind covered windows. She wasn't used to drinking beer and her head felt swimmy and kind of weird but she was feeling really happy, really great. Julie and Holly wanted to hang out with her in the holidays and she'd got a great school report — exceptional results, we have high expectations for Serena's future in the senior classes — and it was holidays.

The lights passed her. She watched as the car did a U-turn in the street ahead, moved slowly towards her and stopped. He got out. She saw him open up the door into the passenger seat. 'Get in. I'm taking you home.'

He stood there waiting, watching her. She said no. 'No thanks, I'm okay to walk.' Except her tongue got caught up and her voice came out blurry.

'Get in.'

He didn't raise his voice, his face looked passive and calm under the street lamp. 'Get in. I can tell you've been drinking so don't deny it. It's my duty to make sure you get home safely.'

He must have been following her, watching her. Her face was burning hot from the sun and the beer and her mouth was dry and she could feel her heart racing. This isn't right. It isn't right. What if she ran? What if she just turned and ran? Across the road and through the park, a couple more streets and she'd be home.

She'd be home except he'd come after her. She'd be in trouble. He could get them all into trouble. Drinking underage. The parents would blame her. Freeman. Serena Freeman.

He stood there, holding the door, holding her with his eyes. She got in. He didn't speak as he drove. She had a quick look across at him and his face was impassive, his eyes on the road. He turned into her street, passed the house and stopped. She already had her fingers around the door handle and she levered it upwards. It was locked. It was locked.

'I'm disappointed in you, Serena.'

He was staring straight ahead, looking out at the road through the windscreen and he spoke so softly, she almost couldn't hear what he said.

'Yeah, well, I'm sorry. I —. Can I just get out now?'

'Drinking underage, and what were you doing with the boys down there? What were you up to with those boys?'

'Nothing. I wasn't doing anything.'

'I thought you were better than that. I thought you were bright enough to know better.'

'I have to go. Mum's waiting for me.'

He turned his face towards her. He rested his hand just below where her skirt ended. 'You want to be a slut like your sister? Just like Lynnie?'

'Let me out. Let me out, now.'

He ran his fingers lightly across her leg. 'Good girls say please.'

'Please. Please let me out.'

Running. Running up the street, yanking open the door, into the house. Mum? Mum?

Darryl was in the kitchen standing over the stove with a beer in his hand, turning over sausages, breaking eggs into the pan. She's away down the boozer with Maureen. Should she tell him? She had to tell someone.

'Fuck.' He rubbed his arm where the fat had spurted up and burnt him. Beer cans on the table, dishes in the sink, the stink of cigarettes and fry-ups and fly-spray.

'Why don't you open a frigging window?'

'What's got up your fucking nose?' His eyes were all fuzzy as he looked at her. It was Friday, probably he'd been pissing up after work, probably had a few joints as well.

What could Darryl do? What could Mum do? What could anyone do?

She went into her bedroom and shut the door. She lay on her bed, pulled the quilt up over her body, tucked it tightly around her chin. She closed her eyes. It'll all come out in the wash. That's what Mum always said. It'll all come out in the wash. Tomorrow's another day.

His flat, pale eyes. His soft, creepy voice and the way he'd looked at her. The crawl of fingers on her skin.

Everything was spoiled. The summer, the holidays, everything. She wanted to go to the river, hang out with Julie and Holly and the other girls. She wanted to talk to them about school and boys and girl-stuff but she was afraid to go out anywhere. Though she told herself it was stupid, she imagined him following and watching. She thought about sitting down at the river in her swimsuit and him hidden somewhere, his eyes on her.

I don't have to talk to him. I don't have to get into his car. What can he do about it if I say no?

Except who he was, what he was, he could do plenty about it. Plenty.

'Thought you'd be out with your friends now it's the holidays.'

Mum was on at her. Every day she was on at her. What're you doing mooching about inside? What're you doing in bed at this hour? If you've got nothing better to do than lie around on that couch all day, you could fold that washing.

Talking to Mum was useless. Talking to anyone was useless. She nearly told Lynnie when she rang up for Christmas. Mum and the dropkicks were eating pudding and watching TV while Serena had her turn on the phone. There was just that bit of time after Lynnie was going on about this new flat she had and her job and her new boyfriend and what he'd given her for Christmas when, finally, she actually asked her something. 'So what's up with you, See?'

'Can I come and stay with you?' she blurted.

'Come here to Wellington, you mean?'

'Yeah.'

'Hey!' Lynnie sounded pleased. 'That would be so cool. How would you get up here, though?'

'I don't know.'

'Listen, why don't you come up later on, maybe Easter? I'll get a Grab-a-seat and shout you. It's just, with buying stuff for the new flat and everything, later on I'll have a bit more spare money and I could get some time off, show you around a bit.'

'Uh.'

Lynnie would know what to do, she could trust Lynnie to tell her what to do. Don't you trust anyone, See. Guys, they can't keep it in their pants.

'Uh, it's just —.'

And then Mum was beside her, holding her hand out for the phone. Come on, my turn, fair's fair.

'Next holidays, Serena. That's a deal, okay?'

Lynnie wasn't so bad. Far as Serena was concerned she was always the best one in the family. She used to dress her up when she was a little girl, wash her hair and put it in curls, take her to the park. Lynnie always looked out for her and meant what she said. But Serena wanted to get away right then. She needed to get away. She felt it like a lump in her gut, a lump of fright and dread. She sat down at the table and scooped up some ice cream, stirring it around and around in her plate, making swirls of pink and white, like she'd done when she was little: ice-cream soup.

'Don't waste it.' Mum was off the phone and Darryl had taken it into the lounge. She could hear him talking to Lynnie while he was glugging down another beer.

'Whatever.' She kept stirring.

'What's got on your wick?' Mum was staring at her.

'I want to go to Wellington and see Lynnie.'

Mum laughed. 'Yeah and I want to go to Fiji. Where's the money coming from, may I ask?'

She heard her voice whining, sounding like a little kid. But she didn't care. She wanted to be a little kid. She wanted to be a little kid and for someone to come along and look after her. 'I never get to go away on holidays. We never go anywhere.'

'Tough.' Her mother rammed the ice-cream lid onto the plastic tub and put it back in the fridge.

But she must have thought about it because just before New Year she asked Serena if she wanted to go away with her and Rob, this new man she had. This different new man she had.

Serena had heard her talking to Auntie Maureen about him: 'Listen, Maur, this one's different. He's really nice.'

Rob didn't look that nice, not with the missing front tooth and all those tats. Mind you, he'd brought them firewood and stacked it under the house for next winter and he'd mowed down the long grass and now he was keeping it short and neat. It didn't look like he was married either.

'Where to?'

'The beach. Whack-a-white.' Serena knew it was called Waikouaiti; one of the kids from school's mum and dad had a cottage there. Mum was sounding casual about it but Serena could tell by the way her eyes were lit up that she was excited. Mum didn't get away much either.

'Where would we stay?'

Mum was off, her voice getting higher and faster the more she talked. Rob had a mate and this mate had a crib and Rob said he said they could have it for ten days. It was just up from the beach. It wasn't very big but it was tidy enough, Rob said, and there was a caravan as well so if Serena wanted she could stay out there, have her own wee place.

'So.' Mum lit a cigarette and puffed on it. 'What d'you think, See?'

'Okay.'

'Only okay?' Mum was looking a bit hurt. 'A bit of a thank-you wouldn't hurt.'

'Thank you.'

It was a way of getting out of town — not having to watch for his car, not having to watch for him — but then she started to get excited. They hadn't been away for a holiday, not since that one time they went to the camping ground in Timaru with Auntie Maureen. She went to the library and got a heap of books out. She bought a torch with her Christmas money, a good strong one she could read by in the caravan.

All the way driving out of town she started to feel lighter, as if that big black lump in her gut was dissolving bit by bit. They drove through Omakau and Ranfurly where the paddocks stretching out for miles from the sides of the road were parched gold but when they came out onto the main road at Palmerston everything was so green. The sea, when they saw it, was all these colours of blue: navy and lavender and aquamarine spreading out beyond the acres and acres of buttery-coloured sand. They followed the coast. There, Rob, there. It says Whack-a-white right there on the sign. They turned off the main road and followed the next sign which said beach. She could smell salt.

The crib was tiny with weatherboards painted yellow and grey roof tiles. There was a giant red wooden butterfly with black polka dots just above the front door. Rob looked tentatively towards Serena's mum. Rob never said much.

'Ooh,' Mum said. 'Ooh, it's so cute.' She sprang out of the car and darted up the path. 'The lawn is lovely. Look at these trees. Look, there's a barbecue! There's an umbrella!'

Serena got out of the car. Her mother was wearing white trousers and Serena could see the outline of her underpants underneath them, could see that they were pink with black stretchy lace but it didn't worry her, not here. She watched her mother waving her hands around. Her fingernails were painted the same bright shiny pink as her top, as her lipstick, as her high-heeled sandals.

Serena felt even lighter here, as if the wind gusting up from the beach was blowing away all that shit she was carrying. She picked up her bag and carried it over to the little green caravan that sat on the lawn, crouched up like some sleeping prehistoric animal. She opened the door. So warm and so silent, it smelled like salt and dry, sweet biscuits.

There was a tiny bench, a built-in, splotchy-red Formica table with red vinyl-covered seats and a divan with a leopard-skin patterned rug spread across it. She opened up her bag and hung her skirt, shorts, T-shirts and swimsuit on the hooks and arranged her books and torch on the shelf above the bed.

She could hear the sea. She lay down, stretched out her arms and her legs, breathed in the sweet saltiness and closed her eyes.

It rained some of the days and nearly every night. But she liked that, liked lying in the hard, narrow bed with the musty-smelling rug cosied up around her chin, listening to the tippy-tap drizzle of rain. It was just about the best time she'd ever had with Mum. They played cards and did crosswords together in a book they found in a cupboard. On the fine days they went to the beach, picked up shells. Serena swam out beyond the waves and lay on her back looking up into the sky.

It will be all right. It will be all right.

Mum wasn't so bad when she was happy, and Rob was okay. He liked to be busy, he said, so he mowed the lawns and cut the hedges. He was quiet and he didn't drink much, only a couple of beers before tea so there weren't any fights. He was good on the barbecue too. There was a butcher down the road who made the best sausages in the world.

She and Mum were lying on the rug underneath the sand-hills, Serena reading her book and Mum flicking through her magazines. A couple of girls were riding their horses further down the beach, cantering in and out of the waves, but other than that there was no one for miles. What if she told her? She didn't want to, even trying to think out the words she might say felt so hard she could almost feel them starting to stick in her throat.

But wasn't telling what she actually should do? What did they say in those classes way back when she was a little kid sitting on the mat and they talked about bad touching?

Tell an adult. Tell.

But telling Mum would mean telling other people and that would make it into this issue that would have to go right out there into the world to be talked about and argued about and for her to be questioned about. It was so creepy, so embarrassing and she didn't want to talk about it. She could see all these concerned adult faces looking at her. She'd be one of those losers who had to be called out of class to go and see Sally Davis for counselling. Maybe she'd have that policewoman, the one with the poodle hair and the fat face, asking her questions.

He followed you? He watched you? He touched your leg? When did this start, how many times, when did that happen, where, when, where, when? Are you sure about this, Serena? Are you certain that this happened? The other kids would start talking about her, looking at her, asking sly questions, 'Hey, Serena, what's up?' It made her stomach clench up and her face hot to even think about it. Telling would make it real instead of something she could shrink until it was very tiny and tuck away out of sight.

Her mum was lying on her back asleep, making this feeble, whistling noise through her nose, her sunglasses covering her eyes. She had got a spray-on tan before they came that Rob shouted her and she was wearing the purple and orange bikini she'd picked up at the op-shop. 'I can get away with it, eh, See? Not too bad for having five kids.' Her belly had kind of collapsed over the pants and her boobs were bulging out of the top.

Right there in her head, Serena could see her mum storming into the police station in her white pants and tight top and her hair with the roots needing doing. Her mum sounded like an out-of-control seal when she got going. Kind of croaky and screamy at the same time. They would laugh at her; right behind their put-on polite faces they'd be laughing at her mum and Serena couldn't stand that. She knew a lot of people laughed at her mum, but Serena had seen her fretting over the bills she couldn't pay, she'd seen the hurt in her eyes when yet another guy left her, she'd seen her cry the first time Darryl went to court.

It had been good here. Over the past days it'd been good and Mum was happy now she had Rob. Telling would ruin everything. And it would bring it all into here, and here Serena could make it go away.

She could manage it on her own. All she had to do was keep away from him. If he did turn up she'd be polite but she wouldn't give in. If he asked if she wanted a ride home she'd just say 'I'm fine, thanks' and keep right on walking, go into someone's house if she needed to and make up some excuse like she felt sick and needed to phone her mum. He couldn't follow her. He couldn't exactly run her off the road. All this was her own fault because she'd been too friendly.

Once he realised she didn't want to be friendly any more, he'd give it up.

She didn't want to leave. She stared out at her caravan as Rob closed and padlocked the gates. The lump was back, churning up her belly the closer they got to Alex. Keep right on walking I'm fine thanks go into someone's house I feel sick can I use your phone to call my mum I'm fine thanks keep on walking keep right on walking.

But she didn't have to worry after all. Maybe he was on holiday, maybe he had other stuff to think about and had forgotten about her because he wasn't in the park, he didn't drive past in his car and she didn't see him parked down the main street. She started to feel okay. She started to go to the river. She lay around with the other kids, baking in the sun on the hot stones, talking, comparing tans, slipping into the water to cool down.

That day. She was on a rock beside the river, getting ready to jump in. She was laughing at Holly who was standing beside her, her arms clutched about her body. I'm not doing it. It's too frigging cold. She heard the car on the bridge. She looked up as it moved slowly across, the yellow and blue glinting in the sun and she saw his eyes in the rear-view mirror looking back.

It happened the next day and the next. The day after that he wasn't there but two days later she watched as his car slowly passed, turned and then came back.

He's checking out the kids at the river. That's his job, isn't it? Driving around, making sure things are okay? It's not like he's stopping me any more, asking if I want a ride.

It's all right. It'll be all right.

School started and though she moaned about it with the other kids she was happy to get back with all the teachers starting the new year by saying the same old stuff; this was an important year for them and they had to work really hard, yada-yada-yada. She didn't mind school; truth was she preferred being there to hanging around at home which was always a mess with stuff everywhere, shirts and jeans hanging over the chairs and the couch, shoes and mugs and plates and beer cans on the floor and the bench and table covered up with crap. At home there was always some drama going on, Mum yelling at the boys because they hadn't done something she'd asked them to, or they'd done something stupid. 'Clean up your shit, Darryl. I'm fucking tired of telling you.'

On her very first day of school when she went into the classroom she saw how everything was properly laid out, everything had its own place: the desks were arranged just so and there was a book corner, a science corner, an art corner. She loved that and she loved sitting on the mat and being quiet. She loved listening to the stories while the teacher read, holding the book up so they could see the pictures and singing while the teacher played her guitar. Most of all, she loved sitting at her own little desk on her own chair, reading and drawing and copying the letters. She was going to be the first of the Freemans to go right through school. After that she didn't know. Maybe she could talk about it to Miss.

Just like every year there was new work and new teachers and the classrooms were so hot by the afternoons everyone was sweating and moaning. She had Miss again. She got this happy, warm feeling when she found that out and Miss gave her a special little smile when she walked in on the first day.

5

They were halfway through maths; she wasn't that good at algebra and she was hunched over her workbook trying to figure out the way to answer the equation Mr Hogg had just given them. She looked up as she heard the tap on the door and the deputy principal, Ms Pringle, came into the room.

'Can I speak with you for a moment, Clar — Mr Hogg?'

Everyone knew that Mr Hogg's name was Clarence so some of the kids giggled like they always did and some dickhead boy from the back sang-whispered it, 'Clar-ence.' Mr Hogg told them to quieten down and carry on with their work. He went outside with Ms Pringle. They closed the door behind them and, while she couldn't hear anything Serena knew, right down in her gut like a thick, black doom that something was happening, something awful and that she was involved. She felt cold and shivery; she couldn't breathe properly.

Mr Hogg came back in and his eyes as he looked over at her were shocked and sad and kind, all at the same time. Mr Hogg always helped her when she got behind in maths. He said he understood she was trying her hardest and maths wasn't everyone's cup of tea and just to come and see him if something wasn't making sense to her.

She liked Mr Hogg. Why was he looking at her like that? He came across to her desk, bent down and said quietly, 'Serena, Ms Pringle needs to see you in her office.'

'Now, you mean?' Her voice shrilled out, squeaky and scared and all the other kids were staring and her face was starting to burn.

'Yes, pack up your books and take them along with you.'

She couldn't be in trouble; she hadn't done anything wrong. She walked along the corridor, outside through the swinging doors and began to cross the quadrangle to where the offices were.

She saw the car in the visitors' car park. She felt dizzy, could feel her heart start to wallop against her chest. It was Mum. Something had happened to Mum. Or one of the boys had been hurt. When Mr Jones' tractor tipped over and he got killed the police came to the school to tell Cassy. An accident. Oh God, there'd been an accident. The ladies behind the glass at the reception office stared out as she bolted past them. Did they know? That poor kiddie.

She stopped outside Ms Pringle's office and stood there, frozen, staring at the door before she knocked.

'Come in, please.'

She hurried inside and he was there, sitting on a chair with his legs crossed and his arms folded, Ms Pringle on the chair beside him.

'Is it Mum?' She burst out with it.

Ms Pringle looked up at her. She seemed surprised.

'Has there been an accident?'

'An accident?' Ms Pringle shook her head. 'No, nothing like that. Sit down, Serena.'

She sat on the chair Ms Pringle was pointing at. A blue chair, blue vinyl like the others. She could feel the edge of it, spongy and sweaty on the backs of her knees.

'Serena, I'm afraid Sergeant Withers and I have some rather serious allegations to talk over with you.' Ms Pringle was eyeing her and her eyes were unfriendly.

'Allegations?'

She'd never been in this room before. The walls and carpet were grey and there were the same kind of blinds covering the windows they had in the classrooms, the kind you can see out of but not in to. There weren't any pictures and the books in the black-painted bookcase looked like textbooks, fat and grey and unfriendly.

What was she talking about? What the fuck was she talking about? Serious allegations. But she hadn't done anything. She hadn't done anything wrong. Except for drinking beer that once at the river. Was that what they were on about? Drinking beer at the river? And now Ms Pringle was eyeing her like she was a piece of shit stinking out her room. For drinking beer?

'I'll let Sergeant Withers explain.' She nodded towards him.

'There've been reports of high school students smoking marijuana at the river, Serena,' he said. 'The information I've been given is that your brother, Darryl, has been procuring the drugs and that you've both been involved in selling them.'

He talked in a smooth, soft voice. Ms Pringle kept her eyes on Serena all the time he was talking and she could see what was in her eyes. What else could you expect from a Freeman? What else could you expect?

Drugs? She didn't know anything about any drugs. Darryl smoked a bit of weed, all of the boys did, but selling it, her selling it, shit, what were they on about? She was so dazed by what she was hearing she had to keep her head right down, she couldn't look at them.

Drugs. Drugs. Drugs.

'Not only marijuana, Serena. Sergeant Withers has told me there has also been reports of pills.' Ms Pringle pursed her lips.

This was a mistake. They'd made a mistake. She didn't do drugs, no way would she do drugs, and the idea of going into a money-making venture with Darryl, well that was a laugh. Except the way Ms Pringle was looking at her, she definitely wasn't laughing. She had to put them right. She had to make them see they'd got this wrong. Lynnie had always told her, 'Keep your head up, don't let anyone put you down,' so she pulled herself up straight and stared right back at Ms Pringle. 'That's not true,' she said. 'I don't know anything about kids taking drugs.'

He and Ms Pringle looked at each other. Ms Pringle gave a little shake to her head and sighed. 'You've been seen at the river,' she said. 'You've been there regularly over the summer, haven't you, Serena?'

All of a sudden she was angry. 'So? Being at the river isn't against the law, is it?'

'Serena,' Ms Pringle's voice was hard and clipped, 'I will not tolerate rudeness.'

She had to try to get her on her side. He was lying, he had to be making it up and she had to somehow make Ms Pringle see that, had to make her see this wasn't true. She'd be expelled if she couldn't make her believe it. She'd be chucked out of school and as for Darryl, she knew the next time he was in court he'd go down. The magistrate had told him that the last time. Even if he was a dropkick Darryl was still her brother and she didn't want him going to prison.

She looked at Ms Pringle, looked her right in the eye, willing her to listen, to believe what she was saying. 'I'm sorry, Ms Pringle, but it's not true. What he said about Darryl and me, someone, someone's not telling the truth, Ms Pringle. Sergeant Withers has got it wrong. I wouldn't do that. I don't do drugs. Anyone will tell you. Please. Please ask anyone. I'm not like that.'

Ms Pringle looked at her. She didn't say anything for a while, then she spread her hands out on the desk and stared down at them. 'I'm sorry too, Serena, but we can't take your word for that.'

We can't take your word for that. Not your word. We've been waiting all along for something like this and, yes, you've been good up until now and, yes, it's a disappointment but —.

'Ms Pringle, it's not fair. I haven't done anything wrong. Ms Pringle, you have to listen. I don't do drugs, I really don't do them.'

'I'm suspending you until we can make more enquiries.'

'But I work hard at school. I just, I just want to keep coming. Please, Ms Pringle.'

She shook her head. 'Serena, I have no choice.'

He stood up. 'I'll make sure she gets home.'

6

She said no. She said she would walk. 'It's not far,' she said. 'I always walk home.'

Was there a flicker in Ms Pringle's eyes? A glimpsed awareness of something not quite right?

Help me, Ms Pringle. Please, Ms Pringle. Don't make me go with him.

'Ms Pringle, I want to walk.'

'Ruth —?' Ms Pringle turned her head back towards him as he spoke softly to her, faintly frowning, shaking his head.

'I'm afraid, Serena, that in this case we can't allow that. It's during school hours and we have to ensure that you arrive home safely.'

He was watching her with his flat, pale eyes and there was a twitch at the side of his face, almost like a grin, as if he wanted her to lose it, as if he wanted her to yell and to cry. She knew, absolutely she knew, that if she started arguing, if she started acting up, the guiltier she would appear and the more Ms Pringle would believe him. What should she do? What could she do?

He was there right behind her as she got her bag from her locker and as she walked across the car park towards his car. Right behind her, close enough to grab, close enough to touch her with his fingers. She could feel him there like prickles on her skin.

Could she run? Just bolt away? If she could get away she could run and hide somewhere. Maybe later on, when he'd given up looking for her, she could make it out onto the road out of town and wave down a car. The caravan would be a good place. She could hitch there and hide. But she had nothing. No money, no food, no clothes, nothing. She was just a kid. They'd come and take her away.

He'd come and take her away.

He drove up the road, past the turn-off to her street. He turned onto the back streets, they were heading out of town, She didn't say anything. No point in saying anything.

She slid her hand down, tried the door handle. Locked. Of course he had it locked. He turned down a side road and they juddered over shingle and stopped.

He undid his seatbelt. She looked over at him. He was staring straight ahead, staring through the windscreen again, this creepy grin on his face. 'You haven't been very nice to me lately, Serena, have you?'

'I don't know what you mean.'

'We used to talk. You used to tell me everything, Serena, all about yourself and your little plans. I thought we were mates.'

'We — we are. I've just. I've just been busy.'

Her hand was frantically working at the door handle. How can I get out?

'We both know you've been avoiding me, Serena. You've been down at the river with your little buddies, haven't you? Pretending not to see me.'

'If we are mates, why are you telling lies about me? What you said to Ms Pringle isn't true.'

'It's true if I say it is.'

If I can get out. If I can just get out of the car.

'No. No it's not.'

'Anything's true if I say so.'

'That's not right.' She was crying now. The door was locked, she couldn't get out, he was still staring through the windscreen and his voice was funny. 'It's not fair. Why are you doing this?'

'Just teaching you a little lesson, Serena, about being nice. About being mates.'

He shuffled around in his seat, he was undoing his belt, his zip, oh God, oh God, he was going to do that to her, he was going to do that. She was screaming, screaming, pounding on the window. 'Someone, help me, please! Help me!'

He gripped her head in his thick, red hands, shoved it down, held it. No no not that, not that, please. Please. She was choking, gagging, her mouth and her throat filled up with him. Suffocating, choking on him and the smell, the sweet-sick smell of the air freshener in the car, the sour sweat smell of him.

When he'd finished he opened the door and shoved her out. She fell onto the gravel on her knees. Gagging, retching, spitting. Spitting.

'Clean yourself up.'

She wiped her tears and her snot and that stuff — that disgusting stuff — off her face with tissues from the box he threw at her.

'Hurry up. Get in.' He drove quickly back towards town, his eyes on the side mirrors, the rear-view mirror. 'Keep your head down. Keep your head down, I said.'

He stopped along from the camp. 'You can walk from here.'

She wanted to get out. She wanted to get away, to get home and lock herself in the bathroom — the pink soap, the flappy, plastic shower curtain with the dolphins on it — and scrub and scrub and scrub her body and her face and her mouth, her dirty, filthy, hurting mouth. But she made herself stay there.

'Go on,' he said. 'Get out.'

'What about Ms Pringle?'

'What about her?' She saw him looking up, checking his rear-view mirror.

'If you don't put it right with Ms Pringle I'll tell.' She heard her voice flat, emotionless.

He laughed. 'Who'd believe you?'

She didn't say anything.

'Just so long as you're a good girl,' he said. 'Give me your mobile number.'

Ms Pringle called. Sergeant Withers had contacted her to explain that he had discovered the evidence wasn't entirely reliable and so they would give her another chance. Only one, though, because if there was the merest hint of anything further —. So she went back to school. She didn't tell her mum. She didn't tell anyone. She felt too ashamed, too dirty.

Sometimes it was once a week, sometimes more. Some weeks she didn't see him and she'd think it was over. Then she'd get a text telling her where she had to be and he'd pull up behind her in his car with that creepy smirk on his face. She couldn't sleep, couldn't think of anything else. She had this itchy, raw, weeping rash up her arms and in her hair.

She was dirty, she was rubbish, she was nothing.

He said he wouldn't put it inside a filthy bitch like her but he made her do that stuff to him. He said, 'You like it, don't you?' He said, 'You're a slut, aren't you? Like your mother, like your sister, you're a slut. Thought you were a bit better than anyone else, well, this is what you are.'

She used to cry, to ask him to please stop. But he seemed to like that, her crying and saying 'No, please no, don't, please. Please.' So she stopped crying and asking. She stopped talking to him at all; she just got into the car with a bored look on her face and did what he wanted. She learned to send her mind way away out of her body, away from the shoving and the grunting and the hurting and the smell. One of the places she went to was when she was a little girl sitting on the mat at school listening to the teacher read stories. Or she'd be back with Lynnie winding her hair up into ringlets with her heated curlers. Sometimes she'd go to Miss's house and drink coffee, sitting on the sofa with the red cushions, or she'd be in Waikouaiti in her caravan or lying on her back with the sea billowing up around her and the sky grey and blue. Anywhere that was safe.

Trouble was, getting herself back from it. Trouble was, nothing was real any more. Get up in the morning, pull on your clothes, take your backpack, along the street, past the houses, across the park, the kids, the desks, the whiteboard. The teacher up the front talking at you. Talking at you at you at you. The desks and the kids and the whiteboard. She couldn't make sense of it. She didn't want to make sense of it. Everything was rubbish. She was rubbish.

Anywhere that was safe, except nowhere was safe.

He tried to make her talk. Tried to make her cry. But she wouldn't, she wouldn't, the red table, the red seats, the salty biscuity smell, the leopard rug pulled up around her chin, the salty biscuit smell. Then he hurt her, he really hurt her, digging his fingers so hard into her head she'd thought he'd crush her skull, shoving so hard into her mouth she thought she'd suffocate.

'Fuck you. Fuck you. If you ever do that again I'm telling your wife. I'll go right to your fucking house and tell her.'

He was breathing hard, wiping himself with the tissues. He said, 'You stay away from my wife.'

She'd got stroppy by then and just laughed right at him, a put-on, shrill, fuck-you laugh. What else could he do to her? Kill her? What did it matter? Nothing mattered.

'Yeah,' she said, 'yeah, I'll go and tell your wife. She's the big, fat, ugly one with the la-di-da voice, helps at the library, eh. That's why you make me do this stuff, eh. 'Cos you've got a big, fat, ugly wife.'

He grabbed her arms and started shaking her. He had his face right up against hers and he was shaking her so hard she thought her neck might snap and his eyes, his eyes were crazy.

He said, 'If you go near her it'll be the end of you and your fucking family.'

That's when Miss saw the bruises. That's when Miss told.

7

He didn't have the smirk. He said, 'Get in.' He didn't say anything more until he stopped the car and then he slapped her hard across the head. 'You've been talking haven't you?'

She stared out of the window. She didn't say anything. Come on, come on, just get it over with.

He slapped her again. 'You little bitch, who do you think you're dealing with? I'll teach you to fuck with me.'

She put her head down and he slapped her a couple more times, then he was shuffling around again, undoing his belt again. She heard the clink of it, that clink of his belt, that clink, and she turned and punched him over and over on his chest, on his arms. 'I won't do it, I hate you, I hate you, you are such a fucking bastard, I hate you.'

He was lifting her, dragging her and she was kicking, punching, screaming but he was too big to fight, she couldn't get away and she was on the back seat of his car, her knickers around her ankles and he was on her, ramming himself into her, his face red and his eyes staring, and the sweat and the car freshener and oh that hurting and tearing and splitting and oh God oh God it was hurting so much.

He slumped down, heavy on her and she shoved at him, shoved until he moved off her and she hauled herself up out of the car. It was, she was, so hurt and her legs and arms were trembling and her head was spinning. She was afraid she might fall right down onto the ground and she wanted to rest for a minute against the car. But it was his car. She wouldn't touch anything that was his.

He got out, doing up his zip and his belt. 'Get in. I'll take you back.'

'Fuck off.'

'Come on.'

'If you ever touch me again, I'll kill you.'

He shrugged but she could tell by his eyes he was frightened. 'Right, then. Walk.'

She started walking. She had to think what to do with her feet. One step after another step after another. It was the beginning of autumn and the leaves were turning golden and red, and she could smell the thyme. One step after another step after another. She felt the sun blazing on her face. All over her body, inside her body, all she could feel was hurt. But it was the last time. She knew that. It was the last time. One step and the next and another.

I hate you.

If you ever touch me again, I'll kill you.

8

She picks up her bag and the case with her laptop inside as the message comes up on the screen: 'Proceed to Gate 27.' She follows the other passengers down the long, narrow aisle away from the cafés and shops of the main airport.

Departures. There's a long queue at security. She puts her bag in one of the grey plastic containers, takes her laptop out of its case and puts it in another. She adds her watch, her bangle, then she takes off her jacket and lays it on the top. Metal buttons. Anything can set off those bloody alarms.

Fuck 9/11.

There's still the metallic beep that always goes off as she makes her way through. Listen, I've only got the one gun up my arse.

'Step aside, please.'

She lifts her arms as a young uniformed guy with a quivering Adam's apple runs the monitor up and down the air beside her body. She glares at him. 'No need to get that bloody close, mate.'

Good to see him turn red. It's the zips on the side-pockets of her jeans. Next time I'll take my pants off. She retrieves her laptop and her bag, slips her watch over her wrist, pulls on her jacket. The woman beside her smiles at her, says last time she flew she had her crochet hook taken off her. She's a sweet old lady, grey fluffy hair and a cherry-red dress.

Lynnie gives her a grin. 'Yeah, well, you look like a terrorist.' They have a bit of a giggle and sit together on the plastic chairs in the departure lounge.

'I'm off to visit my grandchildren in Dunedin, what about you?'

'Oh, family, just family, you know.' Then they're on the move again. She gives her boarding pass to another uniform to check, follows the line up the aisle into the plane. She finds her number, stows her bags in the locker, settles in her seat and clips on her seatbelt.

She's got used to flying. Never even got into a plane until she was twenty but now she's up and down to Auckland all the time. She does training up there. Been down to Christchurch a few times, not so much since the earthquake though. And Sydney. Only the once but she's definitely going back there. She'll go for a holiday next time. She loved Sydney.

Hasn't been on this plane for a while. Not since she came up for the job interview. Far as she was concerned, she wasn't planning on going back.

She liked Dunedin well enough when she lived there. But it was just so fucking cold, and all she could afford was a crap room in this freeze-your-arse-off old villa in North East Valley. Another thing she didn't much like about Dunedin was it was a bit too close to where she came from. Like, she'd be walking along George Street and chances were she'd meet those bitches she'd been at school with, acting like they were her best fucking mates. 'Ooh, Lynnie, how are you, what are you doing here, have you got a job, have you got a boyfriend, where do you live?' And all the time their eyes'd be running up and down, checking her out, so they could have a good goss and bitch about her later on.

'Ooh, Lynnie, we're at varsity, we're at Teachers' College, we're living at St Margaret's College, we've been to the Toga Party, we've been to the Highlanders–Chiefs game, we painted our faces, it was so so fun.'

Silly bitches.

Don't play with Lynnie Freeman, you can't play with Lynnie Freeman.

Lynnie Freeman's dirty.

The plane wheels down the runway, getting ready for take-off. She closes her eyes, there's a lurch, a shudder and they're airborne. She watches as the buildings below grow smaller and the hills and the coast begin to disappear. She loves Wellington. Loves it.

It's a good day, the sea and sky blue, the sun sparkling. She settles back in the seat, opens up a magazine and flicks through the pages: 'Trendy Fashion Under $100', 'Why Weight Doesn't Matter', 'Single and Loving It', 'Super-Quick Salads to serve with Summer Barbecues'.

Going back to Dunedin. She can do that one easily enough; now she's got her shit together she can walk right past anyone she knew from back then, flick them a dirty look. Drop dead, bitch, you're in my way.

What she's scared of is going right back. When she left she wasn't going back. Not ever. No matter what happened, she wasn't going back. Now she has to. No choice. She has to because of Serena.

She knew something was up soon as she heard her mum on the phone. With her you might get a card or a call around the time of your birthday, that is if you were lucky, and maybe at Christmas when she got pissed and started bawling and going on about how much she loved her kids. Her mum was not one for keeping in touch, not unless she wanted something and you could hear that in her voice soon as she got started. 'Hello? Is that you, lovie? How are you doing? Mmm? Mmm? Well, that's good, Lynnie. Good you're doing okay. Uh, uh, listen, Lynnie, I don't like bringing it up but the brakes on the car are stuffed and I need it for taking the kids to school and Darryl needs to go to Cromwell for rugby. So I just wondered, lovie, if you could see your way to giving me a bit of a loan? Only a few weeks I promise, Lynnie, and you'll get it back.'

This time, though, her mum's voice was a bit different as well as what she said. 'Uh, listen love, uh, I've got some news.' She sounded afraid.

Lynnie puts the magazine in her bag and leans back in her seat, stares out of the window. 'All in together/This fine weather.'

The girls with their ponytails and skirts bobbing up and down, the girls jumping the skipping rope with the special coloured handles. 'You're not playing, you're not playing, Lynnie Freeman.

My mother said I'm not allowed to play with you, Lynnie Freeman.'

Don't go there. Just don't fucking go there.

'My mum said your mum's a slag, Lynnie Freeman. Your mum's a slag.'

Though her mum's own version of her fucked-up life is that she's one of the world's true victims, Lynnie thinks the truth is she is a slag. She drinks too much and she smokes too much and she's fucked too many men. Friday-night festivities. Mum, Auntie Maureen and Blenheimer. They'd get just about right through the cask, then they'd pull out the plastic bag from the cardboard and squeeze the last dregs of the wine, like pale yellow urine, into their glasses, Mum and Maureen laughing like chooks, then the kids got to have their own special moments. They got to blow up the plastic bag and chuck it around while The Girls went down to get fish and chips. That's if they made it past the pub.

Her mum waving her arm towards Auntie Maureen. The fag, hanging from her fingers, spluttering ash and sparks. 'Every one of these kids. Every one of them, Maureen, was a mistake and every man I ever loved left me. But I love my kids, Maureen, I love my kids.'

Yeah, right. Get out the fucking violins.

'Uh, listen love, uh, I've got some news. Not good news.'

When has the news from her ever been any good?

Lynnie was nine when her dad left. He'd got home early from work and her mum had some guy in her bed. The kids at school told her who it was. 'Mr Gordon. Your mum was in bed with Mr Gordon.' Lynnie knew who Mr Gordon was. He had the café in town where they went for the takeaways. He was short and fat and he had little, darting eyes and hardly any hair.

'Your Mum's a prozzie, Lynnie Freeman. Hey, Lynnie Freeman's mum's a prozzie!' Well, if she ever got any money for it, none of it came their way. Lynnie was the oldest. She got to be a dab hand at making instant-noodle sandwiches for the other kids. White bread coated with a heap of marg and tomato sauce so that when you put the noodles on they soaked up all the oiliness and flavour.

One after another, the boys all got into trouble. Started out with chucking water bombs at motorists and setting fires in letterboxes, then graduated to nicking stuff and borrowing cars. Stupid little buggers always got caught.

What she remembers, though, were those cute little kids, those handsome little boys they used to be. Darryl especially. She took Darryl to school on his first day. She remembers how little and scared he looked in his striped T-shirt and his grey shorts and sandals. He was so scared he didn't want to let go of her hand. Darryl could write his name and count up to a hundred before he went to school. She remembers the kids running up to her, their voices shrill with excitement and malice. 'Your brother pooed his pants. Your brother stinks.'

Don't go there. Oh, fuck, just don't go there.

She missed the boys. Darryl most of all. He was the next one to her. He used to get in bed with her when her mum and dad were fighting. Never said anything, just got into her bed and snuggled up. He was the one getting into the worst of the shit, though. He said it wasn't him, most of the time. He said he just got blamed for anything going down. 'It's that cop. He's got it in for me.'

She closed her eyes. That cop. He's got it in for me. She'd done her best to make Darryl see he needed to get a fucking life. 'Listen, what you've got to do is get yourself out of that shithole.'

'All right for you, telling me what I should do. Where would I go?'

'Come here. You can stay with me till you get a job. The flat's big enough, I've got a fold-out couch in the lounge. You can stay as long as you like.'

'Dunno.'

'Darryl, you can do it. All you need to do is pack your stuff and come.'

'All my mates are here,' he said. 'Anyway, I don't like cities.'

'How would you know that? You've never lived in one.'

'I don't know anyone in Wellington.'

'You know me.'

They had the same conversation over and over until she was just too pissed off with it to bother any more. Problem was, Darryl wouldn't get off his arse. What he liked was driving around, pissing up with his mates. He had work on a vineyard now, driving a tractor a lot of the time and fixing things. Darryl was good with his hands and he told her he liked the work, enough anyway to stay there a while. Jesse and Todd were in and out of work. In and out of trouble as well.

The plane shudders. The seatbelt sign blinks on. They're over Kaikoura and the mountains still have snow around the tops. The pilot tells them they're experiencing turbulence but refreshments will be served once they're through it.

First time she was on a plane, she was that nervous. She'd got the phone call at work. There was an assistant manager's position in Wellington; they'd like to fly her up for an interview if she was interested.

Interested? Yeah — yes, she was interested. She felt kind of wobbly when she got off the phone. An assistant manager's position. They wanted to fly her up. Wellington. Fuck me. She went into the office and told her boss. He was a good guy, he was pleased for her. 'You've been head-hunted,' he said. 'Good on you, girl.'

She's been working at Les Mills for almost ten years now. She wasn't ever much good at school but she always did okay in sports. More than okay, if she was honest: she was a fast runner, good at gymnastics, so when she saw the job in the *Otago Daily Times* she went for it. They gave her some training and, shit, she could do it, even all that reading; she's good at it and she loves it.

She hasn't done badly for herself. Not so badly.

'Uh, listen love, uh, I've got some news. Not good news.'

She'd just got home from work and was in the kitchen. It had been a long day — she'd had to sack one of the instructors. He hadn't turned up until the afternoon again and from the look of him he had a shit hangover. She'd given him his warnings but she still felt so bad giving him the boot.

'Look, I've been in a really bad space but I'm getting my act together. Can't you give me another chance? I won't do it again, Lynnette, I promise you. And listen, I owe all this money and I really need this gig.'

What she needed was a sit-down and a wine and then something to eat and that was when the phone rang. She sat up on one of the bar stools, screwed the top off the wine and poured herself one while she picked up the phone. 'Lynnette here.'

'I've got some news.'

Shit, why was it always her that got the bad-luck stories? 'I owe all this money and I really need this gig.' So what was it this time? Going on her mum's voice it was something more than the rent behind again, the washing machine broken down again, the power bill, the phone bill, the car. She felt the wine hit her belly, hit her head. Leave me alone, will you? Would you just let me sit here in my own flat, in my own life, and leave me fucking alone?

'Okay, so how much is this one going to cost me?' she said.

'Oh, don't be like that, Lynnie. I do my best —'

'You do your best, all right.'

Her mum was a piece of work. Lynnie had given her money; over and over she'd given it to her, fifty here, a couple of hundred there. Never got a cent of it back. Not that she'd expected it. What would be nice, though, was a bit of thanks now and then.

She'd done it for the kids but she wouldn't need to do that much longer. Serena would be out of school in a couple of years and then Lynnie would be able to say no. She wasn't going to shell out just for her mum, that was for sure. She'd already helped herself to enough of Lynnie's money. At first she'd been stupid enough to send through a cheque and trust her mother to do things right. But after Darryl told her about her mum and Maureen buggering off for a long weekend just after she'd sent a hundred bucks, she got tough. The rule was, any bills needed to be paid, her mother had to send the account and she'd pay it direct herself.

'It's not that. I don't need any money.'

That slightly scared sound in her mother's voice. She hadn't heard that before.

'So what is it then?'

She glugged more wine back. She could tell this was something her mum didn't want to tell her. Something that was her fault and she didn't want to own up to it. One of the boys in trouble again? Well, she was fucked if she was going to be forking out for a lawyer's bill. 'Listen,' she said, 'I'm waiting. I've just got back from work and I'm too tired to sit around holding on for you to tell me whatever it is you want to tell me. So either say it or you deal to it, okay?'

She sipped the wine slowly this time while she waited. Don't want to be turning into a pisshead like her.

'It's Serena.'

She bolted upright on the bar stool, nearly sloshed the wine over the bench. 'Serena?'

'She's missing.'

'How long has she been missing?'

'Uh, three weeks. Well, just over —.'

'Three weeks? Why didn't you call me?'

'I have tried, lovie. Like, I did try to get you last night but I only got your answer service.'

'So why didn't you leave a message? That's what an answering service is for.' She heard her voice rising, she knew there was no point in yelling, losing her rag, but shit, Serena.

God, but she loves that wee kid. Serena has this funny voice, kind of husky and too low-pitched for the size of her body; she's always been quite small and pretty, really pretty, with her big eyes and thick, shiny hair. And she's got this really wicked sense of humour. Really quick; she's always cracking jokes.

Serena was the one she missed most and worried most about after she took off; who'll look after See now I'm gone? But Lynnie'd thought she was doing okay, that she was doing really well at school. See talked to her about this teacher she had — it was all Miss this and Miss that so, to be honest, Lynnie'd felt a bit jealous — and she'd been getting merits in all her subjects, she said, and doing these projects with other kids and she was going to school camps and they were so fun. She even had a couple of friends she talked about. The Freemans didn't have friends as a general rule.

So what the fuck had happened?

She heard her mother, 'I didn't want to worry you, lovie, I just thought she'd come home,' and she was thinking, trying to think. Okay, this last year she hadn't been in touch with Serena quite so much. Whenever she'd phoned Serena sounded moody and grouchy, said she didn't have time to talk, and when Lynnie had brought up that plan they'd had about See coming up to Wellington for a holiday, she'd said she had something else on. But shit, she'd thought, Serena was a teenager, she'd get through all that crap once the hormones settled down.

Then Christmas came and Lynnie went camping up at Taupo with her mates so she didn't call but she'd sent Serena a top. Puffy sleeves with a pink and grey print. Nice. Expensive, as well. See hadn't even texted to tell her she'd got it. When was the last time they'd talked? Properly talked?

'But, well, it's been a while now and I haven't heard from her.'

Serena had told Lynnie she was going to finish school, right through to Year Thirteen. She'd said it with this little question in her voice, this little bit of embarrassment and, yeah, some pride there as well. 'I might go to university. Miss thinks I can.'

University? 'Fuck me, Serena.' Lynnie had laughed out loud, she was that pleased. 'University?'

So when did they talk about that? When?

'I didn't want to worry you, lovie, I just thought she'd come home. I mean, you and the boys used to take off. Used to have me worried sick wondering where you'd got to.'

She breathes inwards. Hard inwards.

They always came in late; she'd hear the back door open, hear the whispers, the giggles, the bed banging against the wall. She heard it all, the married guys, only there for a couple of hours at a time, the losers who stayed until something better came along, the boozers, the beaters. Yeah, she heard the grunts and the squeals and the screams and the crying. 'But I love you!'

When she was little, she used to be scared about the noises. She used to cry. Then she got used to it and screwed up wads of toilet paper to block up her ears. She told the boys not to worry about it. 'Mum can look after herself,' she told them.

'Used to have me worried sick wondering where you'd got to.' So what were they supposed to be hanging around for? Instant-noodle sandwiches and Blenheimer fucking balloons?

Stupid bitch. Fucking stupid cow. What the fuck did she think she was doing? Did she ever even give one thought to what it was like for us listening to her being fucked, being bashed? Did she ever think what it was like for us little kids listening in the dark?

She saw her mum screw everything up time and time again over some prick or other. But if she's somehow screwed Serena up as well —. I shouldn't have left her there, I shouldn't have left her. But what fucking choice did I have?

Take a breath, keep control. 'Okay, so what happened?'

'Nothing happened, Lynnie.' Her mother's voice has taken on that whining tone. Fuck, if she was in the same room, I'd be itching to slap her. 'She just took off. I thought she might be with you.'

'With me? So you're only telling me that my sister's been missing for over three weeks on the off-chance she might be here?'

'There's no point blaming me. It isn't my fault she's gone.'

She poured more wine into her glass. 'So whose fault is it, then? She wouldn't have left for no reason. Something must have been going on. Not that you'd bother yourself about it.'

'There's no need to talk to me like that. Nothing was going on. She just got a bit scratchy.'

'Scratchy.' Her voice sounded flat and bored but she was frightened. Where would Serena go? Why would she go?

'Yeah, went all quiet and moody. Wouldn't eat with us. Wouldn't do anything. She kept missing school. She'd just stay in her room.'

Serena was missing school? 'You didn't think I might like to hear about that either?'

'You're busy, Lynnie. I didn't want to bother you.'

'If it wasn't money it wasn't worth bothering about, eh?'

'Listen.' Her mother's voice is sharp, defensive. 'It's not like you're here, is it? It's not like you ever come to visit your own family.'

Well, she was right there. She'd never been back, though she'd done her best about keeping in touch. It was Serena she worried most about when she left. She knew the boys would look out for each other; in their way they were close, but Lynnie was the one who looked out for Serena. It was Lynnie who made sure Serena went to bed early enough to get the right amount of sleep and that she slept in the sunroom, far enough away from their mum's room. She made sure, too, that Serena had her face washed and her teeth cleaned and her hair brushed before she went to school and that she had the right clothes and the right gear. She used to take money out of her mum's bag, either that or pinch stuff. The way Lynnie saw it, New World and The Warehouse weren't going to miss a few coloured pencils and a lunch box and some undies and sandals and a drink bottle. New World and The Warehouse had plenty, while they had hardly anything.

And while she wouldn't go back, she'd done what she could. At first she had no money but once she got a job she used to send Serena clothes she'd picked up on special or at the op-shops. She wanted her to look right and feel right at school. She wanted See to be able to fit in. She'd only been a baby when their dad left, not quite one year old, and she used to clap her hands when Lynnie got home from school, clap her hands together and grin with her two top teeth looking just so big and weird in her little mouth.

Oh fuck, where is she?

'Did you try to talk to her and find out what was going on?'

'Course I tried. She wouldn't talk to me, though. I did try, Lynnie.'

'Well.' She traced her finger around the rim of the glass. Round and round. Round and round the garden chased the teddy bear.

'You got some guy living with you?'

'Yeah, well, Rob —.'

'He been trying it on with Serena?'

'No. No, he wouldn't. Rob would never. He'd never, I promise you, Lynnie. He's, well, I know he wouldn't do anything like that.'

Yeah, like the others wouldn't do that either.

Atishoo, atishoo and tickles under there. Spidery fingers on her leg. Hey Lynnie, come over here and sit on my knee.

'Have you tried her friends?'

'Yeah, well, I did my best but with school out and everything —.'

'Did she take anything with her? Her clothes?'

'Just her backpack's gone. The one she used for school.'

'Her mobile?'

'Switched off.'

'Did she have any money?'

'I don't know. She might've had her card in her bag. I don't know if she had much money on it, though. That's why I went to see the cops. They could find out if her account's been used. I saw it on TV, this programme about missing people. They can work out from their bank account where they've been.'

'You went to the cops?'

'I had to, Lynnie. I've been looking and ringing around and that, everywhere I could think of. But it's been three weeks, Lynnie, something could've happened to her. I went down to the station and I got Mick, Sergeant Withers, the boss I think he is now and he took a statement, he was really quite nice to me and he said he'd do what he could, he'd look into it and then he'd be in touch.'

She closed her eyes.

'Lynnie, she's only fifteen.'

'I know how old she is.'

She made up her mind. 'I'm coming home. I'll have to work things out here first but I'll be there by the end of the week.'

9

She phoned her boss. 'A few, uh, family problems.'

'Sure, Lynnette, of course you have to go. You take as much time as you need.'

She packed her bag. You went to the cops?

She opens up the magazine. 'Be open about sex with your partner: talk about your orgasms.' 'Vary your workouts: it's easy to get bored if you repeat the same gym exercises so try walking.' 'Join a Pilates class.'

She gives her plastic cup back to the attendant, takes a sweet from a freckly kid who's grinning his way down the aisle. 'We will be landing in Dunedin at approximately twenty past three. The temperature there is seventeen degrees. We hope you have had a pleasant journey and thank you for flying Air New Zealand.'

The airport buildings, the deep greenness of the land, the muffled thud and whine of engines, and they're taxiing across the runway. The wind hits her as she climbs down the steps. She picks up car keys from the rental-car reception bench. She's negotiated a good deal through work and there's a nice little Mazda Sport ready in the car park ready for her.

Where will I look? Where can I even start? What the fuck am I doing here? She loads her bag into the boot, gets into the driver's seat and adjusts it. She glances at the clock on the dashboard. Nearly four o'clock and then there's the two-hour drive. Better to stay here the night, get a decent bed and a good dinner and make a fresh start in the morning.

There's no point in leaving now; it'll be hot as hell in Central, she'll only get there tired and end up fighting with Mum, maybe getting offside with Darryl and Jesse and Todd. Anyway, it's Friday night. They'll all be out on the piss.

Fact is, she doesn't want to go back. She doesn't want to go back so much that every part of her body is telling her that. Her head's rushing with it, her stomach's churning with it. Driving in over the bridge. Seeing it all again. The main street. The pubs, the post office, the houses, the park. She doesn't want to be there. Oh, fuck, she doesn't want to be there. Except she has to find Serena.

Okay, okay, you can do it, you've got through worse than this, girl.

She takes a CD out of her bag, slots it in, turns it up high. Brody Dalle. 'Have you ever been alone fighting your own war?/Someone stole the life from you and now they're back for more.'

Brody Dalle. She is the shit. So. Do it. She's out of the car park, following the road she remembers past the rhododendrons, past the garage, past the little group of weatherboard airport houses and the farmland. She's waiting for a gap in the stream of cars on the main highway.

What the fuck is wrong with you? You've got nice clothes, you get your hair done, you're not too bad-looking. You've got a good job, you live in a nice place, you've got good mates, you've got a boyfriend.

You're not rubbish.

Sean. Her boyfriend, Sean. Shit. She didn't even tell him she was leaving. Up until now, if Lynnie believed anything about guys, it's what she used to tell Serena: 'Don't trust anyone. Guys, they can't keep it in their pants.' So it feels weird for her to have a boyfriend. The first hint of trouble, I'm out of here. But Sean, he's good to her, he says she looks great and that she is great and he loves her. Though she thinks she might love him back she never says it.

You're not rubbish.

Is that what got to Serena? Is that what made her leave? Was she making it all up about school and having friends? Just making it up about this Miss, telling Lynnie what she thought she wanted to hear? Was it the same for See as it was for her? People not looking you in the eye, the whispers and giggles that stopped when you went into a room? Mum down town in tight pants and high heels.

Serena can't stick up for herself. She trusts people. Fuck, she even trusts Mum. What if some of those bitches at the school had started giving her a really hard time? What if some guy had told her a lot of bullshit then dumped her? What if she'd done something stupid? Something really stupid.

Don't think about it. Just don't think about it.

But she's also a sensible kid. Probably she'd got pissed off at home and gone off with some mate somewhere, maybe camping. She's fifteen. Maybe she's gone to Wanaka. All the kids liked getting up to Wanaka over New Year; it's where they all hang out. Lots of parties. Lynnie used to hitch up there herself. Take a sleeping bag and sleep down by the lake. But Serena isn't a party girl. Except Lynnie doesn't know that, does she? The truth is, she doesn't know Serena any more. She hasn't even seen her in the last seven years.

If I can only find her. If she can only be okay. She has to be okay.

Lake Waihola stretches alongside the road, grey and weedy as she drives past and then there's the straight, wide, grey road again. Nearly at Milton. She slows enough to check out the new prison just before the township. The high spreading fences, the gates. 'That cop's got it in for me. Told me, next time you'll be inside where you belong.'

What she'd thought was that when Serena got finished up at school she could come up to Wellington and live with her, at least for a while, so Lynnie could look out for her. There's a university in Wellington, a good one, everyone says. Lynnie wasn't having some guy coming along and screwing everything up for Serena.

If she's okay. If Serena will only be okay.

If — that is when — she finds Serena, she'll take her back with her to Wellington and she can finish school up there. There's a girls' school not far from where Lynnie lives now. She's seen them in their blue blazers and striped skirts. A girls' school would be good for Serena.

She has to be okay.

She's driving more slowly now. There it is just in front of her, the turn-off to Central. She has never driven this road before; it was always Maureen or her mum driving the car if they went down to the city or she'd be in a bus on the way to the school sports tournaments in Dunedin. Staring out the window as the pines and paddocks raced by, pretending it didn't matter she didn't have the right gear, pretending it didn't matter that no one wanted to be in a billet with her. It didn't matter.

The road begins to narrow and twist. She takes it slow through the gorge. There's a car right up behind her and she pulls over to let it pass. Some big arse in his big-arse car. She feels so alone. Okay, she lives alone, she likes to be alone. A night out with her mates, another with Sean, and that's it, she wants a few nights in by herself. Here, though, with the trees hanging down over the road and the ferns and the sky, everything seems so dead, so fucking lonely. She takes a breath, another long one, pulls back onto the road.

'Open sky, the wave of pain the scent of you is bliss/Hungry eyes, they stare at me I know, I know.'

Last time she was here, perched way high up in the truck that picked her up and took her the whole way through. Sitting there rattling on to the driver about how she was going to stay with her auntie and cousins for the weekend and she didn't want to wait for the bus, that was why she was hitching. Feeling so fucking scared. Where was she going to sleep, what was she going to do? She was all on her own but she had to make it work. She was never going back. Never.

She drives into Lawrence. The town has had a makeover, cottages painted up, places to eat and craft shops lining the main street. She pulls over and goes into one of the cafés. 'We're just about to close so there's no meals but there's coffee.'

She can smell it. Good coffee. She orders a long black, takes the last muffin in the glass case, sits at a table and looks around. Polished floors, tongue-and-groove walls, old photographs of miners, a jazzy woman singer on the CD player. The coffee is strong and good and the muffin light and fresh and sweet, filled with raspberries, dusted with cinnamon. Somehow she feels better in here; the smells of coffee and spice, the friendly woman behind the counter, the lavender in the baskets outside, it all makes her feel more at ease. New people with new ideas. She can tell that by the way the whole place has gone ahead. Maybe the same thing's happened in Alex.

When she lived there Alex was the world. Everyone knew everyone else and everyone else's business. Everyone knew who owned the businesses on the main street and who lived in the big houses. That was the world. Alex was the world and if you were important you could do what you liked. If you were important you could take someone little and squeeze them and kick them and stamp them out flat.

But it's years since she left. Of course things would have changed. She gets into the car, checks herself out in the mirror. Things are different. She's different. Whatever happens she can deal with it. Jeez, she deals with clients all day, makes decisions, sometimes decisions other people don't like all that much, she travels, she meets people, she can handle herself.

She waits for the light to turn green beside the Beaumont Bridge, then clatters across. Now the river's below her, the Clutha, moving slowly like some lazy sea-snake monster. The water's the colour of the greenstone twist she always wears. She saw it in a shop in Wellington and there was something about the shape and that colour which made her want it around her neck right away. The name of the artist was on the card beside it and she read the description underneath: 'A Maori twist symbolises the path of life. It is believed to have been based on Maori kete basket-weaving. The path of life takes many twists and turns but carries on regardless.'

She's not into religion and all that spiritual crap; still she liked the curves of the pendant, the feel of the twisted cord around her neck. 'The path of life takes many twists and turns but carries on regardless.' There were two of them in the shop, almost the same, so she took a deep breath and pulled out the credit card and bought one for Serena as well, sent it down for her birthday. 'It's for good luck,' she'd written on the card.

'Carries on regardless.' No matter what bad stuff happens, no matter what good stuff, life doesn't stop, it just carries on. Yeah, well. So long as Serena's okay. So long as Serena's out there somewhere doing okay. Could be she's already back. Could be her mum's doing so much yelling and screaming and crying, she's forgotten to ring her mobile to let her know. She's past the Beaumont pub, coming up to the orchards, the places she remembers. 'Berries, fresh and frozen. Cherries.'

Cherries. She pulls into the roadside stall, buys a small box and puts them on the passenger seat beside her. They don't get cherries like this in Wellington. Fat and gleaming and smooth like wax, so deeply red they're almost black. She pops one in her mouth and it's sweet and thick and fleshy and the juice fills her mouth. That sky. The sky's that solid blue she remembers. 'What colour is the sky? It's blue, it's blue, it's blue. The sun is yellow. The trees are green. The colour of the sky is blue.'

At school, sitting cross-legged on the mat, singing it with the other little kids. She grins as she thinks of her voice, a foghorn droning out beneath and behind the others. Never has been able to sing.

Was it really so bad back then? Didn't she have some friends? Oh yeah, they were the kids no one else wanted to play with, that fat kid with the glasses, the one who had the bad sinuses. But, God, didn't they have some fun? Out with Darryl and Todd and Jesse. The rocks that were their castles and their forts. Climbing up to the battlements, looking out for the enemy. Chucking stones. Riding their bikes through the pines over the tracks, riding like maniacs. Sometimes they found mushrooms, sometimes used condoms they tried to break with sticks. Once they found a woman's underpants, blue with black lace. Darryl stretched them out, started flicking them around like a slingshot. 'Gross. Ugh, gross!'

That year they built the tree house. It took the entire summer holidays, nicking offcuts of timber and nails from building sites, hammering steps into the tree trunk, then the floor, the walls. All that working it out, all that arguing, 'That won't work Lynnie, it won't work 'cos —.' Their mum gave them cracked cups, chipped plates, but Darryl came up with the best thing of all. She remembers him climbing up the steps, remembers the grin that spread right across his face as he handed them the binoculars. They could sit up there and spy. He found them, he said.

Then there was the river. Rushing in after school, hauling on togs, running. Leaping off the rocks, churning through the water. They'd be down there hours in the summer. The smell of thyme, like eucalyptus except fainter, sweeter. The grey-blue colour of it, the feel of it scratching bare legs. The way the soles of their feet toughened up, turned into leather in the summer months. Sometimes Mum came down to find them, Serena under one arm, a packet of fish and chips under the other. Fish and chips, ice cream, MallowPuffs. Thursdays. Benefit days. If it hadn't been for the men, it could've been all right.

It could've been all right but it wasn't.

Roxburgh. The wide main street, the churches, the pubs. She's a bit tired but she keeps on going; not long now. Not long. It's getting towards the end of the day and the sun's lowering, bright and glaring on the windscreen. Past the Roxburgh dam, and she's climbing now, taking the corners gently. Then she's winding downwards. On the last stretch.

There's nowhere else like this with the burnt, golden land and the rocks like great looming ruins glinting silver in the evening sun. Fruitlands, the stone buildings still there beside the road, the pine trees jutting out of sand and rock, the houses dotted up on the rise of hill and there, at last, the bridge.

The bridge was her last memory of the place. Getting up, pulling on her jeans and her T-shirt, her jacket. Taking her bag and moving slowly and silently through the house, turning the door handle, slipping through and easing the door shut behind her. She pulled the hood of her jacket up over her head, wove her way through town, keeping away from the main streets. Along the river, then up onto the bridge. She walked across it, her head down, too afraid to look up.

She was over the bridge, walking up past the houses on the Half Mile. She'd just about got to the top of the rise when she heard the whine of a truck easing into a lower gear. She put out her thumb.

10

She's following the new road extension, past offices, shops, the school and turning onto Centennial Avenue. She stops opposite the park. So what does she do now? She's not staying at her mum's, not among all that mess and craziness. She gets out her iPhone, finds 'Alexandra Accommodation' and scrolls downwards: Alexandra Avenue Motel, Almond Court Motel, Alexandra Garden Court Motel, Centennial Motel.

Not on the main street. She wants to be away from traffic noise; she sleeps lightly enough as it is. Maybe she should look at renting a holiday crib. 'Elderberry Cottage is in a lovely peaceful country setting right beside the rail trail only a 6km car ride to Alexandra. Enjoy a morning coffee sitting out on the lawn overlooking the orchard.' She doesn't want that either. Not being on her own in the fucking country, in the middle of an orchard, rattling around on her own in some creaky old cottage.

He'll know she's back.

In the end she settles for Hideaway Motels, 'quality accommodation at budget prices on a quiet street behind the park'. She phones, negotiates a weekly rate with the manager; it could be a week, maybe even two and she'll clean her own unit, change her own sheets.

'Name?'

'Lynnette Freeman.' She almost holds her breath waiting for the pause, the changed voice, 'Sorry, I've made a mistake. We don't have anything available after all.'

'When will you be in?'

'I'll come now, if that's okay.'

'That's fine. I'll pop over to the unit and make sure everything's ready. I've put you in number three. There's a car park just along from it. I'm Chris, by the way.'

Six grey block oblongs, side by side. A tiny lounge with a couch and a TV and a scarred coffee table. Peach walls, grey vertical blinds that flap when she opens the windows. There's a large white pedestal fan on the floor beside the couch. The bed is covered with a duvet with a grey and pink smudgy-patterned cover. The curtains match. She tries the bed out and it's comfortable enough and the kitchen is well equipped. Everything's clean and there's a little deck outside the sliding doors. It'll do, it'll do just fine.

Chris is hovering beside the door. 'Got everything you need? There's milk in the fridge. Coffee and tea beside the jug. Just ask when you want some more. The heater's on the wall. Not that you'll need that. But you might want to put on the fan.'

It's past seven o'clock and she's tired and she's starving. She looks through the brochures on the coffee table, finds a pizza place that delivers and phones through an order: pepperoni, wedges, Greek salad. She flicks on the TV.

He'll remember.

What she'd really like is a wine, but she's just too stuffed to fight her way around the supermarket; it's Friday, everyone goes to the supermarket on a Friday. Anyway, the food shouldn't be far away. She'll eat, watch a bit of TV, have an early night.

Of course he'll remember. But what can he do?

She drives to the supermarket early in the morning, picks up cereal and yoghurt and juice, a bag of mixed greens, tomatoes, mayonnaise, marg, bread, cheese, a couple of frozen meals she can defrost in the microwave, a bottle of Sav. Back at the motel she fills a bowl with muesli and yoghurt and makes coffee in the plunger, takes it all outside and sits on the plastic chair on the small deck in the sun.

She has to go round there. It's what she's come for. She has to go. Saturday. The boys will be home. It'll be good to see the boys. Maybe there's news by now. Maybe Serena's already back. She and

See could be on their way back to Wellington tomorrow.

She looks up at the hills, the way they wrapped themselves around the town with the clock in the middle up there on Tucker's Hill. The biggest clock in New Zealand, the second-biggest clock in the world. They learned about it in school, did a project about it. Some guy from the Jaycees who'd been in on building it came and talked to them. They had to do drawings of the clock with the facts written underneath in their best work. 'Eleven metres in diameter. 150 bulbs. Each hand weighs . . .'

'We're so lucky in Alexandra, class. If we want to know the time all we have to do is look up at the hill. You can see it from eight kilometres away.'

No shit. She has another coffee, puts on a bit of make-up and does her hair in front of the little mirror in the bathroom. She's wearing her black top, her jeans, her apple-green sandals. She looks good.

She looks good.

The grocery shop on the corner now sells bikes, the hairdresser's gone and there's yellowing paper covering the large window facing the street where she used to stare in at ladies reading magazines with stuff in their hair and towels around their necks. The Pollocks' house is painted green and there's a For Sale sign posted beside the Millers' fence. 'Is This Your New Home? Phone now: 03 448 8888.'

And there it is. Home sweet fucking home. She stops outside and looks in at the grey blocks, the peeling window sills and, oh fuck, the same yellowing lacy curtains looping across the windows, the same parched lawn. She can smell it. Even before she goes inside she can smell the cigarette smoke, the fry-ups, the booze, the fly-spray.

You can do this, okay?

She takes her bag from the passenger seat. Her new black bag she saved up for. It's plain, it's classy and it's leather; she's had to learn those things.

The Freemans, the dirty Freemans, your brother pooed his pants, your brother stinks.

She's walking down the drive past Darryl's Holden, past the oldest Toyota Crown in the fucking world that belongs to her mother, Christ knows how it still gets a warrant, past Jesse's motorbike and she's round the back of the house rapping on the door. The door that squeaked that morning as she left, that door she thought would bring them all out after her, 'Where the hell do you think you're going?'

Darryl's there at the door and he's —. He's actually good-looking, tanned and, jeez, he's so bloody big and he picks her up, twirls her around. He's grinning, his face is one bloody almighty grin and then he lets her down and behind him she sees Jesse and Todd. They're big as well, so big. They're sitting at the table eating toast, looking up at her, they look happy enough to see her but they're a bit wary, she can see that in their eyes. She goes over to them, gives each of them a hug and a kiss on the cheek.

And there she is, beside the bench, filling up the jug.

She doesn't look much different. A few lines around her eyes and mouth. Her hair's still that white blonde and her top and her pants are way too tight. But she's got a good body, Lynnie'll give her that. Another thing she'll give her is her nice eyes, shiny and brilliant-blue fringed with thick eyelashes. When Lynnie was a kid she thought her mother was the best-looking of all the mothers she saw picking their kids up from school. She thought her mum looked like a princess with her blue eyes and blonde hair. Even her name, Charmaine. That was a beautiful name, a princess's name.

. Maybe she should give her mum a hug. They've never been a huggy family, never physically demonstrative, but still, it's a long, long time since she's seen her. It's hard, though. Somehow she can't quite make her body move around the table and get close enough. The idea of touching her mother, of holding, even for a moment, that stiff, thin, alien body against hers keeps her locked there, silent and watching.

Her mum plugs in the jug and looks at her. 'Well, look who's here.'

They eye each other across the table. Welcome home, Lynnie, you're looking great Lynnie, good to see you, Lynnie. Love you, Lynnie.

'Want a cuppa?'

'Yeah, okay.'

She sits at the table, watches as her mother puts tea bags into the mugs and pours in boiling water. 'Still take milk?'

'Yeah. Yeah.'

She adds milk, hands the mug to Lynnie. She indicates the tea bag still floating on the surface. 'I don't know how strong you like it. Sugar's on the table.'

Lynnie fishes out the tea bag with a spoon and drops it onto a used plate. She looks around the room at the plastic baskets filled with washing overflowing onto the floor, the piled newspapers, the —. Shit, what's that on the bench? Looks like someone's dismantling an engine.

'Toast?' her mother says.

'No thanks. Listen, you know what I'm here for. Have you heard from her? Is there any news?'

Her mother shakes her head. The boys start to shift around as if they're about to leave. So they don't want to get into any rows, don't want to get into anything that might turn out nasty? Well, tough. She glares at them. 'You stay right there. Your sister's missing, she's only a kid, anything could've happened to her. I want to know what's been going on.'

'Nothing to do with me,' Darryl says. 'I wasn't even here. I've been up in Wanaka. I'm only here for the weekend. I'm giving a hand to Jesse. We're fixing his bike.' He nodded towards the nuts and bolts bleeding grease onto the newspaper they're sitting on.

'But you must have seen her when you were home. Did she say anything to you? Did you think there might be something wrong?'

'She never said anything to me.' Darryl puffs out his breath and shifts around in his seat. He's a little kid under cross-examination from his teacher, eager to get away from the scrutiny and questions.

'What about you two? Did she say anything to you? Did you think anything could be wrong?'

'Nuh.' The same shifts and wriggles, the same desperate looks towards the door.

'Christ, doesn't anyone ever talk around here?' She hears her voice start to rise.

'It's all right for you to talk.' It's Todd.

'What the hell're you talking about?'

'Well, shit, you haven't been round, have you? You can't come back here bitching and moaning at us.'

Todd always was the fiery one. But he was right. 'Sorry. Sorry, but I'm just worried about her.'

'Yeah, well, we're worried too. We're the ones that've been out looking for her.'

'I'm sorry, okay? But what I want to know is was there anything that could've made you think there was something wrong? Anything she might've said?'

Jesse shrugs. 'She never said nothing.'

'She was fucking moody,' Todd says. 'Couldn't take a joke any more. Like, I told her she was putting on the beef, just having her on, you know, and she went into her room and slammed the door. Wouldn't come out.'

'You shouldn't have said that to her,' she says. 'Girls her age get upset about stuff like that.'

Her mother sits down with her tea and toast across the table from her. 'Well, she was getting really chubby.'

'But Serena's really little.'

'Well, she's not little now. She gave up all her sport and that. Just sat around the place doing nothing.'

'Serena?'

'Yeah, Serena. Serena your sister you never bothered to come and see.'

Ever wonder why? Ever wonder why I left the way I did? Ever wonder how I got on in Dunedin with no one to help me, no one that I knew? Ever wonder if I was scared?

Her mother is chewing her toast. She takes another bite, a slurp of tea. The boys look at each other over the table and, in unison, get up and head towards the door. Let them go. They don't know anything. Serena wouldn't tell them anything. What would be the point?

'I don't want a fight. I just want to know what's happened.'

'Listen, nothing happened. I told you.' She finishes her tea, goes over to the bench, pours more hot water over the tea bag still bobbing in her cup. 'Nothing happened, okay?'

'But —.' She has to stay calm. She can do it at work with some prick yelling down the phone, so she can do it with her mother. 'Serena's always been such a good kid. Doing well at school and all that. But then you said she changed.'

'Yeah, well.' She comes back to the table, butters more toast. 'Kids of that age, girls especially, do change. Like you, Lynnie, going off like you did. Never have been able to get my head around that one.'

'But I wasn't any good at school, Mum. Not like Serena.'

Her mother puts a cigarette between her lips and lights it, draws in hard. 'She'd gone off that, though. Her schoolwork and that. Her school reports weren't much good.'

'Did you try and talk to her? Did you ask her if anything was wrong?'

She breathes in hard. 'I've told you, Lynnie. Course I asked her. Course I tried to find out. But she shut me out. All you kids've done that. Shut me out. I've done my best. It's not easy on your own bringing up five kids, you should try it sometime.'

As if I'd be that fucking stupid.

'And it's not like you made it any easier, taking off like that. You're the oldest, you could've given me a bit of a hand.'

Pick up Serena, would you Lynnie, get the washing on Lynnie, I just have to go out for a couple of hours Lynnie, you can put the tea on, eh?

'Like this now with Serena. If you'd been here —.'

'I've worked hard over the past few years,' Lynnie says, 'and it's been bloody tough trying to make something of myself. I've got a good job now but I've had to work for it.'

Her mother sniffs. 'Well, good for you. But don't you go coming down on me. I've done my best for all of you kids.'

The door opens and there's a man heading towards the bench: singlet and shorts, tats up one arm, pot gut hanging over the elastic waistband. 'Rob,' her mother says, brightening up. 'Lynnie, this is Rob.'

He turns around. 'Pleased to meet you.'

She sees his missing tooth. Fuck, Mum, is this what it's come down to?

'Another brew?' He points at Lynnie's cup and she shakes her head. All she wants is to get away. Back to the motel, pack up her stuff and fuck right off out of here. But she can't, not until she finds something out and there must be something.

He sits down beside her mother. She pats his hand. If he's touched Serena, if he's been touching her, if he's been fucking her, I'll find out and I'll kill the bastard.

'We've been talking about Serena,' Lynnie says, eyeing him across the table. 'Something was wrong. From what Mum's told me, it's obvious she was upset about something. I just think, if we can figure out what it was, we might be able to work out what's happened to her.'

Is there a flicker in his eyes as he shifts them away from her gaze and reaches across the table for toast? She watches him spreading it, slathering on the marg, the jam. 'Not my business,' he mutters.

'But you've been living here, right?'

'Yeah, but she's not my kid, eh.'

'There's been nothing that's happened? No trouble?'

'Well,' he chews, 'just that bullshit story. I had to straighten that one out —.'

Her mother has her hand on his arm, she's shaking her head, 'It's got nothing to do with that Rob. Nothing to do with it. That was months ago.'

'What was months ago?'

'Nothing.' Her mother looks flustered. 'It was nothing.'

'What?'

'Better tell her, Char. We've got nothing to hide.' His voice rises, booming out across the table. Nothing to hide.

Her mum won't meet her eye. 'Only a bit of trouble with one of the teachers, Lynnie. It was nothing, really.'

'Could you just tell me what happened?'

'Well.' She lights a cigarette. 'This teacher. This teacher, well, she thought she saw marks on Serena's arm. You know, uh, bruises? So she told the counsellor at the school. Sally Davis, her name is. She came around here —.'

'Throwing her bloody weight around,' Rob mutters. He reaches for more toast.

'Serena had bruises on her arm?' She stares at her mother.

'Listen, it was nothing. Serena said she'd fallen over. But Sally Davis said she had to talk to me. She had to visit Serena's home, she said. Just, just, what'd she say, Rob? Just fulfilling the requirements of her job.'

'Just making a bloody nuisance of herself,' Rob said. 'Stupid bitch thought I might've done it.'

Her heart is juddering, her mouth is dry. And did you? Did you? Oh, Serena, poor little kid, who hurt you?

She looks directly at her mother. 'What did Serena say?'

'Just like I told you. Said she'd fallen over.'

'Here? Did she fall here? Did you see her fall over?'

'No. Not here. It was —. I don't know, she didn't say, did she.' Her voice is harsh and irritable.

'Did she have bruises anywhere else on her body?'

'I don't know. How would I know that? She's fifteen years old. Not like I'm going to be in the bathroom with her, is it.'

'Did you ask her, Mum? Did you talk to Serena. On your own?'

Rob slams down his mug and stands up. His face is scarlet. 'Here's another one thinks I did it!' he shouts. 'Listen, I never touched her. Never. I don't hit bloody kids. What the hell do you take me for?'

Her mother is standing now as well, clutching Rob's hand.

'Course you didn't, babe. Course you didn't.' She scowls at Lynnie. 'You've got your wires crossed there, Lynnie. Rob's a good guy. He'd never do a thing like that. See liked Rob.'

Darryl has come in and he's by the door, his arms crossed, looking at them. 'What d'you mean, See liked Rob? She's not dead, Mum. See's not fucking dead, is she?'

11

See's not fucking dead is she?

Is she?

Her mother's crying now. 'She can't be dead. Serena's my baby. The best-natured of the lot of you, See is. I love See. I love all my kids and look where it's got me.'

Lynnie has to get out. Her mother is bawling onto Rob's shoulder and he looks as though he wants to hit her and now Maureen's turned up: puffy face, white pants, glittery top. 'Just look what you've done. You never come near the place then you turn up upsetting everyone. Your mum's got enough on her plate without you on it as well.'

'I'll see you later.'

She has to get out, has to get away from them, the whole sad-loser bunch of them. What's that new name they call fucked-up families? Dysfunctional? Dys-fucking-functional, that's them all right. But she has to do something. Even if it means knocking on every door in Alex, she has to do something. She drives around the streets, the main road, around by where the old swimming pool used to be, down the narrow streets by the river. She sees girls walking along the footpath, hanging around the park, giggling together. Girls talking about clothes and boyfriends, all that stuff girls like to talk about, normal girls from fucking normal families. Not the girls with bruises on their arms, not the girls people don't even notice are gone. Where is she? Where is she?

What if she's been taken by someone? She could've been out biking or walking along Dunstan Road, Earnscleugh Road, there are plenty of places where someone could be snatched up off the road without anyone seeing.

Some bastard pulling up alongside her, 'Can you tell me the way to —?'

And knowing Serena, she'd go right over to the car trying to help, leaning in close so she could hear where he wanted to go. 'Could you just show me on this map? I've just got it here somewhere —.' She's trusting, far too trusting. Shit, she's told her often enough, you can't trust men. They can't keep it in their pants. She's told her.

Or is it something to do with that tosser Rob? What do they always say on TV? Look at the family first? Well, she doesn't like the way his eyes shift around the room, anything but look back at you. He could've been at Serena, at her all the time, and her mother wouldn't have had a clue. A few too many wines, she'd be snoring her head off, and there he'd be creeping along the passage to See's room.

There were bruises on Serena's arms. Why wasn't I told about that? And why isn't anyone out looking for her? If it was someone else's kid, wouldn't they be out looking? She could be dumped somewhere; in the lake, in the pines, up in The Nobbies way off the road. Still, way down in her gut she's certain that if Serena was dead she'd feel it. She'd know. Serena's alive. She's sure of that, except where the hell is she?

She goes back to the motel, makes coffee and a sandwich. In the afternoon she drives out to Clyde then over to Cromwell. She knows it's useless but she slows to scan the faces of hitch-hikers and drives slowly around the streets.

It's a waste of time, of course. She phones her mother, keep it light, no drama, just ask the questions. 'Can you make me a list of Serena's friends?'

'I told you. I've already rung around.'

'Well, now I can ring around.'

'I can't say I like your attitude, Lynnie.'

'Please. Just do it, Mum, okay? A list of names and any phone numbers and addresses you have.'

'Must be this job you've got making you so bossy. Too big for us now, eh?'

'I'll be around later to pick it up.'

Maureen's sitting at the table with her mother when she calls in, the wine bottle between them. 'Hey, stranger. Didn't get much of a chance for a yak this morning, Lynnie-girl. How are ya?' Maureen wraps her soft, dimpled arms around her. 'Look at you! All grown up and gorgeous. Isn't she gorgeous, Char?'

Lynnie hugs her back, that long-ago smell of tobacco and sweet wine and Tabu. Maureen's not that bad, Lynnie knows she's kept an eye on her mother and the kids over the years. She looks hard as nails with her dyed red hair and she's got a mouth on her but she's a softy underneath it all. Got a bit more sense than her mum, sense enough to give her a bloody good talking to when she has to.

'How long are you here for?'

'As long as it takes to find Serena.'

'Ah, no need to worry about See. She's a sensible kid. Probably needed to get a few things off her chest. She'll be back any day.'

'Did she talk to you?'

'Me? No. If she had I would've said. Want a wine, Lynnie?' She holds out the bottle.

'No thanks, I'm driving.'

'You're driving? Where you going?'

'She's not stopping with us,' her mother says, filling her glass. 'We're not good enough for her now she's got that fancy job and lives in Wellington.'

She can't get angry, can't snap back. 'I just called in to get a list Mum's made for me. I'm going to talk to Serena's friends,' she says to Maureen.

'Even though I've already talked to them,' her mother says, sighing loudly. 'Doesn't trust me to do it right.'

'Won't do any harm to check them out again,' she says lightly, 'just in case someone's heard something. Nice to see you, Maureen. Mum, I'll stay in touch.'

She sits in the evening sunshine with a glass of wine in front of her on the fold-out table, looking through the list. There are only six names. No numbers or addresses. She looks them up on her iPhone and writes the details beside them. She'll call around to their houses in the morning; she can easily cover them in a morning. After that? Well, she doesn't know what she'll do. She's hoping something will come out of her visits that she can follow up on. She goes inside, locks the sliding door behind her, switches on the telly.

She's running, the pines dark and thick pressing in on her. She hears the dull thud as her feet hit the ground. Run, keep going, watch out you don't fall, there are rocks, tree stumps buried in the sand. Falling smack into the sand. Into sand creeping, covering her, heaping up over her can't move can't move in her nose and in her eyes and in her mouth in her mouth gritty smothering filling up her mouth.

The hoarse cry, half-strangled in her throat, heaves her out of sleep, back into this unfamiliar room. She opens her eyes, stares into the shadows. There's a crack of light flickering through the curtains from the street lamp outside. She feels her heart, the rapid, hard throb of heartbeat against her ribs.

Where are you, Serena? Where are you?

12

She gets up early. The shower drums down strong and hot on her body. She takes extra care with her hair and make-up and wears her stripy shirt, jeans and sandals and her earrings like wide, curved leaves. Maybe if she dresses herself up a bit, maybe if they see she's okay, she's respectable, they'll take this more seriously and try to help.

Her first call is in the new Molyneux Estate, Wildflower Way. It's a cream block place which spreads across almost the entire width of the section. She walks up the perfectly white and even concrete drive and rings the doorbell. She smiles at the woman who opens the door and holds out her hand as she would with a business associate. 'Hello. I'm Lynnette Freeman. I'm Serena's sister. I was wondering if I could speak to Julie.'

The woman looks at her for a moment then takes her hand, 'I'm Sarah. Julie's mum.' She turns her head and calls, 'Julie. Someone here to talk to you.'

She turns back to Lynnie. 'Can you tell me what this is about?'

'Serena's missing. I'm checking with her friends to see if they've heard anything.'

She looks alarmed. 'Serena's missing? Have the police been notified?'

'Well, yes they have. They're looking for her.'

'Oh, you poor thing. You'd better come inside. You must be so worried. Please, sit down. When did she go missing?'

They're in a room with smooth grey carpet, a fireplace with a schist rock wall behind it, family photos on shelves attached to the walls. She sits on the spongy leather seat Sarah is ushering her towards. 'About three weeks ago.'

'Three weeks ago? But —.'

A girl comes in. Tanned legs, a blonde ponytail. She looks questioningly at her mother. Lynnie sees they both have the same startled-looking, pale blue eyes.

'Julie, this is Lynnette Freeman. Serena's sister. Did you know Serena was missing?'

Julie sits beside her mother on the sofa and looks at Lynnie, her eyes wide. 'Serena hasn't come home yet?'

Her mother turns to look at her. 'You knew about this?'

'Serena's mum rang Cindy to see if she was there and then Cindy rang me. I told you.'

'Well, you did say something about it but I didn't realise she was missing. Three weeks —.'

Lynnie asks the questions she has worked out. Yes, Julie and Serena were in the same class. No, she wasn't a close friend but they knew each other fairly well. They'd hung out quite a bit when they'd been on this project together, this mural they did at school. But that wasn't this past year, it was the year before and she hadn't talked to Serena, not for a while really, and she hadn't heard anything about her, not since school broke up for the summer holidays.

Did Serena have any particularly close friends? Not really, not that she knew about anyway. They just kind of all hung.

Last question. The most important question. 'Julie, do you know anything that might help us? Do you know if Serena was in any sort of trouble?'

She shakes her head. 'I don't know. Like, I don't really know her that well —.'

But, Sarah says, cutting in, they'll take Lynnie's mobile number and let her know immediately if they hear anything, they'll let her know the minute they find out anything at all. And they will ask around. Though they are going away in a few days. The Gold Coast.

It's the same at the other houses she visits. Cindy, Melanie, Holly, Mandy. Houses with the sun coming into the living room through the vast windows, the pale carpets, the hefty, cushioned chairs and sofas, the wide glass coffee tables, the family photos. The shocked, wide eyes, the offers of coffee, the exchanges of mobile numbers.

The same answers: 'Like, I don't really know her that well. I don't really know . . .'

I don't know.

They're telling the truth. She's certain of that. Their mothers are concerned and helpful, they feel for her. 'Oh, you poor thing.' But nobody knows anything. Whatever was wrong, Serena kept it to herself.

She asks the last question of the final girl, Janine. 'Do you know if Serena was in any sort of trouble?'

'No. No, I don't really know her that —.' Then she stops, turns a little red and starts fiddling with her bracelet. 'Uh, you know about Serena being suspended?'

'Suspended? No, I didn't know that.'

'Oh.'

'When was this?'

'It was way back at the beginning of the year.'

'Do you know why she was suspended?'

Janine looks at her mother. 'It was about drugs. How I know is some kids got called in to talk to Ms Pringle. Everyone they knew who'd been down at the river over the holidays got called in and she — Ms Pringle, that is — asked if anyone had been offered drugs.'

'By Serena, you mean?'

She shakes her head. 'She didn't say it was Serena but it was easy to work out who it was because she'd been called out of class and then she didn't come back.'

'What kind of drugs?'

By now Janine's face and neck are flushed red. 'Uh, marijuana. And, uh, P.'

'Were you called into Ms Pringle's office?' Her mother's voice is alarmed.

'Yeah, well, Mum, I was at the river. Just swimming and —.'

'Had you been offered any drugs?'

'No. No, Mum. Anyway, Serena came back to school a wee while after that so the school must have found out it wasn't true.'

'You're telling me that Serena wasn't involved with drugs? You never saw her with any?'

'No, I didn't, Mum, I promise. Listen, it wasn't true, it never happened. It was just some stupid story that got spread around. Serena isn't like that.'

No smoke without fire. Lynnie sees it in Janine's mother's eyes as she abruptly stands up. Obviously she wants Lynnie out so she can interrogate her daughter.

'Thanks,' Lynnie says, standing up as well. 'You've been really helpful.'

'Well.' Her eyes are hard as they head towards the door. 'I hope you find her soon.'

Lynnie drives without thinking, past the golf course, past the block of pines, takes the turn-off to Clyde. Ends up parking at the lookout staring out over the dam. The great banks of concrete, the swell and spread of water.

Serena was on drugs? Lynnie's seen enough people hooked on crystal to know what it does to them. Even weed can fuck you up. She was moody, she stayed in her room, she slept a lot. Maybe that's it. She doesn't like it but it could explain everything. The changes in her behaviour, the falling grades at school, even the marks on her arms; she could've got on the wrong side of whoever was dealing it to her, or the bruises could be from needles.

But Serena? Yeah, Serena. Serena your sister you never bothered to come and see. She leans back against the seat and closes her eyes. If See has a drug problem anything could've happened to her. She could be anywhere. Taken off with some wanker.

She could've done too much, done the bad stuff and freaked out, could be down there somewhere, down among that mass of oily green.

She has to face up to it: Serena could be dead. Even if she's alive, if she's into drugs she's in trouble. No nice girls' school, no university, no nothing. Except Janine denied it. Denied, anyway, that she'd had anything to do with it. But that flush on her neck and the way her mother was watching her like a hawk, ready to rip right into her, she might have been just covering her own back. The backs of her friends as well.

Think. Think. Who could tell her something? Who would know? There was that school counsellor her mother had mentioned, Sally. Sally Davis, that was it. She must know something; anyway it's worth a try. She takes out her iPhone: Davis, A, Davis, T and then there it is, Davis, S. She selects the number.

'Hello?'

'Is that Sally Davis?'

'It is.'

'I'm Lynnette Freeman. Serena's sister. Serena's missing. You might already know?'

'No, no I didn't. Gosh that's —.'

'I was wondering if I could come and talk to you. I know it's the holidays but —.'

'Well, by all means. But I don't know if I'll be able to help.'

Lynnie takes her address and drives there. 'Earnscleugh Road. Just look for the name on the letterbox, it's a wee cottage not far off the road, white with blue around the windows, fruit trees out the front, chooks running around.'

Sally's a large, soft-and-comfortable-looking woman, floaty skirt, grey hair pulled up in a twist. 'You must be Lynnette. Come in, please come in. Tea? I've got green tea and apple and plum, ginger and orange? I don't do caffeine, I'm afraid.'

'I'm fine, thanks.' Lynnie can barely hold back the grimace; she hates herbal teas with a passion. They're in a tiny room smelling of pot-pourri and the jasmine which billows out of a china tea-pot. There's the fattest tabby cat Lynnie has ever seen asleep on the armchair Sally indicates for her to sit in. 'That's Wilberforce, just give him a shove and he'll move.'

She shoves. Wilberforce gives her a withering look and moves slightly, looping himself across the arm of the chair. Sally smiles. 'Is that all right? Have you got enough room? I hope you're a cat lover.'

She's not a cat lover, but she nods. Sally leans forward, frowning slightly. 'Now. Serena is missing,' she says. 'How long has she been missing'

'Three weeks.'

'Three weeks. Oh dear. Why hasn't the school been notified?'

'I suppose because it's holiday time. I really don't know. I've only just found out myself and I've come down to see what I can do.'

'But the police know?'

'My mother told them last week.'

It's all there in Sally's eyes: oh, the slackness of this family which has only just woken up to the fact of a missing teenage girl weeks after she's gone, which has only just come to the realisation that this could just possibly be serious. 'Well,' she says, 'how may I help you?'

'I talked to one of Serena's friends. Janine Whitely. She told me Serena had been suspended.'

'There was an allegation that Serena had been selling drugs to other students. The story was that her brother was involved as well. I never quite got to the bottom of who'd made the complaint but in the end the school was reasonably confident that the accusation was unfounded and so Serena came back to school.'

Reasonably confident. 'Which brother was supposed to be involved?'

'I believe it was Darryl. Of course, we already knew Darryl.' Her face puckers enough to indicate that the school's knowledge of Darryl had been disagreeable.

'How sure were you it wasn't true?'

Sally purses her lips. 'As sure as we could be. The other students were asked about it and denied knowing anything about it. Adamantly denied it, in fact. Serena was questioned, of course, and she denied it as well.'

'If all of this was just a story, why was she suspended?'

'The school has a zero tolerance to drugs policy. We pride

ourselves on running a very good school and, well, there's the other students to consider.'

'I understand you spoke to my mother about bruises on Serena's arms?'

'We do have to follow these things up, but Serena told me herself that she'd fallen.'

'You believed her?'

'I had no reason not to.'

'But her grades were falling. She gave up sports. She was really good at sports and she was missing school.'

Sally sighs. 'Girls go through tremendous changes over those years. If they choose not to disclose —.'

'Weren't you worried about her?'

Sally is silent for a moment. 'No more,' she says stiffly, 'than about the other five hundred or so students under my care.'

'But Serena was a good student. She was doing well. Didn't anyone notice when all that started changing?'

'Well, we do rely on backup from the home and when that's not there —.'

'Are you saying when a kid comes from a shit home they're not worth helping?'

'Of course I don't mean that. That's not the policy at all.'

'Look, here we have a kid, a really good kid, who gets suspended for something she didn't do and then her grades start going down and then she's got bruises on her arms. Didn't it enter into your head that she might be in trouble? Didn't you think it might be your job to try to find out what was going on?'

'I take great pride in my job.'

'Yeah, like Mum said. Fulfilling the requirements. Sounds to me,' Lynnie says, 'like no one at that "good school" of yours gave a fuck about Serena.'

Sally's face flushes and she stands up. How dare you use that word in my nice little cottage with its genuine coal range and the sweet cross-stitched pictures on the walls? Interview over.

'I don't think that's at all fair. As I said, if students don't wish to disclose . . . But rest assured I will notify the school.'

Lynnie starts up the car. Rest assured. She'd like to grab Sally Davis by her fat neck and shake all that smug fucking niceness out of her. She'd like to shake all those teachers with their running-a-good-school crap. They didn't give a fuck about Serena. What she'd said to Sally bloody Davis was right, though she hadn't liked hearing it. Oh, if it'd been a dentist's daughter or a lawyer's daughter or the fucking mayor's daughter it would've been different. And if it was one of those kids missing, they'd be doing something, all right. The fucking TV cameras would be there. They'd be out in their thousands, there'd be fucking church prayer meetings. 'Oh, we're so concerned, oh, this wonderful girl, oh, we're doing our very best. We'll bring her home.'

Rest fucking assured.

She's back in the motel. She's run out of ideas and she's angry, so choked up and angry she's got tears running down her face. Drugs. Bruises on her arms. Chucked out of class. Chucked out of school. No one to talk to, no one to help. Oh, that poor kid. I should've been there.

She punches in Darryl's number. 'What's this I hear about you and See dealing drugs?'

'Me and See dealing drugs? That's a new one. What the hell you on about now?'

'I'm on about Serena being suspended from school because of you two selling drugs to kids down at the river. Whose idea was that, dickhead?'

Now he's laughing. 'Where did that come from? First I've heard of it. I might be a dickhead but I'm not a stupid dickhead.'

'She had bruises on her arms, she was missing school —'

'So she didn't want to go to school. Listen, Lynnie, if See was taking anything I'd know, okay? She's too straight to do that kind of stuff.'

'But something's happened.'

'Yeah and whatever it is she'll get over it.'

'Darryl, I'm just so —.'

'Scared. Yeah. I know.'

He's growing up, Darryl. She can hear that in his voice. Straightened himself out a bit as well. Looks like this Wanaka job might be doing him some good.

'She'll be back. Don't worry about it. Listen, we're going out to Galloway for a barbecue. Todd and Jesse and a few mates. What about coming down with us?'

She hesitates, but what else is she going to do? Sit in this hot motel room watching TV? Search the streets? Interrogate people who don't know anything? Why not have a bit of fun with the boys? 'Okay, you're on.'

'We're heading there now. We'll pick you up.'

She changes into shorts and a T-shirt, grabs her swimsuit. And jeez, but it's actually fun to be rattling along in Darryl's Holden, the windows wide open and the CD player blasting, ker-chung, ker-chung, Lynnie in the front passenger seat, Jesse and Todd in the back. They laugh a lot. They tell jokes, tell her their stories about scumbag bosses and tosser workmates, they brag about their chicks, about how wasted they got last Saturday night. Darryl drives too fast and she tells him to slow down but she's laughing as well.

Darryl takes the barbecue, Todd carries one chilly bin, Jesse the other, she's given the blanket and the bag of towels. They set everything up under the trees near to the river. Darryl pops the top off a can of beer and hands it to her. 'Cheers, Lynnie.' Their mates turn up in another Holden, ker-chung, ker-chung. She recognises some of them from school. They were just little kids when she left. One of the girls Jesse was talking about, Leigh, is there. She looks good in her orange bikini. Lynnie sees Todd grin at Jesse.

She changes into her own swimsuit, the new red one with the black straps. Darryl whistles and she flicks her towel at his legs. She's got a good body, the gym makes sure of that. She lies on her towel, drinks a couple of cans, listens to the talk, laughs along with them. They're all jumping off the river bank into the water and she joins them. The water's freezing but it's good. It's so good.

They eat the sausages and lamb chops Darryl and his mate Jason cook on the barbecue with thick white bread and butter and tomato sauce. The meat's salty and slightly charred, dripping with grease. The sun, the ripple sounds of the river, the trees sheltering them: she could sleep here, just sleep and sleep.

Darryl comes and sits beside her, 'You okay?'

'Yeah.'

'I did think about leaving, Lynnie. But like I said, all my mates are here.'

'It's all right. I understand.'

'This job I've got. They said they'd like to take me on permanently.'

'So what do you think about that?'

'Yeah, I'm keen. I'm staying out of trouble as well.'

'What about this story I heard about you and Serena selling drugs?'

'It's bullshit.'

'But how could a story like that get started?'

He shrugs. His chest, arms are tanned and smooth; drops of water cling to his skin and his hair is wet. She sees one of the girls watching him. I'd watch him too. He's bloody good-looking and he's actually quite sweet.

'Some bastard got it in for us, I suppose.'

'Serena ever come out here with you guys?'

'A couple of times last summer.' He grins. 'She never drank anything so she got to be our sober driver.'

'Serena has her licence?'

'No. She can drive, though.' He winks and she laughs and takes a swipe at him. He's a larrikin, Darryl, him and Jesse and Todd, just total fucking larrikins.

She swims and they eat more, drink a few more beers. She lies in the sun, she'll be burnt more than likely but jeez that sun feels good on her body. She hasn't done this, laid out in the sun, drunk beer, just chilled out in so long.

It's dark, starting to cool down when they load up the car. Jesse is still down at the river with Leigh and Todd has his arm around one of the girls. 'We'll make our own way back. No sweat.'

They're silent on the way back. It's been so good and she's tired. Still, she can't help thinking about Serena. 'Where do you think Serena's gone?' she asks Darryl. 'Where would she go?'

The muscle in the side of his jaw tightens and he rubs his hand across his forehead like he used to when he was a kid and worried about something. 'She'll be all right. Has to be, eh?'

'Yeah. Yeah, she has to be.'

13

It's Monday. She's been here three days and she's found nothing. Fucking nothing. Oh yeah, Serena was accused of selling drugs but it turned out to be nothing. Serena had bruises on her arms, missed school, stopped talking, stayed in her room. But that was nothing as well.

Something was going on. But if anyone knows about that something they're not saying. Was it some boy or was it drugs or was someone bullying her? She knows that's big right now, kids writing crap about other kids on Facebook, sending them shit texts. She trawls through the Facebook pages. The kids she's talked to, links to their friends. Nothing. Nothing but photos of grinning kids and likes and 'awesome'. 'That's awesome, babe.'

What about that teacher she talked about? What was her name? She called her Miss. Miss said. Miss told me. Who the hell is Miss?

She phones her mother. 'That teacher Serena used to talk about. What was her name?'

'Wouldn't try her. Totally up herself, that one.'

'Mum, I just want to know her name.'

'It was yonks ago Serena used to talk about her. Never hear a word about her any more.'

'I just want her name.'

'It's Klein. But I'm telling you, she won't want to talk to you. She lives with her mother. Bitches, both of them, think they're better than anyone else. They're Germans.'

'Okay, thanks.'

She finds the number and it rings, over, over. She's about to hang up when it's picked up. 'This is Gerda Klein.'

'Hello, my name is Lynnette Freeman. I'm Serena Freeman's

sister. I know that you taught Serena, she talked about you a lot and I was wondering if I could come around and speak to you. Serena's missing.'

There is silence and when the woman speaks her voice is harsh, the accent more pronounced. 'I am not this teacher.'

'Oh. Is Miss Klein your daughter?'

There is a long silence.

She raises her voice. 'Hello? Mrs Klein? Could I speak to your daughter, please?'

'She is not here.'

'When will she be back? Could I come to your house and talk with her later?'

'You cannot come here.'

'I'm sorry?'

'We do not wish for visitors. You cannot come to this house.'

The phone clicks. Shit, maybe Mum's right for once. But there are other teachers. She phones Julie's mother, gets a list of the teachers who taught the class last year. Phones them one by one. Some are away, others sound surprised, even shocked but they can't help. 'Yes, her grades went down and she was quiet in class but —. No. I really don't know —.'

How can a fifteen-year-old girl disappear without anyone knowing anything?

Except it happens. Kids take off. They live on the streets, they steal, do tricks, do drugs. And sometimes, sometimes, they're actually okay. Like Lynnie. How long was it before she called home after she took off? One, two, three months? She was busy finding a job, finding somewhere to stay. And she didn't want them to know where she was. Maybe it's the same for Serena. Maybe she'll phone when she's ready.

Lynnie walks into town, buys a couple of magazines, leafs through them sitting outside on the little deck. She can't think what to do next. Maybe she should go to that teacher's house, that Miss Klein. Just turn up and knock on the door. Maybe the mother's gone a bit loony, got dementia. Tomorrow, maybe.

Or she could drive back to Dunedin, get on the next plane, piss off out of here and just wait. Though she knows how that would drive her crazy. Every time her phone rang she'd think it was news — but being here is driving her crazy as well.

She goes for a run, has a shower, washes off the sunblock she's slathered on her skin and pulls on her trackies and T-shirt. She heats up a quiche from the deli section at the supermarket and empties the rest of the bag of salad greens on her plate. She'll need to get more food if she stays. Doesn't fancy sitting in one of the cafés on her own, maybe seeing people she might know. 'Lynnie, oh it's Lynnie isn't it? How are yoo-oou?'

If she stays. She's about to switch on the TV when her mobile rings. 'You better get round here. They've found her.'

'They've found her? Is she all right?'

'You better come round.' Her mother's voice is flat and the phone goes dead.

She grabs her keys, runs to her car, turns on the ignition, pulls fast out onto the road. They've found her. What does that mean? That she's home? That they know where she is? That she's in hospital? That they've found her body?

Her hands are shaking as she grips the steering wheel. Come on. They've found her. That's good, right? They've found her. If she was hurt or dead her mother would be screaming. They've found her.

Serena, you've got to be okay.

She parks outside the house. There's a cop car in the driveway. She gets out of the car, feels the bile rushing up in her throat. She hurries down the driveway, almost running, opening the door.

He fills up the room. That big red face, the blue shirt, the belly bulging over the belt looped through his trousers. He turns and slowly looks her over. The piggy eyes. 'Lynnie.'

She straightens her shoulders, stares back at him. 'Where's Serena?'

Her mother's voice is shrill. 'That's what Mick, Sergeant Withers has been telling us, Lynnie. She's over on the West Coast.'

His voice is flat, his eyes stare steadily into hers. 'We've had reports of a girl answering to your sister's description hitch-hiking on the Haast Road near Jackson Bay.'

She turns towards her mother. 'Is that all there is?'

'It's a start,' she says. 'At least now we know she's okay.'

'When was this?' Lynnie looks back at him, keeping her gaze steady and direct.

'The driver picked the girl up at Wanaka and dropped her off over at Haast two weeks ago.'

'But. She didn't tell him who she was? Did she tell him where she came from?'

'He said she got in the back seat and slept all the way there.'

'Why do you think this girl was Serena?'

He shrugs. 'I said. Answers to her description.' He opens up the folder on the table. 'Young girl, dark hair, carrying a backpack.'

'That could describe most of the girls around here.'

'They're not missing, though, are they?' He flips the folder shut.

'Okay,' she says, 'so you think this girl could have been Serena. What happens next?'

'We've made contact with police up the coast. They'll put out the word and keep an eye out for her.'

'And that's it? Listen, this is a fifteen-year-old girl we're talking about.' Her voice is raised but she doesn't care. Let him see that she's angry, let him see she won't be pushed around. 'I don't understand why this isn't being taken more seriously. Why isn't anyone looking for her?'

'We're making enquiries,' he said, 'but if someone chooses to leave and doesn't want to be found there's not a lot can be done about it.'

'Chances are this girl isn't even Serena. Why would she be going to the West Coast?'

'She could have her own reasons to go there.' His voice is measured and calm but she sees the anger flickering up in his eyes.

'She could have a boyfriend over there. Or —.'

'Or what?'

'She may be involved in the selling of illegal substances.'

This is so outrageous that she laughs out loud. 'She's going over there to be the leader of a drug ring, right? This girl who might be Serena might be heading over to the West Coast because she might be involved with drugs? Come on, this is bullshit.'

He eyes her as he picks the folder up off the table. 'We'll be in touch.'

'You shouldn't of talked to him like that, Lynnie,' her mother says, lighting a cigarette. 'It doesn't pay to get on the wrong side of cops.'

'Yeah, well, you'd know all about that,' she says. 'Anyway, they should be out looking for her instead of coming here with crap stories about hitch-hikers.'

'It could've been her, though. It sounds like See. What we have to do is just wait. She'll be all right. She'll be in touch when she's ready.'

Yeah, that's right, Mum. It's sure to come out in the wash.

'I've been thinking there's not much point in me sticking around,' she says. 'I may as well go back.'

'Yeah, yeah,' her mother says. She's flicking through the paper, finds the TV guide and runs her finger down it. 'There's meant to be a good movie on tonight. Think me and Rob'll stay in for the night. Darby and Joan, eh?' She laughs.

'Yeah, well, I'll see you.'

'See you, Lynnie. You'll call in before you go, won't you?'

'Yeah, yeah. Tomorrow probably.'

She goes back to the motel. She's hot, flustered and she goes into the bathroom, splashes cold water on her face. Her greenstone twist is on the cabinet. She took it off when she had her shower and now she clips it around her neck. Many twists and turns many twists and turns many twists and turns.

She finishes off the quiche. It's bland, the texture like soft butter, but she's hungry. She makes a pot of tea and turns on the TV.

Watches as cars roar after villains, someone climbs a ladder and jumps from building to building. More speeding cars. More crims. She boils the kettle, makes more tea.

It's dark when she hears the knock on the sliding door. She goes over and peers through the blinds. It's late but people are still around; she can tell by the lights and the sound of the television that someone's up in the next unit and Chris's unit across the drive is still lit up. She turns on the outside light, opens the door, steps out, pulling it shut behind her and stands there, her arms hanging loosely at her sides. She knew he'd come sooner or later. 'What do you want?'

He steps towards her. 'I don't want you stirring up trouble, you hear me?'

'What do you mean?'

'You've been asking questions. Pestering people. It's our job to find your sister. You keep out of it.'

'She's my sister and I'll do what I like. Doesn't look like you've been doing much, anyway.'

'Appropriate procedures have been put in place.'

She laughs. 'Don't give me that police-talk bullshit. Serena's just not important enough, eh? A fifteen-year-old kid's missing and you can't be biffed getting off your arses to look for her.'

'You don't know what you're talking about. Your sister's trouble. That's why she's gone.'

She doesn't let her gaze waver an instant. 'That's bullshit. I don't believe you.'

'You better believe me because what I'm telling you is the truth. She's bad news. She's got herself into all sorts of bother with booze and drugs.'

'Yeah?'

'Yeah, and what you need to do is go right back to where you came from and hope like hell she comes out of it all right.'

She smiles. 'Yeah? And maybe I should just hop right into your car and we can sort it out at the police station, eh?'

'I'm warning you.'

'You're warning me? Guess what? I could tell.'

He steps forward close enough that she can see the pores potholing his face, the veins like red spider-webs on his cheeks. 'Tell what, Lynnie?' he whispers. 'That you're a lying bitch and your sister's a slut?'

He's close enough to grab her, close enough to put his big meaty hands around her throat. She feels his breath on her face, feels his spit as he forces out the words but she stands her ground. 'Get the fuck away from me.'

His eyes flicker as he hears a car turn into the drive and he steps back as it passes them slowly. The light catches her face, makes her want to blink but she keeps her eyes on him. His pale eyes sweep her face, move across her neck, her shoulders and then his mouth twists, almost as if he's trying not to grin. 'See you, Lynnie.'

He's gone, striding across the path. She pulls open the door, locks it, closes the windows. That weird look on his face, as if he knew something, as if he had some sick plan. It'd be easy enough to break in here late in the night, wouldn't it. Anyone could just smash the glass in the door, put his hand through, turn the lock.

But she'd hear it, wouldn't she? Or other people would. Someone would hear. There's no need to be afraid. His breath on her, that bulk of him. For a moment she wanted to run. Scream and run.

Sometimes when she's having a few wines with her mates she tells the story: 'So this is how I left home, right? It was Friday night and I was up the main street in town, just walking along minding my own business. I was going to meet some mates, pick up a takeaway, then this cop car pulls into the side of the road right alongside me.'

He slid across the front seat and opened the window, 'Hey, Lynnie, what's this I hear about you shoplifting? We need to talk about that.'

It was Sergeant Withers, the cop who came to school when there was any trouble, so she knew who he was and that she hadn't any choice except to stop and talk to him. She didn't go closer to the car, though. She said, 'Mr Johnston said they wouldn't be pressing charges.'

He looked at her through the open window, 'He told you that, eh? All I know is there's been a crime committed and it needs dealing with.'

'I told him I was sorry and it wouldn't happen again. He said they were giving me another chance.'

'That's not what I heard,' he said. 'You have to come down the station and talk about it.'

She stood there looking in at him.

'Come on,' he said, 'hop in. You're coming with me. This needs sorting out.'

She told him something she'd heard at school. 'If you interview me I'm supposed to have a parent present.'

He laughed. 'A parent present? You mean your mother. She'll be down at the Bendigo pissing it up with her mates. I think we can work this one out without your mother.'

He got out of the car and opened the door. She didn't want to go with him, what was happening didn't seem right but, well, he was the cop, after all, so . . . So she got into the car. He said he had one other call to make first and he started heading out of town, down Dunstan Road. She had this short skirt on. She saw him glancing across at her legs. He pulled up off the road, juddering in under pine trees, stopped and undid his seatbelt.

He put his hand right up under her skirt, squeezed the top of her leg. 'I've heard you're a nice girl, Lynnie, so how about we just sort this little problem out between ourselves?'

Her heart was thudding. 'How're we going to do that?'

'Well,' he said. 'Well, I've got an idea.'

He undid his belt and unzipped his fly, grabbed her head and shoved it downwards to where she could see his cock sticking up. She put her mouth around it and she put her hand in his pants and gave his balls a bit of a tickle, just at the back of them. 'Oh yeah, oh yeah, baby, that's good, that's so good, mmm-mmm.'

Then she bit him. A good hard bite, enough to leave teeth marks, enough so he'd have to explain it to his wife, the fucking sleazeball bastard. She got a grip on his balls and squeezed and twisted hard as she could. While he was doubled over, moaning, she reached across him and pulled the keys out of the ignition.

She got out of the car, chucked them off into the pines, and looked into the window at him. 'That's us sorted.'

And she ran. She ran and ran.

'Day after that, I got out of town. Never went back.'

What she doesn't tell is how his eyes flared as he watched her leaving. What she doesn't tell is how her heart was thudding and how she couldn't get her breath through the hard, raw sobs as she ran through the pines, through the sand, lurching and stumbling. If he catches me, he'll kill me.

She doesn't tell how she packed a bag that night and hid it under her bed and waited through the night, listening for a car outside the house, listening for the car, for someone banging on the door. She doesn't tell how, as soon as it was light, she slipped out of the house and walked up over the bridge. Keeping down in case it was his car. Ready to run. Ready to run.

And she'd never tell, ever, about the hurt she felt that night after she got home. She filled the bathtub up with the hottest water she could bear and scrubbed at her skin. She drew her knees up tight against her body. The way he looked at her. That way they all looked at her. Like she was dirty, like she was nothing. That teacher she had when she was just a wee girl, that pretty teacher everyone loved. She used to wear this pink and black skirt, long with little pleats, tiny little pleats, and when they were sitting on the mat the girls would push to sit close so they could reach out and touch those pleats, take the bottom of that skirt in their fingers and press the little pleats together. Then, that morning, she got close enough and she reached her hand towards the silky sheerness of that skirt, the wee, tight pleats, she almost had it in her fingers and then the teacher, that pretty one who everyone loved, drew back her skirt and crossed her legs.

'Your sister's a slut. She's bad news.'

Well, I've got bad news for you, buddy. I'm staying.

She switches off the TV and the main light, sits there thinking in the half-dark with only the lamp on. She picks up her phone and dials.

'Yeah, what?'

'Listen, it's me.'

'Listen yourself. It's bloody half-eleven. What you doing calling this late?'

'I just need to ask you a question. Who was it reported that Serena had those bruises?'

'What you bringing all that up for? I told you, she fell over.'

'Yeah, but who reported it?'

'It was that teacher. That German bitch, okay?' The phone goes dead.

She switches off the lamp. That pretty one, the pretty teacher everyone loved, drawing back her skirt, crossing her legs, like she was nothing.

Well, she's not nothing now.

In the morning she knocks on the door.

Part Two

1

They are quiet. Although she knows this will not last — one will cough, another whisper — for now there is the silence; all twenty-nine of them bent over their books, burdened by this task of reading a short story. English Curriculum, Year 12. Response to text.

The spindly hands of the large clock on the wall move slowly. She goes to the windows and shoves, pushing them as far open as they will go. At this time of the day the sun is ferocious, beating onto the desks and whiteboards so that the black sun-filter blinds must be pulled. And now, a wind has come up, it's slight but enough to cause the blinds to tipper-tap against the window frames.

'Mi-iss?' Their eyes leave their books and gaze up at her.

Those exasperated voices. 'Mi-iss?'

A beam of sun falling across a desk, the jangle of a blind, causes unendurable disturbance to these kids. More than ten minutes of solitary, unrelieved attention to a task is intolerable. She ignores the clatter of the ruler falling to the floor, the chitter-chatter which is slow and soft now but threatens to erupt. Soon, she will answer the questions. Soon, she will once again ask Kyle Stratton, hunched over his mobile, texting, to switch it off, to put it away, but for now she will stand beside this window with this slight coolness of breeze on her face. Beyond is the concrete-block wall, covered by dark imprints from the ivy which was, some months ago, torn down. Random wanderings, marks that weave and meander: there is no pattern to the trails left behind.

This is her day-world. This concrete wall with its marks and scars, this room with the children coming daily, changing year after year yet never changing. There are few fluctuations in this town, only small variations in the business of living.

'What I want,' her mother said when they came here, 'is for each day to be the same as the one before it.'

She turns to face the class. 'Okay, now we will discuss this passage,' she says. 'Kyle, give that to me, please. Last chance, eh? Mel, let us start with you. What is this boy telling us in this story?'

She hears her voice, the slight hiss, the rise and fall of it so different in this land of flattened vowels. The 'th' she can never quite master falling somewhere between an 's' and a 'z'. She was ten when they came, too old to entirely lose her accent. But they quieten when she talks; they respect her. She does not beam at them as certain other teachers do in some vain attempt to become friends; there are no chummy barbecues in after-school hours or first names bandied about.

Oh, there are the sweets she occasionally hands out for good work but she is their teacher. That is her job, her role, and, when it is necessary she can summon steel into her eyes and voice and bearing. Kids are like a pack of wild creatures: if they detect the smallest waver in your voice, the slightest flicker in your eye, they will be onto you, they will bring you down.

'Well, uh, well. He's telling. About himself, Miss.'

'Of course, but what is he telling us? Seamus?'

'He's telling us, uh, how he's good at everything and how his life is so perfect.'

'Yes, and can we believe this boy?'

'No.'

'No? But why not?'

'Because of everything else that happens. What the other kids say and how they talk to him and all that. And how he tells it. Kind of skiting. So you like him at first and then you start thinking he's a wank —. A cheat.'

'Uh-huh. A cheat. Does everyone agree this boy is a cheat?'

They all nod agreement. 'So this boy is a cheat. Now, how is this story told? What method is used?'

It is Janine's hand again, triumphantly waving in the air, 'First-person narration, Miss.'

'Very good, Janine. So here we have this story. This boy telling you his own story, just as we would tell our stories. I did. I saw. I felt. And yet we cannot believe what he tells us since gradually the truth of his story is disrupted by the reactions and words of those around him. Does anyone remember what this method is called?'

The faces are blank. She shakes her head. 'So, no chocolate fish prizes today, huh?' She writes 'unreliable narrator' on the whiteboard.

'The motive behind using this method is to demonstrate either ignorance on behalf of the character or self-interest in distorting the truth. What's the case here?'

'Self-interest, Miss.'

And so it goes.

'You have twenty-five minutes before the bell to write a short paragraph about the narrative device used,' she says. 'Remember to give examples.'

She allows the muffled groans. It is Friday, after all, and so hot. Besides, they are nearing the end of the term and eager to be out of the classroom claiming the freedom of the next six weeks. She allows her eyes to brush over these kids. Though they would not suspect it, she has come to know them well over the past year. Writing gives away the spirit behind the words.

Some of them will not return to school in the coming year. Dean Harris, Che Sullivan: brains enough but wanting the money and ease that a job which is not too taxing will bring. Cindy Baker, Holly Cook, Mandy Brown: all waiting for something to come up at a café, perhaps a vineyard and there is always the supermarket. Cindy has her long tanned legs stretched beyond her desk; her hand is over her mouth as she whispers across the aisle to Dean. No matter. These kids will do okay. These are lucky kids in their safe world with their good-enough lives ahead of them. Here the sun shines and the fruit ripens and the clock on the hill sedately marks the time.

Some, like Janine and possibly Julie, will leave to go to the university in the city. Others, she's not so sure of. Serena, for example, hunched over her desk, alone at the back of the classroom. Despite the heat, she is swaddled in an oversized cardigan.

What has happened to the Serena who flew into the classroom, so lithe, so pretty in her summer uniform of the red checked dress, her arms slim and tanned against the white cuffs? The Serena who whipped through her books answering more questions, dark eyes cracking, than the rest of them together, whose laugh seemed too big and too loud for such a little body. Such a quick, quick mind. So eager.

Serena was her mistake. For her, Ilse broke the rules.

Despite what any teacher, scrupulous to the equal rights of the students under her care will say, there are students you will like more than others. She liked Serena more, much more, than the others and so didn't mind when Serena began to come to her classroom after school while she was marking or preparing work to ask about assignments. They chatted about books and Ilse began to lend her own to Serena. One afternoon Serena called by their home to return a book she had forgotten to take to school and so Ilse made thick, strong coffee and shared with her a plate of Mutti's ginger and cinnamon cookies. There were not many such visits but there were some.

Then came the grim Serena, the Serena with the dull, sullen eyes. Why did she no longer answer even the easiest of questions? She forgot her homework, she missed her classes. What had happened? What had cut her down? Ilse understood that Serena's family was not as affluent as others. Perhaps problems with money were creating anxiety and tension within this family. Should she speak to her? But what would she say? Her own background made such an undertaking almost impossible. Where she grew up people did not speak of personal difficulties outside of the family walls.

She spoke to her mother about the girl.

'Ach, Ilse, she will have a boyfriend. Do not become involved.'

Do not become involved.

But when she saw the marks she believed she must become involved. This is New Zealand. Here citizens are free to report what they have seen. And so she told about the listlessness, the falling grades, the purple blotches on the girl's arm, to Sally Davis, the school counsellor. And Sally said she would deal with it: she would talk with Serena.

'She tells me there's nothing wrong,' Sally reported back to Ilse. 'School is boring, that's all. Oh, and the bruises? She said she fell. There's a bit of a family history there, though, so I'll be talking to the family and CYFS. Just to cover us.'

It would be confidential, of course it would be confidential, but in this little town a whisper will fix itself, like ivy to a wall, creeping and sliding and slithering. It was so late that Ilse was asleep when the pounding on the front door and the long, shrill peals of the doorbell began. She switched on the light, pulled on her wrap. Her mother was already in the hallway, her fingers fidgeting at her mouth, at her neck, that old signal she was afraid. 'Ilse, what shall we do?'

Ilse checked the safety chain on the door and opened it up with a bravado she did not feel. And there he was, looming up at her from the darkness, this man who was shouting, his face and voice distorted with rage. 'What lies have you been telling?'

His body was thick and beefy and he was close against the door.

'Get off my property. I will call the police.'

'I've never laid a finger on her. Never.'

She shoved the door shut.

'Kraut bitch.'

Her mother was breathing hard, her face ghost-pale under the lights. Ilse put her arms around her, tried to stop the shuddering which came in rhythms, trying to calm the body which trembled and shivered.

'It is all right, Mutti. Everything will be all right. He has gone away.'

'You should not have drawn attention to us in this way. They will come for us.'

'It is not like that here, Mutti. You know that.'

'Ilse, it is you who should know you cannot trust anyone. This girl you brought into our home. She has turned on us.'

'He had no right to come here. Tomorrow I will go to the police.'

'No. No.'

'But Mutti —.'

'Promise me you won't. Promise me.'

And so she promised. What did she get for her concern and desire to help this girl? That battering on the door in the night? That man, reeking of alcohol, with his shouting and his insults? And now, this sullen girl in her classroom who lowers her eyes each time Ilse looks towards her.

She has learned her lesson. When Sally asks how Serena is doing she simply shrugs and smiles. 'As well as all the others,' she says.

'Fifteen,' Sally says, smiling in return, raising her eyebrows. 'Fifteen-year-old girls, eh?'

But when Ilse looks at the other girls she sees the usual things of being fifteen, the longings to be pretty, to be popular and free from the boredom of this classroom with its silly ideas and stultifying tasks. To have fun. That is not what she sees in Serena's eyes. Serena is not doing as well as all the others.

You must not become involved. Promise me.

The clock's arms hover on 3.15 and the bell pierces through the heat and the smell of sweating kids. But they know they must stay in their allocated places. This piece of training is her small victory: she will not have them, as other teachers do, exploding from their desks, shoving and shouting, knocking over seats and leaping over tables on their way to the door. Her eyes are on them as she waits. 'You may go.'

She hands Kyle his mobile. He grins mischievously and she shakes a finger at him. He is not a bad kid. Not so bad. She sits at her desk and marks their papers. At five o'clock it will be time to unlock her bike and ride home. This is her routine.

2

For most of the time her car is parked in the driveway, swaddled in the 'triple-layer car cover, fabric provides maximum water-repellence and resistance'. The words sing to her as she skims along the streets and around the corners so familiar to her. 'Two durable buckle-clip belly straps for secure fitting. Maximum protection from UV, rain, pollution, snow, dust, dirt, bird droppings and tree saps.' Oh, but she loves the way words tangle through her mind, twisting and weaving and chanting. She is fortunate in this way. 'Ilse has a talent for languages.'

She knows they laugh at her, in the town, pedalling this old-fashioned bicycle with the cane basket strapped to the front in which she places groceries, books from the library, students' papers to be marked during her evenings. She does not tell them that back home everyone rides bikes, that back home there are special places for the riders of bicycles beside the tram tracks and the pedestrian lanes.

If it's so good there why don't you go back?

Neither would she tell them that when this staid and tight-lipped teacher they see rides beyond town, passing by the opulent houses crouching on the Bridge Hill, and begins to pedal harder, to speed as fast as this old bike will take her along the Earnscleugh Road, the speed is for the sheer hell of it. Along that grey and quiet highway with the orchards and the vineyards at each side and at last clattering over the bridge into Clyde, the river heavy and green below her.

As she would not tell them that sometimes in her mind she is feeling not sun on her face but an air which promises snow. She is breathing in the smoke of thousands of stoves pumping out the heat needed to warm a winter city. She is jolting across cobbled streets, clutching the handlebars of her bike in her woollen mittens with her red scarf flying. She is back.

There is Thomaskirche with the sounds of the Thomanerchor spilling into the street, the organ muttering beneath those soaring voices. Bach was Thomaskantor at our church. This is where Bach himself played. And there, the Mönchs- oder Beichtglocke is calling the time as it clangs from the tower on the hour.

She could not tell them because even the most sympathetic would stare back, astonished and uncomprehending. 'You've lived here over twenty years now, haven't you? Isn't this your home?'

They escaped, didn't they? You'd think she'd be grateful. New Zealand is a paradise. Everyone says so.

But yes, even after these many, many years, she is homesick for the acridity of smoke in her mouth, for the lurch of cobbles beneath the wheels of her bike, for high-peaked buildings with little-paned windows. Heimweh, a yearning for home, and yes, she yearns, for that city, for chestnut trees and the sound of voices and music coming from the cafés and for words which cannot be translated.

These New Zealanders with their clean air and natural beauty, their safety and their newness. How could she explain to them what it is to live in a place where your parents were born and their parents and their parents before that? How could she explain that along with shame and grief and ugliness there is also beauty? Yes, she has still a longing for her past city and friends, Anja, Klaus, Hansi, Ilse, the four of them, that inseparable four. Klaus and Anja and Hansi turning their heads to look back at her as they biked away. 'Bis morgen.'

'Bis morgen.' See you tomorrow.

She never said goodbye to them. Neither could she write. Who are they now? What have they become? As for Ilse, she has attempted to instil in herself the benefits of living in the daily world of now. The students she has come to feel mild affection for, the solidity of this town with its glass-fronted shops, post office and banks, the New World supermarket, the houses built from bricks and plaster surrounded by lush, well-tended gardens on wide flat streets. 'This sunny, low-maintenance split-block home is well worth your inspection.'

They left in the summer, climbing into that first aeroplane and then the next and the next. She slept and woke, half-opening her eyes, sticky with tiredness and grief, to see her papa always awake, his eyes staring steadily ahead of him. She remembers the muscle that twitched in his cheek. She remembers her alarm as she realised she could no longer understand the voices which murmured around them.

For some weeks they lived in rooms in a city where wind careered about the streets and buildings. She followed her parents into offices where they filled out forms with the help of people who spoke in slow shouting, grimacing and gesturing as if the Kleins had not language difficulties but problems with their hearing and intellect. And then came the news there was a job for Papa and so there was another aeroplane and then a bus that passed through farmland into a moonscape of bone-dry land and sinister rock formations. Her mother, who up until that time had tried to cheer Ilse by pointing out features of the landscape or the houses they could see tucked off the road, fell silent.

They got out of the bus into the kind of cold that reaches through your clothes to finger your bones. They stood close together peering out at the huddle of shops, the empty street. There were people to meet them, this man, this woman with the smile that did not waver, who leapt out of a car parked beside the bus stop, welcome, welcome to your new home. This man who vigorously shook Papa's hand, 'Bill, it's Bill,' and this woman, 'Myra, please call me Myra,' who first hugged Mutti and then pulled Ilse tightly against her, 'Oh, what a little sweetie.'

Ilse squeezed into the back seat of the car with Mutti and Papa. Bill, with Myra smiling back at them from the front seat, drove past rows of houses through a tangle of streets. There are no people in this place. Where are the people? And stopped, finally, outside a square grey house.

Bill inserted a key into the door at the front and opened it. Papa and Mutti nodded and smiled and whispered their English thank-you words as they were led through rooms where flowers leapt across the carpets and walls and curtains. The bathroom was pink, the kitchen green. There was a bedroom for Mutti and Papa, another for Ilse. Bill showed Papa the way the shower taps should be turned, Myra demonstrated to Mutti the way the switches turned on the cooker in the kitchen. In the largest room, Bill bent down to open and light the wood-stove which was already filled with paper and kindling. He took the handle of the stove, turning and locking it, turning and locking it, his eyes checking that Papa was watching. He pointed to the wood stacked on the hearth and demonstrated with gestures the action of reloading the fire and then held out the box of matches to Papa as if bestowing on him a grave responsibility. Then there were the switches for lamps which lit the front porch to be found and observed and then they trooped out to the back garden where there was a small tin shed and a high fence that surrounded the bare, frozen earth.

Myra opened the doors of a cupboard and the refrigerator to point out the supplies of tea and tinned goods, margarine and cheese and milk. She took, from the basket she had placed on the kitchen bench, green soup in a plastic container and white sliced bread. After they had left, Mutti prised the lid off the container and poured the soup into a pot she found in the cupboard beneath the sink. They watched nervously as she switched on the cooker and waited beside the stove as it began to spit and bubble. Mutti poured it into bowls from yet another cupboard, and they sat at the table. What was this soup? Ilse had never before tasted soup like this.

Mutti put down her spoon and stared at Papa. 'These bowls are too small and too shallow.'

'We must be grateful, Gerda. These bowls, everything here, has been given to us.'

Ilse had not seen her mutti cry before but now her eyes were glassy with tears. 'But the soup becomes cold and there is no taste. The taste is lost in these bowls.'

'Hush, now,' Papa said. 'We will find new dishes once I begin to work. We will buy whatever is needed.'

'But I will not be able to ask for the correct crockeries.' Mutti's voice was thick and the tears had begun to spill down her face. 'We have practised our English so hard but still this Myra and this Bill, they do not understand us, Horst, and we cannot understand them.'

'Gerda, listen to me now. We must have patience. We will understand them soon enough.'

Ilse went into the bedroom with the pink roses on the floor and yellow roses on the walls. She took off her clothes and put on the pyjamas which had belonged to her cousins and which her aunt had given her in Berlin. This bed. It was so wrong. There was no duvet, the pillow was the wrong shape, it was too small and it was filled with something that felt spongy and foreign. At home her pillow was an immense soft square stuffed with goose-down. At home she could nestle into her pillow.

Mutti had filled a hot-water bottle for her and slipped it beneath the sheets but Ilse could smell the new-rubber reek of it and, although it was wrapped in a towel, she could not bear the heat of it on her feet. They had left everything behind them. They could bring nothing, there was nothing in this house she could touch and remember. What she longed for now was the hot-water bottle Oma had given her when she was little. Shaped like a lamb with little black button eyes, it was covered in thick, soft wool.

Oma filling up her hot-water bottle. Oma tucking her into her bed. 'Schlaf gut, Liebling.' Falling to sleep with the night-light on, the rise and fall of their voices; Oma, Papa, Mutti, Opa in the living room just beyond the door of her bedroom.

That first winter she was cold from the surface of her skin to deep within her bones. Each morning, she trudged with Mutti along the flat, empty streets to the school where she tried to make sense of the odd-sounding voices around her. In spring there was white and pink blossom on the trees behind the house and the roses which had been dull twigs burst out into colour and scent. Papa was coaxing her out.

'Come. You must not be sad forever. It is not so bad here, eh?'

3

It is yet another point of strangeness to this town that a woman over thirty years of age should live with her mother. Not so strange where they came from, where apartments were only rarely squandered on only one person. But where and how else should she live? Alone on the other side of the town, simply for the sake of independence? She and her mother live together well enough. Papa has gone and they are company for each other; there is space enough in this house for both privacy and companionship.

Ilse has had men; despite what some seem to suspect she is no frosty virgin. While she was at the university and occasionally, secretly, even in this town, she has had men. Nice enough men, some even attractive enough to make her heart beat a little faster. But she has never been tempted by thoughts of always and forever. She believes such a notion odd in a world that regularly tips and shakes.

As for children, by the end of each day she has had enough of them. So much better to shut the door behind those oversized, sprawling boy-men and the girls with their eyes slanting towards them in the afternoons, and to have only their essays and papers to keep her awake at night. Her mother, too, who has remained beautiful, strong and slim and straight with her sea-eyes still dazzling, has had suitors; widowers and divorcees who bring to her their offerings of vegetables or sometimes ducks they have shot in the season or trout they have laboured for in the nearby rivers. Her mother thanks them politely, gives them coffee, sends them on their way and smiles at the forlorn hope behind the carrots, cucumbers and corpses which spread across the kitchen table. She tells Ilse that Horst was the only man for her.

Will Ilse be here still in this grey, split-block house of theirs in another twenty years, by then almost the age her mother is now?

Will she be still riding her shabby black bike, the basket attached to the front with worn and faded leather straps? The idea makes her smile a little as she runs up the steps.

Into this house which, despite her parents' intention to transform themselves into solid New Zealand citizens, indistinguishable from anyone else on the streets, has in fact, little by little, been transformed into a small part of Germany. There is the piano tucked into the corner, the plain wooden furniture, the cushions and the rugs, the smell of good coffee; there is the Schwibbogen, already in its place for Christmas, the arch with the cut-out star shapes above the small figures which stand around the tiny Christ child in the manger, the candle-holders at each side. Papa discovered it in a Dunedin shop on one of his visits to the city and returned beaming as he placed the package in Gerda's hands. Ilse remembers her expression of startled joy as she pulled the paper aside, as she stroked the pale and dark woods carved so intricately.

And here, now, is Mutti taking Apfelkuchen from the oven and placing it, her lips curving into a smile of welcome and triumph, onto the table. They talk a little as they eat. Her mother tells her that while there may be a new contract for her in the new year she has finished up for the moment. No matter, there is work to be done in the vegetable garden and the fence at the back of their property needs repainting. At home, her mother was a nurse of high status. Here, since qualifications gained in their home country were not recognised, she has worked short contracts caring for the elderly at the nearby old people's home. The pay is poor but the work is, in the main, good enough, she says. Her mother chooses to dwell on the positive side of things.

That is when she is well and that black beast of misery is not riding her shoulders. He, like the hoar frost which descends on this town, enclosing all in ghostly dimness and silence, has been a habitual visitor to this house. On such days, her mother is unable to move from her bed where she lies, her eyes sometimes closed, sometimes fixed on the ceiling.

Now his visits are fewer, though each year when the arms of the clock set into the hill are pushed an hour forward and the waking hours grow darker, Ilse crosses her fingers that this will be one of those winters where the mornings begin with sharp, crisp frosts followed by afternoons of beaming sunshine. That it will not be a winter of consecutive days where greyness and cold hover over the town making her mother's bones and spirit ache.

But for now it is summer and this year Mutti has been well. It is summer and it is Friday and the weekend is before them and then only another week until the long summer holiday when six weeks will spread ahead. She has no plans; only to read the books she has been saving and perhaps spend some days hiking across the rocks and hills which surround the town. And while she still, at times, yearns for those tiny-paned windows lit yellow by the lights in the rooms behind them, for chiming bells and bakeries smelling of spice, and for those winds of ice blowing up from the steppes of Russia, she has now a deep affection for this place. For the pale fragility of spring blossom. For the blistering force of summer sun, for the way the hills and mountains glint gold, for the feel of rock beneath her boots. For the purity of air, the smell of thyme and the glimpses of mountains still swathed in snow. Then autumn with that sky, so flawless and blue above the new vibrancy of colours: scarlet, orange, the brash, shameless gold; a rainbow of the earth. And in winter, though she fears this time, she sees also the beauty of the smoke-grey days, the ice crystals suspended so gracefully.

When they have finished their meal and she has eaten at her mother's bidding — 'Ilse, you are thin' — two generous slabs of Apfelkuchen, they watch television together. When they first came here, arriving from the East where food was restricted, her mother was, first of all, astonished by the availability and variety of foods. 'Bananas, Ilse, bananas and oranges and all this . . . meat.' Her surprise at this abundance was soon supplanted by the way in which food was prepared and cooked. The flavourless sausages, bland white bread, the plastic-covered lumps of insipid cheeses.

But now New Zealand has been swept with an intense interest in cooking. Her mother has become immersed in one of the programmes presently dominating television, where hopeful cooks may win the title of MasterChef. Mutti has her favourite on this programme and tonight she is tense. Her champion, Gerald, has been admonished in the past weeks over failing to plate his meals in the acceptable voguish way and she watches intently as he warily arranges his fillet of venison with potato and celeriac mash, his rosemary and his apple sauce, on the square white plate. 'Ach,' she says, 'he is a good cook. Who wishes to eat a sculpture?'

But Gerald has made it through into round three and both he and her mother are smiling. They switch off the television set and read. It is almost dark. Soon they will go to bed.

Her mother's name is Gerda, so given because her grandmother loved the Hans Christian Andersen story 'Die Schneekönigin'. In this story, Gerda is devoted to her friend Kai, whose eye and heart is pierced by slivers of glass from a wicked sprite's broken mirror: 'And when they got into people's eyes, there they stayed; and then people saw everything perverted, or only had an eye for that which was evil. Some persons even got a splinter in their heart, and then it made one shudder, for their heart became like a lump of ice.'

The Snow Queen takes Kai from their village, carrying him by sleigh to her home. But of course, in the way of fairy tales, Gerda searches until she finds him and then restores him with her love: 'But then little Gerda shed burning tears; and they fell on his bosom, they penetrated to his heart, they thawed the lumps of ice, and consumed the splinters of the looking-glass.'

Ilse also has loved this story. She remembers her Oma reading from the book she had kept safe through all the years following her own childhood. 'Now then, let us begin. When we are at the end of the story, we shall know more than we know now —.'

'I chose to call your Mutti Gerda,' Oma told her as she brushed then plaited Ilse's hair, binding up the ends in bands which she then covered with small, neat ribbon bows. 'Because I wanted my daughter to be sweet and good and brave like this girl in the story.'

And, of course, her mother is sweet and good and brave. Still, those tears she sheds during her silent battles do not have the strength to wash away the coldness that pierces her heart and distorts her vision. Ilse knows that her mother was insistent that they leave Leipzig. She herself felt the ferocity that drove her and which, in the end, drove them all. Perhaps it was that force which took so much of her mother's strength, leaving her with little to face the conflicts of later years.

Her mother had taken her out of the apartment to the park across the street. She had looked around as if checking for someone, then gestured for Ilse to sit with her on a park bench. She and Papa had decided, she said. They were going to a new country to live. A beautiful country. Perhaps Canada, perhaps Australia.

She could not believe the words Mutti was saying. Leaving Leipzig? Leaving their home? 'I don't want to go.'

'It is decided, Ilse. We will go.'

She began to cry. 'I want to stay here with Oma and Opa and Hansi and Anja and Klaus. I don't want to go to another country.'

Her mother did not put her arms around her and tell her everything would be all right. Instead, she sat stiffly beside Ilse, her face stony-hard. 'There is no point in tears,' she said. 'Now, listen to me, carefully. You must not tell. Not anyone, do you hear me? If the Stasi hear any word of this, anything at all, then we will be in the most terrible trouble, both ourselves and the people who are helping us. Even those who have found out and informed on us would be under threat.'

Ilse watched her without speaking.

'Do you hear me? If the Stasi find out then everyone will be assumed accountable. Innocent people will be taken away. We will be taken away.'

Ilse had heard stories of people who disappeared. An older boy from school had whispered about his older cousin who came back a week later, but would not speak of it, was never quite the same afterwards. She had heard, also, that sometimes people never came back.

'Do you understand what I am telling you?'

Ilse did not know this Mutti with these empty eyes and this iron voice. She tried to push her head and her body against her belly, to try to coax those stiff arms to encircle her body — 'Mutti, Mutti, come back, hold me, carry me, I am so afraid' — but she was unyielding, despite those pillows of softness around her belly and hips from the baby. 'I will not go.'

'You will go.'

'I will tell. This is wrong, Mutti. You are wrong.'

'You will go and you will not tell. If the Stasi discover anything of this, they will come for us and we will be separated. Your papa and I will be put into prison and you, Ilse, will go into an institution for the children of criminals of the state.'

She was ten. Her mother was her world. Her small rebellion faded. She began to listen as her mother sat on her bed before she went to sleep and whispered of where they would live and the opportunities they would have. 'Far away from here. A beautiful country. Far away.'

Her mother left to go with Papa to the hospital. When she returned, a long time after, it was without Ilse's promised brother or sister. The baby, a boy, had died, Papa told her, his arms around her as she sat on his knee. 'Do not speak of it to Mutti. Your mutti is so sad, Ilse, so sad.'

Was this dead boy the cause of her mother's black days? Or was it a longing for the home and family and the friends she had left? Was it feelings of strangeness in this town where people, coming with their gifts — those plastic containers filled with soup, their casseroles of tinned spaghetti mixed with eggs and bacon and pineapple pieces, the clothing that was too large and the worse for wear — had cast their eyes up and down their faces and bodies as if they were aliens from outer space? Was it finding out, after Germany's reunification and the letters had been sent and the agonising, stuttering phone calls that echoed back their voices had been made, that Oma and

Opa were now dead, that many of their friends had moved away and could no longer be traced?

Ilse does not know. She remembers Papa sitting on the bed he shared with Mutti, clasping her hand as tears drifted unchecked down her cheeks. 'Talk to me, Gerda. Please talk to me.' She remembers the wretchedness of his face. 'When we are at the end of the story, we shall know more than we know now.' It is not so with her mother. Her lump of ice is her own secret.

But now it is Ilse's time. For while their house holds a minute part of Germany within its walls, just along the concrete footpath and over the bridge is the wild openness of New Zealand. She goes to her room, takes off her clothes and pulls on her swimsuit. Her jeans and T-shirt go over the top and into her backpack go a towel, underclothing and a torch. She slips her feet into her sandals.

Each evening she waits until it is too late for the families with the young children who must be fed and put to bed, and for the teenagers who will move on to other occupations of the night. This is the time she anticipates during those classroom afternoons when the Cindys and the Hollys and the Katies are stretching out their bare, long legs as if the cultivating of the tan on these legs and the colour they have painted their toenails are of the greatest possible consequence. The time she anticipates when the Kyles and the Deans are staring blankly and the Serenas are brooding.

The curtains in the houses above her are all drawn and she sees the flicker from the television screens as she walks the few metres down the street and crosses the bridge. She feels the accustomed motion of it, this shaky bridge, suspended by wires attached to the beams of wood at each end, rocking her body. She clambers down over rock and through scrub to the small clearing by the river, feels the sandy soil beneath her feet, hears the movement from the willow branches that hang over the river.

The delicious, icy jolt as she lowers herself into the river in the dark. She glides forward, her eyes tight shut, letting the motion of the river take her, her body easing, warming as it recovers from that first jar of cold. She flips over and floats on her back.

Here she has the aloneness in which she is at ease. Within the staff room, the township, the classroom, aloneness is caused by her voice and her forthrightness, by her differently moulded face and her height. In this river she is herself only. In this silken water, swimming through the deep, cold pockets and sun-warmed shallows, she is only skin.

Only skin within this night of cooling rocks and the soft, crooning whrr-brr, whrr-brr of the pigeons that nest beneath the bridge. Only skin within this ripple and muttering of river. Here, her body and her mind can float and glide and drift without will or intention.

'Our Ilse. She has become a water sprite.' Her father is looking fondly at her as she comes into the house. It is yet another of those searing days when the tar on the pavement has blistered and turned to liquid and the sky is as blue and the sun as yellow as in a child's picture, still glossy from the paint which has not yet dried.

Another of those days she is only now learning about, only now becoming accustomed to in this first summer on the other side of the world. Watching closely, she has taken the examples of other children and now she walks home from the pool in her togs with the new yellow-and-green striped towel with the bobbly white fringe around her neck and the new pink rubber jandals on her feet.

In Leipzig, Ilse and her parents had occasionally visited the Stadtbad, a bathing pool of grand columns and fairy-tale arches and mosaics. In New Zealand she learnt that it was usual in the summer months to swim every day, and each afternoon she lined up and trekked with her class to the town pool. The sun glimmered on the long, unadorned length of blue, the high and low diving boards and the concrete dolphin situated in the adjoining small paddling pool.

Ilse has an aptitude for swimming; she discovered after only a few lessons that she could swim cleanly and strongly. She taught herself to dive, first by crouching at the edge and falling face-forwards and then by springing up on the balls of her feet. And not only did she have the aptitude, she loved to swim. She could hold her breath and skim a full length along the bottom of the pool, could curl her body into a ball and spin again and again beneath the water. She began to go to the pool in the early mornings so that she shared it only with a few devoted swimmers or, better still, had that glorious expanse of water entirely to herself.

Her mother believes that to walk in a public place half-dressed like this is uncivilised, scandalous even, but for now she will allow this behaviour. Because this Ilse, with water dripping from her tanned and glowing skin, has replaced the sullen spirit of misery which crept and huddled around their winter house. This summer, whatever she asks for will be given: the ice-cream treats, the pink ra-ra skirt, the spaghetti jeans and the television programmes that play until the impossible hour of ten o'clock. Her parents are so pleased to have this new configuration of Ilse that they will coax her with gifts to ensure that she stays.

That was the Ilse who blasted through the door like a savage, semi-naked and sopping wet, whose eyes were permanently reddened by the chlorine which reeked from her skin. That was the Ilse who silently watched and listened as her classmates told their jokes, always too afraid to join in but who told these jokes to her parents trying out her new brash Kiwi laugh.

Walking to the pool on those early mornings, the air warm and sweetened by the blowsy roses nodding over fences, paying her money to the woman behind the glass window, pulling on her swimsuit in the damp-smelling, concrete-block changing rooms then diving into the stinging coldness of early-morning water. While she was not at home with her new surroundings, that summer she saw a way of making the best of them.

She gets out of the water and treads carefully across the stones. It is so dark tonight with the moon a mere sliver in the sky. She switches on her torch, takes off her swimsuit and towels her body.

4

She has driven herself hard during the past weeks to complete preparation work for the next term so she can be free to enjoy this coming holiday. Now she puts down her bag and throws herself onto the sofa, her head on a cushion and her feet resting on the far end.

'Ah, Ilse,' Gerda says, laughing. 'Freedom for you.'

'Six weeks,' she says, breathing in hard. 'Six weeks.'

'You must rest, Ilse. You work so hard. And here.' She opens the fridge and takes out a bottle. 'Look, I have wine tonight. To celebrate.'

She polishes two wine glasses with a tea towel, pours wine into each of them and hands one to Ilse. 'Prost.'

They drink the cool, delicious wine, eating together the light meal of cold meats, bread, cheeses and salad. 'Remember,' Gerda says, 'when we first came and Papa used to make us play the game?'

Ilse smiles. 'Das Silbenrätsel.' Charades. In English but he insisted on the German version where each syllable of the word, and then the whole word, is acted. Each evening during that first year he was so firm that they must play the game. Those evenings when they were tired and disheartened from negotiating their way through yet another day of the difficulties of language and customs of this odd little place, still they must play Papa's game.

Gerda shakes her head, smiling. 'How you hated it, Ilse.'

Every day she returned home from school feeling weighed down, worn out by listening so carefully to this language, trying so hard to first of all find the words then to arrange them, in her head, into the correct English order before tripping her tongue around the sounds. She wanted to speak her own language, her home language but instead Papa said that they must not only speak English at each meal time but that they must also play the game. 'One hour. Only one hour.'

Each evening they were to have three new English words ready to act out. They must have them ready and be ready, also, to explain the meaning.

'Ro-ta-tion.' She remembers Papa making the rowing motions, then the gesture which indicated 'sounds like'. She and Mutti sat watching, perplexed as he threw his arms about in a series of meaningless gesticulations. If they offered anything in German, he would frown and shake his finger.

Ach, the game. She hated that she was made to play it but at the same time she always ended up laughing. And although Papa had been strict in his demands that they all work hard to speak and write English fluently, he had been right.

He was a good man, her papa. In Leipzig, he was a senior teacher of chemistry. In New Zealand, he became an orchard worker. In later years he was given the opportunity to use his knowledge and expertise in one of the many vineyards which sprang up in the 1980s. His name was Horst, his own father's name. Here they called him Horse. 'How ya going, Horse, you old bastard?' That is how they spoke to him. Her mother said it was disrespectful but he smiled. He always smiled. 'Ach, Gerda, they mean well.'

Going out into those bitter winter mornings wearing, instead of his suits, a ribbed woollen hat, thick overalls, checked woollen jacket, pulling the gloves over his gnarled hands, his fingernails split, no longer those clean, fine-fingered teacher's hands Ilse remembered. Coming home, his face reddened and chafed by those long days outside, putting on the kettle, making the tea. Smiling always, his eyes steady and kind, seemingly at ease with this new world and the place he had made in it for himself.

'Und Ilse, was hast Du heute Schönes erlebt?' And Ilse, what beautiful things happened to you today?

Only once she saw him lose his temper. It was 1989. The day the wall came down. They watched the images on the television news: the bulldozers and the banners flying, people crying and embracing. They heard the cheers and the chanting.

'We can go back,' Ilse said. 'Papa, now we can go back.'

He turned on her with such anger, such anguish on his face and in his voice that she dared not question what he said. 'Ilse, we will never go back. Do you hear me? Never!'

Papa threw himself vigorously into this New Zealand life. That first spring he set himself the task of learning about gardens. When the ground was no longer frozen, he carefully measured and then dug a vegetable plot and planted seeds which he cared for with all the watchfulness and nurturing of a mother hen over her newly hatched chicks. When the first shoots appeared, Mutti and Ilse were ushered out to admire them. Then came the abundance of lettuces and cabbages and spinach and beetroot. The glory of the potatoes. At last the fruit trees began to flourish: the apple, the peach, the pear, softening the stark tin fence and offering up a quantity of fruit which increased with the years.

And, of course, there was the day of such pride when Mutti and Papa signed the papers that made them the owners of this house. The careful saving and the preparation, the visit to the bank manager and the lawyer. 'We are land owners, Ilse.'

Was he happy here? He seemed content enough with his work and his garden and Ilse knows he had friends who loved him. After he died, so suddenly, shockingly — who could have thought that her strong, tall Papa could be felled like that by his heart? — there were so many at the funeral, the men who had known him in stiff dark suits and shirts brought out for weddings and for funerals, their wives in fitting skirts with matching jackets worn on visits to the city, perhaps to church. Such a multitude of cards and flowers; so many flowers Ilse and her mother didn't have enough vases and were forced to place the large bouquets bound in ribbon and encased in cellophane in water jugs and bowls and finally, since there was nothing else for it, in the bath. And then came the pies and casseroles and cakes because what else can people do when they know a most precious loved one has gone than to try to fill the deep chasm left with their gifts of macaroni cheese, cakes made with carrots, and shepherd's pies?

How ya going, Horse, you old bastard? Ilse saw tears in the eyes of those men at the funeral as they held and shook her hand and tried, at last, to swivel their tongues around his name.

'Hors —. Horst was a good man. A good mate.'

Ach, they mean well. And so they did.

She and Mutti followed the black, shining hearse along the narrow road into the cemetery. The silence of that place, the line of spindly poplars where they parked their cars, the bright flowers, the ribbons and balloons and toys on the graves of children, the row on row on row of graves which spread to the dark fringe of pines on the hill beyond, jagged against the milk-white sky. The earth they lowered him into was so cold. The first frosts had come, and the air was pungent from the mat of pale gold leaves shed from the poplars. Her mother took Ilse's gloved hand in her own. 'So far away,' she whispered. 'Horst is so far away from home.'

And there he lies up in that silent place amongst the Kinneys and the Keans and Mees and the McKinstries. Horst Gerardus Klein. Of Leipzig.

It is dark. Ilse is bone tired after this week of teaching and turning in final marks, of balancing roles and filling in forms for the planning and requirements of the New Year. She is almost reluctant to swim. They have had a surprising cool spell this week with winds and rain and days of grey cloud. The river, without the warming of the sun, has been icy this week. Perhaps she would have a long, hot bath and go to bed early instead. She could swim in the town pool in the morning and wait a few days until the river again warms.

The old baths have now closed, replaced by the Aquatic Centre, a series of pools situated on the outskirts of the town. Though these pools cater better for the town people who can now enjoy all-year swimming within the comfort of heated water, they do not have spreading lawns and trees to sit underneath on hot days, the pleasures involved in swimming on your back, your eyes fixed on the rocks and the hills that fringed the pool's enclosure. It is only on days when the river is dangerously high or impossibly cold that she goes there. Still, the water is warm; so much kinder to a tired body. She stares unseeing at the television programme her mother has switched on, the sound of the voices a muffled blur. She is almost too weary to move.

A long hot bath. Dozing against her pillows, falling into sleep knowing that there is no work tomorrow, or the next day or the one after that.

Ilse, you are turning yourself into an old woman with your thoughts of hot baths and bed at 9 p.m.

So, then. A swim.

Already, as she pulls her swimsuit on, she can feel and smell the river water on her skin, in her bones. The clouds are so low they seem to be pressing down on the street as she walks and the houses are silent, muffled up in their heavy curtains. Across the bridge and down over the rocks to the place she has claimed. She is reluctant to remove her sweater and sweatpants and expose her body. She shivers in the night air and eyes the pale, rushing water.

She walks through the shallows feeling the intense chill on her ankles, on her thighs and then there is nothing for it, but to hold her breath and plunge in.

Oh Gott. So cold. But even in this chilly water, she loves the sensations she now experiences: the first frozen surge, the oh-so gradual process of her body becoming accustomed to the temperature, and then the contentment of being enfolded and held. She is both enlivened and tranquil as she swims through the silver rippled shadows as if gliding through iced silk.

So what will she do with her six weeks of freedom? Tomorrow she will allow herself a lengthy sleep-in. She will make coffee and take a large mug and warmed rolls spread lavishly with butter and honey back to her bed. She will spread the newspaper out and read each inch and then, perhaps, begin on one of her books. Then there is Christmas only a short time ahead: she and Mutti will cook a celebratory meal together and exchange gifts. She has her books to read, she will walk, she will swim. Other than that, no plans.

Sometimes she wonders at herself, questions this life she has made. The girl who rode her bike, scarf flying, with those close-knit friends through alleyways, over cobbled streets. The girl with her ra-ra skirt and her spaghetti jeans mimicking so carefully those around her. And now this oh-so-cautious woman. She asks herself often, should she go back to Leipzig? It would be easy now. All she need do is take leave from teaching, a few months to visit the places so fixed in her memory and in her heart. She could visit her old home, the church, the streets and cafés, she could find Hansi and Klaus and Anja. Oh, Anja, her best friend. How they talked. How they giggled.

But the truth is she is afraid to go back. She knows that the country she belonged to is no longer there now that reunification has occurred and she imagines the places she loved being diminished by her adult-self's scrutiny. She imagines her friends' faces, no longer the carefree faces of children; she imagines the stilted, uncomfortable conversations as she observes their homes, their partners, perhaps their children.

What I want is for each day to be the same as the one before it.

Better, perhaps, that way.

And so Christmas and the books and the walks and the swimming. The river is deeper after the days of rain. Deeper, darker. Now that her body has warmed she gives herself up to it, kicking out rhythmically with her feet, slicing though the water with her arms. And breathe. And breathe. And breathe. And —.

And then it comes to her. A sound. A sound like a soft, low wail.

She is motionless in the water, all her senses concentrated. Is there an animal somewhere in this darkness, hurt and needing help? Somebody's injured pet which has stumbled down by the river to lick its wounds? But there is nothing. Whatever it was, it has stopped. She swims again but that easy absorption and obliviousness has gone. She cannot help but listen for the sound within the murmur of river, the clatter of lupins as the breeze catches them.

And there. This time the sound is slightly louder. It is almost human, she thinks, this trail of low whimpers and sobs. Does it come from over there where the shrubbery grows almost to the river? It is difficult to tell in this dark and among the whispers of the river.

Over there is movement. So slight, so barely perceptible, it could be the wind moving in the scrub but she must find out. She cannot leave an animal alone and suffering. And so she swims to the bank, dries herself swiftly and pulls on her clothes. What to do? She will take her towel. If she finds a hurt animal it may lash out with claws and teeth — she may have to wrap it in order to carry it. She creeps along the bank to where she knows the river is shallow enough to cross on foot, carrying the towel and her torch. She must not yet switch it on in case she alarms the animal. She must approach quietly then attempt to soothe it with her voice and slow, gentle movements.

But there is no sound. Other than the river and the low crackle of the lupins there is nothing. She hesitates, turns to go back. Just go back, climb up the track, cross the bridge and along the street and home, leave this sound, whatever it is, behind.

And there it is again, beginning with a muffled moan and then rising to a cry of such hurt and terror that every nerve in Ilse's body is quivering. That sound and the thought of the blood and suffering that may go with it twist her gut; she could so easily turn her back and carry on up the track. But then there is a yelp, a low shriek of agony. She must try to help. For the animal's sake and for her own, for she knows that if she takes the coward's way out, she will lie awake this night and for many after thinking of the poor creature she left to die in pain.

What if it is beyond help, too broken to mend? She tells herself firmly if this is the case she must put it out of its misery. She will press the towel to its head, she will hold on, applying enough pressure so that the cries, struggling and writhing stop, the breathing stops and this poor creature is left in peace. She returns to the shallow place in the river and begins to cross, feeling among the gravel and the rocks with her toes for safe footholds; it would be so easy to slip in the darkness. Then she is at the other side clambering up the soft, clay bank.

The sound has again stopped and she stops also, listening and cursing herself for the softness of her heart which has brought her here, straining to hear the moans of a creature she will most likely be unable to help and which may hurt her. There. She moves towards the sound, as silently as she can, across the flat rocks, through the scrub. The sound is louder; she is getting closer. Ragged breathing; a moan; a cry. She is edging towards it, holding her breath, treading softly, feeling with her hands for undergrowth that may hiss and crackle.

There, up in front of her. She flicks on the torch and her gasp is audible as a head turns blindly towards the light.

5

'**M**iss?' Her arms are wrapped around her belly, her eyes glassy, her face smeared with tears and snot and sweat. She stares up, dazed by the light. 'Oh, Miss.'

'Serena. What —. What is happening?' Ilse blurts it out, yet it is clear, even through her shock and confusion, exactly what is happening. The girl is in labour.

Ilse is by nature reticent and inhibited. By the time she has considered the whys and wherefores of physical contact with another human being the moment, generally, has gone. But now she moves without reserve to take Serena in her arms, this poor, hurting child, and holds her, rocks her, whispers to her in a mother's way. 'I'm here now. It will be all right, it will be all right.'

Serena's body is so tight, so rigid, but then she leans into Ilse with a great sigh and sobs. Ilse takes her face into her hands and brushes her hair from her forehead. 'Serena, listen to me. I will be gone only minutes. I will call the ambulance and then I will come back and wait with you.'

'No. No. Please, Miss, please.'

She is wailing, incoherent, her eyes wild and her hands like vices on Ilse's arms. Ilse's mouth is dry with fear. There is no time for this. I cannot deliver a baby. She keeps her voice calm and steady. 'Serena, I must get help. But then I will stay with you. After that, I will not leave you.'

'It's hurting. Oh, it is hurting.' She doubles over. This is a contraction and although Ilse knows about contractions from her mother and from the television and her books she has not known about the agonised cries, the thrashing and writhing of the body.

How can she leave this terrified child, even for a few minutes, to suffer alone?

'It's hurting. Make it stop. Make it stop. Miss. Oh, please.'

Out here in the dark this contraction seems to continue on and on for an eternity, though Ilse cannot tell, truly, how long it lasts. But she knows that these contractions must be monitored, timed and charted. Serena rests against her, breathing hard. How long since the last one? How long before the next?

'Serena, listen to me, we cannot stay here.'

Her face is stubborn, she shakes her head, clutching Ilse's arm.

'We cannot stay here. Do you understand me?'

'I won't. Go.'

'If you insist on staying, I must leave you while I call for help.' Her brisk, no-nonsense teacher's voice.

'Don't leave me. Please.'

'Can you walk?'

Serena hesitates. Looks into Ilse's face and sees the resolution there and nods.

'Let's try now. Before the next contraction hits. Okay?'

Serena breathes hard, nods again. Ilse places her arm across Serena's shoulders, tucking her hand under her arm supporting her and they hobble forward. When they get to the river bank, Serena shakes her head. 'I can't do it.'

'Come on. I'll keep you from falling.'

They are halfway across when she doubles up. Ilse rubs her back, supports her body as best she can. 'It's all right, it is all right, we will make it together; it will be all right.' What if she can't make it? What if the baby comes?

'Put your arm around my shoulders.'

They stagger again across the river stones. Slippery. It is so slippery. What if she falls? Ilse won't be able to hold her if she falls. 'Good girl. Not far to go, now. You're doing well. Good girl. Keep going.'

Ilse keeps up an endless stream of words, encouraging, soothing words. 'It's fine, it's going to be just fine, you're doing well, so well.'

They are at the other side of the river. Not too far now. Another contraction. They're coming so quickly. Breathe slowly, breathe slowly now.

They are on the track, Ilse following, her hands planted hard on Serena's back, helping her climb when Serena stops and cries out, clutching at her neck, looking around.

'What? What is it?'

'My necklace.'

Ilse almost laughs. The girl is in labour and she's worried that she has lost a necklace?

'Lynnie gave it to me. I have to find it. It's for good luck.'

'Hush now. We will find this necklace later. For now we must keep going.'

They rest and climb and there, ahead of them, is the bridge. 'Only a few minutes, Serena, and then I will phone for the ambulance and you will be looked after. They will help with the pain.'

'Please', she whispers. 'Please, Miss. No.'

Ilse is almost carrying her as they stumble up the path. She has no key; her key is in her bag at the river along with her swimsuit. She cannot risk alerting the neighbours by ringing the bell so she slaps at the door with the flat of her hand as loudly as she dares. 'Mutti.' Her voice spills rough and anxious into the darkness. 'Mutti!'

The passage light switches on and her mother is there behind the small pane of glass, fumbling with the lock, pushing open the door. Her body is solidly planted in the doorway as she peers out into the night. 'What is it, Ilse?'

She recognises Serena and raises her hands, palms upward. 'No.'

Ilse is supporting Serena, keeping her steady and upright but then the girl buckles and the sound comes again, that sound which comes from some secret and deep-rooted place within her body, that sound which is black and greedy and cavernous.

Gerda's mouth and eyes fly open and she pulls them inside and closes the door and then she is on her knees beside Serena.

'I must call for the ambulance,' Ilse says.

'No!'

'Serena, you need proper care.'

She is gasping, thrusting out the words, one by one. 'They. Will. Take. It. Away.'

Gerda's eyes narrow as she massages Serena's back with clean, practised strokes. 'Breathe,' she says. 'Breathe. Slowly now.'

And when this agony passes Gerda stands up briskly taking Serena's arm. 'Come, Ilse,' she says. 'You must help me.'

'But Mutti, we must get help. Serena must go to the hospital. We cannot —.'

Serena is shouting, 'No! No, no, no!'

'We need fresh sheets on the bed in the visitors' room. Fresh sheets and towels, please now quickly, Ilse. Serena, listen to me. You must put yourself in our hands, eh? We will do what we can for you. First you shall have a bath. The warm water will relax you.'

And so here is Serena now resting against the pillows in the visitors' bed, thirstily drinking the iced water from the refrigerator. Her body and face are clean and her damp and soiled clothes have been replaced by a fresh cotton T-shirt of Ilse's.

'So now we will see, eh?' Gerda has Serena lying on her back, her knees up and legs apart. 'Good,' she says. 'Good girl. The cervix is opening nicely. You are doing well. Not long now.'

Ilse catches Gerda by her elbow and pulls her from the room. 'Mutti, what are you doing? We must call a doctor.'

But Gerda's face is set. 'I have been in a delivery room many times and I know what I am doing. We must listen to what this girl is telling us.'

'But she is a child.'

'Even so,' Gerda says, 'she is a mother.'

'We must — at the very least we must contact her family.'

And yet Ilse cannot help but think of fingerprints on Serena's arms and remember how her eyes hollowed into the blankness of this past year. The police, an ambulance, a doctor — what should be done?

'We will help her,' Mutti says, 'and then we will see.'

'You are not thinking straight. Something could go wrong. We would be responsible.'

'Aber wir müssen etwas tun.'

6

'It is what we must do. It is what we must do.'

In the apartment where they had always spoken openly and laughed freely, there was silence. At night Ilse would listen, her ear pressed against the wall, trying to make out the words they whispered in their bed on the other side.

In the mornings her father and mother would prepare to leave for work as usual. But their faces wore different expressions and before the door was opened they would clasp each other and Ilse in hard, tight embraces. And then they would, as was normal, go out into the corridor and walk down the stairs, passing others who also lived in the apartment block, greeting them and smiling.

As was normal.

'Nobody must observe any differences in our behaviour, nobody must find in our words or manner cause for comment. Everything must appear exactly as it should be.'

Ilse heard the whispers. The Stasi. At least one informer was allocated to each apartment block to report on the movements and behaviour of residents. To report, also, on the visitors to residents' apartments. What were their names, what were their occupations, how many times did they come and how long did they stay?

Who, in their own apartment block, was this informer? Was it Frau Beicke who lived only along the passageway from the Kleins? Frau Beicke was unfriendly, only curtly nodding in the mornings then following them with her small, lifeless eyes as they passed by. Or was it Herr Altenhoff who came out of his apartment to shake his finger at Ilse and Hansi, Anja and Klaus if they talked too loudly or made too much clatter with their boots on the open wooden staircase? It could be anyone. Someone you would not suspect, someone you might even like and trust. Someone like Herr Fuhrmann who lived with his smiling wife and pretty children on the next floor.

Phones were tapped, letters intercepted, small holes drilled in apartment walls so that occupants could be kept under surveillance: in some cases, filmed. All of this the Kleins knew through the snippets of information which flew through the air to be seized and whispered over. But for Ilse this scrutiny was not wrong. In school, they had learned that the Ministry for State Security was there to watch over and protect the citizens of the state. The Ministerium für Staatssicherheit was the Schild und Schwert der Partei, the shield and sword of the Party. The methods of surveillance used were necessary to prevent the enemies of the state from contaminating others. These enemies must be stopped and punished, then guided towards correct thinking.

But her mutti and her papa were good people and Ilse was a good girl; hadn't she received a Good Conduct Award in the Young Pioneers and didn't she carefully listen to the lessons taught in her school about the Party, about the state? No, she was never one of those students who had to be admonished for fidgeting during the lessons, for allowing their gaze to wander aimlessly around the classroom over the walls, the ceiling, the faces of other students. Nor was she one of those students who asked questions that made their teacher frown and respond sharply.

'The wall of protection against imperialism has been built at our borders to protect our citizens from people trying to break in from the West.'

'Sir, please sir, why does the barbed wire face inwards?'

'Your papa and I will go to prison and you, Ilse, into an institution for the children of criminals of the state.' But how could that be when the state prided itself on fair dealings to all citizens? When the state was incorruptible?

Later, she learned that Papa had spoken indiscreetly. Naturally schools were under strict surveillance and a fellow teacher who had made a pretence of befriending him was an informer. From then on, the family was under observation.

She could make out, but could not comprehend, her parents' whispers in the night. The words repeated by her mother, the words which she did not and still does not understand. She has asked but her mother has brushed her off, tells her she cannot have heard correctly, perhaps she dreamed these words. Yet she remembers those words whispered in the night.

'There is no choice. Ilse will go and then we will follow.'

Those words which sent her to the railway station, holding her Uncle Jürgen's hand. This uncle from the West had been granted a two-day visa to come to the East to address a conference at Leipzig University. He came to the apartment. Papa opened the door and brought him inside but they did not speak other than to greet each other, the awkward hearty greetings of those who do not know each other despite family connections. The strange artificiality of this meeting: could this man with his smart Western suit and coat truly be her mother's brother? 'Guten tag, Gerda. Horst.'

This Uncle Jürgen from the West stood uneasily looking at Mutti who raised her finger and placed it across her mouth as she pointed with her other hand to a place where their living-room wall met the ceiling. 'Shall we walk in the park? It is pleasant at this time of year.'

They went silently to the park and there, while her papa remained silent, the words began to fly between them. 'You realise, Gerda, the risk you are taking? You realise the consequences of failure?'

'Do you not think, Jürgen, that I have not thought of this? Do you not understand we are doing this only because there is no choice?'

Ilse's eyes were stinging and blurry because she was wearing her cousin Lena's old spectacles. Her hair was darkened and curled and she was wearing the Western clothes, right down to singlet and knickers, that her uncle had brought with him.

Still, she did not cry. Mutti had told her over and over, she must not cry. 'You must not cry, Ilse. You must hold your uncle's hand, you must smile and talk to him as you would to your own papa.' Although she must speak very, very softly and not too often since her Leipzig accent could give them away and if anyone spoke to her and asked questions she must pretend to be shy and allow her uncle to answer for her.

'Ilse, you must go with your uncle.'

'I don't want to go with him, Mutti. Why can't I travel with you and Papa?'

'This way is safer. You will stay with your uncle and your aunt and cousins until we come for you.'

And you must tell no one. No one.

They travelled in the late morning, the busiest time, and in second class since they would be less likely to be singled out among the crowds of travellers. They sat together, Ilse beside the window and her uncle between her and a woman wearing a dress covered in flowers. Her uncle offered her a cookie and an apple, and she remembered that she must call him Papa. 'Danke, Papa.' She whispered it.

She watched through the window as they moved through the central parts of the city and then they were passing the rows and rows of apartment buildings which had been built by the state to accommodate the citizens of Leipzig. These apartments, each with a fitted kitchen and central heating, were grand homes for the workers, they were told at school, who in the West were not honoured in this way but forced, by the greedy capitalists who own all the businesses and factories, to live in miserable conditions on meagre wages.

The state is just. The state is always right.

They were crossing now through the country, through small villages, moving all the time towards the West. She felt fear and horror rising up in her belly. Her parents weren't thinking straight; her parents were wrong. The lessons she had learned at school and in the Young Pioneers told her she must report any suspicious behaviour. 'Even if it is your friends or family who behave in a way which causes concern or doubt, you must tell.' You must tell.

'These people, once they have learned the error of their ways, will be grateful to you.'

A man in uniform came down the aisle of the train, checking tickets. He stopped beside them, looking first at the ticket the woman in the flowered dress held out, then he nodded at her uncle and held out his hand. He looked at the tickets and then at her uncle's transit visa. Perhaps she should stop this ticket collector, tell him that she was being taken away? That against her will she was being taken to the West? Your papa and I will go to prison and you, Ilse, into an institution for the children of criminals of the state. The ticket collector nodded, moved past them and Uncle Jürgen put the papers back into his wallet.

She was an enemy of the people. That is what she had become, an enemy of the people. She curled up, her head against the window, and closed her eyes. An enemy an enemy an enemy of the people.

She woke. Uncle Jürgen was gently shaking her. 'We are at the border now. We are at Friedrichstraße, Ilse.' This would be the most difficult part, her mother had warned her. This was where they were to leave the train and go through passport control. 'Hold your uncle's hand and say nothing, Ilse.'

Uncle Jürgen took his small suitcase from the rack above their seats and she followed him down the aisle of the train and stepped out onto the platform. She felt the tension in his grasp as he took her hand.

They lined up with the other passengers. There ahead of them were the officials. She watched as a man in uniform nodded to the next people in the row to come forward, then checked and stamped their passports.

The Ministry for State Security is our friend and will protect us.

She should tell, she must tell. This was her last opportunity to make things right. An enemy an enemy an enemy of the people. If she could force the words out everything would be all right; it was not too late. Her parents would be reprimanded but then they would be shown the wrongness of what they were doing, they would understand how mistaken they were in their thinking. She could go back home. They could stay in Leipzig.

And then it was their turn. The man in the uniform nodded and they stepped forward. Her uncle was gripping her hand so tightly; her hand was sore and sticky because this uncle she did not know was clasping it so tightly in his sweating hand.

Uncle Jürgen held out the passports to the man who scrutinised it, his eyes running down over the details, flicking back and forward between Uncle Jürgen and the photograph on his passport.

Ilse's heart was beating up into her throat: now he was looking at her, considering the photograph on her cousin Lena's identity card then examining Ilse's face, his narrowed eyes scrutinising her, flicking back to the picture.

Tell. Tell. You must tell. The Ministry for State Security is our friend and will protect us. Enemy of the people. Enemy of the people.

His eyebrows were drawn together, his eyes flicking back and forward, back and forward. Was there a question in his eyes? Was he taking longer with her than with others? Tell. Tell. Now is your chance. Tell.

Papa and Mutti would go to prison.

She felt the grip of her uncle's hand, felt the clammy sweat. She forced her voice upwards into her throat, whispering the words, finding the words her mother had told her she must say if the inspection of their papers was prolonged. The words she had practised over and over ensuring her Saxon accent did not give her away: Papa, ich fühle mich krank.

'Papa. I feel sick.' She pressed her hands to her mouth as Mutti had said she must do. But the heaving sounds which came deep from her belly and the yellow puke which spurted from her mouth splattering her clothes and the grey concrete floor beneath them were entirely spontaneous and utterly real as she vomited her terror and her grief and her guilt again and again. Her uncle ineptly tried to wipe her face and clothes with his handkerchief. The man swiftly stamped the passports, they were through.

They were through, hurrying alongside other passengers down long, winding corridors, dark corridors, shoes clicking along the floors, voices echoing, the clicking, the echoing; the sour smell of vomit clinging to her, filling her mouth. Hurry, hurry.

They were on the U-Bahn where her uncle led her to the toilets, held paper towels under the tap and mopped at her face and her dress. They moved towards the door as the U-Bahn shuddered to a stop. They were safe, her uncle whispered as he led her across the platform, they were safe but they must keep moving.

He still held her hand as they queued for a taxi. Now she could take off the spectacles and as they drove through the city she stared out at the brightly lit buildings, the windows filled with mannequins dressed in coats with fur trimmings and elegant dresses, the gleaming Mercedes gliding through the streets. Everything here was so new and so vivid, too bright, too colourful for her eyes which were accustomed to the soft greys of a Leipzig where buildings were heated by coal which drifted into the atmosphere and where the range of paint available was limited. They passed through avenues and parks. 'This is Berlin-Zehlendorf, Ilse. This is where we live' — and stopped outside iron gates. Her uncle now appeared cheerful. 'Well, we are here at last, little niece.'

She looked up through the gates at the large building in front of her. 'How many people live here?'

'Only us. This is our home.'

'You have a whole house?'

'Yes,' he said, smiling. 'This house belonged first to your Aunt Anke's grandparents and now it has passed to us. And here are your cousins, Lena and Hilde, and your Aunt Anke to meet you.'

The cousins were older than her, much taller, and Hilde wore Levi's. Levi's! They stared as the aunt kissed her. Uncle Jürgen indicated the stains on her coat and on her dress. 'Ilse got a little travel sickness on the way.'

'I will find some clothes and you can shower, Ilse. Come, I will show you your room and the bathroom you will use and then we will eat.'

The room her aunt showed her was too big for her alone, with two large beds covered with shiny green fabric, flouncy curtains, a cabinet and a dark, large wardrobe. She stood under the shower, shivering despite the heat from the water which poured over her, dressed herself in the checked skirt and the yellow sweater her aunt had given her and walked slowly along the passage — five bedrooms, two bathrooms — down the stairs to the corridor and into the living room where her uncle and aunt and cousins sat together on the sofas, looking up at her as she came through the door. 'Coca-Cola, Ilse? Would you like Coca-Cola?' She sipped at the glass they held out to her. So sweet. Too sweet. She much preferred the more bitter taste of the Vita-Cola they had at home, she decided, placing her glass carefully on the table.

You must be a good girl, Ilse, until we come for you.

Her aunt and uncle and cousins were kind and she was good; she remembered the manners her mother had reminded her of — 'Say thank you, eat slowly, do not interrupt when others are speaking' — but she was a stranger with these people. She was helpful and silent and polite; she did not express her shock at the number of rooms and the surplus and newness of the furniture and trinkets in this house, nor did she allow any expression to show on her face as she opened the food cupboard when she was helping her aunt set the dinner table and saw the excess and extravagance. There on the shelves were row on row of sauces and pickles and cans. Boxes of cereals, different varieties of jams, Nutella, Milka chocolate. She leapt back as if she had been stung.

And there on her aunt's bench one day after she had been grocery shopping were four packets of Jacob's Kaffee. Frau Sommer's Jacob's Kaffee. She had seen Frau Sommers on television — blonde, smiling, chic — holding out this coffee in her manicured hands, speaking of the aroma and the flavour. Once, at home in Leipzig, she had seen her mutti measuring it out in tiny amounts, making it last for months, after a precious packet had been slipped to her by a grateful patient.

Ilse did not have her own clothes: everything she wore had belonged to somebody else. And she must call them different names. When she had referred to her shirt as a 'nickie', Lena and Hilde had laughed at her. 'It is a T-shirt, Ilse. That is a T-shirt.' Oh, how long must she go on being this good girl and stay in this place where she felt strange and awkward, where she had to wait until the nights to quietly weep into her aunt's duck-down pillows?

It was a week, then three weeks. She watched her aunt lift her eyebrows at her uncle as he returned from work in the evenings and saw the slight shake of his head, heard his whisper, 'No word.' Another week, a month. Her aunt took her to a store where she bought her sweaters and skirts, a dress, shoes and, yes, jeans. These jeans she had longed for at home yet now seemed so inconsequential.

Her aunt bought her a Barbie doll so that she could play with Hilde. She accompanied her cousins to their school to sit among other girls who talked in their strange accents of television programmes. But what about The Olsen Gang? What about Egon and Benny and Kjeld? She thought about curling up on the sofas and chairs with Anja and Hansi and Klaus laughing at the Olsens' crazy adventures.

One month, two months. Three. What if they don't get out?

In the night she heard her uncle say quietly, 'Then we must keep the child until they can. There is plenty of room. She's well-behaved, isn't she?'

'That's not the point,' her aunt replied equally quietly but with some heart. 'She's not our child and she's unhappy, Jürgen. Can't you see that?'

'There is no choice. We will have to make the best of it.'

'You should never have agreed to this. The girl is pining for her mother.'

'Horst and Gerda have explained why it is they have to get out.'

'Oh, all these stories which come from the East. There is no crime there, I have heard there is plenty of order and that is not such a bad thing. That man should have kept his mouth shut. Gerda should not have married him. I told you so at the time.'

'Hush now, Anke. You know you do not mean what you are saying.'

'Well, I do know this. Next time you see your sister it may very well be in her coffin. That is if you ever do see her again.'

'Anke, that is enough, I say.'

Next time you see your sister it may very well be in her coffin. These were the words Ilse carried with her as she went with her cousins to school. As she followed them to the parks, to the ice-skating rink, to all the places they took her. That is if you ever do see her again. They were being kind, she knew they were being kind, wanting her to settle, wanting her to smile. What if they never get out?

'Ach, the girl looks so miserable. I try to get her to eat properly but she says she is not hungry. And those circles around her eyes! She is not sleeping. Jürgen, I am worried. The responsibility —.'

And then at last they were there. Mutti and Papa were there coming through the door following Uncle Jürgen. She lurched up out of the chair where she was sitting watching television, she was fixed to the floor on which she was standing, opening then closing her eyes. Papa? Mutti? Was this a trick, a dream?

She gave a great cry of joy and she was running across the room, throwing herself at them and Papa picked her up, as if she was still a little girl and he held her so hard against him and then they were all embracing, all crying, Ilse and her cousins, her uncle and aunt, her mutti and her papa. There was Butterkuchen and Zwetschgenkuchen and juice and coffee; they were all speaking at once. The cousins and Ilse listened with wide eyes as Mutti and Papa told the story — this must never, never be repeated beyond these walls, girls — of their escape in a Volkswagen van with a hiding compartment beneath a false floor driven by Americans posing as tourists. Mutti spoke of how cramped they were and how they could not make a sound for all those hours of travelling. How afraid she was that she would cough or sneeze.

'When?' Ilse said. 'When did you come?'

Papa looked at Mutti. 'We have already been in Berlin a while, Ilse.'

'But why didn't you come for me?'

'We could not,' her mother said. 'We longed to see you but we could not.'

'We had to wait until it was less likely we would be followed,' Papa said. 'And then today our friends decided it was safe to contact Jürgen.'

But already they were standing, making moves as if to leave. 'Where are you going?' Ilse cried out.

'We cannot stay,' Mutti said. 'It is not safe to stay here. But soon we will be together. It will not be long, Ilse, I promise.'

There were forms and documents, Uncle Jürgen explained to Ilse, many documents and forms which must be filled in and taken to official places to be stamped and submitted and then once those were approved, still more to be filled in and taken to other places. 'We must wait,' Papa told her during one of the infrequent visits her parents made to the house. 'We must be patient. It could be Canada. How would you like to live in Canada, eh, Ilse?' Each day Ilse was afraid to go to school — what if she returned one afternoon and her uncle and aunt were to tell her that Mutti and Papa had gone, that they had been sent off to this Canada or Australia with no time to wait for her?

'Why can't you stay here?' Ilse heard her aunt asking Mutti as they prepared vegetables for the evening meal. 'Germany is your home. Horst would easily find work in Berlin. You could be near to us. It is good for the girls to have their cousins.'

She heard her mother's voice, hard and bitter and final. 'This is not our home, Anke. Our home is gone.'

7

Her mother has remained consistent. 'We must live a quiet life. We must not complain or draw attention to ourselves.' And so when those boys at school raised their hands towards Ilse in Nazi salutes, when those girls in their exclusive groups asked, their voices dripping honey, if she had read *The Diary of Anne Frank*, Ilse remained silent. Although she understood that their minds were filled with the atrocities they had been told and read about, that they had seen in the series *Holocaust* which had recently replayed on television, she did not repeat to them what her Opa had said to her: 'Many of us, Ilse, did not want the Nazis. We did not want another war. It is little people who are swept away by the ambitions of big men.'

'Horst, we must tell people we are Dutch,' Mutti had said. 'That way they will like us more.'

'But we are not Dutch,' Papa had replied, smiling at her.

'Ach, they would never know the difference.'

'Gerda, I have changed my country but I will not change my nationality. Not even for you.'

But here, now, is her mother, this woman who would deny even her birthright to fit in, saying Ilse cannot call an ambulance, cannot call a doctor. It is her mother who is insisting that they take this girl in, that they alone must bear this responsibility. Ilse stands watching as Gerda coos soothing words, as she cools Serena's face with a wet towel. She doesn't know what to do. She knows full well she should make the phone call which will remove this burden from them but how can she stand against these two women, one so obstinate, the other so afraid?

There is hardly any time now between the contractions. Ilse feels sweat on her own face, feels it trickling down her back; she is so afraid as she watches Serena who is upright one moment, crouching on all fours the next, writhing and bellowing, her face red and contorted. 'I can't do this, make it stop, make it stop, make it fucking stop.'

This level of pain cannot be normal. How can anyone survive such agony? But Gerda's face is calm as she takes Serena's arm when the pain dies away for a moment. 'Listen to me,' she says evenly and firmly. 'All this shouting and tossing about is only wearing you out. You must concentrate and save your energy. When the next contraction hits, breathe with me. We will breathe through it together and we will beat it, okay?'

Gerda kneels on the bed beside Serena, placing her hands on her shoulders. 'Breathe normally. Don't hold your breath. Your baby needs all the oxygen you can give for this journey. You understand this, hey?'

Serena has her eyes on Gerda's face, seeming to calm, as she breathes in and then out.

'That's it. Now keep it rhythmical. In then out, easy, yes?'

Serena nods and then begins again to grimace, the muscles in her shoulders tensing and drawing up towards her ears as the pain begins again. 'Oh, I can't. I can't.'

'Hush, now. You must watch me and we will do this together.'

Gerda breathes in through her nose, blows out softly into Serena's face. 'Breathe with me. Now in, and let us count it together, slowly together, one and two and three and four and now out and, very good, you are doing so well, a little pause now and then keep your mouth very soft and sigh this breath out and aah, yes, let it out and now a little sip of water, nearly there, it is nearly passed and, yes, this is good, you have done so well.'

Between contractions Gerda is beside Serena, speaking quietly. 'No, it will not be long now. Yes, it will hurt but you are young, you are strong, it will happen quickly and then you will have your baby. We will be here to help you. Remember the breathing, the breathing will get you through.'

Here is the mother Ilse remembers from so many years ago. The respected nursing sister in charge of a large, busy ward in Leipzig main hospital. This is the woman Gerda was, so forthright and unafraid. Whatever comes of this, Ilse understands that her mother is doing what she believes must be done for this girl. She moves closer to the bed, no longer afraid, but caught up in this drama of turmoil and power. She takes the towel from Gerda, cools it beneath the cold tap and sponges Serena's hands and her face. She fills the glass with fresh, chilled water and holds it to her lips. Serena's face no longer holds the panic and fear of a child but is profoundly and fiercely concentrated as if she has summoned from deep within herself the courage and strength required.

There is little time for her to rest between the contractions which are coming hard and lasting minutes at a time. And now she is grunting, gasping, 'Push, I have to push.'

'Push with the contractions,' Gerda tells her. 'Wait for the contractions.'

Then, 'Push, good girl, push and now pant, pant, good girl, you can do it, good girl.' Serena is roaring, bawling, her face swollen and glistening with tears and sweat and she is grunting, panting, grunting, bearing down. And, now, a long, low growl of agony, of exultation and here, at last, is the miracle of the roundness of a small head, eyes open, there between the legs.

'One more push,' Gerda says. 'Just one more push, push down, down into your bottom, you're almost there, you can do this, just one more push.'

The head is out, properly out this time and oh, such a marvel, this small head with the fuzz of dark hair. 'Easy, easy. Just little pants now, just little pushes.' And out Serena's boy slithers, out purple and bloody and streaked in grey-white film. He is breathing, on his own he is breathing, and now he lies blinking as Gerda tenderly wipes his body, ties and cuts the cord.

'Is it all right?' Serena says.

'Your son is perfect,' Gerda says.

She lifts him into his mother's arms, settles him at her breast and he nuzzles, sucks, his eyes wide and open, this most wondrous and tiniest of creatures. Serena strokes her finger across the child's cheek. They are all smiling together, smiling in wonderment. Ilse feels tears running down her cheeks, a knot of emotion like a deep, choking sob in her throat.

They are silent, smiling and watching.

Yes. He is perfect.

8

Shrilling through the silence. The insistent chiming of the doorbell. Serena clutches her boy tight to her body. The doorbell shrieks again. Again. 'You must go, Ilse,' Gerda whispers.

Ilse closes the door to the bedroom. Her heart hammers as she moves down the hallway to the front door. She checks first that the safety chain is in place, then turns on the outside lamp.

'Mr Taylor.' Ilse says it calmly.

Their neighbour is standing under the light, peering through the half-open door. Each day, Ilse reluctantly waves her hand to this man, this Jack Taylor and Linda, his wife, sitting inside the room they have built onto the front of their house; the 'observation tower', Ilse and Gerda have named it, since it is made primarily from thick, transparent plastic through which Jack and Linda, on their cane sofas, may observe the comings and goings of the neighbourhood.

'We heard noises,' he said. 'Linda thought I should come over, check things out, you two ladies being on your own.'

Naturally, Ilse and Gerda, the German ladies, come under his ever-watchful gaze, the gaze from those small eyes which are presently sparking with anticipation.

She says, smiling, 'We are perfectly safe.'

'But we did hear something.' He is peering into the passage behind her.

'I promise you we have not been threatened on this particular evening, Mr Taylor.'

'It sounded as if somebody was screaming.' His eyes darting along the passageway.

'We are watching a film,' she says, laughing a little. 'A DVD. Perhaps that is what you heard. My mother has trouble with hearing.

I'm sorry that we have disturbed you.'

The brightness in his eyes fades. There are no outrages to be witnessed, no scandal to pore over with Linda in the conservatory after all. He turns reluctantly away. And now it comes. The faint mewling cry of a newborn. His eyes are again alive with curiosity as he turns back to her.

'Ah,' she says, 'we are on to a most interesting part of this film. The birth scene. You must excuse me.'

She shuts the door. Her breath is coming too quickly, her face burning. She goes into the bathroom, splashes cold water onto her face, catches her image in the mirror. There is a bright splatter of blood on her T-shirt. She goes back into the bedroom. The child is sleeping in his mother's arms; Gerda is cutting towels into squares. 'These will do for napkins for tonight but tomorrow we must buy clothes and proper napkins.'

Although the idea of going into the township and buying tiny clothes and napkins — all the paraphernalia and equipment Ilse has observed accompanying infants — seems extraordinary to her, she nods. She is so dazed by the happenings of this night, she thinks, that whatever she is asked, whatever further occurs, however outlandish, she will simply continue to nod.

'And Ilse, could you bring the picnic basket from the shelf? This will make a good bed.'

She climbs up on a chair and lifts it down from the laundry shelf. Although the basket looks clean, she takes a towel and wipes it down carefully and thoroughly. She cuts a sheet into quarters and covers the small pillow she has found which fits inside and takes a small, soft blanket from the back of the linen cupboard.

She lifts the bed she has created into the room. Serena is sleeping, Gerda is holding the child, rocking him in her arms, her head bent over him. He is dressed in a white, brushed-cotton gown with blue smocking at the neck and cuffs. Gerda looks at Ilse, sees the question in her eyes. 'I brought it with me,' she says. 'There were the three of us but of him there was nothing. I had to bring something of him.'

The house is silent. Everyone is sleeping. Tomorrow there will be the questions of what is to be done. But for now Ilse can only lie awake in the dark, thinking of this night. She hears through her bedroom wall Serena's soft breathing, the faint mew and snuffle of the child.

How has this all come about? How has Serena hidden this? The baby is small, Gerda said, and Serena is young, her body taut and fit. But why has she hidden this? She is still a child. Can a child be so alone that she cannot ask for help? And what of the father of this child? Is he some frightened boy who has denied Serena and run away from what he has done?

If she had not gone to the river this night. What would have happened? This does not bear thinking about. She thinks of Serena as she found her in the darkness. This poor girl, alone and terrified. Was there nowhere for her to go? What of her family?

But, she, Ilse must also take responsibility. She abandoned Serena when she should have seen her despair. Serena, that brave girl, her cheeks pink and eyes bright, her fingers tracing her boy's cheek. Ilse will never again abandon her. She will stand beside this girl. Nobody will hurt her or her boy. Nobody. At this moment, staring into the dark, anger and sadness and love blooming like hot blood inside her, Ilse knows she would kill for this girl. Yes. She would kill.

She wakes to a sound so unfamiliar and so strange that, for a moment, she cannot think where she is. She hears Gerda murmuring in the next bedroom, hears the bed squeak slightly and the sound stops. She slips her robe over her pyjamas. So early. The sun is barely up.

'He is feeding well,' her mother says as Ilse goes into the room. The child is at Serena's breast. There is a cup of tea placed on the chest of drawers beside her and Gerda drinks from her own cup.

Ilse goes into the kitchen and pours herself a cup from the pot sitting on the trivet on the bench. She looks around her at the red, blue and white checked curtains, the clock on the wall, the striped tea towel hanging from the hook. She almost wants to touch these things to ensure she has not been caught up in a dream. Yesterday everything was exactly as it had been the day before and the day before that. And now.

And now there is this fugitive they have taken in along with her newborn. They have taken in a fugitive, birthed her baby and now here they are, she and Mutti, concealing them in their house. For this she would lose her job. She knows it. Still, it does not seem to matter. She fills the kettle to make more tea and slices the dense, dark rye bread they always buy from the bakery and puts it into the toaster. She's hungry. Probably Mutti is hungry too, Serena as well. She slices more bread and toasts it, spreads it with butter and honey and carries it through to the visitors' room on a plate.

The sun is coming into the room, brighter now, through the pale blue curtains. They eat the toast quickly. 'I want to call him Kai,' Serena says. 'Mrs Klein told me the story last night about how she got her name.'

'Kai is a fine name,' Gerda says.

'Kai,' Ilse says. First there is this child being born in their house and now they are naming him? Next, are they to be planning his education? And here is Serena, wearing Ilse's nightshirt with the faint grey-blue stripes lying against the large white pillows, the baby sleeping at her breast, Gerda sitting on the chair near the bed. The baby makes a soft mewing sound and stretches his arms up above his head, his face screwed up and grimacing and they all smile. Ilse's job is likely to be lost, there will be accusations and trouble and here they are in this sunny room munching on honey and toasted bread and smiling at a baby? 'I think,' she says, 'I think we should talk about —.' She waves her hand. 'We must have plans.'

'Yes,' Gerda said. 'We need napkins and clothing. Oil, also, for his skin to prevent rashes. We need cotton buds and methylated spirits for the navel cord.'

'So,' Ilse says slowly, 'I am to go to town and buy clothing and provisions for the baby and we are to keep him and Serena hidden in this house? This is what you want?' She looks at Gerda and at Serena who is gently rocking the boy and gazing rapturously into his face. 'Do you not see,' she says gently, 'that we cannot hide you? Your family will be worried about you, Serena, there will be people looking for you.'

Serena is unperturbed. 'Lynnie just took off,' she says. 'Nobody looked for her.'

'But you are a fifteen-year-old child. You cannot just disappear. And you have a baby. Somebody must have known.'

Serena shrugs. 'I didn't tell anyone.'

For Ilse, this discussion is so strange, so odd. To have a baby at fifteen and tell no one? 'But your mother,' she says. 'Your mother must surely know.'

Another shrug. 'She said I was getting fat.'

What can she say to this girl? What should she say? 'The father of your baby. Surely he must know?'

'No.' Serena flushes and her voice rises. 'No!'

Stay away from that. For now, anyway. Some boy has disappointed her. 'We want to help you. But we must do what is right. Your mother —.'

'No. No! Just —.' She begins to sob. 'Just let me stay here until I'm a bit better, Miss. Please. Just till I'm better and then I'll sort it. I'll be okay then, Miss, please.'

She cannot bring herself to stand against this child with the anguish in her eyes and tears running down her face. 'Of course you must stay here,' she says gently. 'But Serena, I must ask this. How was it that I found you giving birth on your own? How could this happen?'

Serena lowers her head, sobbing. Gerda shakes her head. 'Ilse,' she says sharply, 'these questions must be asked at another time.'

'I was going to go to Lynnie's,' Serena says, 'I had some money to get there. I was going to take off next week. But then it started off early.'

'And so,' Ilse says, 'you went alone to the river?'

'I didn't know what was happening, Miss. I didn't know what to do. I looked on Google and it said first babies always come late so I didn't think it could be that. I thought I had some flu or food poisoning. I got out of the house because I thought if I had some fresh air I'd be all right. I kept on walking and then it got worse. Miss, I thought I was going to die.'

The boy is sleeping and Ilse takes his wrapped body and places him into the basket beside the bed. She sits on the bed and holds Serena's head against her shoulder, smoothes her hair back from her head. 'It's all right, Serena. It's all right.'

Her voice is raw. 'I didn't know what to do. I kept thinking it wasn't going to happen. I kept pretending it wasn't. I thought if I didn't eat anything it would just die, and I kept going on these runs and bike rides trying to —. Trying to stop it from happening but it was, I could feel it there. I could feel it.'

'Did you tell your sister?'

'If I told her she'd tell Mum. I thought I'd just get to her place and she'd know what to do. I had to get away.'

'Such a secret to keep. Could you not tell your mother?'

'Miss, I couldn't tell anyone. I couldn't.'

'But there is help. Sally —.'

Serena sits upright, spits out the words. 'You can't tell her. Promise you won't tell. They'll take him away from me.'

'Shh shh. Nobody will take him and we will not tell, not yet anyway. The time will come when we will tell but you, yourself, will choose that time. I promise you.'

Serena closes her eyes, tears are seeping through her eyelashes and down her cheeks. 'I have a baby. I have a baby and I never wanted him. I just wanted him to not be there, just to never have been there at all and now I feel so bad about not wanting him.'

'Becoming pregnant is not a crime.' Ilse keeps her voice low and calm. 'This happens often to girls. When it is time to tell about your baby there will be help for you. You will see this.'

'I can't tell ever. I can't tell and I can't stay here.' Serena heaves herself up on the pillows and looks wildly about the room. 'This is your house. It's not fair.'

'You will stay until you are stronger and things become clearer in your mind,' Gerda says firmly. 'In the meantime, you must get some sleep.'

Serena is already dozing as they leave the room and close the door.

'What are we to do?' Ilse holds out her hands.

'The child is terrified. She is exhausted and terrified. For now, we will look after her. When she is stronger, we will talk of what is to be done.'

'I don't understand this fear she has,' Ilse says. 'Other girls at the school have become pregnant. There is no shame about these situations. It is simply a matter of working out with the girl and her family what is to be done for the best.'

'Whatever she is feeling it is heartfelt. We must wait until she is ready to tell us.'

'Why wouldn't she tell her mother? Is it this man her mother has there that has done this to her? In that case it's the police and social services we should be turning to for help.'

'The family? The police? The social services? Serena does not trust any of them and we must not either.'

'But she is fifteen. She is under-age. Are you proposing that we keep her hidden here forever?'

'We will look after her until we know what to do and who we can trust. That is all I can say. And now that the shops are open, I have made a list.'

This is another thing. How is she, Ilse, this spinster schoolteacher, whom most people in this town know at least by sight, to go into a shop and purchase the articles on this list? Clothes, cotton buds, a bottle of methylated spirits to dab onto the umbilical cord so it will dry and can be easily removed, baby oil, talcum powder, disposable nappies?

It is laughable to think of her chatting to the girls she has taught in her classes as she selects, yes, three cotton singlets, three gowns and wool, please as well, three-ply wool, three skeins white, two blue and size-3 knitting needles. Oh yes, and then she will pile it up in the basket on her bike and begin to cycle home with the eyes of the town watching.

'Ach, Ilse, what is the matter with you?' Gerda says. 'Go to The Warehouse. Nobody will care what you buy. If anyone is curious, tell them your cousin is coming to stay. Your cousin and her baby. Tell them whatever you can think of. Take the car. There is too much here for the basket.'

And so now Ilse is in the aisles of The Warehouse, her fingers moving through the clothes on the racks, her eyes scanning for clothing to fit the smallest person she has ever seen. There are motifs of ducks and rabbits and small fluffy dogs she imagines may be termed 'cute' but is this clothing suitable to put against the skin of a baby? The fabric feels harsh and coarse to her fingers; everything smells to her of plastic.

Kai, his skin so soft, so tender. She discards the clothing she holds in her hands and pays at the checkout for a stack of disposable nappies. She puts them into the boot of her car and walks further into the town to the shop she has noticed. 'I wish to buy gifts,' she announces to the woman behind the counter. 'A layette.' Where does this word come from? How is it she has this word in her vocabulary? 'Yes, a layette, for my cousin who to visit comes.'

As always when she is nervous, her accent is markedly pronounced and the word order incorrect. She knows she is speaking too loudly and her face is flushing.

'A layette?' The woman smiles. 'It is a long time since I heard that word. Such a lovely word. What did you have in mind?'

What did she have in mind? What do babies wear? When she thinks of a baby, if she ever thinks of a baby, it is completely submerged in wool. 'What would you advise?'

'Well, how old is the baby?'

'Small.' Ilse holds out her hands to indicate.

'Boy or girl?'

'Boy.'

'So, you wish to purchase a gift for your cousin's baby? She will be bringing her own clothes with her, I imagine.'

The words blurt out. 'My cousin has lost the clothes. The airport has mislaid her suitcase. So she needs —.'

'Oh dear. She will need singlets. Does she prefer gowns or stretch-and-grow suits? We have sleep-bags, just in, and merino hats and socks and —.'

But oh, just look at these tiny perfect things, a striped hat, blue and white with a jaunty knot at the top, socks, singlets, the articles the woman calls onesies. Three little wrap-rugs and this sleep-bag striped also, lemon and blue. 'Merino, it keeps a baby so warm,' the woman says. 'It's all that is needed, really, for sleeping.' And two cross-over jackets with ties at the side, tiny pants to match and all so soft in her fingers.

Though she gasps when she hears how much all this has added up to she feels exultant as she pays and places the bags in the car. She goes to the pharmacy, tells the same story, 'My cousin, her bags all lost,' and buys with the shop assistant's help the best and softest of creams for a baby's skin.

They are in the guest room, which is now Serena's. The clothes are spread across the bed, blue and white and navy and lemon, holding them up and smiling: these most beautiful of clothes for the most beautiful of babies. Kai opens his eyes. Will his eyes be blue, brown or green? His hair is now quite dark but that may change. Generally the first baby hair falls out, Gerda tells them, and the new hair that comes in can be quite different. But, oh, just look at him. The hand which he cannot get into his mouth, the unfocused but curious eyes. Gerda deftly puts a nappy on him, pulls a singlet over his head, then comes the merino gro-suit and the hat. 'Oh, he suits blue,' Serena says. He stretches and grimaces; so funny, so perfect, so handsome.

In the following days it is the baby, the baby. He takes so much care and attention it no longer seems odd to talk of this new being in their house; the baby. It surprises Ilse how much care this small person requires. The feeding, the changing of clothes, the washing, drying and folding of those clothes, the creams and oils which must be applied to various parts of his body with Gerda carefully overseeing it all. 'Take care, Serena, that you do not allow the methylated spirits to spill onto his skin and keep it away from his eyes. Your eyes as well. Oh, do not look so afraid. It would not cause any permanent damage but it would sting.'

They bath him together. Gerda has cleaned a plastic washing basket which they fill with water — Gerda has demonstrated to them how to dip an elbow in to test the temperature — and place in their own bathtub. Kai is such a tiny fellow yet he kicks his legs in the water, gazing up at them. His eyes are less filmy — already he will see more clearly, Gerda says.

They love this baby, all of them love him, and this also surprises Ilse. She sees Serena's love for him in the light in her eyes as she feeds, strokes and dresses him but this love is natural: Serena is his mother. Yet Ilse too feels love for this child, she who is not even a relation. She sees this, also, in Gerda's face as she holds the child and watches him sleeping.

Ilse will not have a child of her own. Why that is she does not know but always she has known this. Perhaps the intensity of feeling she has for this child is simply a rerouting of her own maternal feelings. For Gerda, perhaps he is the grandchild she will not have. But this is too much introspection. There is washing, cooking, the uncomplicatedness of the tasks which must be completed, the simple pleasure of sitting in a sunlit room watching a sleeping child. And, oh, look at the way this small body is filling out and at these little cheeks puffing up.

Nothing happens to worry or threaten them. There are no messages from the school warning that a student is missing. Ilse hears nothing when she is in the supermarket, nothing in the streets. Serena is calm. The only concern she expresses is for the necklace she has lost: 'It's special. Lynnie gave it to me. She's got the same one. It's for luck, she said.'

Ilse returns to the river and looks for it but it has gone. Still, this is not so important and it seems at present they do not require a necklace for their luck. They know this cannot go on forever, they know eventually they must be found out or they must tell, but the days pass and it is a week since she came upon Serena and then it is two.

They are careful, of course. They keep the wooden blinds on their windows down and only half-opened during the day. The tiny clothes, wraps and sheets are dried on racks inside, away from prying eyes. Ilse knows that with any provocation at all the eyes of the Taylors, watching from their observation tower, will be upon them. Linda, who complains to anyone who will listen of the noisiness and rudeness of children in the neighbourhood and of the smoke which fouls the neat rows of washing she pins out on her line each morning at eight-fifteen. Jack, who keeps watch for trees threatening to become overgrown and for weeds that may creep through his fences and infest his level patch of lawn, his impeccable rose plot. What would they do with a story of a young girl and a baby living at the Kleins'? In the past, she and Gerda have laughed together about these Taylors. Now Ilse understands that they are dangerous.

It is Saturday morning and they have drunk their morning coffee, toasted slabs of bread and eaten it dripping with honey and butter. Kai has been fed and changed and is sleeping in his basket while Serena is in the laundry folding the dry washing, Mutti is cleaning up in the kitchen and Ilse fluffs up duvets and makes the beds.

There is the sound of a car stopping outside. Ilse looks through the window of her bedroom. It is an official car, the blue and yellow squares on white of a police car.

9

So this is where it all must come out. It is a local police officer — she knows him by name, this Sergeant Withers — who has got out of the car and is looking up and down the street. She has seen him at the school; he regularly comes to the sports events and the plays and concerts. She has been told by other staff that he is friendly and helpful, though she herself has spoken to him on only one or two occasions. Ilse watches as he turns towards the house. Well. There is nothing for it. She leaves her bedroom, goes out into the passage.

'Miss.' Serena is beside her, her face grey, her breath coming in short, terrified gasps. She reels back against the wall as they hear his footsteps on the gravel approaching the house. She starts to collapse onto the floor, her body trembling and her eyes glassy. Ilse grabs her arm, pulls her up and supports her, half-lifting her down the hallway and into the living room at the back of the house. This is not simply the anxiety of disclosure; the girl is terrified and Ilse cannot and will not give her up. Afterwards will be the time for questions. In the meantime, there is no time to waste. 'Mutti!'

Gerda comes, from the kitchen, wiping her hands on her apron.

'The policeman is here. Take Serena into the bathroom. Take Kai as well. Lock the door. I will get rid of him.'

Mutti does not question her but seizes Kai in her arms and hustles them all in. Ilse hears the lock click in place. She tosses towels, sheets, anything she can put her hands on across Kai's makeshift bed, gathers up everything of his she can see and shoves it all into the wardrobe. She switches on and turns up the volume on the radio; that way he will not hear anything if Kai wakes. Please God he will not hear anything. Her heart is wildly beating. Deep in her gut she

152

knows that she must keep Serena and Kai hidden from this man, that if she does not, something dreadful will happen. Mutti has turned on the shower. Good, that will muffle any sounds too.

The doorbell shrills and Ilse walks back along the passageway. Not too slow or he will think I am reluctant; not fast or he will think I am afraid. She opens the door and looks out at this man who has so terrified Serena. He is a big man. His bulk almost fills the small porch but he is also nondescript with his thinning hair and small eyes. He holds a black plastic bag.

'Can I help you?' Friendly enough, but she must not appear ingratiating.

'Miss Klein?'

'I am Ilse Klein, yes.'

'We've had a report of a missing girl. Serena Freeman is one of your students?'

'She is, yes.'

'I understand she visits you.'

'You are quite wrong. I do not welcome visits from my students.'

'We've had reports she comes to your house.'

'Some time ago she came once, perhaps twice, to return a book. That is all.'

'I see.' He is eyeing her. She finds his gaze impertinent, disturbing and now he is moving towards her, only slightly forward but almost as if he intends to slip by her and go into the house. As if he believes he has the right to go into her house. She stays, planted solidly in the doorway, her eyes on him steady.

He scribbles something in his notebook. 'To return a book, eh? So when would that be?'

She shrugs. 'This would be many months ago.'

'You haven't seen her recently?'

'I have not seen her.'

Lying to police. This is yet another nail in her coffin. But even if Serena had not reacted in this way, there is something about the manner of this man which disturbs her.

'It's been reported to us by the counsellor at the school, Sally Davis, that you were concerned about the girl.'

She shrugs again. 'These girls. Always there is something wrong.'

He persists, his eyes still on her. 'But you were concerned enough to speak to Sally?'

'I was mistaken. This was all cleared up.'

'You have no idea where she may have gone?'

'I do not.'

'And you say you haven't seen her?' Again he is asking this. Slipping in this question with those sly eyes watching.

'That is what I have told you. I have not seen this girl.'

He scribbles in his book. 'Mind if I have a look around?'

'I do indeed mind,' she says. 'There is no reason for such an inspection.'

Now his gaze on her is even more intense. 'Not an inspection,' he says. 'But never mind.'

She nods and begins to shut the door.

'Ilse,' he says. 'Miss Klein, that is.' He pauses on the 'Miss', only slightly but enough to give it emphasis.

'Yes?'

'Are these by any chance yours?' He holds the black plastic bag out towards her.

She looks inside. It is her swimsuit and towel, discarded by the river when she found Serena. In all the busyness of the past days she has not thought of them. She feels a slight flush on her cheeks. 'Ah, yes. I have been swimming. I must have forgotten —.'

'Something interrupted you?'

She takes the bag. 'Only absent-mindedness. Thank you for returning them.'

He turns to go, then hesitates and turns back to her, holding out his hand. In the palm is a greenstone pendant in the shape of a coil. 'This was found further away.'

'It is mine.' She says it without thinking, reaching out her hand because surely this is the necklace Serena has been concerned about, and he drops it into her palm. She closes the door and watches through the bubble glass as he walks down the gravel drive and then turns and opens the gate into the Taylors' house. She waits. It is almost ten minutes before he comes back out. There is something in his face she does not like. She steps back from the glass as she sees him pause beside the car and scrutinise their house before he drives off.

She goes to the bathroom, taps on the door. 'He has gone.'

Gerda opens the door. Serena is crouched in the alcove beside the bathtub, Kai clutched against her. Her forehead is covered with sweat; she is breathing too rapidly. Gerda leans down close beside her, rubs her back gently. 'It is all right, everything is all right, now let me take Kai, let me have him now.'

Serena gives him up into Gerda's arms almost as if she is moving in her sleep and now she is rocking, back and forwards she is rocking, her arms wrapped around her body, her breathing shallow, she is shuddering, her eyes are staring. Ilse kneels beside her, puts her arms around her and holds her firmly. 'I understand. Do you hear me, Serena? I understand. This man has gone. He will not hurt you. Listen to me now. I promise, this man will not hurt you again.'

Gradually Serena's breathing slows, gradually her arms held so rigidly slacken and she begins to cry, great juddering sobs shaking her body. 'Oh, Miss. Oh, oh Miss.'

Ilse helps her to stand. She helps her into her bedroom. This room is private from the neighbours or the road, nobody can see into this room and so the sun is shining brightly through the wide windows onto the pretty pink-and-white quilt, the white cushions on the chair beside the window. Ilse pulls back the covers. 'You must rest now. You have had a great shock and now you must rest.'

'Kai?'

'Mutti will look after Kai. He is in good hands.'

They both manage a tiny smile. They both understand how Mutti dotes on Kai, how she will hold him in her arms, rock him, sing to him for hours if need be. 'It's not his fault. It's not Kai's fault,' Serena whispers.

Ilse brushes Serena's hair from her forehead. 'Kai is perfect.'

Serena stares up at her, a lost child, 'He won't be —. Kai won't be like him, will he?'

'Never,' Ilse says. 'Never, Serena.'

Serena closes her eyes, then opens them again, tears welling up. 'Miss, you don't think —. It was never —. I never wanted to.'

'Hush, Serena. There is no need to explain. I see what he is and what he has done.'

Ilse sits on the chair beside the window watching her sleep then she joins Gerda who is sitting in her rocking chair. The treads squeal softly against the floorboards as she sings to Kai who lies sleeping against her shoulder: 'Schlaf, Kindlein, schlaf. Der Vater hüt die Schaf.'

Ilse measures coffee into the pot, places it on the stove and sits opposite Gerda. 'You understand what has happened?'

Gerda nods. 'Kai is this man's child.'

Ilse stands, adjusts the heat beneath the coffee pot, takes cups from the cupboard, milk from the refrigerator. She takes biscuits from the pantry: the coffee is not ready, the coffee is not yet ready. She paces, picking up the newspaper, folding it, closing a window, opening it again. 'Sit down, Ilse,' Gerda says. 'Please, you must sit down.'

'I am angry,' Ilse says. 'I am so angry. This man. Such evil, a man preying on a child. I am so angry I do not know how to manage myself.'

'Hush, now.' Gerda's gaze is calm and level. 'Here, Ilse, you hold Kai and I will make the coffee.'

Ilse is reluctant, she wants to pace and shout, she wants to smash and stamp and bellow, but she takes Kai, that small, light bundle, and feels his face burrow into her neck, feels his small nose and his mouth against her skin and smiles. In spite of the rage boiling inside she smiles.

'There.' Gerda places the cup filled with coffee on the table in front of her. 'That is better.'

They eat and drink silently. The good strong coffee, the cinnamon biscuits warm her belly and the child's moist face against her — yes, she is calmed, a little she is calmed.

She places her cup on the table, faces Mutti across the table. 'I think he will come back.'

Gerda's face is serious, her voice grave but she does not appear frightened or alarmed. 'What makes you think this?'

'It is a feeling I have. Before he went away, he looked into the house as if he was curious.'

'Then we must make sure he has nothing to be curious about.'

'We must have help. This is too big for us.'

'Ilse, listen to me. We are two women, a mother and a daughter who live quietly together. We take care of our house and our garden, we are pleasant to our neighbours. We keep mainly to ourselves and there are no upsets or scandals. We must give this man no reason for questions or suspicion.'

'We cannot continue to hide Serena and Kai. Someone will see them or, at least, hear Kai crying.'

'Kai does not cry.'

Ilse smiles again. She must admit to that. Kai does not cry since there are three women hovering, anxious to scoop him up into their arms to soothe and comfort him. 'But eventually he will cry. As, eventually, he will need to be taken outside this house, to go to the doctor for his immunisations or if he is ill, to be taken to the park, to meet other people. We cannot shut a child up in a house forever, Mutti. You know this.'

'So.' Gerda runs her finger around the rim of the cup. 'What do you propose we do about it?'

Ilse sighs. 'I don't know. This is rape. Rape of an under-age girl. But he is a policeman so who can we turn to? We must talk to someone in authority, but who that would be I do not know. Perhaps a lawyer. Perhaps Child, Youth and Family could help us.'

Gerda leans forward in her chair. Her voice is harsh. 'One word of this, Ilse, and it will be around this town like wildfire and he will be here with his threats and intimidation. You saw how afraid Serena was. Imagine how it would be if she came face to face with him?'

Ilse shakes her head. 'I don't know what else we can do.'

Gerda reaches across the table, clutches her hand. 'We cannot trust the people here. This man is big in the eyes of the town. He will lie and he will use his power to hurt Serena and Kai.'

'You cannot know this. There are good people in this town who will support us.'

'Good people,' Mutti says bitterly. 'Good people are swayed by the unscrupulous. I have seen this time and again.'

'So what do we do?'

'When Serena is strong and Kai a little older we will take them to Dunedin. In the city we will find the right people to help us and then we will tell our story.'

Ilse thinks hard. Perhaps her mother is right. Serena must not face this man. Not yet, anyway, and when she does face him she must have strength behind her. 'Yes,' she says. 'Yes, I will agree to this. But we must make a time. We must decide when this is to happen.' She watches her mother as she thinks, her fingers still tracing the edge of the cup.

'Let us say two months,' Gerda says. 'Serena must be strong to withstand the questions she will be asked, the people she will have to speak with. You saw her today. She is in no state yet to stand up for herself.'

'Two months,' Ilse says. Kai nuzzles against her neck and she laughs at the strange and sweet feeling as he butts his head, tries to suck her skin. 'This little man needs his mutti,' she says.

Gerda turns her head away but Ilse can see that her eyes are bright suddenly with tears. 'Ja, he needs his mutti,' Gerda repeats quietly.

10

So that is the plan. They agree to this, talking also with Serena. Ilse gives her the pendant later, as if she has found it herself, and they do not speak of the man again. Instead, they talk about Kai, about how he is now smiling at them, this toothless smile that stretches across his small face. They talk about how he reaches his hand out into the sunlight, how he is growing, if his hair will be dark or blond or red and if his eyes will remain blue.

'What will happen in Dunedin?' Serena asks as she nurses Kai.

'Just as we said. We will find the right person or people to help us find the right ways to manage this.'

'I don't want him to know about Kai. He'll try to take him away from me.'

'He must come to know about Kai. But he will not take him.' Gerda says it firmly, folding a small sheet into a tight, neat square.

'How can you stop him?'

'If I have my way,' Ilse says, 'he will be in prison.'

'In prison?'

'What he did to you is against the law. You must know that.'

'Yes, but he will say I agreed to meet him. That I —.'

They have heard her story. 'Only because he threatened you,' Gerda says.

'He blackmailed you,' Ilse says. 'That, also, is against the law.'

'But it'll be my word against his. Everyone will believe him. I'll have to go to court and it'll be him against me. No one will think I'm telling the truth.'

'You have your baby to prove your truth,' Gerda says gently. 'You are under-age and you have his child. If he denies this there are medical tests to prove it is so.'

'I won't be able to come back here, though, will I? Not with everyone knowing. I'll be on my own.'

'We will be with you,' Ilse says. 'Whatever happens, Mutti and I will be with you. We will not let you down.'

For Ilse sees that their time left in this town is about to end. With a court case and everything that hangs ahead of them, they will not be able to live here. She cannot continue to teach at the high school.

She does not know what will happen. Would Mutti settle happily in another place? What will Serena's wishes for herself be after the shock of all that has happened has passed? She says now that she will not return to her mother's house, that she does not wish to see her family. But that is now. Circumstances change; circumstances always change.

'Where would I live?' Serena says.

Ilse has been considering this, talking of it with Gerda. 'You must not worry. Perhaps, if this was your wish, you and Kai could continue to live with us. When you are older you will, of course, want to have a place of your own but for now you can stay with us — that is, if you would like to — and if we cannot remain here in this town, well, then there are other places.'

'You would do that?' Serena stares at her. 'You would do that for me and Kai? You would give up everything here and move to another place?'

Gerda answers swiftly, 'Aber sicher! Du und Kai, gehört jetzt zu uns.'

'Of course. You and Kai belong to us,' Ilse repeats it to her, smiling.

They lock the doors at all times. The blinds remain down in the front-facing rooms and Kai's clothing and bedding dry inside the house. They resume their ordinary lives; nothing must be seen to change. Gerda works in the garden and sometimes Ilse helps. Sometimes she reads in the deck chair in the garden and Serena joins her, bringing Kai out in his wicker basket to sleep in the shade. The high fence, the trees Papa planted protect them from view. Here, in this garden, they are safe.

Ilse goes each night to swim, lazily lifting her hand towards the Taylors who hover, like large nesting birds spying for food, in their plastic capsule. The cool of the river, the surge and lap of it, soothes her body and her mind. When she is swimming the worries slide away; the police car which sometimes she sees passing slowly up the street, turning and moving back past their house before it drives out onto the main road. That nagging concern that the key to the front door which had been in her bag was not there when she tipped her clothing out. She has searched for it by the river. Probably it slipped out and is lost amongst the lupins and the scrub. She does not mention it to Mutti who would be troubled. This is nothing to fret about but, still, she ensures each night that the safety chain is in place.

You must not worry. You must not worry.

But in her bed, alone at night, when there is nothing to take her attention but her thoughts, Ilse does worry. What if somebody notices something? They are careful, of course they are careful, but just a voiced suspicion, just one word and everything could be set alight. The police. CYFS. She has heard the bad stories, children taken away from families, from young mothers. But Serena has her, she has Mutti. Could this not be viewed as a stable household?

Yet they are harbouring a runaway. They have delivered a child and hidden him; they have not registered this child. Is this against the law? She does not know. She does know, though, that if this story got out, if it became public, her reputation would follow her, she would not get a teacher's position anywhere in this country. Then how would they all live?

And if she and Mutti were found to be guilty of crimes against the law of this country, they would be seen as incapable of providing a stable environment for Serena and Kai. Who would look after them then? Would the state step in, take Kai, place him in a foster home? She cannot have that. She will not have it. This little man needs his mutti. Kai and Serena, they need each other.

And so the thoughts go. Round and round in her head. She jolts awake sometimes. Is someone outside the house? Is someone spying into our windows?

'But think of the joy Serena and Kai have brought to us,' Mutti says when she voices some of her concerns. 'Es wird nichts so heiß gegessen, wie es gekocht wird.' Things are never as bad as they appear.

Don't think of it. Do not think of it. All this worry and supposition over happenings which may never occur. They must hang on. For another few weeks they must hang on and then they will take Serena and the child to Dunedin.

She is holding Kai who is gazing up at her with such wonderment on his face. 'O brave new world that has such people in it,' Ilse says, laughing as he stares, almost cross-eyed at her.

'That's Shakespeare isn't it, Miss? I mean, Ilse?' Serena asks. Ilse has asked that she call her by her name but she is having trouble with this.

'Of course. How did you recognise it?'

'I read it.' She shrugs and turns her eyes away. 'Tried to, anyway.'

'You are clever, Serena. The cleverest of all my students,' Ilse says firmly.

This man has taken so much from Serena: her confidence, her bright spirit, her love of learning. A man who preys on children; such cowardice, such cruelty. But, still, Serena is doing well. She looks healthy and now she has begun to talk more freely and to laugh. There have been no more visits.

And then comes the afternoon when Kai and Serena are napping and Ilse is in the kitchen preparing a chicken to be roasted for the evening meal. Gerda's voice reaches her, shrill with alarm: 'Ilse, there is a woman outside. A woman looking into our house.'

Ilse goes to the front door and looks through the glass. The image is distorted but still she can see a woman with dark hair looking up and down the street — and then she turns and Ilse sees her face. She throws open the door and she is running, catching this woman by her arm. 'You! It is you!'

The woman draws back and they gaze at each other. 'Anja. It is you.'

She is tall. Like Ilse she is tall and she is lean in her jeans and white T-shirt. Also like Ilse she has pale olive skin and her cheekbones are high, like the thick edge of a knife. Her eyes are bright and blue and her hair dark. Anja. The girl she was, the woman she has become, Anja is home to Ilse who sees in her eyes and face the streets, the alleys, the houses, the churches. She has thrust home so deeply inside, been so fearful of drawing home up into her consciousness but now here it is in front of her. Anja. It is Anja. 'Come in. Oh, come inside.'

Gerda stares with disbelief, then folds Anja into her arms, this girl she so often referred to as her second daughter. 'There is no need for concern,' Gerda calls to Serena. 'This is Anja, our friend from Leipzig.'

Serena comes out of her room carrying Kai in her arms. The coffee must be brewed, the Nusszopf sliced and placed on the table and all the time they are talking, talking. 'How did you find us? How is it you are here?'

'It is no longer difficult to visit other countries,' Anja says. 'How I found you? I found your brother's name, Tante Gerda. The records are easily procured these days. I phoned him in Berlin and he told me you had gone to New Zealand. After that it was easy.'

Tante Gerda. Ilse had also called Anja's mother tante. Tante Gitte. She remembers the Meyers' kitchen with the pattern of hens and cross-stitch on the curtains. She remembers the smell of cinnamon and eating Thüringer Rostbratwurst at their wooden table.

'We could not write,' Gerda says, tears in her eyes. 'You understand we could not write to you? To Gitte and to Carl —.'

'They are well,' Anja says. 'They send you their greetings. I have letters and photographs.'

Ilse is silent, drinking Anja in. Is she dreaming? Is this Anja sitting at their table? Her English is good. Only an occasional fumble for words. Where did she learn to speak English? At school they were taught Russian. There is so much to talk about and to find out.

'Letters?' Gerda says, her eyes bright. 'I must see these letters.'

'Where is Onkel Horst?' Anja asks.

'Papa died some time ago,' Ilse says softly.

Anja's face fills with grief, 'Oh, Ilse, no.'

'But when did you get here?'

'I flew into . . . Ock-land?' Anja makes a little face as she gets her tongue around the name. 'And then the plane to Queenstown. I stayed there for a night and I caught a bus.'

'Where are your bags?'

'I found a place for staying.'

'No,' Gerda says. 'No. You will stay with us, Anja.'

'But do you have enough room?'

'There are two beds in my room,' Ilse says. 'There is room enough.'

'It will be like it was before,' Anja says, smiling. 'Do you remember, Ilse, our sleepovers?'

'Of course,' Ilse says. 'Of course, I remember.'

Anja turns to Serena, who is silently watching them. 'And this little chicken? What is this little chicken's name?'

'Kai,' Serena says, looking down at him.

'A beautiful name. May I hold him?' Serena passes him to Anja who takes him gently and holds him against her shoulder.

'Who would have thought this?' Gerda says, a wide smile spreading across her face. 'Who would have thought it? Serena and Kai and now Anja,' she laughs, offering the plate of Nusszopf again to Anja and Serena. 'Ilse and I were to have such quiet holidays.'

Ilse watches her mother. Before the baby, before the whispers, on warm days, Ilse and Mutti and Papa would visit the gardens and parks in Leipzig. She remembers Mutti running with her across the lawns, pushing her on the swings. She remembers the light summer dresses her mother would wear and how, over the hot days of summer, her face and arms and legs would turn slowly golden. Mutti's face now has that young woman's softness and the happiness Ilse remembers.

'We have a chicken for dinner, we have salad vegetables and new potatoes of the season. We have wine and I will make a cake. We will have a feast,' Mutti says, throwing out her arms. 'Ilse, you will go now with Anja and carry her luggage to our house. I cannot wait to see these letters.'

'You have not changed,' Anja says, smiling at Serena. 'Always one for a celebration was our Tante Gerda.'

Mutti cooks, the cover is removed from the car and Anja and Ilse return with the baggage. Mutti takes the letters, strokes the envelopes in her hand. 'From Gitte and from Carl, and oh, here is a letter from Hanna. You remember Hanna, Ilse.'

Ilse remembers. She remembers Tante Gitte and Tante Hanna and how they would come to their apartment for coffee and pastries. Oh yes, everything she remembers as they sit, that evening, around the table with the fresh roses in the vase, with the candles burning. Serena listens, smiling, sometimes talking with Kai in her arms. 'Kai is restless this evening. He wants to be part of us, at this table with us,' Gerda exclaims. 'He wishes that he is not excluded.'

They eat, they drink wine in the softness of the candlelight; they pore over the faces of the people in the photographs. 'Gitte? She looks still so young. And Hanna, these are her grandchildren?' Gerda reads to them small pieces from the letters. Hanna's daughter-in-law Lore is pregnant again. There are good stories and stories of sadness: friends who are ill, who have experienced misfortune; friends who have died.

'Hansi?' Ilse says. 'And Klaus?'

'They are well,' Anja says. 'Hans I do not see so much since he relocated to Berlin with his wife. Hans is a doctor now.'

'A doctor? Hansi? And he has a wife?'

'Yes. Not Klaus, though. He said I must say hello to you Ilse. He sends you his greetings . . . He said I must ask, when will you come home and marry him?'

Ilse laughs. They had a pact, the four of them. Ilse was to marry Klaus and Anja was destined for Hansi. They would live in adjoining apartments.

'And you, Anja? What is your work now?' Gerda says.

'I am a psychologist, Tante Gerda. I work with children.'

'Oh. That is so marvellous.' Gerda shakes her head. 'Our Anja, a psychologist.'

And at night she is there. Anja, only a metre and a half away, she is in the next bed. They reach across, clasping hands as they did so many years ago when, as children, they slept in each other's homes. 'Gute Nacht.'

Ilse wakes in the night. She hears Anja breathing softly in the next bed, she looks across and can make her out within the shadows. Her hand is hanging limply from the side of the bed and Ilse reaches over and lightly touches it. So she is here. Anja truly is here.

In the morning, she tells Anja about Serena and Kai. No need to explain to her the need for secrecy, not to a past citizen of Stasi rule.

'But here in New Zealand?' Anja asks.

'This man has power. I cannot trust that we would be treated fairly in this town. In the city it will be different. But first Serena has to become stronger.'

She tells her, laughing, about her nervousness over shopping for the child. Her story of the visiting cousin.

'But,' Anja says, 'I can be that cousin. If there are any questions to be answered, Kai is mine.'

'A few enquiries at the immigration department would soon set that right.'

'Oh yes, but for the neighbours, for buying things that are necessary, that will be our story.'

And so that day Kai has a proper bed and a bath instead of the basket and the plastic tub which he is outgrowing. He has a soft stuffed bear, he has a rocker-chair and a baby gym and a mobile of butterflies and birds which hangs above his crib. Anja has been introduced as Ilse's cousin to the baby-shop owner and to anyone who has greeted Ilse on the street. In the evening they bath Kai, all of them watching, as Serena tests the water with her elbow and lowers him in, her hand behind his head.

Will he cry? They are all almost holding their breaths as he lies so still, his face screwed up as if he is carefully considering this new enlarged environment which gives him the freedom to stretch and spread his limbs. He kicks his feet, gently at first, then enough to disturb the water. He kicks and looks up at Serena and his eyes are sparkling.

11

Although Ilse does not feel easy about leaving Mutti and Serena and Kai for long, some days they slip away for an hour, sometimes two, and hike up into the hills. Anja marvels at the rock formations like strange gigantic animals, like citadels and palaces. They climb high and sit looking over the town and the river; from where they are they can see to the pine trees which edge the town, to the new subdivisions stretching towards Clyde.

In the house, Ilse and Mutti rarely speak German; Papa's admonishments to speak English somehow have prevailed. But now she can speak her mother tongue again. At first it is not easy; she must listen so closely to Anja, almost translating what she says into English, and then as Ilse answers she must pause to think of the correct words, the correct expressions, and as she forms them her tongue slips and stops on sounds which are no longer familiar. She laughs at herself but she feels sad that somewhere in time and place she has lost her Muttersprache.

Then, at last, the words are there, rushing out as if there is a flood which will not be contained and they are talking and talking of past school friends, of Ilse's journey to Berlin and to New Zealand; there is a wealth of present and past to cover and discuss.

In the mornings Gerda sends them off. 'Go. We will be fine.' Ilse has become less cautious about leaving them alone and they begin to walk further, taking sandwiches, and apricots from the tree in the garden, and drink bottles in their backpacks. On this day, Gerda has made a special lunch and waved them away — 'Go for the day, so hot and beautiful, go and have fun' — so they have taken the car and driven beyond the town, following the highway to Cromwell. They park then walk around the old part of town, looking into the buildings and the cottages.

'Built 1913,' Anja says, reading the plaque outside a building. 'Only one hundred years old. Almost brand-new, this house.'

Ilse smiles. Again Anja is teasing her. They walk to the edge of the town and follow the track alongside the lake. 'Here,' Ilse says. There are trees for shelter against the midday sun which is scorching down and the water glistens as they spread out towels and the rug. Ilse takes off her shorts and T-shirt, sprays sunscreen on her arms, legs and back and hands the bottle to Anja. Beneath her shirt and shorts, Anja wears a blue bikini, the brazen blue of an electric sky, which fits tautly across her lower body, revealing the blades of hip, her flat, tanned stomach. The top is cut low and held in place by narrow straps which fasten around her neck. Anja looks wonderful in this bikini, Ilse thinks, and here she is in her swimsuit with its high neck and wide straps, its barely scooped back. She looks like a flat, black tube in it; she dresses like an old lady. Why does she do this, why this need to hide herself away?

Perhaps she should buy a bikini. Miss in a bikini? She smiles to think of it as she lies on her stomach watching as Anja sprays, then smooths the sunscreen into her skin and lies close to her. It is so still here, so silent, Ilse could almost sleep but there are questions she has been waiting to ask. Questions she is afraid may upset Anja but even so she must try.

'We have not talked of this,' Ilse says carefully, 'but we saw on the television when the Wall came down. How was it at home at that time? What was happening then?'

'Did you ever hear before you left, Ilse, the talk that there were people who would meet at Nikolaikirche after the Monday service, to talk about politics and to pray?'

Yes, she had heard the whispers, seen the meaningful looks. 'I did hear of the meetings and I thought these people were very wrong.' She thinks back to the way it was in Leipzig. 'It frightened me that I'd heard such things. I thought I could be implicated.'

'I was afraid also when I heard the rumours.' Anja looks across at

Paddy Richardson

Ilse. 'Like you, I was against these people. But we were only children. We believed what we were taught to believe.'

'I still believed it when we left. I did not want to go. I never wanted to leave. It was my parents —.'

'They must have been aware of things that you did not know about. You remember the Runde Ecke?'

Ilse sees now that elegant, round-shaped building close to the walking pavement which created in her, always, feelings of fear, of unseen things, like waking in the dark still clutched by dreams of unknown places. She remembers how she would be washed over by dread as she rode past on her bicycle, how she would lower her head and pedal swiftly past. 'Of course I remember the headquarters of the Stasi.'

'After the Stasi left, the building was stormed and some people were able to find their dossiers. They wept as they came to understand what had been done to break their lives.'

'What do you mean?'

'It was widely known,' Anja says slowly, 'that the Stasi had their own people in the post office who opened and read mail. It was also known that they planted bugs and monitored what happened in people's homes so they could suppress discontent.'

'We were told that the Stasi kept our citizens safe, that no one who was loyal to the state had anything to fear.' Ilse hesitates. 'But, of course, there were many lies.'

'We were told terrible lies, Ilse. Everything we believed was founded in lies.' Anja sits upright and stares ahead of her into the water, 'What wasn't so widely known was that the Stasi had special methods for persecuting those they suspected. Lies and rumours would be spread to destroy these people who, without explanation, would lose their jobs. In many cases their children also were punished by being barred from education. Do you remember Erich from our class? He was so much brighter than the rest of us? Erich was prevented from having a place in the university.'

'Erich? He should have —.'

'Of course he should have. Many, many people who should have had different lives had those lives stolen from them. I heard a story, Ilse. A terrible story of a doctor. First he was demoted within the hospital and then his wife began to receive letters from someone purporting to be his lover. In the nights the phone would ring and there would be a woman asking for him. This man denied it, but his wife, after some time of this, well, she left him and demanded a divorce. After the Stasi had gone she discovered this had all been fabricated, that it was members of the Stasi who had sent the letters and made the calls. She could not even ask for her husband's forgiveness. He had died.'

Ilse turns onto her back, stares up at Anja. 'There is no doubt this story is true?'

'It is true,' Anja says. 'But it is only one among many such stories. Worse stories, if that is possible. People who were tortured, people who were executed, parents who were separated from their children and sent to the work camps and died in terrible, brutal conditions. Forty years of killing, Ilse.'

Despite the heat Anja is shivering. Ilse reaches across and takes her hand, holds it in her own. 'I did not know.'

'You were lucky that your parents took you away.' Anja's voice is bitter. 'As we got older, there were students from our class who were taken. Some returned but there was the look in their eyes of an animal which has been beaten and has lost faith in life. I was afraid. We all were afraid.'

Ilse is holding in her breath; she almost does not want to listen to any more, she is so fearful of what she may hear.

'Herr Wosser from the apartment next to us was taken. Then it was Hansi's uncle,' Anja says, her voice shaking. 'Who would be next? What was being said along those lines of whispers? A chance remark picked up and repeated could have dreadful consequences. We discovered after the wall came down that in East Germany there were ninety thousand Stasi and a hundred and seventy thousand informers.'

'So many?'

'We did not know there were so many then but what we did know was nobody could be trusted. Even children were being used as spies. Children, once they were thirteen, who came from families with good party values, would be recruited.'

'Children,' Ilse whispers.

'Oh,' Anja says bitterly, 'such an honour to be chosen and to have the distinction of spying on your neighbours and teachers and other students. Once they were selected, if they performed well, they had such a good future all set in place ahead of them, working among the Stasi. Liesse-Lotte Schmidt, Piet Wagt from the classes above us? They were spies.'

'Did you talk with your parents about what was happening?'

'How could even a family speak in privacy? We may have been under surveillance. We did not know. If we said anything or asked a question that was even mildly subversive, Mutti would shake her head and place her hand against our lips.'

'You were so afraid?' Ilse murmurs.

'Oh yes, we were afraid. As the Stasi began to see they were losing their hold they became even more rigorous in their attempts to control.'

'Did you know, did you sense it was ending?'

'We were too nervous of that talk to listen. Our family, Ilse, we were cowards.'

'Anja, no. That is not fair.'

'It is true. The people who talked and prayed at Nikolaikirche all those Mondays, all those years. The people who stood up to the Stasi. If it had not been for them —.' Shrugs.

'But,' Ilse says, 'your parents had to take care of you. They had to keep you safe. How could they put your lives at risk?'

Anja shakes her head. 'I don't know but this is the way such things happen. People are afraid for themselves and for their families and so they say nothing and the atrocities continue. After it was all over, Ilse, we went to the Runde Ecke. We saw the interrogation rooms and the cells where people had awaited trial. They were so ugly and bare. To think of people locked up in such conditions, separated from their families, perhaps never to see them again. Mutti and I were weeping. But then —.'

These words which sweep over Ilse. These terrible stories. She remembers marching with the Young Pioneers, saluting with her arm at that special angle across the top of her head, bellowing out the songs. 'Now I am a Young Pioneer everyone congratulates me. Dad comes home, he says "my Young Pioneer".'

'There were rooms filled with machines,' Anja is saying, 'and large objects like papier-mâché rocks, the sorts of things children at school make as props for a play. I could not work out what these objects were and that was when Papa cried. Ilse, I had never heard him cry before and I was so afraid, it was as if he had turned mad. He began kicking these rocks, kicking them over and over again. "This is what they have made of good people's lives?" He kept repeating it. "This is what they have made of them?" And then I understood. The machines were grinders. The Stasi had tried to destroy the records by shredding them and mixing them with cement and water. That was what Papa was saying.'

'Oh, Anja,' Ilse breathes.

'The Runde Ecke is now a museum. I went once to visit and I heard tourists laughing at the wigs and the false noses and the glasses used for disguises. There is a false stomach made of padded fabric with a hole in the middle to hide a camera. There are jars that hold the preserved body scents of suspects they held in the interrogation rooms. People the Stasi were suspicious of would sit on a chair on which a cloth would be laid and then this cloth would be removed and sealed in jars so that dogs could later track them. All so comical, but this comedy ruled our lives.'

'Were you at the protests?' Ilse asks.

'The first one,' Anja says. 'October the second. Mutti and Papa had forbidden me and Klara from going but I watched and followed from a distance. The protests were to be peaceful but Papa said that the Stasi would not accept this and they would use firearms against the crowds. I thought if I heard shots, I would run. There were eight thousand people moving through the streets carrying candles. I went home and told. I would not be kept quiet, even with Mutti shaking her head and shushing me. Papa listened. He said we would go. Next Monday we would go as a family. He said to Mutti, "It is time we were heard, Gitte. We have been silent for too long."'

Tante Gitte, Onkel Carl. They were both tall and self-assured with wide smiles and confident voices. Ilse cannot imagine the Tante Gitte she remembers shaking and shushing. The Onkel Carl who told the marvellous jokes, crying. How could that be?

'Were you frightened?' Ilse reaches across and takes her hand.

'I was only a child, only just turned thirteen, but we grew up quickly in those times. We learnt fear and silence in our mother's arms. I was afraid, yes, but more than that I knew that this was the people's time and chance and so we as a family had to move with the others. Each week the protest grew stronger. One week it was eight thousand, the next a hundred and twenty and then more than three hundred thousand people were out on the streets. Despite the news which got out that Eric Honecker had issued a shoot-to-kill order to the military, despite the talk that Tiananmen Square had happened only months ago and that this would be another massacre, three hundred thousand people were there. Imagine it, Ilse.' Anja's eyes shone bright. 'Three hundred thousand of us holding our candles and chanting through the darkness, "We are the people".'

In her mind Ilse sees rivers of darkness lit by candles and hears the sound of voices which soar above the faces made radiant by that light. 'Wir sind das Volk. Wir sind das Volk.'

'We led the country,' Anja says. 'It was us in Leipzig who led the way by holding those Monday protests. All of the Eastern cities and towns, Berlin, Dresden, all of them followed. In November the government crumbled. In November the people tore down the Wall.'

They lie silent, holding hands. The sun shines and the river glistens and beyond them are the rocks, so beautiful these rocks.

Those other rocks; such ugliness.

'It is why I trained in psychology,' Anja says at last, 'and why I chose to work with children. For a long time I wished to go into politics. I felt it so deeply that we, our family and others like ourselves, had been liberated on the backs of the people who had been brave. But I do not have the strength and forcefulness to stand against powerful people. This way I can try to give strength to children.'

'But, Anja, you are strong. What you have lived through —.'

'Not me. It is all pretence. Come.' Anja is on her feet, looking down at Ilse and smiling. 'Come and swim. And then we will eat Tante Gerda's bread and the cheese and the eggs and the sausage and pickle and the Apfelkuchen.'

'You've sneaked a look, have you?' Ilse grins up at her.

'What is this "sneak a look"? Come on, first one in, hey?'

They swim, they eat. They lie in the sunshine. 'You know,' says Anja, 'that the Stasi built bunkers for that nuclear war we always thought was coming? Bunkers for the Stasi so they could save themselves and repopulate the earth? Imagine that. The whole world populated with little Stasi.'

'Grey uniforms,' Ilse says, smiling. 'And crew cuts.'

'And big bellies. I wonder if they would have remembered the necessity of taking women with them into these bunkers.'

'But who would dare to impregnate a Stasi woman?'

'For you, Ilse, life has been good here?'

'It is good.'

Ilse closes her eyes. She knows she must be thankful for this sun on her body, for the river and the rocks, for the life her parents have given her, free of the fear Anja has told her of. Yet she is lost in a world away amongst those nights of the many thousand flickering candles. Oh, that she had been there, a part of the liberation of her home. 'Wir sind das Volk. Wir sind das Volk.'

12

They drive silently through the gorge, the pine trees rising on one side of the road with the rocks perilously poised above and the water oily and silent below them. Ilse's head is buzzing with what has been said.

Anja glances across at her. 'You are quiet,' she says.

Ilse smiles. 'Thinking,' she says. 'Just thinking. Shall we stop for coffee? We could make a detour, go into Clyde. There are cafés.'

'Yes,' Anja says, 'and will they have the, the crunch of ginger?'

Ilse laughs. Anja has discovered already the pleasures of New Zealand baking. Custard squares, Louise cake, yo-yos and ginger crunch. 'Perhaps,' she says, 'or a chocolate brownie. You haven't had a chocolate brownie yet.'

It is late afternoon when they turn back into the drive. They are laughing. Anja has eaten both a brownie and a slice of ginger crunch and is discussing the merits of both. 'The ginger crunch, this is so tasty. It is, at the base, so chewy and the top is creamy and the little pieces of ginger inside. Ach, it is so good. But the chocolate, oh, that is wonderful.' Anja holds her arms out wide and puffs out her cheeks. 'In New Zealand soon I will be the size of a pig.'

Ilse closes the car door, still laughing. She sees the car parked outside, close to the curb. A car she does not recognise and now she is running. Up the drive, turning the key in the lock, drawing Anja quickly inside, hearing the voice she does not recognise.

They are in the living room, looking up at her as she bursts into the room, Anja close behind her. A strange woman holds Kai against her shoulder. Ilse sees that her eyes and face are inflamed as if she has been crying.

'Who is this?' she asks Gerda.

'Lynnie,' Serena says. Her face and eyes are also red and swollen. 'This is Lynnie. My sister.'

'Sit down,' Gerda says. 'It is all right, Ilse. Everything has been talked out today.'

'How did you find us?' Ilse blurts out. If Serena's sister could find them others may also and now that this woman knows, she may tell others and those others will come and they will talk and —. And now this Lynnie is closely scrutinising her.

'Serena talked to me about you. This Miss she was always talking about. So I found out who you were. I'd tried everywhere else. It was the only place left.'

'Almost I sent her away,' Gerda says, 'but Serena heard her voice.'

'You know everything?' Ilse asks.

Lynnie nods, tightens her hold on Kai.

'You know our plan?'

'That you're going to Dunedin to talk to people there?'

'Perhaps we should go sooner.' Ilse looks at her mother, at Serena. 'She has found us. So will others.'

'No,' Serena says. 'I'm not ready yet. Just a few more weeks.'

'I didn't tell anyone I was coming here,' Lynnie says.

'But —.' Ilse shakes her head. 'You have questioned people. Somebody has told you who I am, someone may make a connection and begin to ask questions. I am afraid for you, Serena. Think of how you were when that man came here, how you would be if he came back. We could go now to Dunedin and find somewhere to stay and wait there until you are ready to speak out.'

'I feel safe here with you and Oma.'

Oma. In spite of herself, Ilse smiles.

'I found you because I was looking hard,' Lynnie says. 'I don't think the cops give a shit. There's some crap story of Serena hitching to the West Coast.' She pauses, thinking. 'But there's another possibility. Serena and Kai could come home with me. I've got my own apartment. Nobody'd be asking us any questions.'

Gerda looks at Serena. 'Would you like this?'

'You'd be working, Lynnie,' Serena says, 'And I'd be by myself every day. What if something went wrong with Kai? I wouldn't know what to do.'

Ilse says, 'It is dangerous for you and Kai to remain here. We can hide you if we must, but it is impossible to hide a crying baby.'

Anja has been frowning, following the conversation as closely as she is able. 'What is this danger?' she says. 'I am the niece of Gerda, the cousin of Ilse. Kai is my baby. This is easy. Already we have told people.'

'So,' Gerda says, 'there is an explanation for a baby who cries in this house.'

'Of course,' Anja laughs. 'We can parade him up and down the street. We can show him off to these Taylors in their spying tower.'

'I wish you would come with me, See,' Lynnie says quietly to Serena. 'I've let you down. Our whole family's let you down. I want to help you.'

'Plenty of time for your help,' Gerda says gently. 'Years and years ahead for this. You have come, this is the main thing. You are here now with your nephew and your sister.'

'That bastard.' Lynnie begins to cry again. 'That bastard. If you'd told me, See, I'd have been on the next plane. I would've. Shit, I would've sorted him out.'

Kai began to squirm in her arms. Serena stands and takes him. She unbuttons her shirt and tucks him against her breast. 'But I have Kai,' she says.

'And so,' Gerda says, 'all we must do is to continue to keep Serena's presence here a secret.'

'Ilse and I,' Anja says, 'will take Kai out in his buggy. The proud cousin and the proud mutti of this beautiful baby.'

Serena looks up at them, her eyes suddenly filling with tears. 'I wish I could take him out in his buggy.'

'But you will,' says Ilse, 'of course you will. When we get to Dunedin, the very first day we get to Dunedin, you will take him out. We will get Kai a whole new outfit for this wonderful occasion, this outing with his mutti.'

'I'll have to get back to Wellington for work,' Lynnie says, 'but I can stay until the beginning of next week.'

'You, also Lynnie, must be a secret in this house,' Gerda says.

'Yeah, I've been thinking about that.' They work it out. She will conceal her visits by coming on foot early in the mornings, leaving late in the evenings. As an extra safeguard she will use different routes to get there and back. This will be so easy.

A strong wind has come up and Ilse moves quickly to close the windows. She is in the bedroom that faces onto the street and a car is nosing past, slowing, slowing down and then it keeps on going. It is not a police car but she watches as it turns at the top of the street and again passes. She pulls the window shut and goes back into the living room. 'Your car,' she says to Lynnie. 'Would anyone recognise it?'

'I don't think so.'

'There was a car passing the house,' Ilse says. 'Passing slowly.'

'Shit.' Lynnie looks alarmed. 'He might have seen my car when he came to the motel. It's got a Hertz logo on the side. But it was dark —.'

'It was not a police car,' Ilse says. 'Probably it is nothing. But we must be careful.'

'I'll park further away from my unit in case he comes back,' Lynnie says, 'and I won't drive here.'

They are at the table, eating dinner and drinking wine. 'I'm coming to Dunedin with you,' Lynnie says, holding up her glass. 'I'm going to tell them my own story, back up what Serena tells them. So here's to bringing that bastard down.'

Gerda reaches over, clinks her glass against Lynnie's. 'Ja. We will bring that bastard down.'

13

As Lynnie goes out into the night, Ilse locks the door behind her and attaches the safety chain. She checks that the back door into the house is locked. Anja comes in from the bathroom and gets into her bed as Ilse goes into the bedroom. 'I am so tired,' she says, yawning. 'Too much sun and swimming and good food and surprises. Ilse, I did not imagine that your life could be so eventful.'

Ilse listens as the house gradually falls silent. She hears the click as Gerda switches off her bedroom lamp, the slight creak as she turns over and makes herself comfortable. It is too old that bed, yet Gerda refuses to replace it: 'It is good enough, I am used to it, why would I waste all that money on a new one?' Ilse understands the real reason is less practical. The bed has been here ever since they arrived. It is this bed that her mother shared with Horst, his arms holding her and his body warm against hers in the coldness and loneliness of many nights.

Ilse hears the two or three faint cries Kai always gives before he settles into sleep. She hears Anja breathing slowly in the next bed. She is sleeping, sleeping so peacefully. But for Ilse, sleep is far away. Still she is there in Leipzig amid the stories Anja has told her.

Ilse has read enough and seen enough to know that humanity is capable of cruelty, so vicious and so merciless. It is almost beyond belief. She is, of course, German, and as such she is part of a people held to account for much of the destruction and slaughter of the past century. When she was old enough to understand this, she believed that she had a responsibility to educate herself about how this had come about and what was done. East Germans had little sense of sharing collective guilt for the Holocaust. The common thought was that they, in the East, had been Communist at heart and their Soviet comrades had liberated them from the brutishness of Nazism. Since she has been an adult, she has discovered the truth. Take ownership, find closure, move on, step up. How wonderfully these psychobabble terms appear to make possible the impossible. This truth she has found has had her hanging her head in horror and in shame. She has read many of the ever-increasing array of books. She has a grasp, she believes, of the politics. She knows the justification. Crippled and broken, blamed and punished for the first great bloodbath, Germany was ripe for a dictatorship which promised to give the people hope and pride.

In a nutshell, that was it. If the victors had not kicked the badly injured and suffering animal, the National Socialist party may not have risen. The regime of thugs and madmen, the war, the camps, the years of brutality and death; all of this may not have come about. She sees this interpretation may very well be correct, but the mothers and children with their suitcases, the suffering faces and hollowed eyes, the skeletal bodies and the ovens and the piled bones: all of this was done by her own people, her fellow countrymen. This horror was perpetrated not only by those monsters at the death camps but by ordinary men and women who averted their eyes as the trains with the crammed cattle trucks rolled away. This is what she has learnt from these books, this is what she has forced herself to recognise.

They were afraid. It is natural, it is human nature to wish to protect oneself. As it is natural to wish to protect children, family members and friends. The people at the death camps, they were forced to follow orders; also it is human nature to accede to a greater power. But is cruelty, so vast, so horrible, so staggering, also human nature?

She sees meanness among her students, also among the hierarchy that is the staff room. Petty jealousies and conflicts, bullying which occasionally intensifies into harassment. But how could these solitary difficulties escalate into an all-encompassing barbarism? How does a collective mind-set arise where another's humanity no longer is seen?

Those Stasi behind the doors of the Runde Ecke, deciding together that Erich, that small, quiet, clever child who could spit out the answers to mathematical problems long before his classmates had moved beyond even the first step, would be denied the opportunities that his talents deserved? Would they not feel ashamed, these big men in their uniforms? Yet, this action of denying Erich his chance is barely significant in the larger scheme of things. 'Forty years of killing, Ilse.'

In the end, she put the books away. There was a lifetime of reading in those books and yet, at the end of that lifetime what would she have? Only sorrow, only bitterness. A country of cowards and thugs. Is that what she should think?

Didn't her country suffer also? Did her people deserve such suffering? Is that what the rest of the world thought? That they deserved whatever happened? The three thousand tonnes of explosives dropped on Germany by the Allies on a daily basis compared to the thirty on England. Their children slaughtered and burned while their beautiful cities were smashed. Dresden. There were no factories to destroy; there was nothing there that was important other than a city filled with old people and women and children. Did they deserve Dresden? Did they deserve the slaughter of citizens, the women raped by the Russians, the orphans and old people left to scavenge and die of the cold and starvation and disease? The stink of rotting corpses, the exchange of family treasures for a bunch of carrots. Did they deserve forty years under the boot of the Soviets?

But she must consider, also, the suffering of the Russian people under the hands of her own countrymen. The raids on the Russian countryside which left nothing: no wood, no food, no animals, nothing. She must consider the seven hundred thousand civilians — two hundred thousand of them children — who starved to death in the Leningrad siege. She must consider the statistics that suggest between sixteen and twenty million Russians died in a war instigated by Germany.

Oh, why such cruelty? Even here, in this country renowned for safety, there is this man who has preyed on Serena. This man so small in his spirit that he requires a child to make him feel important and powerful. He must be punished and prevented from hurting Serena again or from hurting other girls. This she can do. This she will do.

The house is silent. While she knows about cruelty she knows also that this, like so many others, is a house of gentleness and love and it is this she must hold on to. Better not to think of viciousness but to consider the goodness that also is in this life. The tenderness which shines so naturally and honestly from her mother's eyes for Serena and for Kai. The care and protection of strangers.

In the morning Ilse and Anja buy a buggy. Serena straps Kai in, covers his body with a light blanket and places a hat on his head — 'Oh, he is so beautiful, this little man' — and Anja and Ilse saunter slowly together to the shops and then across the park.

'This is my cousin, Anja. This is her son, Kai.'

And so the days go. These are tranquil days, days that follow a pattern. There is early breakfast and the washing to see to and then walks with Kai through the park — but not for too long, neither Serena nor Gerda can bear for these walks to be long. Serena has a look of such longing and envy in her eyes as she tightens the buggy straps and clips them together. 'I so want to take him out,' she says.

'Of course you do,' Ilse says, hugging her. 'You are his mother. It will be soon, Serena.'

'I'll be able to take him out in Dunedin?'

'You will choose that special outfit and you will take him out. Perhaps you would like to go to the Botanic Garden. You could sit with all the other mothers with their babies and show Kai the ducks.'

'He's noticing things more and more every day, isn't he? Oma says he's very observant.'

'He is very clever,' Ilse says smiling. 'There is no doubt of that.'

And he is clever, Ilse thinks, as she and Anja sit together in the park and she sees his bright eyes open and peer through the black mesh over the buggy that protects him from the sun. So clever, so handsome. Already he has Serena's inquisitiveness.

Yes, there is a routine and a rhythm to these days. There are the feeds and the sleeps. Lynnie comes early and during the mornings she talks with Serena and Gerda and helps with the work around the house while Ilse and Anja and Kai take their walk. In the afternoons Serena naps or sits in the garden with Lynnie, talking, their voices soft. They play with Kai, they eat their evening meal together. Gerda generally cooks but Ilse and Anja also take their turns. Anja has made, one evening, her mother's recipe for meatloaf with sour cherries and the soft, warm evening was filled with memories. Gitte and Carl, Gerda and Horst and the three little girls, Klara, Anja and Ilse. A world away and a lifetime.

During the easy flow of these days with the talking and laughter and eating together, Ilse has made her decision and has emailed the principal of the school. Also, she has written a formal letter of resignation and tomorrow she will post it in the letterbox along the street.

What she will do, she cannot yet tell but she will not return to the high school. This life she and Mutti have lived together has been safe but too narrow. Now she sees her mother come back into her own. She sees this each day, as Gerda talks and laughs so easily, as she cares for Serena and Kai, and knows they will not go back to that life they had.

She cannot go back. Not to that classroom, not to those blank eyes and faces, not to that wall with the ugly blemishes suggesting a map that turns forever back on itself, going nowhere. She too must come into her own. She has enough money that they can live, Serena, Kai, Gerda and herself, for a while. Let things take their course and then she will see. She will see.

These days of walking with Anja in the park, of Kai's bright eyes, of Serena, and now this brash yet warm-hearted Lynnie. She is so brave, Lynnie, leaving this town with nothing but her few clothes and her few dollars. What this girl has made of herself. What she has done. The stories she tells them over dinner, making Ilse choke with laughter. The places she has lived in, the people in these places. The clients at the gym she works at. The man who used liquid soap instead of Vaseline for his friction areas and began to bloom bubbles as he sweated. The woman who physically attacked her personal trainer when she did not lose weight, the man who asked Lynnie to give him a massage every time he came in and finally demanded his money back.

And after the food, after the laughter and when it is finally dark, Ilse and Anja go to swim. As on this night when they are later leaving the house than usual. The evening meal has stretched with the talk and the stories. After they have passed the Taylors' house with the lights still on in the conservatory, the street is unlit other than the irregularly placed street lamps. Still, Ilse could find her way blindfolded, she has followed it so many times. Across the bridge which swings and clanks as they walk. Ilse sees movement beyond them, a rabbit scurrying in the scrub. Anja follows her down the track and across the rock formation to the small clearing beside the river. The rocks are still warm beneath Ilse's feet and hands as she climbs and finds her footholds.

They swim naked. Ilse has not swum naked before: always she has shuffled her body into her respectable black swimsuit. Not that she is a prude: it is only that she has been cautious. What if her students saw her? It was unlikely, but on occasion kids came down here to drink and to smoke away from the prying eyes of adults. If they saw Miss swimming naked? Imagine the whispers, the uproar in the classroom. But now she is liberated from all that. She is no longer Miss. Who or what she will be in the time to come she does not know. Nor does she care at this moment as she pulls off her clothes and steps down into the river.

'How is it?' Anja is not so fond of this cold Central Otago water.

'Wunderschön.' Ilse moves forward to where the water becomes deeper and lowers her body until there is nothing but the top of her shoulders and her head above it.

'I don't believe you,' Anja says, sitting on the bank dipping her foot in. 'This river is ice.'

'You spoilt European types,' Ilse calls back. She remembers a phrase from her students. 'Toughen up.'

'Toughen up?' Anja lunges in. 'Toughen up, hey?'

This night, this water, is alight with stars. They swim silently in the deep hole that has formed this year beneath the bridge. Ilse lies on her back, closes her eyes, lets the water take her. Anywhere. Anywhere. There is river-smell in her nostrils, the soft sounds filling her ears, the cool sweetness that holds her body.

They swim for longer than usual; the day has been so hot and the river is warmed more than usual by the harshness of the sun. Ilse swims over to the bank and Anja holds out her hand and pulls her up. 'Perhaps we should walk home naked,' Anja says. 'It is warm enough.'

Ilse looks at her. Anja's face is serious. 'I don't think —.'

'It would give these Taylors reason for both their vigil and the expense of building their post of looking out.'

'Oh,' Ilse says. 'You are joking.'

'Oh,' Anja says. 'So serious, Ilse. You were not always so serious.'

Somehow those words uttered so lightly slice deeply and Ilse feels tears rush up into her eyes. She turns her head away, blinks them back.

Anja is towelling her body. She glances at Ilse, looks back at her again. 'Ilse? Please, I did not mean to hurt you.'

'It is nothing.' Ilse's voice is husky. This is so stupid, so crazy. Now I am behaving like a schoolgirl, spoiling everything between us. All this fun and the easiness and the joking spoiled by this seriousness which sticks within me like grey winter fog.

'Ilse?' Anja takes her hand. She kisses her hand, the palm of Ilse's hand with her warm full lips and Ilse turns to her. Anja is kissing her eyes, kissing the tears around her eyes, gently licking them away.

Ilse is afraid and awkward. Never in her life has she kissed a woman, not in this way and yet, how wonderful to feel Anja's soft full mouth against her own and to reach out her hand and tentatively touch and then stroke Anja's skin. It is so smooth, this skin on her arms and, now, on her back and, oh, this firm curve of hip, this concave hollow of belly.

Her breasts. Oh God, her breasts. They are so firm, yet also so soft. The rounded curve of them. The lushness of her skin.

And Anja is touching her. They kneel on the ground, kissing, they are kissing, the warmth of Anja's mouth and her tongue and Anja's hand slides across her thighs and she is following, following Anja's lead.

Everything. Everything she has she now gives to Anja. Her breasts, her arms, her mouth and her tongue, the warmth and moistness between her legs. All of this is for Anja. Her sighs, the arching of her body, the cries she cannot keep back which spill into the night. All of this for Anja.

Afterwards they lie in each other's arms, holding, touching, stroking. They do not speak. Ilse is afraid to speak. And then she says it. Into the dark, she says it. 'Ich liebe dich, Anja. Ich werde dich immer lieben.'

And Anja's arms tighten around her. 'Ich werde dich auch immer lieben.'

I love you. I will always love you.

14

They go out into the dark, slipping together within river shadows. Ilse hears Anja moving in the water, hears her breathing: sometimes they brush together, reach out their hands and touch. Afterwards they make love in the soft hollow of sand, protected by the overhanging branches of the trees. The drift and ripple of river, the gentleness of Anja's lips, the touching and tasting, those soft gasps of surprise and delight.

Oh, this love she feels for her Anja, this urgency to touch and to hold her. Does every lover take such pleasure in the body of their beloved? That marvel of this curve of the underside of her foot, the soft fleshy padding of her heel. The wonderment of Anja's lean, long toes, her narrow, bony ankles, the small raised scar on her knee, the curve of thigh, the dip from hip to taut belly. So much to discover in a body. This body she cherishes. This body she has known from childhood when, in their homes in Leipzig, she sat behind Anja in the bathtub, soaping her back, trickling water from a sponge down her knobbly spine.

In the nights they sleep, pressed together, in Ilse's bed. Although, for the sake of propriety, Anja slips into her own bed in the early morning before the others are up. Does Gerda know? Surely she must see the way Ilse now looks at Anja, for how can she hide behind her eyes the love and desire which surges through her body and her spirit as she looks at her?

What will her mother think? What will others think? Ilse is not ashamed of what she and Anja have and feel together but she knows there are problems with such a relationship. Problems and labels and judgements; all of this in other people's minds and eyes but still there, nonetheless. Not her mother, never her mother who loves her and who has always wanted what is best for her. But if it was Hansi who had come, if it was Hansi whom she had fallen in love with, this would all be open, she knows this.

She does not want to see concern or perhaps alarm in her mother's eyes, not yet, for Ilse feels such joy that she does not want it marred by others' reactions. So for now, she will not tell, they will not tell, for now it is us. She and Anja. Ilse and Anja, together.

'Do you have a tent?' Anja says to her one morning as she pulls the curtains back in the bedroom.

'A small one,' Ilse says.

'Then let's go camping. Just for one night. I would not like to leave Gerda and Serena and Kai alone but while Lynnie is here, she will keep them company.'

'Yes,' Ilse says. 'Of course, we will go.'

'You must take Anja to Wanaka or to Queenstown,' Gerda says when Ilse tells her. 'But why only one night? Stay the weekend, a long weekend, and give yourself a holiday. You have not had any time since school ended.'

'But what if something happened?' Ilse says.

'What could happen? Lynnie will be here. We can take care of ourselves.'

And so on Thursday morning they drive off. Past the golf course, past the spread of dark pines and they are on the wide highway passing through the gorge, the hills overhead, the sun glinting on the rocks and on the water below the road.

'What is over there?' Anja points to the other side of the river. 'Does anyone live on the other side of the river?'

'Not now. There is only a road along the river and a few tracks up into the hills. Before the dam went in there were orchards all along there. When we first came here the dam wasn't finished and the river was only a narrow strip of water at the bottom of the gorge.'

'That is hard to believe. What happened to the orchards and the people who lived there?'

'People were resettled. Some of the houses were taken away to be re-situated. Some of them are still there under the water.'

'That gives me the shivers down my spine to think of houses and the living of people down below that water. What if there was a drought and all of those concealed houses came up again into the light? It would be horrible for those people who once lived there.'

'It would be horrible,' Ilse says. 'But there is far too much water for that to happen. Besides, there is so much silt down there, the houses probably are submerged within it.'

They have passed Cromwell, where they smiled at the giant cluster of waxy, gaudy fruit hoisted beside the signpost, and are passing orchards and spreading vineyards. 'So beautiful,' Anja breathes, her eyes on the hills in front of them, the sun reflected in pockets of gold and cinnamon and deep lilac shadows. Ilse drives slowly into Wanaka, around the lake, towards the camping ground. 'Oh,' Anja says. 'Oh, Ilse. So ein schöner Ort.'

This lovely place. Edged by a sun-glitter of stones, the lake is a satin quilt smoothed into perfection stretching to the rise and the soar of the mountains where there are glints of snow, the seamless stretch of sky. They call into the office at the camping ground where a woman with a face flushed by the heat allocates them a site. 'Warm enough for ya?'

Anja looks blankly at Ilse who nods, yes, it is warm enough. They find their site, put up the tent. 'It's so hot,' Ilse says, wiping sweat from her face. 'Shall we go to the lake and swim?'

Anja's face has an odd expression. 'I wish first to go to shop.'

'You want to shop?' Ilse is incredulous. Shopping? On such a day? But Anja is determined. 'Yes.'

And so they drive back towards the town, park beside the lake and walk across the wide highway to the row of shops. There are people everywhere, sitting outside the cafés, sauntering along the footpaths in their shorts and inscribed T-shirts — OMG; And Your Point Is?; Next Mood Swing 6 Minutes — all these people. The sun burns fiercely and Ilse feels the sweat that has begun to trickle down her back settle around the waistband of her shorts. As she manoeuvres her way around the tables and seats spreading across the footpath a boy knocks into her as he passes, studying the phone which is in his hand. She looks at Anja who is striding ahead, that resolute and concentrated expression as she stares around. Well. This must be the give and the take of relationships Ilse has seen featured in the headlines of those magazines which are piled in the waiting rooms of hairdressers and doctors and dentists: 'Mend Your Relationship: Find Out How Other Couples Compromise.'

'In here.' Anja grasps her arm, pulls her into a shop. There is music, so loud, and with that reverberating boom of bass sound Ilse hates. Ka-boom ka-boom ka-ka-boom; this shop is filled with the tanned bodies and tiny shorts of young, chattering girls. She turns to flee but Anja has a grip on her elbow.

'Why are we in this place?' she hisses at Anja but she is grinning. 'Ssh. Over here.'

Over here are rows of colours, rows of stripes and flowers and polka dots and squares. Row on row of minuscule scraps of fabric cut and sown into triangles.

'Oh no.' Ilse's hands rush to her mouth and she shakes her head. 'No, Anja, I cannot.'

'Yes, you can.' Anja is flicking through the rows. 'This is my gift for you.'

'No. I am far too —.'

'Far too what? Far too beautiful to be wearing a swimsuit designed for an old woman. Here. Try these.'

She holds up three of the dangling triangles. Red, yellow, and green. Ilse is still shaking her head and yet she feels such longing for these bright scraps of colour. But Miss wearing a bikini? She has never exposed her body in such a way. 'I could not wear red. Perhaps black? And bigger?'

'Not black. Not bigger. This green is my favourite. The colour, so pretty. It will suit you.'

And so Ilse goes into a cubicle and pulls the curtain firmly into place, checking that there are no gaps at either side. She takes off her clothes, keeping her eyes averted from this menacing mirror which shows the full length of her body. She eases the bottom part of the bikini over her hips, hooks her hands around her back to clip the top into place. She feels that the fit is good but is afraid to look; involuntarily she has closed her eyes. She is too old for this, this wearing of a bikini; too set in her ways. Ach, she is over thirty, after all. She does not wear bright colours that draw the eye; the clothes she chooses are functional. Smart enough and functional.

She keeps her eyes tightly closed. All of this: Serena, the child, Anja. It is too much, too much movement and change and risk. Anja will leave and then how will it be? She will be alone again. No kisses, no bikinis. She must face this or she will make a fool of herself. As she is making a fool of herself here in this shop for babies. This ka-boom ka-boom ka-ka boom. These voices outside, these squealy, silly voices. 'Did he? Was he? Oh. My. God.'

But, oh so young, so filled with fun and, yes, that is the word, glee. Filled with glee. Ilse has not been young in that way; never has she been publicly gleeful. This is not her nature, she is serious; a serious and careful person. It is too late for this glee.

But still, she opens her eyes and there is her long, spare body, her slim hips. This colour is so glorious, this green with the touch of blue which is like the river. Anja has slipped in behind her and places her arms around Ilse's waist and looks over her shoulder into the mirror and they are reflected together. Anja smiling, Ilse so anxious.

'Look at you,' Anja says. 'Du bist schön, meine Liebe.'

Ilse's eyes fill with tears. She tries to blink them away. You are beautiful, my love.

'I feel —.' Her voice is thick and hoarse with the lump which has grown up into her throat. 'I feel so afraid, Anja.'

Anja tightens her arms around Ilse's waist. 'I will look after you,' she says.

Ilse closes her eyes, rests her head back onto Anja's shoulder. Oh, to be looked after. Such a luxury, such a shield. Such peril. But they giggle together as Anja pays for the bikini, explaining that it does not need to be placed in a bag since it is now placed on the body of her friend.

They spread a rug beneath a tree and lie together in this glory of sunshine, run across the stones and into the lake, plunging into the water. Gasping. Gasping and shrieking. It is so cold, so cold they can almost not bear it.

Three days.

Ilse is proud that her belly and shoulders and the tops of her breasts have turned pale gold. They find the best chocolate cake in the whole of Wanaka, the best coffee and Anja discovers hokey-pokey ice cream. They hire kayaks and paddle around the edges of the lake. They swim and read and swim again. They return to the shop and Ilse buys a dress: such silky-smooth fabric and so prettily patterned in these little red and blue flowers. She buys tight black pants, matador's pants with slits at both sides just above her ankles, and a shirt, so soft and such a delicious pink that she must stroke it with her fingers. Gleefully stroke it with her fingers.

Three nights.

They zip their sleeping bags together and sleep naked, close. They make love with such ease and joy. Ilse wakes in the night and listens to the sounds of the night, the cars that pass above them on the highway, the lake hushing and slapping onto the stones out there in the dark.

Du bist schön, meine Liebe.

Yes, Anja must leave and Ilse must let her go. But for now, just for now, Anja sleeps, warm and softly breathing beside her. This is now and for now Anja is here.

15

They leave late in the afternoon, almost evening. After the early -morning kisses and the swimming and the sun. After the breakfast of eggs Benedict with smoked salmon at the café on the corner and after the coffee and the slabs of dark, rich chocolate cake. Anja must visit the shop she has admired to buy a printed velvet cushion: pink and crimson roses on a background of citrus green. 'Tante will like this,' she says. And then, of course, they must buy a small red-and-white-striped suit and matching sunhat for Kai and handmade soaps for Serena and Lynnie.

'This has been our own little home,' Anja says as they take down the tent, fold it and place it in the boot of the car. Ilse manages a half-smile and shrugs. What can she say in response? That she would like to live forever in this tent on the shores of Lake Wanaka with Anja? That she cannot bear to think of the day when Anja will go? That she has lost her heart? What? Better to remain silent.

And they do remain silent, as they drive out of the town, past the airport and through Luggate with all the holiday cribs and the growing settlement across the bridge. They have already passed Cromwell with its fruit when Anja at last speaks, her voice thin with hurt. 'Ilse, don't you want to be with me? Do you not love me?'

'Of course I love you. How can you say such a thing?'

'Well then,' Anja says, 'come back with me to Leipzig.'

'But how can I, with Mutti depending on me as she does? She has been so ill in the past. And now I have Serena and Kai to consider as well.'

'And are there not also Anja and Ilse to consider?'

'Do you not think?' Ilse says, her voice thick again with this lump which is growing so persistently inside her throat. She never cries, not for years and years has she cried, but these last weeks, always there are tears she must try to hold back. 'Do you not think that if I could have my way I would come with you and live with you and have every day and night of my life with you?'

'Then, come. Come!' Anja cries.

'I cannot,' Ilse says. 'You must understand that. Perhaps later. A holiday —.'

'A holiday?' Anja turns her head away and stares out the window.

They are driving through the gorge, those rocks looming up above them, the river below. Soon they will be back and soon Anja will be gone. 'Please,' Ilse says. 'Please. We must not quarrel. This is now and we must not spoil it. We will talk of this again. I will try to. I will think.'

'You must think.' Anja places her hand palm-down on Ilse's thigh. 'Because I cannot be without you.'

These wonderful words she has so longed to hear; at the same time these words so insistent, compelling her to act in a way she believes would be wrong and selfish. How could she leave her mother, how would Gerda manage without her? They have not only the love between them of mother and daughter but they have been good companions; they have stood together. And if a winter came where Gerda became again ill, what would become of her? Perhaps she could come with them. Yet in her heart Ilse feels that this is not possible. She does not know what caused them, but Ilse is certain that there are dark shadows Gerda left behind which are too fearful for her to face.

Though it could be that now she has listened to what Anja has told her of the new Leipzig, the new Germany and now that she knows of friends who are still there and would welcome her, Gerda may reconsider. But then, what of Serena and Kai? Ilse has made a promise to Serena that she means to keep. 'I promise you this man will not hurt you again.' How could she keep such a promise from the other side of the world? Yet Serena is becoming so much stronger, so much more capable and there is Lynnie.

Lynnie who is busy, who is young and must build her own life. She may forget Serena. Certainly she has done this in the past.

'Yes, I will think.' She reaches down, squeezes Anja's hand. 'Here is Clyde. Shall we stop for coffee?'

And they stop and all is easy again as they walk along the main street with its substantial stone buildings. They point to the signs: this once was the bank and here is the grocer's shop, the post office, the Masonic lodge. They look into the hotel with its second-floor veranda resting on thick posts tethered to the street. They choose a café with tables and chairs and sun umbrellas on the street outside and order beer. 'Good,' Anja says, 'but not so good as the beer at home.'

Though they say nothing, they are reluctant to go back to the house and have these perfect days behind them and so they sit for a while then walk again together, pausing beside a cottage, beside a garden. Anja takes lavender from a clump spilling out over the walkways and crumbles it up, rubbing it into the palms of her hands. 'Smell, Ilse.'

Ilse takes her hands and breathes in the sharp, oily sweetness. She kisses Anja's hands then holds them against her face. 'We must go back,' she says.

It is twilight, almost dark as they walk back to the car. Ilse switches on the ignition and the lights and pulls out into the road. When they reach the turn-off she drives left onto the main highway.

Part Three

1

One day at a time, Oma says. One day at a time, Serena.

Sometimes it's too big for her. She's a kid. She hasn't even finished school yet and she's got a baby. She didn't want the baby. The first time she missed her period that dull hurt of terror in the pit of her stomach started. For weeks after it was due, she'd go into the toilet, shove toilet paper up inside her and sit there waiting and hoping so hard there'd be a spot of blood on it when she pulled it out. Then she'd be all right. She'd be all right.

Then when nothing happened she hoped she'd lose it. Even people who wanted babies lost them, right? So why couldn't she? She went running, she got on her bike and rode around for hours. What she hoped is she could dislodge it and then she could forget all that shit and be back to who she was.

It wasn't fair. She hadn't even kissed a boy, not properly kissed him. And now she had this thing inside her. She thought about going to Sally Davis. That's what other girls did; they went to Sally and she sorted it all out for them. They went to Dunedin for abortions, down and back on the same day most of the time. She used to hover around Sally's office. But she couldn't make herself go in. She just couldn't go in there. Because this can't be happening, it can't be true.

Even though she tried to pretend it wasn't true, the thing was growing. She had to get big tops and pants with elastic waistbands from The Warehouse. She got some stretchy fabric like a great big bandage and wrapped it tight around her belly and pinned it with safety pins at the side. She made sure the bathroom door was always locked when she was in there. Most of the time she hid out in her room.

It wasn't real. What was happening inside her wasn't real, even when it started bucking about, she knew it wasn't real, it would die inside her, it would, it had to, it would die and then it would come out like a big blob of blood and she could hide it and nobody would know.

That night when she saw the knob of dark jelly-blood on her underpants she knew it was happening and she'd been right. It had died and now it was coming out. She'd googled pregnancy and birth and it said it was thirty-eight weeks; well, she was thirty-five weeks so it couldn't be alive any more. Anyway it said first babies were usually late so it couldn't be that, it couldn't be an actual baby coming.

She'd looked up miscarriages as well and it said they caused 'mild to extreme discomfort'; 'pain in the lower pelvis and back similar to the kind of discomfort experienced during menstruation'. Well, she could handle that okay. When she saw that blood she just took off and walked to the river and, at first, it was okay, it only hurt a bit, this funny tightening feeling she had running across her belly and her back.

Then it got quite sore, I can do this, shit I have to do this. But then, oh God, oh fuck, then it really hurt, it hurt so fucking much, far more than she ever thought anything could hurt, as if her spine was being twisted around and around and around by giant claws and, at the same time, as if those claws were inside her belly tearing it apart. When she was down at the river, before Miss came, she knew they were both going to die; she and that big blob of blood were going to die down there together.

When Oma put the baby onto her, when she saw his eyes were open and he was looking at her and she felt him so still and light and slippery, she couldn't believe it. She had a baby. The baby was alive.

And she loves him. She can't believe how much she loves him. She's still a bit frightened of him: he's so small she's so afraid she might hurt him by mistake. But now she picks him up, holds him, jiggles him up and down playing with him. She blows onto his tummy. He watches her, his eyes so bright, and when he smiles, well, he's so little the smile takes up his whole face.

She loves him now. She loves him so much and she feels so bad about wanting him to die, to slip out of her like rubbish. Oma tells her it was natural for her to feel that way: 'You were alone and you were afraid.'

She loves Oma as well. She loves Oma and Miss and now Lynnie is here and Anja. She's got through the shit, there's a bit more to go but she doesn't have to do that on her own. She's got through most of the shit and now she's a mum. One day at a time. She can do it.

One thing, though. She so wants to take Kai out in his buggy. It's not that she wants to show him off, she just wants that feeling of pushing her own baby in his buggy. Sometimes she takes him around the garden, but it's not the same. She loves Miss and she likes Anja a lot but when she watches them through the blind pushing Kai in his buggy, chatting together and smiling, she feels so jealous and a little bit angry.

She's putting Kai into his buggy to take him out into the garden when she has the idea. Anja and Ilse are away. Oma is asleep. She was reading in the armchair but now she's fallen asleep. Lynnie is at the supermarket.

Just a wee way. Just a wee way along the footpath, just to see what it feels like. She could cut through the side path and that way she wouldn't see any of the neighbours; she'd only be on the public footpath for three minutes, four at the most.

She pulls Miss's straw sunhat down over her head, puts on sunglasses. She opens the door quietly. Only a few minutes; she'll have to be back in the house before Lynnie gets here. If Lynnie sees them out she'll go off her head at her.

Just a wee way. She keeps her head down, pushes the buggy onto the side path. It feels so great. By the time she can really do it, in Dunedin like Miss said, Kai will be so big. He's getting bigger every day. So it's nice to have this little try while he's still quite tiny.

Around onto the public footpath, she's nearly back, nearly made it. She won't do it again. One time's been enough. She won't do it again and she won't tell them. Her and Kai's secret.

She hears the car. She pushes the gate open, scurries up the path, pushes the buggy inside the door and shuts it behind her. She's breathing hard, her stomach is a tight knot. She lifts Kai into his bassinet.

She had the hat pulled down, the sunglasses covering most of her face. He wouldn't be able to see, he wouldn't know it was her.

His eyes looking back.

2

'Get over yourself.' Isn't that what people tell you? 'Get over yourself. Get on with it. It's not about you. Get over it.'

But, oh fuck, she wanted to hurt that bastard, she wanted to fucking crucify him. She wanted to get a fucking sharp knife and stick it into his fat gut; she wanted to get a shotgun and shoot him right in the fucking balls, wanted to go up to his house, bang on the front door and stand there shouting out to his wife and the whole fucking neighbourhood what he'd done. She wanted to get a fucking loud-speaker and stand in the middle of fucking Centennial Avenue broadcasting it.

She wanted to destroy him.

Except this wasn't about her. It was about Serena.

But that bastard. Preying on a kid, torturing a kid.

She feels so fucking guilty. Because she can't help thinking it's all because of her and what she did. Sometimes she used to worry that Darryl getting into all that trouble with the cops was because of her as well, because of that bastard holding a grudge. But she thought Darryl could get out of town if he wanted to — he was old enough and big enough to look out for himself.

But not her little sister. Not Serena. She doesn't cry. Never has. But, Jesus, seeing See holding the baby, watching her face, hearing her voice break as she told her. Lynnie cried then, first time in years. She cried so much it hurt, her whole body hurt.

Get over yourself. It's not about you. Get over yourself.

What she has to do is to listen to Serena. Listen to what she wants. One thing she saw straight away is how much she loves Kai. That love shines right out of her eyes, it's there in the way she cuddles him and talks to him. So that's the first thing she had to get her head around. Serena has a baby and she loves him.

That's something Lynnie can help her with. See's only fifteen and she's going to need a lot of help. At first she wanted to gather them both up and take them right away so she could look after Serena the way she should have. She thinks about last Christmas, she goes over and over that in her head; how Serena talked to her on the phone, how she asked if she could come and stay, how her voice sounded, sort of quiet and really wanting to come. She thinks about how she was going to phone back a few days later, talk to her, find out if anything was wrong. I should have. I bloody should have.

But she was busy: they were short-staffed at work; she'd only just moved into her apartment. She didn't even have a bed yet, for herself let alone for anyone else. And she was excited about the job, about the apartment, first time she'd had a place all to herself. See can come some other time. If she'd only phoned back, if she hadn't only been thinking of herself, if she'd only listened. I wish I'd. I wish.

She loves Gerda. She loves how she smiles and that funny singy-songy way she talks. At first Lynnie kept saying that to her, 'I should have, I wish I'd listened more carefully, I so so wish I'd.'

'Ach,' Gerda said in the end, 'Wenn das Wörtchen wenn nicht wär, wär mein Vater Millionär.'

Lynnie stared at her. 'Sorry?'

'If there wasn't the little word "if", my father would be a millionaire.' She shrugged her shoulders and smiled. 'Perhaps it does not translate so well.'

'I get it,' Lynnie said.

So get on with it. No ifs, no sorries, just do what you have to do now. Okay, Serena wants to stay with Ilse and Gerda. Lynnie loves Ilse as well. She comes across kind of stern at first but underneath it all she's just so kind. Like Gerda she's really gentle. They both want to help Serena and Kai and they both want what's best for them. Lynnie didn't want to leave Serena here but she sees now it's for the best; she trusts Gerda and Ilse and she knows they'll look after them. And Lynnie will go down to Dunedin when the time comes.

She'll stand by Serena. She'll tell her own story, back her up. After that she'll see what has to be done.

But, God, to see Serena with Kai. She's so careful to do everything right. She seems so grown up. She's a mother. Other times she's like a kid again.

Like today. Lynnie came back from the supermarket and Serena was standing beside Kai's bassinet. Just standing there looking down at him. Then when she came out to the living room she was quiet, hardly said a word. Didn't want the Pixie Caramel bar Lynnie had brought back from the supermarket even though she'd asked her to get her one. That went on all afternoon; Serena looking all moody and worried and hardly saying anything and when Lynnie asked her what was wrong, was she feeling sick or anything, Serena shook her head. 'There's nothing wrong, okay?'

Same thing right through dinner and then she just burst out with it. 'I did this stupid thing. I took Kai out in his buggy.' She had her head down. 'I had on a hat and those big sunglasses and it was only a few minutes. I cut through the walkway and then I came back.' She burst into tears. 'I just wanted to wheel him in his buggy. I'm really sorry.'

She was just a kid; a little girl wanting to wheel her doll in her pram. Gerda moved closer to Serena and rubbed her shoulders. 'Ach, it is all right. Only the once, hey, and no harm done?'

She was silent as she sliced up the pork chop on her plate. She forked a piece up towards her mouth and then put it down. 'A car went past. Not a police car but I think it was him. I think it was him. Looking.'

Fuck. Don't get upset. Don't get angry. Deal with it. Lynnie keeps her voice level, calm. 'You think it was him but you're not sure?'

'I think —. I really think it was.'

'You said he was looking at you. You had a hat on and sunglasses? Could you tell, did it seem like he recognised you?'

'It was only for a few seconds. Then he turned the corner and I came in here. I was so scared. I pushed the buggy in fast as I could.'

Lynnie looks at Gerda. Fuck. Fuck. What do we do now? Though her expression is concerned, Gerda's voice is calm. 'The doors are locked and soon Ilse and Anja will be home. If he returns with his questions, Kai is Anja's child and we have not seen you, Serena. It will be all right.'

They eat but they are silent. Though they don't speak of it they're all waiting for the knock on the door or for the doorbell to peal along the passageway. But if he was suspicious, wouldn't he have come straight away, wouldn't he have been at the door the moment he had seen them? As the time passes, they begin to chat again, to relax. Gerda and Lynnie wash and dry the dishes while Serena baths Kai.

'See shouldn't have gone out like that,' Lynnie says, 'but I can understand her wanting to walk her own baby in his buggy.'

'Of course,' Gerda says. 'And she has been here shut up in the house. She has been so good about that.'

Lynnie dries a plate and places it inside the cupboard. Yeah, Gerda's right. See's been really good, really patient and good, but at the same time, she's a kid and kids make mistakes. What it makes her think is that the sooner they get Serena and the baby out of here away from all the shit and get things sorted the better. She's going to talk to them soon as Ilse gets back. Lynnie's going back to the motel tonight, leaving early in the morning so she needs to get it settled before she goes.

They finish the dishes, Gerda settles into an armchair with the jacket she is knitting for Kai and Lynnie folds the washing which has dried during the day. Shit, there's a lot of washing to do with a baby. Can't believe that tiny little kid could produce so much washing. Yeah, if she has her way they'll be out of here and on the way to Dunedin by the end of next week. It's just too dangerous, all this fucking about. Serena and Kai, both of them are doing just fine. Anyone can see that. Just look at them over there — Serena looks like a bloody madonna with Kai tucked up against her in the big armchair while she feeds him.

Serena is looking down at Kai so she doesn't see her watching and

Lynnie feels a big, daft grin spreading across her face but she can't help it. That kid's so cute; the way his little cheeks are filling out, getting quite fat, the way he's resting his hand on Serena's breast, the way he's sucking so hard and breathing inwards as though it's the last feed he'll ever get. Serena is so pretty with her hair on her shoulders, the curve of her arm, that besotted look she gets on her face every time she looks at Kai. He's almost asleep against her breast and she lifts him onto her shoulder, rubs her hand over his back until the milky burp comes. She sits there holding him, rocking him gently against her shoulder. They're both so, so beautiful.

It is almost dark. They hear the key in the front door lock.

'There they are,' Gerda says. There is relief in her voice. 'Ilse and Anja are home. I will make coffee.'

3

So beautiful that it scares Lynnie. They have to stay like that. Beautiful like that with nothing hurting them.

When she hears the key turning in the lock and the front door opening, she's pleased they're back and that she can get this stuff talked through and sorted before she leaves. She sees also the relief on Gerda's face as she stands and turns to go into the kitchen. She thinks that Gerda will understand about not waiting any longer and Ilse will agree as well; it will be only Serena who she'll need to persuade. She has to work out the best way to bring it up. She needs to make Serena see she can do it, can talk to people and make them see what's happened and get their help but she needs to come at it quietly and calmly so Serena won't panic. If she panics she won't budge. She'll say they promised her more time and she'll freak out.

She's working out what to say as the footsteps come up the passage. Maybe just start it off by saying how well she's doing, how well both of them are doing. She needs to see it's not safe to stay here but I don't want to frighten her, she's been through enough. So it doesn't register at first that there's one person rather than two walking, that the steps are soft and cautious and then it hits her: no one's talking.

With Ilse and Anja, it's chatter-chatter-chatter, never stops, but no one's talking. She's up on her feet and the door flies open and he's there, he's there, and, she's frozen, she's stuck, can't move, can't talk, can only stare. What the —? What the fuck?

Go. Go. She feels her body surge forward across the room and she plants herself solid, feet apart on the floor and now her voice is coming, loud and hard and strong. 'Get out. Leave!'

His eyes are fixed on Serena and Kai. Kai has turned his head towards the sounds and is staring, unblinking, across the room. Serena's face is as white as chalk, white as paper. 'No!' She holds Kai close against her body. 'No no no no no.'

'You little slut,' he says softly. 'You little bitch.'

No fear. Lynnie feels no fear. 'Leave. Now. Fuck off. Do you hear me? Fuck off!' She feels no fear. Just white-hot anger and she's brimming with it. She slaps at his arms as he stands there staring at Serena and Kai. She's slapping, thumping, shoving at his body. 'Get out. You've no right to be here. Get out!'

He looks down at her, lazily, as if he's only just aware that she is there and he grabs her arms. She sees the menace, such menace in his eyes. 'I've got no right to be here, huh?' His hands grip her wrists and he shakes her, brings his head down towards her, his face red and his eyes glassy. 'I've got every right. That little slut over there's reported missing and now I find out she's got herself pregnant and got a kid? You think Social Welfare won't want to know about that? You and those bitches that've been hiding her are in trouble, you hear me?'

'You're in trouble,' Lynnie shouts. 'It's you that's in fucking trouble. My sister didn't get herself pregnant, you bastard.'

She feels the slam against her face, the whack of pain and force which makes her stagger. 'You be careful what you say.' His face is close to hers, his hands are against her throat.

'We're going to tell what you did. You won't get away with it.'

'You'll tell, will you?' He tightens his grip and shakes her. 'You'll tell what? That you and these stupid bitches have been harbouring an under-age runaway? That you threatened a policeman? That you assaulted a policeman in the execution of his duty?'

She can barely force out the words but she keeps her eyes on him. 'I'm going to tell. What you did to me. What you did to my sister.'

'No one's going to believe some story two dirty sluts've come up with about where that little bastard's come from. I'd keep my mouth shut if I were you, Lynnie.'

'There're blood tests. We can prove —.'

'Voluntary, Lynnie. Blood tests are voluntary. You think I'm going to dignify your accusations like that?' He moves away from her and shakes his head. 'No way is a respected police officer in this town going to do that.'

She's frightened now. 'People will believe us. Ilse and Gerda believed us —.'

'Those two freaks? That's a fucking laugh.'

She throws herself against him, punching, kicking, get him, get him in the balls. She wants to hurt him, wants to kill him. It's an urgency burning in her gut, in her bones, filling up her head, it's a thick, cold stone stopping up her throat, the hatred she feels for this man. She's kicking out, walloping, pounding with her fists.

He slaps her hard across the side of her head. The pain is white-hot, her ear rings, black rings open and close in front of her eyes. He grabs hold of her arm. 'You think you're clever, eh? Well, sorry to give you the news, Lynnie, but it's you that led me here. You and that thing around your neck. Soon as I saw it, I knew something was up. All I had to do was follow you.'

Black rings opening and closing, opening closing in front of her eyes. She swallows, trying not to vomit, trying to stay on her feet.

'Here's what we're gonna do,' he says. 'I'm calling for backup and you'll be taken down to the station and charged.' He nods towards Serena and Kai. 'CYFS'll be keen to hear about those two. I'll take them where they need to go.'

He moves towards Serena. She stands, holding Kai tight against her body.

'Don't think you'll be keeping that kid much longer. CYFS won't like what I have to tell them. They won't like it at all.'

Kai is crying. Serena's voice is a wail of fear. 'Lynnie, don't let him. Don't let him take us!'

4

'They are home.' Gerda herself can hear the relief in her voice. 'I will make coffee.' She goes into the kitchen, measures the coffee beans into the machine and switches it on. Better than the old-fashioned grinder with the handle which must be turned, so much more efficient, so much faster. But that noise, g-rrr-rrr, g-rrr-rrr. She closes the kitchen door because Kai does not like this sound — she has seen how his little body tenses when the machine is running. Because of this sound she misses the solid heaviness of the footfalls in the passage and that these are the footfalls of one person rather than two. She only hears the voice as she switches the machine off, the voice of harsh authority which has come into her home. This voice has come for them. This voice has come, as she knew it would, to take their child.

Her legs go first and then it is her whole body which is crumpling, slipping downwards, and she tries to hold fast to the kitchen table, this table which Horst searched for and brought to this house where he stripped away the paint and sanded and oiled the wood to a satiny, golden sheen. Though he did not tell her this, she knew it was for her, this table, since it was similar to the one left behind. Because he believed such a table would, to her, signify family and safety.

Safety. But they are here. She knew they would come.

She leans against this table, gripping it with her hands. Her heart is bursting through her chest, her breathing coming in short, shallow gasps. The voice is here and now she hears it rising, thundering above the little voices which whimper their terror and their helplessness.

Listen.

The baby is crying.

She loosens her hands from their grip on the table and slowly straightens her body. She stands for a moment quietly breathing. She must move carefully and slowly.

She is there. She is beside the door.

Listen.

Listen.

She hears it through her sleep, opens her eyes to the darkness of the room and heaves herself up so she is half-lying, half-sitting in this strange bed. Pain. There is so much pain. She switches on the light on the wall above her and looks around. What has happened, where is her baby? And again it comes, the thin wail, the short silence for the intake of a breath then the shrill, craving cry.

She is attached to a tube fastened to a bag filled with blood. She turns off the filter and manoeuvres the catheter out from beneath her skin and replaces the dressing, pressing it down hard on the blood which blooms and seeps over her wrist. She cannot be concerned with this. Where is her baby?

Listen. Listen. There it is again.

She is nauseous, feels bile rush into her mouth and for just a moment she must rest back on the pillows, breathing slowly to clear the black dots that rush and scurry in front of her eyes before she pushes back the cotton quilt and lowers her feet to the floor. She gasps at the wrench of pain which judders through her body as she stands, her head is swimming with it, but she can move, despite this still she can move. Outside the room she stumbles into the dimly lit corridor. Bent almost double, she is shuffling like an old woman.

Ahead of her, at the end of the corridor, a gleam of light spills out onto the walls, onto the dull green linoleum, down, down the cavernous mouth of this corridor.

The lighted room. One step. Another, another. The cry. The silence. The cry.

The pain makes her stop and rest against the wall. It is hurt, she has worked this out now, from the wound. The pain comes from where they cut her. This pain. It is deep inside her belly, raging in her belly and up into her rib cavity, stopping up her breathing. She is dizzy and so weak. Her legs are shuddering.

Lie down and sleep. Just lie down on the floor and sleep now. Anywhere will do. Here will do.

Lie down. Sleep, now.

Schlaf, Kindlein, schlaf.

Der Vater hüt die Schaf.

The baby is crying. The room is ahead of her. She is there. She is beside the door. She is beside the door looking through the large glass pane into the nursery. She places her hand on the doorknob. Blood drips from her wrist, down her hand and onto the floor.

Open the door. Open the door.

5

But why is he telling her this? This baby has started its journey into this world in the normal way with the small tightenings in her belly; these are still only the edges of the pain which will come and she is young and strong. Neither has this labour been long. It is a few hours only and she is managing well.

And yet, despite her questions and objections, she has been wheeled into a room and into this room has come a doctor in his green scrubs and with a mask covering the lower part of his face and, now, what is this foolish fellow telling her? That a Caesarean must be performed?

'You have made a mistake,' she says, smiling and looking up into his face.

'There is no mistake,' he says. 'This baby is in trouble.' His voice is terse. He does not look her in the eye and, all at once, she feels a small twist of fear.

'No,' she says. 'No. There is a mistake. The heartbeat, everything is normal. The cervix is opening well. I am a nurse. I know this.'

'You are not qualified in obstetrics, Frau Klein. The baby is in trouble,' he repeats.

Another doctor has joined him. More green scrubs, another mask. There are two nurses, silent at the edge of the room. 'Why are you saying this?' Gerda asks. 'Please tell me what is wrong.'

She snatches away her hand as the second doctor, the anaesthetist she understands now, attempts to take it. 'Please,' he says. 'Your wrist, please.'

'No. You must explain what is happening.' She looks towards the nurses for support. 'This pregnancy has been normal. The labour has been going well. Nobody has expressed concern.'

She sees the creases above the first doctor's eyes, sees the coldness in these pale blue eyes. 'You are questioning our decision, Frau Klein?' His voice is incredulous, 'Do you not want what is best for your baby?'

She looks around the room. The nurses, the doctors watch her. All are masked. How can she tell what they are thinking beneath these masks? She is afraid, suddenly so afraid for this child in her belly who until now has been a source of such joy for her and for Horst and for Ilse. The excitement of telling her, 'Ilse, you will have a baby brother or a sister. The baby will be born in the spring.'

She has waited for this baby. She did not fall pregnant as easily as she had with Ilse. Such excitement when she knew without doubt that she was again pregnant. Such delight in her changing body; her breasts tingling, she even welcomed the nausea and extreme tiredness she experienced in those early weeks. And then her body began to thicken and become large and heavy. She was so much bigger than she had been with Ilse; she walked with her back arched, her belly tilted to carry this child.

'Perhaps this time it is a boy,' she had said to Horst and he had said smiling, 'If it is not, she will be a great lump of a girl.'

'Ach,' she had said, 'whatever it is, this baby will be beautiful. I know it will be beautiful.'

And now there is something wrong with their baby? But what could be wrong? What do these people know that they will not tell her?

'I would like to call for my husband,' she says firmly.

Horst will know what to do. And if something has gone wrong they can face it together. Already, she feels more relaxed. Horst will hold her hand and the baby will be all right. These doctors will realise they have made a mistake and then everything, after all, will be all right.

'There is no time for delay. Now, please. If you want what is best for your baby, you must cooperate.'

Tears flood her eyes, her mouth is dry, her body shivering with sudden dread. This is something serious, something too serious for them to tell her. She sees from the manner of the people surrounding her there is something badly wrong. They appear remote as if they do not wish to be involved in future grief. This is not the atmosphere of imminent celebration but of apprehension, even dread.

Is it the size of the baby which is causing difficulty? She knows of babies which have become lodged in the birth canal and deprived of oxygen. She knows that babies affected in this way have died or suffered brain damage whereas a Caesarean section performed earlier would have saved them. She must cooperate with these doctors who must, after all, know what is best. They will take care of her and the baby. She will wake and Horst will be there with her. Their baby will be all right, their baby will be beautiful. She holds out her arm. The anaesthetist finds the vein, slips in the needle.

Count. Now count. It will be all right. This baby. Our baby.

Gerda wakes into such dizziness and pain. She tries to pull herself up, begins to retch over and over, bringing up thin yellow bile over the bed and then into the pan the nurse brings.

The baby?

The nurse offers her a cup with a plastic straw attached to it and she sips, coughs. Starts again to retch. 'Where is my baby?'

The nurse slips out of the room and returns with the ward sister. 'Frau Klein, your baby is dead.'

Dead? Dead? 'No. It cannot be true.'

The sister looks away as if she cannot bear to look at her suffering. 'I am sorry.' Her voice is clipped.

'My husband —.'

'Not until you are stronger, Frau Klein. When you regain your health we will allow visitors.'

'I want to see my baby.'

'That is not possible.'

Tears pour down her cheeks. This cannot be true. All the hope and the love she has felt for this child. It cannot be true. She is dreaming? Is she dreaming?

'Is my baby a boy or a girl?'

The sister hesitates.

'Tell me please.'

'It was a boy, Frau Klein. Now take these, please.' She holds out pills and a plastic cup filled with water. 'This will help you to sleep.'

Gerda drifts. In and out of sleep. In and out. The baby. She hears something in the blackness. A voice. A cry.

A voice a cry a voice a cry.

The cry.

A cry she is certain she knows as she pulls herself from the blackness as if from a murky river. Her breasts tingle at this cry. There is milk for this cry. She drags herself up in the bed, collapses back into sleep.

Gerda, you must wake up. Sit up in the bed now and switch on the light, you know where the switch is, you have switched on such a light in a thousand such beds and now pull this thing from your wrist take no notice of the blood which blossoms and spills and turn your body so that you are supported by your knees and your arms now your legs to the side of the bed and your feet now lower your feet on the ground these feet the pain, oh, the pain so stop for a moment this pain your hands on the bed holding you let your legs take your weight.

She is trembling. Circles of black. She breathes in. Breathing.

The cry. Oh, the cry.

One step after another step and another, shuffling down the corridor to reach the yellow light, the window of the nursery gleaming in the darkness, the sliver of light beneath the door. The dull green linoleum in the light beside that door.

The cry again. She has a sudden surge of strength. The cry, the silence, the cry and, through the window, there, look now at this nurse holding the baby wrapped in a white cloth.

She remembers how her fingers slipped in the blood seeping from her wrist as she grasped the doorknob. She remembers the baby swaddled in white, the fuzz of dark hair at the top of his head.

She remembers what she said. 'This is my baby.' That is what she said. She remembers that the baby's head turned at the sound of her voice. The baby turned his head and for just an instant she saw the brightness of his eyes.

6

'This is my baby.'

That is what she remembers. That small instant, so tiny in the course of a lifetime but yet she has held onto it, the turning of that small head, the brightness of the eyes.

She remembers also the alarm in the nurse's eyes as she stared at her, the swiftness of the way in which she turned her back shielding the baby from her gaze. 'What are you doing here, Frau Klein? You must not be in this room. You surely know this is for medical staff only.'

The ward sister crosses the room, hurrying towards her, pressing the alarm button in the wall. She stands in the doorway, preventing Gerda from moving further into the room and Gerda tries to push past, her eyes riveted on this nurse with her back turned to her, on the baby in her arms, my baby, my baby, she is sure of this. The fuzz of dark hair beneath the light. He turned his head.

'He knows my voice,' she cries out. 'He knows my voice.'

She hears a door bang, footsteps hurrying down the corridor, someone seizes her arm. 'Take Frau Klein back to her bed.'

She struggles against the hands holding her. Though she feels the menace of authority in the hands which grip her arm, still she struggles. 'No. No. He is my baby. He is mine. You know he is mine.'

The sister's face is grim, her voice hard as she stands her body solidly guarding the door. 'You are unwell, Frau Klein. Your mind is not stable. Do you understand me?'

'Give me my baby.'

She feels the grip tighten on her arms, hears the power in the voice which addresses her and although with every part of her body and her mind she longs to shove this woman out of her way and snatch the child from the arms of the nurse, to press the small body against her own, she is powerless. She is falling back into the blackness, so unsteady and so feeble, and her body is slumping and those hands which held her back are now supporting her.

'Come now, Frau Klein, you must rest.'

One step and another and another, moving back into the darkness, the hands draw her away from the cries, from the light, from the small head which turned to her voice. She weeps, she hears the faint moans which come from her body as she is led down the corridor. She feels the hands bracing her, hoisting her upwards into the high bed which grinds and creaks. She lies there, numb, as the nurse who has appeared whispers with two male porters who unlock the braces at the side of the bed and begin to push.

Through the door, into the corridor, she feels the motion of the bed as it passes swiftly through the gloom of the long, long corridor, the orderlies on either side, the nurse pacing beside it: she cannot fight against these strong hands and bodies. She does not ask where they are taking her; there is no point in asking. There is nothing she can do to stop what is happening. There is nobody she can call on for help.

Nothing and nobody.

The clattering of the wheels turning on the linoleum, nothing and nobody, nothing and nobody. They stop beside the elevator, the nurse presses the button. She hears the grinding and clanking as it wheezes its way up, the doors crank open and they push her in. Nobody speaks as it moves upwards, as the doors open and they wheel her out and into another corridor.

Nothing and nobody, nothing and nobody. She is in a room with green walls and a tiny window.

'Better for you to be here, Frau Klein, away from things which will upset you,' the nurse says. 'You must not wander about. It will not be good for you. Do you understand?'

She nods her head. She does not argue. Neither does she argue as the injection — 'Your arm, please, this will calm you, Frau Klein'

— pierces her skin. She feels the faint buzz in her head which turns into a swarm of bees as she lurches into the blackness.

She wakes and her belly is cramping, her breasts are hard as bricks and aching; all over her body she aches; the bruising is livid, around the wound and her breasts, oh her breasts. But there is a remedy even for this. The nurse comes and winds thick bindings around her body, tightly swathing her belly and breasts: 'This will take the milk away.' These bindings, these pills, 'Take these pills now.' Pills to take away the milk, pills to ensure that she is composed and that she sleeps. She takes the pills obediently, one after another, swallowing them down with the water the nurse holds out to her. She does whatever she is told. If she is obedient and does not ask questions they may allow her to see Horst. She cannot fight them alone. If Horst comes he will stand and fight beside her.

How many floors up? Two? Three? Then along the corridor to the room, to the small head that turned, to the fuzz of hair beneath the light. He will still be there. He must still be there.

And so she takes the pills and eats all of the meals on the plates they bring her and smiles and thanks them and waits. Waits until at last as she wakes, she feels the clasp of his hand on hers. She feels a rush of tears. But there is no time for tears. She turns her face close to him and whispers it. She knows there will be surveillance but if she is quiet. Anyway, before their baby is taken away and given to the waiting couple, this couple who have been deemed by the state as more worthy to raise their son, she must tell him. 'Horst, they have stolen our baby.'

She sees the astonishment, the sudden fear in his expression. Does he doubt her? What lies has he been told? Herr Klein, your wife has lost her mind.

'Gerda schatz, our baby has died.'

'No,' she whispers. 'No. I have heard of this. If there is doubt about the parents' political allegiances sometimes they will take away their children.'

He shakes his head, his eyes filled with grief and alarm. 'Gerda, no.'

'I saw him,' she says. 'I saw him. He was in the nursery. He looked at me.'

'No. You are mistaken. Gerda, listen to me. This has been a terrible blow for you. They would not let me come in. They told me you were ill. Very ill with the shock of losing the baby.'

She stares incredulously at him. 'You think I do not know my own child?'

He tightens his hold on her hand but he does not answer.

'You think I am crazy?'

'You are not crazy.' He presses his lips to her hand. 'Of course you are not, but this has been so hard for you to bear. I am here now and we will face this together. We must accept what has happened.'

'I will not accept it,' Gerda says. 'Have you seen this dead child?'

'No, but Gerda —.'

'Don't you see?' she hisses. 'That is the proof. If there was a body we would see it. We are the parents. You must ask to see him. We have the right to see the body of our child.'

Horst shakes his head again. 'I do not want to cause you more pain, my darling. But I think you must know this. They told me the child was deformed. Quite quite badly deformed. They told me he could not have survived.'

'And where is this deformed body of our son?'

'They told me they wished to spare us from seeing him. The body is disposed of, Gerda.'

'And you believe what they have told you?'

'I do.' Horst's face is anguished and his eyes filled with tears. 'My darling, I do.'

Gerda lies back on the pillows, closes her eyes. She cannot fight them. She has no proof, no authority, no power. The small head that turned, the fuzz of hair beneath the light. The cry.

'And so we have lost our son?' she says.

'Yes, Gerda. Yes, we have lost our son.'

She feels the cry from deep inside her, raging up into her throat, shaking her, erupting into such an explosion of wailing. It is as if she is beyond her body, beyond this sound which now emanates from her. He holds her, rocks her, she feels the wetness of his face against her own, the strength of his body against hers. My baby. My little boy.

'I want to go home, Horst. I must go home to Ilse.'

But she cannot go home; the hospital authorities forbid this. 'You have been seriously ill, Frau Klein,' the doctor tells her, his voice curt and uncompromising, 'both in your body and your mind. We must keep you here, under observation, until you are fully well again.'

Do not protest. Simply nod and agree. She thanks the doctor for his concern. She feels his eyes on her, coldly scrutinising, long after he leaves the room. She closes her eyes. Under observation. She understands what that means. She is a nurse. She has experienced those situations where patients are placed under observation and watched carefully. She knows that depending on how they behave, some will eventually be permitted to leave the hospital while the others are transferred to the Dosen Asylum. She is cold with fear. She wants to run from this place, to escape and yet, how would that seem to the authorities? The proof of her craziness, she would land this right there in their laps. This woman, this very ill woman has run in her nightwear out into the streets. A risk to herself. A risk to others.

Her dress, her shoes, her underwear, all are in safe keeping. 'There is no room for the storage of clothing within the wards Frau Klein,' the nurse says when she asks. 'Your clothing will be returned to you when it is required.'

Was that another mark against her? Questioning this nurse? Did she record this in her notebook to be brought out and laid on the table at the next meeting?

She had brought with her the blue dress her mother made with the buttons down the front for breast-feeding. The dress and the summer sandals, the new underwear, the new maternity bra. Oh, she was to look so smart, so happy, as Horst took her home wearing her new blue dress, her baby wrapped in the fine white shawl in her arms. The little white jumpsuit, the pale lemon jacket with the matching mittens, the soft shawl, once Ilse's, and now carefully washed and dried out of the sun in case it turned yellow. These also are in her suitcase. She closes her eyes, feels the tears again spilling down her cheeks, feels her belly contract, her breasts prick and tingle and ache; still agony, her breasts.

She must harden herself. Think. Think, Gerda, of who may help you.

7

It started so innocently; and they are innocent, Gerda, Horst and their friends. All they wanted was for the betterment of their country. Does it not belong to them? Her family, the Silars, and Horst's family, the Kleins, have lived here for generations. She and Horst have talked of a loosening of the restrictions that confine this country. They talked of the possibility of more choices and independence for the citizens. They talked of there being, ultimately, less power for those in authority. The Stasi.

The Stasi.

Horst is a teacher and where else should this independence of thinking begin than in the minds of children? 'How can this country progress, Gerda, when our children are fed lies?' Lies that she was taught and believed as an innocent girl who trusted unthinkingly in the good of the Party and the State. Now she has seen too much, heard too much to believe the lies she was told. This poor country of theirs: the fertile land and formerly magnificent buildings scarred and broken, the country divided up by the victors of the war. Families divided: East or West. Even her own family is now divided. Gerda's older brother, Jürgen, had been awarded a scholarship for postgraduate study at the Freie Universität Berlin in the American section of Berlin when the Wall went up and he chose to remain in the West. Still, before Horst told her of the meetings, she preferred to put all that to one side. She had her work and her friends and her family; this was enough for her. She had seen people who involved themselves in politics becoming angry and frustrated, sometimes placing themselves and their families in danger. What was the point of this? Better to live your life as best you can. Be content in a state which provides comfortable living conditions:

food, clothing, a home and work.

So, there was not the choice of food that is over there in the West? But here you knew which foods were best and where you should go to buy your food and, besides, there were always gifts and the means to barter. So, the choice of clothing and shoes in the shops was restricted? You could sew and knit, you could alter clothing to your own taste with buttons and trimmings. The citizens of the East were not only well provided for, they were resourceful with what was available. As for the restrictions, better to skirt around them than go at them full on, like a charging bull full of bluster and stupidity.

'There is no danger,' Horst told her. 'Only a few of us talking together. Only a few of us who believe changes are needed at the school.'

'What kind of changes?' she asked.

'If our students are to be successful in this world there must be more liberality in the way they are allowed to test what they are doing and to think for themselves.'

'You must take care.' She rested her hand on his arm. 'You know I agree with you but —.'

'I know what you are thinking, but if it is true what the authorities say, that the children of East Germany are to be the scientists and innovators of the future, then they must have the tools which will allow this to happen.'

'But how can you trust that these people you speak with are not informers?'

'These are people I have worked with for years. I know who they are and how they think. I would trust these people with my life.'

She started to speak, then turned away. What was she worrying about? Horst was a careful man, cautious in his words and in the people he trusted to be his friends. He would not put his family in jeopardy. And, besides, he was a good citizen. What he wanted was for the best of this country.

Jürgen. Perhaps he can help them. Perhaps Jürgen could get them out.

Gerda remembers the shock on her parents' faces as they read the letter. The letter from Jürgen, already opened and read by others on its way across the border. He had decided to stay in the West, his work was too important for him to leave, and he could not give up the prospects which he was certain would open for him so long as he stayed on. Although he had considered applying for a place at the Humboldt-Universität zu Berlin in Eastern Berlin he would not have the same opportunities. The university was under the strict control of both the Soviets and the Socialist Unity Party of Germany and the ideological strictures would limit his ability to pursue his chosen career in physics. Anyway, despite his excellent qualifications he could not be assured of a place there. He had heard that students were selected according to their compliance to following the party line and his own situation of having lived and studied in the West would be a sure black mark against him.

'Besides that,' he wrote, 'I have changed. I am no longer in agreement with the governing principles and restrictions of the Eastern bloc. I cannot live and work freely and happily with those restrictions. Forgive me, my dearest parents, but my life now is here with my work, my friends, my girlfriend.'

'We have lost him.' Her mother folded the letter and placed it back in the envelope. She took her pen and wrote the details on the back of the envelope as she did with all the letters which came to their apartment. 'Jürgen, 18 August 1961.'

My work, my friends, my girlfriend? What were such matters compared to your own family and country? Though Gerda would not have expressed her thoughts aloud to her parents, she saw him as a traitor, this brother of hers, to his family, the Silars, who had lived for generations here in Leipzig and to his country, to all the friends who had cared for him, to the many teachers who had guided and promoted him. She knew that this girlfriend of his came from a wealthy family in Berlin and, oh yes, why would he not stick with them since such families ensured success and ease? A traitor. That was what he was.

That girl she was; that girl who took in the doctrine they were taught in school as easily and thoughtlessly as she breathed in the air and just as unthinkingly thrust it out in ready-made convictions and disapprovals and censures. She does not like that girl who at the age of fourteen knew and had an opinion on everything. But that girl was safe. And now the distrustful woman that girl has become during the twenty years that have passed is not safe. Neither she nor her family is safe.

Could Jürgen help them? That girlfriend, Anke, of the 1961 letter now is his wife but Gerda does not know her, nor her brother's children: the little girls she has met only briefly the few times her brother has brought his family across the border. Gerda's mother and father, their own Oma and Großvater, have barely met these little girls. While it was not difficult for Jürgen to procure a visiting visa, social calls from Westerners, even family members, were monitored. Too many visits, too many letters would lead to strict surveillance — perhaps a summons from within the corridors of the Runde Ecke.

And why should he help them? Whenever she has met with her brother, they have both been aloof and composed; there is no warmth between them. She does not know this man in his Western suit and shiny leather shoes, his Saxon accent obliterated. Neither does she have strong memories of him from her childhood. He was older than her: when she was a girl, he was almost a man.

There have been letters over the years to her parents that her mother has passed on to Gerda. Letters about his work, the news of his marriage, the birth of the children. A scattering of photographs. After that first letter, he was careful; he knew better than to criticise or even to mention the differences of life here in Leipzig with the West. Only that once, when her mother wrote to him the news that Gerda had completed school and was to begin her nurse's training he wrote back with obvious disapproval. Gerda could do better for herself. Why was she limiting herself in this way when she was so clever and capable, scoring the highest marks in her final examinations? If it was medicine she was interested in, why was she not training as a doctor? There were better opportunities, he wrote. Much better opportunities, elsewhere. He and Anke could help. This letter had been fingered, crumpled slightly at the edges, the envelope torn, a sticker holding it together: 'Damaged in transit'.

'Elsewhere,' Mutti whispered. 'Does Jürgen wish to bring more trouble to us with this elsewhere?'

For already there had been questions raised about this son who chose to live within the capitalism and corruption of the West. There was reason to suspect that this was why Gerda had been denied a place in the faculty of medicine at the Universität Karl-Marx.

'I will write to him,' Gerda said. And so she wrote. She was content with her chosen path, she told him, and had no inclination to study elsewhere. He must not be concerned about her: she was happy and satisfied; she had made her decision freely. As freely as he himself, she wrote, had made his own choices. She folded the letter, placed it in the envelope, fixed the stamp to the front of it and placed it in the mailbox near their apartment building.

Why would she choose to be elsewhere? This was her home. The marketplace with the City Hall, the clock in the tower high above the ground. Thomaskirche, Nikolaikirche, the Leipzig Botanical Garden. The Zoological Garden, the rollicking trams, Karl Marx Square with the billowing flags. Roller skating with her friends beneath the chestnut trees that lined her street.

Born six years after the war, she was accustomed to the regular sound and sight of the building sites, the hammering and drilling and heavy machinery. The citizens of Leipzig were proud of their city; everywhere there was progress. First of all there was the industrialisation creating a strong economy and providing employment in the rows of factories in Wolfen and Bitterfeld and the coal mines that ran along the southern perimeter of the city with its cranes looming against the skyline. Yes, this was a city of work and advancement; even through the night the blue lights from conveyers at the mine could be seen. Then there was the building of the ten-storey apartments to provide accommodation for the city's workers. Already sixty thousand Plattenbau apartments had been completed, each with a bathroom, fitted kitchens and central heating. And all of this so that workers were no longer obliged to live in cold, cramped and frequently damaged pre-war apartments and forced on winter nights out into the darkness and chill of outside bathrooms.

Gerda had also seen the reconstruction of buildings laid to waste by that war. Hitler's war. The war made by the barbarians of the Third Reich. She was not a daughter of this Third Reich but a daughter of the now, of the present. She did not know, nor had any desire to know, who within her family or the families of her friends had supported or, for that matter, had opposed National Socialism. Questions about the past were not encouraged. Even within her own family they were not encouraged. 'Such questions are hurtful,' her mother told her.

Rühre nicht an alte Wunden. Do not touch old wounds.

Gerda understood this. She had seen the deep crevice edged with shiny purple skin and the wasted muscle in her father's lower leg, the discomfort on his face on cold days when the dull ache became a throbbing torment. But in spite of the pain he suffered and the crutch he had to use when he walked, he was fortunate, he said on the rare times he mentioned it. Her father went to war with two brothers who did not return.

Then there was her mother's younger sister, Liesle, the adored baby of the family, killed with her three children in Dresden during the bombing. There were the cousins, friends, neighbours remembered by her parents and all now lost. Rühre nicht an alten Wunden.

Better to think, as she was instructed, that her generation belonged now to a wholly new country, that the shame and mistakes of the past had been extinguished within this newness. This generation belonged to the country of the Socialist Unity Party, a state by and for the workers, led by Walter Ulbricht, and carved out of the brutishness of Nazi rule by their Soviet comrades uniting with their own German citizens' heroic resistance to overthrow it.

That girl she was. The girl who sang 'Risen from Ruins', the national anthem, with such gusto, who threw herself wholeheartedly into competitive sports since the GDR wholeheartedly supported sporting excellence, who worked so hard in those classrooms with the pictures of Lenin — his immaculately clipped beard and moustache, his white shirt and flawlessly knotted tie, the firmness and courage of his expression, the dark intelligence of his eyes — in pride of place.

The girl who set herself the task of making more red carnations from crêpe paper than any other student in the school for Workers' Day. Who, at the age of thirteen, pledged herself, along with the other students of her class, in the decorated local hall to give herself to the noble cause of socialism, to deepen the bond with the Soviet Union and to fight for the interests of the international proletariat? The Jugendweihe. She remembers the days of excitement before the ceremony, the sleeplessness of the nights. The pride she had when her father hung the framed certificate to the wall.

That girl. That stupid girl. That safe girl.

The nurse comes. Gerda smiles, thanks her for the pills she tips into her hand, the glass of water. Gerda places the pills in her mouth, manoeuvres them beneath her tongue and sips the water. When the nurse leaves, she spits the pills out into a handkerchief. She will think, later, how these pills can be disposed of. She must have a clear head. She must think.

When did the questions begin?

The training of nurses was exacting and carefully regulated, their education of medical procedures conducted on the wards. They learned to pay strict attention to the hierarchy: the doctors, the senior, middle-grade and junior nursing staff. Nurses were at the bottom and must learn their way upwards from the depths of the foundation: bedpans, bed-making, ensuring patients were clean, comfortable and tidy, the careful monitoring of temperatures.

Oh but she loved wearing her white tunic dress, she loved even the ugly lace-up shoes she wore within the wards. She ensured that she appeared always immaculately clean and tidy since the ward sister had stressed that a professional appearance was of utmost importance. She had always been eager to please her teachers and to succeed at school and now she worked hard to become a fine nurse. All of the girls she became friends with worked hard, skivvying in the hospital throughout the days and studying into the nights.

But then there was the girl she had not made friends with. Hanna Schwarz. She was older than the others yet far less conscientious. Her bed-making was sloppy and she appeared unworried about the exams which were approaching. Besides that, she spent too much time on her tasks, laughing and talking with the patients, joking with the men as she worked. She was under the sister's eye, everyone could see that. And so, although Gerda was attracted by and slightly in awe of Hanna's sophistication and self-confident manner, she knew it was better to remain distant from any overtures of friendliness. The other girls, she was sure, felt the same way. When they arranged, at the end of a day, to go to a café for coffee or hot chocolate Hanna was not invited.

'Fraulein Schwarz, I have arrived at the opinion that you are not suitable for the nursing profession.' Gerda heard it as she passed by the open door of the ward sister's office. Not suitable for the nursing profession. Even hearing that said to another girl made Gerda's heart thump. She had not approved of Hanna's behaviour but still she felt sorry for her, and so the following afternoon when she was on her way home and saw Hanna also at the stop waiting for a tram she smiled at her. Hanna looked at her closely, then smiled back. She was wearing the bright lipstick, the Western black leather jacket she always put on as she left the hospital, and waved the cigarette she was smoking. 'Hi, Gerda. On your way home?'

'Yes. Just in time for dinner and then more study.' Gerda made a little face though, in fact, she did not mind the study. She realised what she had said and felt her face flush. How could she complain about study to Hanna who had lost her place at the hospital?

Still, Hanna did not seem to mind. Perhaps, after all, she had been given another chance. 'You live with your parents?' Hanna asked.

'Yes. How about you?'

'No.' She flicked ash from her cigarette onto the ground. 'My grandparents.'

'Oh.' She would not ask about Hanna's parents. Such questions could result in unpleasant revelations.

'My parents are dead,' Hanna offered matter-of-factly. 'I was raised by my Oma and Opa.'

'Oh. I'm sorry. About your parents, that is.'

'Don't be. I didn't know them. My father was killed on the Eastern Front in 1944. My mother in 1945, not long after I was born.'

'The bombings?'

'No.' She did not even bother to lower her voice. 'My mother was raped and murdered by Russian soldiers.'

Gerda gasped. She could not believe she had heard the brutality of these words splattering out into the ordinariness of the evening. To say nothing of the insult to their liberators. She looked around. Who has heard, who has been listening? She wanted to move right away from Hanna, to pretend she had not heard, but she could not be so rude.

Hanna had her eyes fixed on her. 'You do not like to hear this?'

'The Red Army released our country,' Gerda said stiffly. Oh, where was the tram?

'They invaded our country and their soldiers raped our women. Both my mother and my grandmother were raped along with tens of thousands of women. Even little girls, even the women in the maternity hospitals. Ask your mother.' She dropped her cigarette butt onto the ground, grinding it out with her boot.

'Why are you saying this?' Gerda hissed, looking about her. 'This is dangerous talk, don't you understand that?'

'I am not ashamed to be saying this because it is true. You are so smug, Gerda Silar, you and your little friends. Is the truth too dangerous for you? Then I wish you well with your lies.'

A tram came. Hanna stepped onto it and seated herself beside the window. Her face was turned towards Gerda, watching her with her bold eyes and she gave a jaunty wave as the tram jerked then moved forward, gathering speed. Gerda could not move, she was so mortified. She knew her face was flushed red. She glanced quickly at the people standing near to her. Could they be thinking — please let this not be so — that this girl was her friend?

How could Hanna speak this way? So rebellious and undignified. The tram came at last and she climbed on and sat alone. She opened up the manual, turned to the part she was to memorise by the next day. She could make an early start on the way home and she bent her face over the book though her thoughts and heart were racing.

Hanna did not return to the hospital. There were rumours of a boyfriend in the West who had helped her to escape. Perhaps that was why she had been so disrespectful.

Tens of thousands raped. Even little girls. Even women in maternity hospitals. I wish you well with your lies. Ask your mother.

Hanna's eyes, the expression within them of anger and of challenge and of something else. Was that pity in her eyes? Pity for Gerda? In her eyes and in that jaunty wave, in that smile on her red, glossy lips and the words she said? 'Ask your mother.'

But although she tried several times when they were alone, Gerda could not bring herself to broach this subject with her mother. She imagined the shock and reproach in her mother's face in response to such questions: 'Where did you hear such scandal?' And so she went to her aunt, her mother's older sister, who she had found was more straightforward about awkward issues. She sat in the kitchen as her aunt made tea and arranged Lebkuchen onto a plate. Perhaps it was better to leave this, after all, and to simply have a nice visit with Tante Marte talking of her nursing training and of her cousins and the weather.

Rühre nicht an alte Wunden. But she needed to know this. She could not let this challenge go by. She was not, as Hanna suggested, afraid of the truth. In fact, part of the reason she was there is that she was certain that Tante Marte would brush it all away with one wave of her hand. The girl is lying to you, Gerda. She is trying to cause trouble.

She had to ask. She said bluntly, 'Tante Marte, I have heard talk that women were raped by Russian soldiers when they entered our country.'

Her aunt poured tea into the cups, pink with a green rim, to match the pattern of flowers on the plate. 'This talk is true,' she said.

Gerda took the cup and saucer her aunt held out to her. Her hands were shaking slightly as she carefully placed it on the table. 'This happened here?'

'In Leipzig, in Dresden, in Berlin. Everywhere in the East. First the Americans came to Leipzig and then they gave it over to the Russians. We were terrified of them coming and those who could not leave and had houses still standing barricaded up the windows and doors with timber from the bombed houses.' Tante Marte's voice was as unemotional as if she was speaking of the baking of a cake, the setting of the table. 'We took in the neighbours whose houses were gone and we hid in the cellars. Oma, your mother, me and other women from the neighbourhood locked ourselves in with the children. Your mother had Jürgen with her and I had Trude. It was difficult keeping the children silent.'

'I did not know this,' Gerda said. 'Why has no one told me?'

'Ach, little Gerda.' Her aunt smiled at her. 'Why should we talk to you of such sad times?'

'Because it is the truth.'

'You want truth, Gerda? Take care with this truth. You may hear things that are too painful to bear.'

'I want the truth.' She looked her aunt squarely in the eye. 'Tell me.'

Her aunt sighed. 'I will tell you this. We did not have enough food. We had tried to save some. We knew the end of the war was approaching and that Germany would lose. We did not know what would happen after that but we understood we may have to leave or hide and that we would need food. But there was barely enough even for our day-to-day living since food was severely rationed because the soldiers at the front had to be fed. We pooled our resources but it did not last, of course. Although we knew women were being attacked on the streets someone had to go out to look for food.'

'One of you went?'

Her aunt nodded, her eyes staring straight into Gerda's.

'She, whoever it was who went, she was all right? She came back safely?'

'That is all I will tell you.'

Who went for the food? Mutti? Oma? Tante Marte? One of the women from the neighbourhood? Who went for the food? She could not ask it. There was a darkness in her aunt's eyes she was afraid of. 'But,' it burst out of her, 'the Soviets are our friends. They helped us to rebuild our country.'

'They helped themselves to our country.'

'In Dresden I have seen the plaque which commemorates our liberation from Nazi oppressors by our Russian brothers. I thought —.'

'You thought what? That the Russians were met by smiling German comrades waving the Soviet flag? That we, here in the East, were at heart socialists and were saved by these heroes from fascism? No, that is what you have been told, Gerda, but it is not the way it was. These soldiers were bent on revenge for what had been done by our own soldiers in Russia. What happened there was brutal and shameful, just as what happened here was also brutal and shameful. This is your truth, Gerda, but what is gained by knowing this? What is gained by thinking back to that terrible time? Nothing of good comes from bitterness.'

Gerda brought the cup of hot tea to her lips but could not bring herself to drink. She could not believe what her aunt was telling her; her pretty aunt, always so loving and happy.

Who went for the food?

'But people are well looked after here. They are content.'

'Do you think this is so?' Tante Marta sipped her tea. 'Do you think people are happy the way things are with our country divided up and governed and occupied by foreigners? Why are there so many suicides here in the East? Why do so many people risk their lives to escape?'

'But, Tante Marte, are you suggesting that everyone, even our own family, is unhappy with the way things are? Because it does not seem that way to me. Mutti and Papa attend the celebration days. They say they are proud of what our country has become.'

'Gerda, this is what we do for our children so that they may be happy and successful.' Her aunt smiled at her. 'Our generation, we have been through a war, our parents through two wars. We have lost too much and there is no fight left in us. We make the best of what is left to us because we have no choice. This is the way things are. Now drink your tea, have a piece of ginger cake, it is freshly made this morning, and tell me of yourself, of your nursing —.'

Well, then, I wish you well with your lies.

Digging out the truth from beneath the topsoil of propaganda became Gerda's mission in the following months. She was taking a risk, she knew that, but there were those who were eager to whisper their stories of refugees herded like animals, people beaten and shot. Of the girl from the next street who said she would go to find food because she could run fastest. Raped so many times she lost consciousness and left like rubbish amongst the rubble: 'She had to have an abortion, she could not have children after that.'

They told their stories and they showed her the hidden publications where she read of the lost sons, husbands, fathers; hundreds upon hundreds of them taken between 1945 and 1950 when the Russian secret police imprisoned those who may have caused trouble for them, using former concentration camps, building new prisons or simply sending them off to Russia to ensure their silence. She read of the forced emigration of German people living in Poland and Czechoslovakia; thousands driven from their homes. The plunder and takeover of East Germany, the demands for war-reparation payments, the equipment seized from the factories sent to Russia. The rules and regulations that brought ruin to privately owned businesses, to farms that had been owned for centuries by families, now forced into collectivisation. The 1953 uprising was not, as Gerda had been taught, a machination of the West attempting to destabilise socialism but a response to the inequality within East Germany. The poor working conditions and meagre wages had sent the workers into the streets. The Russians came with their tanks and fired into the crowds.

She almost regretted what she learned in those months and yet some instinct kept her turning over that thick topsoil to see the corruption and smell the stink of decaying flesh beneath. Yes, she regretted the loss of her innocent beliefs but these truths brought with them a shrewdness and watchfulness and she believed that finding out made her not only more resilient but a more compassionate nurse. Her mind had been prised open: she was less inclined to judge.

In the end, she had let it go. Nothing of good comes from bitterness. These evils were in the past and she must live in the present and look forward rather than back. Present conditions were good enough for those who were uncomplaining and worked hard.

8

In the night there is the clanking of the trolleys passing along the corridors, the torch that wakes her for her medication. In the daytime she dutifully eats and drinks what is placed before her and waits for Horst. He explains to her that he comes every day, that sometimes he is allowed to come into the ward but at other times they tell him she is sleeping and cannot be disturbed. She does not argue. She does not tell him that, no, she was not sleeping, that every day she waits for him.

They come with their shut faces and their soups and coddled eggs and pills and bindings; they come with their bedpans and bowls of water and towels. 'No, Frau Klein, you are not yet well enough to go to the bathroom.' They are making her an invalid and she is too weak to stop this. There is nobody who can help me. Nothing and nobody.

Why is this happening when, for all of these years of her adult life, she has been compliant, telling herself and everybody else that life is good here, as long as you do not ask questions or criticise, as long as you do not speak out? It is good. We live in a beautiful city, there is work, we are cared for. What more could anyone ask?

She graduated proudly, her parents there among the crowd of other parents, hands clapping, faces filled with joy. At the hospital they saw how efficient she was in the operating theatre, that she was neat and quick and skilful and had the ability to detect, almost before the surgeon directed her, what tools the procedures demanded. It was generally considered, the sister in charge of graduating nurses told her, that she had the potential to accomplish the role of a senior theatre nurse in the future. She was very well thought of, the sister said. 'Keep working hard, Nurse Klein, and you will achieve your goals.'

She went with other nurses to a dance and met Horst, so handsome with his fair hair and blue eyes. So handsome. He walked with her across the park to her home, his large, firm hand holding hers. The chestnut trees were blooming, the flowers gleaming and white, the soft sweet smell of them, the soft sweet feeling of his lips on hers before he left. Horst.

Of course life was good with all the excitement of falling in love, of talking, talking, talking to Horst, of kissing and kissing until they were breathless with wanting. Then the planning of their wedding, the dress, the celebration, finding their future home and the plans for furnishing it. They were fortunate enough to secure a two-bedroom apartment: teachers and nurses were appreciated by the state and rewarded for their hard work. But so lucky to be there at the top of the building so that they could look down from the windows, their own windows, across the rooftops. They saw other young couples as they walked up the stairs of the building; perhaps these couples would be their future friends? There was a park across the road where they saw young men and women walking together, some pushing prams.

Mutti gave her the china which had been her own Oma's, the Meissen china with the rich blue borders and edgings of gold. She and Horst placed it carefully in the cupboard of the heavy dark dresser which had been given to them by Horst's uncle. 'I will be too afraid to eat from such treasures,' Horst teased her.

Such happiness, such excitement. She and Horst, both of them were doing well in their careers. During the week they were so busy, almost flying in and out of the apartment on their way to catch trams to work. In the evenings they had so much to talk about, on the weekends so much to do. Often they invited their parents and friends for coffee and cake or to eat dinner. Gerda loved to keep their apartment just so; she loved to set the table nicely with the white embroidered cloth and the special china and to make cakes.

Then Ilse came. Baby Ilse with her grasping hands and watchful blue eyes. Ilse. She must get home.

This is what we do for our children so that they may be happy and successful. And it is what she and Horst did, also, for their Ilse. Although some of the notions Ilse has brought home with her from school and repeated to them — such force and passion and, oh, that aggravatingly fervent gleam in her eye — have made Gerda inwardly cringe, she always listened silently.

'Our teacher says the West is corrupt and Americans are the most evil force on this earth. Our teacher says everyone in the GDR must be prepared for the struggle against Imperialism. Mutti, why has Papa not built a bomb shelter? Our teacher says we cannot rely on the charity of others on the occasion of a nuclear war.'

Our teacher says. Yes, Gerda has nodded and agreed even when her stomach is churning at this bitter, hate-filled Dummheit which has been poured into the mind of her child. Even though she has asked herself time and again, 'What is this doing to our girl?' Ilse has listened to such lessons from her first days in Kinderkrippe and Kindergarten. What is it doing to this world when babies are learning the lessons of division and hostility? Ach, these men and their threats, their nuclear weapons poised like toys in the hands of reckless children.

But what can she do but bite down hard on her tongue and nod? And, although she dislikes, almost to the point of revulsion, the sight of her Ilse in the Young Pioneers cap and scarf, hates that silly song they sing, 'Take your hands from your pocket/Do some good, don't try to stop it', hates the way her Ilse disappears among these marching, saluting, singing toy soldiers, still she has attended each and every one of the celebration days. She volunteers regularly to be one of the three chaperones required for the organised outings, she has demonstrated basic first aid including the winding and application of bandages to the Young Pioneers in preparation for the Imperialist-driven nuclear war which is certain to break out at any time.

Good work, good friends, a loving husband, a beautiful daughter: make the best of what is here. And when you meet them in the street, the grey faces of the Stasi, look ahead and continue walking at the same pace. Do not draw attention to yourself. Remain invisible.

The clanking of the trolleys passing along the corridors in the night. Another day has passed when Horst does not come. Another night, another day.

Do not draw attention to yourself. Remain invisible.

Why did she not remember these lessons that night when Horst, in bed beside her, told her of the meetings? Why did she not tell him that life was good for them and that if other people wanted changes, well then, those other people must take the risks?

For days, Horst has been silent and inattentive; sometimes he has spoken sharply to Ilse which is not the usual way for him and now, while they are lying close together in their bed he tells her. 'You won't like this,' he says and she feels his body tense beside her. 'I know you will be against it. But there are such injustices at the school, so many bad things that I feel there is no choice, Gerda. I must join with the others.'

She lifts her head from his shoulder where she has been resting and props herself up on her elbow so she can look into his face. 'Join with the others?' She says it slowly, trying to make sense of his words. 'What do you mean? Who are these others you are speaking of?'

'Teachers,' Horst says. 'Other teachers.'

'You mean teachers at your school?'

He hesitates. 'Our school and some of the others within Leipzig. We are simply meeting and talking, Gerda. There is nothing for you to worry about.'

She sits upright and switches on the lamp. 'Of course there is something to worry about,' she says sharply. 'This could mean serious trouble for us all.'

'These are people we can trust,' Horst says. 'I would trust any one of them with my life.'

'I'm sure those words have been said many times,' Gerda says. 'But would you also trust these people with my life and with Ilse's as well as your own? You know there are informers everywhere.'

'We are doing nothing wrong. We are teachers and we want the best for our students.'

'What is so bad that you wish to join with these others?'

She knows about many of the issues of which Horst speaks. There are the little girls, talented in sport, who are selected for the specialist academies and given the 'vitamins' which develop broad shoulders and masculine features. There are the boys, still children, taken into military service. And, yes, the policy in schools is that children will be indoctrinated to become Marxist to the core. But this is what they have here and they and the people they know are not powerful enough to generate change. This is what they must live with if they are to be safe and comfortable within their home.

'It is not too bad for me,' Horst is saying. 'The equipment and the books I am given to work with are adequate only but since the area of my teaching deals with data and specifics I can teach with truth and honesty. It is the others I am most concerned for.'

Then let these others deal with their own problems. 'If you are happy, why involve yourself?'

'I am not happy,' Horst says, raising his voice, 'when the children of this country are fed lies.'

'But you are now the head of the science department. This is what you have wanted for many years. Why jeopardise this position you have worked hard for?'

She hears her words and feels ashamed. Look after yourself, forget the troubles of others, is that what she has become? Is that what this administration is making of her? A selfish woman who cares for nothing but her own concerns? 'I am sorry,' she says. 'It is just that such talk frightens me. You have heard the stories, Horst. It is unwise to speak against the state.'

'I am not speaking against the state. I am trying to speak for the country. Our country, Gerda.'

She settles back against his shoulder and takes his hand. 'Tell me,' she says. 'I will listen.'

The main problem, he explains, is the history curriculum which is designed to entrench in the students a sense of socialist patriotism. 'And so,' he says, 'teachers must instruct their students that history prior to Karl Marx merely demonstrates the depravity of the ruling classes and the exploitation of capitalist systems. The expanse of socialism is, in comparison, a triumph of advancement and the just conclusion to the working class's battle.'

'There is no change. This is what we ourselves were taught in history,' Gerda says.

'To reduce the complexities of the development and fall of civilisations to this simplistic jabber is nonsense.'

'But these students will learn to think for themselves, just as we did. They will grow up and things will change.'

'How will things change if we stand back and wait for someone else to do it? How will it change with young people growing up filled with hatred and lies? When our children are told that the Cold War began with the American nuclear bombing of Hiroshima and Nagasaki, an action that was unnecessary to victory but was instead designed to warn the Soviet Union? When they are told that the Berlin Airlift was uncalled for since the USSR had offered to take over the care of the Western sectors of Berlin? When they are told that the construction of the Berlin Wall was a necessary response to West German aggressiveness, instigated by the warmongering successors to the Nazi Wehrmacht?'

Horst's face is hot with anger, his voice is shaking. Gerda places her hand on his arm. 'Horst —.'

'No, Gerda. No. I am sick of it. Sick of all these lies. That Hitler and his Nazi thugs came to power because of the degeneration of a decaying capitalism. That all is rotting and evil in the West but well for us in the East. I am sick of it, I tell you. I ride my bike to the school where there is sand and dust in my mouth all day from the mines just beyond the gymnasium, where the children are forbidden to walk on land edging the school because of ammunition left over from the war. Is this what we should be giving our children, land and air fouled by industry and war and lies about how these situations have come about?'

Gerda squeezes his arm. 'You are right, but how —?'

'There will be a way. We are not rebels, Gerda. We do not want to overturn the system. All we want are some changes.'

Some changes? What harm could a few changes bring about? Yet in her belly are stirrings of dread. Horst could lose his job if this came out. Their apartment would be taken from them. He would be forced to find work in one of the factories. Their hopes for Ilse, all of their hopes as a family, would be denied them. 'You must be careful,' she says. 'You understand what we could lose if things went wrong.'

'I will be careful. Nothing will go wrong. You must know that you and Ilse come first with me. You do trust me, Gerda?'

'Certainly I trust you. It is other people I do not trust.'

'I must have you with me on this.'

Her stomach is churning with dread. 'I am with you.'

That night is what she thinks about as she lies alone in the dark, as the clattering of trolleys passes her door in the night. It is what she thinks about as the first glimmers of light streak the sky. Should she have behaved differently? Should she have told Horst that he must not become involved with these rebels? Should she have shouted at him that he would bring them to ruin, him and his big ideas, that he was risking not only himself but his wife and his child?

Should she have forbidden him to take this path, reminding him that a divorce was easy to acquire in the GDR? That when one spouse was found to be disloyal to the state, the state would take special care to meet the other spouse's needs? She could not do this. Horst was a good man. He believed what he was doing was for the best of the country. How could she stand in the way of a course of action he believed with all his heart was right? Horst was a good man and she loved him.

She wants to go home to Horst and to Ilse. She craves the

comfort and familiarity of their wide wooden table, of the sofa and the chairs and the beds, the bright rugs they had saved for and now cover the floor, the cushions that bring colour to the rooms, the cherished dresser, the special china; all of those objects that fill their apartment and give her pleasure as she touches them and holds them in her hands. She longs for these objects that will remind her who she is, will persuade her that what she and Ilse and Horst have together is real.

It is dark in the room and in the ward outside. Horst has not come for some days. What has happened that he does not come? Lying as she does through the nights, through the days, in this high narrow bed in this small green room with the tiny window and the curtains around the bed, she cannot quite believe in that home and in that life which is waiting for her on the other side of the city. Yet she must believe in it, she must hold on to it. The apartment with the views across the rooftops and the park, soon she will be there at home with the windows thrown open. She will be back at home tucking fresh sheets onto the beds, fluffing up the quilts, polishing a sheen into the dark wood furniture. Soon.

She must believe in this. As she must, also, believe in her own ability to remove herself from this room. She must keep hold of herself. What they have, she, Horst and Ilse, what they have is real. It is real.

This is what she does on Saturdays. In preparation for the week of work before them she cleans the bathtub, sweeps and washes the floors. She changes the sheets and the covers on the beds, washes and irons Horst's shirts, Ilse's school clothes, her own white and pink coveralls. Everything clean and tidy for the week ahead.

Did they listen as she worked, humming to herself as she always does? Did they listen as she and Horst and Ilse sat around the table eating and chatting of this and that? Did they listen to the sounds they made, she and Horst, as they made love?

They were careful with the meetings. Very careful, Horst said. Ach, these teachers thought they were so clever, meeting always in places different from the one before. There were no notes passed, no records made of the meetings: this was the rule. Without records, they said, there was nothing to incriminate them.

Nothing to incriminate them other than the weakness of those who would be questioned. Nothing to incriminate them other than those listening and watching and waiting.

'But what are these meetings for?' Gerda asked. 'What are you hoping to achieve?'

'Nothing at this stage,' Horst said, 'other than solidarity. If we are talking, others also will be talking. Things are changing in the world, Gerda. There is talk that the Soviets are beginning to lose strength and will in time pull back from the countries they are presently controlling. When that happens there will be room for change here and we will be ready.'

Gerda frowns. 'If that happens.'

Horst smiles back. 'When, Gerda, when.'

Did they hear those particular words? Did they hear the teachers speaking together at the one meeting which was held in their own apartment? Were they given away before or after that particular meeting? And who gave them away? Who was the informer? Was it the quiet man who sat drinking the coffee Gerda handed him and thanked her so politely? Was it the woman with the strident voice and the too-bright lipstick? Who?

So easy for them to come with their wires and machines when Horst and Gerda were at work and Ilse at school. Who would tell if they looked out of their own door and saw them coming up the stairs and letting themselves into the Kleins' apartment? Quick, shut the door before they see you are watching. Shut the door before they come to you with their questions and accusations.

They were finishing breakfast when the phone rang the first time. Gerda was busy, taking the plates over to the bench for washing, calling to Ilse to hurry, it was almost time to leave, and so she did not notice the seriousness of Horst's face until he replaced the phone and turned to her. 'I am to go to the Stasi offices this afternoon,' he said. 'They say they wish me to clarify certain issues.'

Gerda went to work numbed by fear. All day she wondered whether Horst would be detained, if he would be arrested. If she would be, as were other women she had heard of, left waiting with no news, no communication, ostracised by workmates and neighbours who feared they too would be suspected because of their connection with her.

She heard the footsteps running up the stairs, the key in the lock and then he was there, pulling her against him, that cocky grin on his face. She pulled away. Could this man of hers take nothing seriously? 'What happened?'

'They played their games, kept me waiting in one of their interrogation rooms. It was all designed to frighten me. They have no subtlety or intelligence in their methods, Gerda. Any fool could tell what their intentions are. Well, at last one of them appeared. Big belly, smelling of tobacco, you know the type. This buffoon pretended he was my friend. He told me what a fine fellow I was, what a fine teacher and then he began asking about my views on the school, my fellow teachers, the curriculum. All very cheerful and kindly, as if he was an agreeable old uncle taking an interest in me.'

She sat beside him on the sofa and took his hand. 'What did you say?'

'We have talked of this at the meetings. The rule that we made is that we must say we are satisfied with the school, the curriculum and the entire education system. We agreed to deny anything they may throw at us, to admit to nothing.'

'Did this man believe you?'

Horst hesitates. 'I think they suspect something is up. Whether it is our particular school which is under question or they think this is a general problem, I do not know. One thing that gave me confidence is that many of the teachers they asked about are not part of the meetings.'

Admit to nothing.

Some of the others were taken in for questioning. They received the same treatment: the wait, the questioning from the friendly officer. Then Horst was taken in again, picked up outside the school gates by a waiting car. This time when he returned late at night, there was no self-assurance, no grin. He sat on the sofa, his head resting on his hands. 'I didn't think they would let me come home. This time it was two of them, the same man and another. The friendly man tried to persuade me to tell the truth about the people I worked with. When I said I didn't know what he was talking about the second man butted in and said they knew I was lying. They said, both of them said, that I am likely to lose my job. They talked of treason, of the severe penalties for crimes against the state.'

Gerda's hands fly to her face. 'Horst, no.'

'They said others had talked and if I knew what was best for me I must also tell them what I knew. They tried to turn me into an informer.'

'What did you answer?'

'Understand, Gerda, that this is a trick they play. To pretend that others have talked and that they know what has happened is a way of forcing disclosures.'

'So you said nothing?'

'I said nothing.'

'You must stop all of this.' Gerda moves close to Horst and grips his arms. 'You must stop it now. Ilse and I need you. This new baby needs you.'

Horst averts his eyes. Gerda sees that he is afraid. 'I will stop. I promise you.'

The meetings cease. But is it their imagination or are there people on the street who watch and follow? There is the car which is sometimes parked opposite the apartment. Then Horst does not return at the end of the day. Gerda delays their evening meal and then keeps it warm for him, placing it over a pot filled with gently bubbling water, the pot-lid covering the plate.

'Where is Papa?' Ilse is curious rather than alarmed.

'He has a meeting at the school. It must have continued later than he expected.'

Ilse does her homework and Gerda goes into her room, kisses her goodnight, pulls the quilt up and tucks it tightly around her. 'Sleep well, my darling.' Does Ilse hear the quaver in her voice?

At last Gerda removes Horst's meal from the stove. She waits. She is so afraid and, as well, so angry. How could he do such a thing to them, how could he put his family in danger in this way? Sometime in the night, she wakes, cold and stiff in her chair. She goes into the bedroom; although in her heart she knows he would not return without waking her, still she hopes. The bed is, of course, empty. She draws back the blinds and stares down into the wet, dark streets.

When Gerda returns from work next day, he is still not there. Again she delays their evening meal. She hears unease in Ilse's voice this time when she asks, 'Where is Papa? Why is he not home?'

They are eating when she hears the footsteps on the stairs, slow this time, and now there is the key in the lock. She rushes to him and he shakes his head as she sees then touches with rising alarm the bruising on the side of his face.

He shakes his head, also, when Gerda asks later when Ilse is in bed. 'I will not speak of this,' he tells her. 'Please do not ask me, Gerda.'

Later, he tells her, his eyes and voice filled with guilt and pain, that Jonas Biermann, the head teacher of history, has been detained and that the school informed he will not return to his position.

There are rumours, always rumours, about people who disappear. Rumours of bodies taken to the mortuary in the Southern General Cemetery and cremated so that any injuries remain secret. Rumours of the prison in Berlin-Hohenschönhausen with conditions so brutal that those sent there rarely return.

Incidents begin to happen, small incidents that make up the whole. Luck has deserted them; they are no longer the type of family which is desirable within the GDR, visible only through their health and contentment and cooperation, their willingness to work hard. Horst is demoted to a junior position, Gerda does not receive the promotion she had been assured was hers and neither is she allowed the transfer to the ward which she had applied for. Her body grows larger and more awkward — but she is not granted the usual flexibility of working hours allocated to pregnant women. Even little Ilse is not awarded the Young Pioneer medal she is entitled to. Gerda thinks, but does not dare say aloud even within the privacy of their apartment, that she and Horst have expected the punishments which have come, but to penalise a child in this way? What has their country come to with these petty-minded monsters in control?

Still, they were together and they were safe. This was what mattered now. This game Horst had played was not a game for little people and they had been fools to believe they could battle against the power of the state. But at least, she had thought, they had come through it largely undamaged, that they would sit tight and play by the rules and they would be safe. And all that time another strategy was in play. These monsters had been waiting. Oh yes, they had been waiting. What to do? What should she do?

She falls into sleep and the dreams come again of her boy lost, crying. She feels the grip of terror in her belly as down a shadowed tunnel and another and another she listens for the cries and searches for those eyes which will turn to her. She hears her own shrill yelp as she jolts from sleep, her heart vibrating against her ribcage.

These tears again. These pathetic tears running down her face. This is what she has become? A woman who is afraid of sleeping? Who allows herself to lie here each day, becoming more feeble and more helpless? Who waits each day for Horst to appear and grips his hand as tears trickle from her eyes? She must get better for Ilse. For Ilse.

Yet what if Ilse has already been turned against them? Already they may have told her their lies; perhaps they have come for her, perhaps she too has been given to a more deserving family? Perhaps this is why Horst has not come, because he cannot face her or perhaps he has again been detained. Perhaps . . .

She has a home, a husband and a daughter. This is what she must hold on to, this is what she must believe in. When it is light she lowers her feet onto the floor, takes the bag with her toiletries from the locker then, holding herself up as erect as she can manage, she walks to the bathroom. She takes off the coarse nightgown with the tapes opening at the back. She removes the safety pins and unwinds the binding from around her breasts and belly.

She feels the rush of nausea, sees the black pinpoints in front of her eyes — she is weak, so weak — and she leans against the wall. Gerda, you must do this. Now the shower; she reaches in and turns and adjusts the taps then stands beneath the stinging hot water. The scar across her belly is not so livid, her body is healing, she will again be strong. She lathers the soap in her hands and scrubs her body, scrubs her head with the shampoo; her skin and scalp are clean and smell of lemon.

She wraps herself in a towel and rests on the plank seat outside the shower and towels her hair. She drags the comb through it and twists it into a knot which she fastens with the pins from her bag. Her pink bag with the luxury soap and shampoo. She packed this little bag so carefully and so lovingly — here is the special cream for nappy rash which worked so well when Ilse was a baby, and here the talcum powder, the skin oil — and now again these tears which rush so hot into her eyes and are forever drifting down her face. She brushes them away with the towel. She has her girl. She has her daughter.

She observes herself in the mirror; she is pale and her face is thin but with her hair washed and pinned she does not look so bad. She goes to the large cupboard situated, as in every ward in this hospital, opposite the bathroom and takes a clean nightgown and a robe and dresses herself, walks along the corridor to her room and sits in the chair beside the bed, gathering strength and resolve, yes, I can do this, I must do this. She rings the bell. A nurse hovers at the edge of the doorway. Good, she was young and appeared new to her position.

'I wish for my clothes to be brought to me immediately.'

'Frau Klein, you should be in bed.'

'As you can see, I am well. Please bring me my clothes. I am leaving.'

'You cannot leave, Frau Klein, not without permission from the doctors.'

Gerda smiles kindly at her. 'I am a senior nurse. I know my rights. I know that a patient can leave whenever they wish so long as they take responsibility for their decision. Now, please, bring me my clothes.'

'I must get the sister.'

'Yes, by all means get the sister but bring my clothes at the same time.'

The young nurse returns and stands anxiously behind the sister who glares at Gerda while making firm motions with her hands, shooing her towards the bed. 'Return to your bed immediately, Frau Klein.'

'I am leaving immediately, Sister Brandt.'

'You cannot leave. You are unwell.'

'I am perfectly well, Sister Brandt, and I will return now to my home. This is my right.'

'I will not allow you to leave. You must at least return to your bed, Frau Klein, until I am able to consult with the doctors.'

'I will not. Now, please, will you bring me my clothes or shall I go out into the streets barefooted and in my nightwear? I cannot imagine that would work well for the reputation of this hospital, Sister, so let us be sensible about this.'

She knows that they can restrain her, she knows that patients' rights can be effortlessly swept aside if it is deemed necessary; she herself has been taught with other nurses the methods of overpowering an unruly patient. What she is bargaining on is that this sister will not want the irritation of such an incident: there will be forms to fill in, questions to be answered, the routine and order of her ward will be upset. Sister Brandt stands close, her frown and stance intimidating, her eyes locked on Gerda's. I will not back down. I will not back down. She waits and then lowers her eyes, heaves an audible sigh and stands up. 'Very well, if you deny me my clothing I will go without. But I must warn you, Sister Brandt, this will not look good for you.'

Again she meets the sister's glare and for some time they stare at each other. Do not let her see I am afraid, do not let her see. Then Sister Brandt drops her gaze and turns to the nurse. 'Get her clothes,' she snaps.

Gerda waits — will someone of a higher authority appear and prevent this from happening, will she again be ordered to her bed? But at last the nurse reappears with her small suitcase. She dresses quickly — underclothes, the blue dress, sandals — and takes the suitcase. Along the corridor, into the lift, along another corridor; she must keep going. And outside, beyond these hospital doors, which she pushes open, here it is, the world. She hurries down the steps, across the grounds that edge the buildings. She crosses the street, more fearful of being followed than of the cars and bikes which rush towards her.

Across the street to the tram stop where she has waited so many times in her life. The tram stop where she had met Hanna. She fumbles around in her purse for coins as the tram surges in and stops beside her. She stumbles slightly as she climbs up the steps and the older man standing behind her catches her arm. 'Are you all right, dear lady?'

Her eyes fill with tears at the concern in his voice, the old-fashioned courtesy of his address. 'Thank you. I am all right,' she whispers. As the tram lurches forward, she sits beside a window and for a moment, rests her head against the glass, and closes her eyes. She breathes inwards; she has been so afraid that until now she has not allowed herself the luxury of taking it all in. The air of the city is so different from the stuffiness and the reek of cooking smells mixed with antiseptic mixed with cleaning fluid she has become accustomed to. Oh, the freshness of this air, jumbled up as it is with coal and petrol and, yes, she can decipher among these smells the chestnut flowers. As the tram pulls in to another stop, she breathes again, hard inwards, this sharp, clear scent of early morning. She drinks in the sight of people coming out from the apartment buildings on their way to work, filling the streets, filling the trams. There they are, the schoolchildren, chattering and laughing together, the mothers holding the hands of the children on their way to crèche. She is dizzy with the sounds of the tram moving, all of these people and their talk, the breathing in of the air; all of this fills her senses to an almost unbearable level of love and loss.

For she has lost not only her baby but her country. How can she stay here now, knowing what she knows? How can they live with the fear that at any time any one of them may be taken? She watches as they pass the places she has loved, the graceful buildings, the streets, the parks, the trees.

Her own stop is coming up and she stands, makes her way to the door and steps down onto the footpath. She crosses the road and walks along the narrow street into the next. Across this street is their apartment. She looks up into the windows. Who is watching? Who has seen her? Who is signalling to another using the signals she and Horst have heard about and laughed over?

Subject coming; touch nose with hand or handkerchief. Subject moving on; stroke hair with hand. Subject standing still; lay one hand against back.

Observing Agent wishes to terminate observation because cover threatened; bend and retie shoelaces.

She knows from the talk that they have crew cuts; that they wear old men's clothes, never jeans or sneakers; that they take photographs with small, disguised cameras; that they usually drive a Moskwitch, a car inaccessible to most people in the GDR. She knows they wait, parked in these cars, outside the homes which are under surveillance. She knows she cannot run away from them, that they will always be there.

Perhaps they have already decided her fate; she will talk to others, she will ask questions, make a fuss. They do not have to have reasons; at any time, they may simply pick her up. She straightens her shoulders, crosses the street, opens the door of the building, climbs the stairs and inserts the key into the door of their apartment.

Her baby has gone. She has one child left. She will keep her.

9

Gerda walks from room to room. She and Horst had set up the crib that had been her own and then Ilse's in their bedroom for the baby before they had left for the hospital and she sees that it has been removed from the place close to their bed. Horst and Ilse have left the apartment tidy and clean but there are not the touches of care which is the way of a woman. In a while, she will take care of these particulars, but for now she breathes in the smells of this place which has been her home: the cooking of meals, the drinking of coffee, the soap on the pedestal basin in the bathroom. She pushes open the windows. The tree below her is filled with blossom. Later she will go outside with her kitchen scissors and cut some for the empty vase on the table.

She sits on the sofa, draws up her feet, stretches out her body and rests her head on the red cushion she stitched so long ago before . . . Before. She feels the morning sun on her face and closes her eyes. Yes, there are matters she must later attend to but for now she is here alone. At the end of the day Horst and Ilse will also be here and then she must be strong, must be firm and uncompromising, must prod and shove them as harshly and brutally as a lioness with cubs who do not understand the danger of unseen, circling eagles.

Perhaps this is the last time she will lie here in this way breathing in the smells of this home she and Horst have together made, mingling with the faint honey-smell of blossom and spring air. All of their possessions are here, all that she or Horst have been given or have made with their hands or saved for and bought; here they are, all these things which now surround her. Such love in creating this small home. Such trust and hope.

The last time she will lie here in this way, her face and body warmed by morning sun, her eyes closed. She remembers the first time she and Horst made love in the apartment. It was before they were married and they had only just collected the keys. They came up the stairs together, almost running, so excited and so young. They unlocked the door. 'This will be our home. Gerda, we have a home,' Horst said. There was almost fear in his voice at the responsibility ahead of him. A wife. A home. But Gerda took his hand and led him through the rooms and soon he was smiling again.

The room that would be their bedroom was not large but there was ample room for the bed they had ordered and a wardrobe could stand in the corner and there under the window they would place the cabinet Gerda would bring from her home. Gerda stood at the empty space where their bed would lie. 'Horst,' she whispered.

He turned from the window and looked at her. She watched his eyes as she unbuttoned her blouse and unzipped her skirt. She took the hem of her slip in her hands and lifted it over her head. She unhooked her bra and slipped her knickers down over her hips and stepped out of them.

Up until then their love-making had been a furtive and hurried thing, they had not seen each other naked, but now he came to her and slowly and carefully touched her body as she undid and tugged off his shirt then his pants.

He lifted her. She was against the wall, her legs around his waist as he thrust inside her and she was crying out in a way that had never before been possible. He lowered her to the floor, his head was between her legs as his tongue found her.

She was almost embarrassed but then her body took over from her mind and she was rigid, utterly still and then that trembling rush of sweetness, of the sense that all she was was sensation and pleasure. It was the first time that had happened for her, here in their home. Later came the adult responsibilities of the placement of furniture and kitchen equipment but that first time all there had been was themselves.

She thinks of the joy of that time. For now, she will think only of joy. There have been many celebrations in this place; good food, wine, the laughter of friends and family. This is where she and Horst brought Ilse shortly after her birth, both fussing that she was wrapped well enough, that she had had enough milk. She remembers them tiptoeing around Ilse's crib, both she and Horst surreptitiously touching her cheek, checking that their child was still breathing. She remembers the worry they experienced when she had a fever or a cough.

She opens her eyes and gets up slowly from the sofa. She walks around the room examining the walls closely with her eyes and fingers. She takes a chair from the kitchen and climbs up on it. There, at the edge of the ceiling, a tiny drilled hole. She takes the chair into the bedroom and, yes, there is another one. There will be a mechanism, also, in the phone.

It is late morning now and she busies herself, dusting the furniture, fluffing up the duvets and pillows on the bed, the cushions on the chairs and sofa. She cleans the bathtub and the pedestal hand-basin. Finally she places her favourite red and green checked cloth on the table, washes and dries the large glass vase, and goes outside. There is a car parked along the road from the apartment, a white car. She cuts slim branches of blossom from the tree beside the entrance to the apartment and goes back inside.

She slices potatoes, onions and carrots and the meat she finds inside the refrigerator, rolls the meat in a little flour seasoned with salt and pepper and paprika, tips it all inside her cast-iron casserole pot, adds liquid and makes dumplings which she arranges across the top. She puts the lid on and places it on a low heat on the stove-top.

She is tired. So tired. Still, there are words which this day must be said and processes put in motion. She sits again on the sofa and allows herself to doze until she hears the key turning in the lock. She looks up at Horst as he comes into the room and he crosses it swiftly, his face beaming and incredulous. 'Gerda; you are home. How —?'

He kneels beside her, taking her hands in his. 'Why wasn't I told you were coming home? I would have come for you.'

'The ward sister agreed that I was well enough to return home on my own.'

'But are you well? You look so pale.'

'I am well,' she says firmly. 'I have had good care and now I am well.'

He holds tightly to her hands, keeps his eyes fixed on her. 'Now that you are home, I will take good care of you. I want you to take time off work until you are completely recovered.'

'I am completely recovered,' she says. 'I intend returning immediately to work.'

His eyes are puzzled as he looks at her. 'But you have only just lost the baby.'

She keeps her voice flat and calm though inside she feels her heart splintering. 'What has happened has happened to many women before me. The best way of dealing with such an experience is to return to normal life.'

'If this is what you want we will get back to the way things were.' His voice is hesitant. 'Gerda, we are still young. Perhaps in the future we —.'

'There will be no more children.' She hears her voice hard and resolute. 'The doctors told me that after what happened they were forced to perform a hysterectomy.'

'But I was not told. Nobody contacted me or asked for my permission.'

'I had good care,' she says sharply. 'The doctors did what they had to do and, now, Horst, I would like some fresh air. Fresh air will be good for my health following the weeks in hospital. I would like to walk with you in the park.'

He follows her. They shut the door behind them and walk down the stairs and out through the main door. Gerda moves as quickly as she is able, glancing around her as she walks. Across the road, through the gates of the park, across the grass, passing the gardens with the spring flowers starting to bloom, across the flat grassy area, climbing up the hilly bank to the copse of trees. She cannot see anyone close by and here among the hanging branches she hopes they will not be seen.

'Horst,' she says, fiercely. 'You must listen to me now. Our apartment is bugged. There are listening devices. I have not imagined all of this. I am not unstable as they tried to tell you. We cannot stay here. It is not safe for us.'

He stares at her, begins to slowly shake his head. 'We cannot leave. This is our home.'

'It is no longer our home. We must make somewhere else our home. First we will get Ilse out and then ourselves.'

'You are saying such things because this has been a terrible ordeal for you,' he says. 'But this is our country. Our family and our friends are here. We cannot give up everything we have.'

'Do you not see that by taking our child they are telling us that we have no power, that they can take anything and everything from us? For now, they are watching and listening to see what we know and who we see. Next, they will ask that we become informers and when we say that we will not, our jobs will go and our apartment and, after that, it will be Ilse.'

'Do you want us to abandon our country? Things will get better, in time they must get better.'

'And so we wait for this time when things get better and in this time we lose our daughter?' She moves closer to him, grips his arms, gazes squarely up into his face. 'If you will not come, I will take Ilse and we will go alone.'

'I will not let you go. Gerda, I promise you —.'

'I have listened to your promises,' she says. 'But it is you who has brought this trouble on us. It is you who has lost us our child. Now you must do what I ask.'

She watches as his eyes absorb what she has said. Watches as he stares back at her, stricken by the hurt and shock of her words. She watches the hopelessness and misery in his eyes as he says it. 'I have failed my family and I am sorry for it. Yes, we will go.'

She cannot take him in her arms and tell him she is sorry and that she did not mean these words. It is done now. What needed to be done, she has accomplished.

10

He's moving towards Serena. She stands up, clutching Kai tightly against her, wailing, 'Lynnie, don't let him! Don't let him take us!'

But he shoves Lynnie out of the way, shoves hard and she staggers backwards, she falls. He lunges across the room, his face dark with blood and his eyes gleaming under the light.

Serena snatches up the bottle of methylated spirits from the table where Kai's equipment is carefully laid out, throws it up into his face, into his eyes and as he howls with the pain of it and raises his hands, she pushes past him, the weight of Kai against her, his body heavy, his head jiggling against her shoulder, running as hard as she can, the sound of his crying in her ears, in her head. Kai never cries. Kai never cries.

And now Kai's crying is screaming. Her Kai is screaming in fear and she feels his tears wet against her face as she runs. The door slamming behind her. Runs. The street is dark. Runs. Along the street. Nearly there. Nearly at the bridge. Running for their lives. Across the bridge and —.

And slow down. She has to slow down, to keep her balance. If I fall I'll hurt Kai. She sits at the top of the track, holds him tightly, slithers down on her bum. 'Ssh, ssh, it's okay, Kai. Ssh, ssh now.' If she gets across the river. If she can make it across the river they might have a chance. The scrub and rosehips tear at her arms and at her legs as she moves along the bank listening for the sounds of someone behind her, someone following. 'Ssh ssh, Kai, ssh ssh.' Because he will follow her. She knows that.

So dark she can only just make out the glimmer of water. She's close to where she thinks the water is shallow enough to cross. What if I slip? Will I be strong enough to hang on to him? What if I slip and hit my head?

She can't let him take Kai. She slips him under her T-shirt and ties it tightly around her midriff. Holding him against her, she steps into the water. You can't. I won't let you. Bastard. You bastard.

Gerda is there. She is beside the door. Where is the baby? Where is the baby?

Serena steps into the water. She remembers the rain of the night before and how it surged, like a tropical storm, so unexpectedly from the sky. She remembers Oma running to close the window and the thrum and rumble of thunder. The slash of lightning. Oma running her finger across Kai's cheek. 'This little one's first thunderstorm.'

Perhaps the river will be up. She stands still, testing the feel of it. Is it deeper, is it moving more swiftly? She takes another step, feeling for a safe foothold.

Gerda is there beside the door grasping the door handle. Slippery — is it blood or is it the sweat from her hands?

She is in the room, he has his back to her. He is standing with his back to her and Lynnie is against the closed door, guarding it with her body, saying, 'Fuck off. I won't let you. Leave her alone.'

She slips across the room, silent, cautious. She places her fingers to her lips as Lynnie sees her. And now Lynnie lets out a wail as he raises his hand. 'Don't hurt me! Please! Please don't hurt me!'

Lynnie's hands are covering her face, her body is hunched over and she cries out, 'Please, please, please! I'm sorry, just leave me alone, okay?' He reaches out to shove her out of the way — 'All piss and wind, that's all you are, Lynnie, just piss and wind' — and as he reaches for her she uncoils, plants her legs and punches him hard in the gut.

He staggers slightly. Gerda hears the whumph of the breath going out of him. Now. She braces herself. Now.

A world away. A lifetime away. Twenty-six young nurses.

'In your future career you may come up against patients who will become abusive, sometimes physically aggressive. This technique must never be used lightly but if it is necessary you must be swift and strong. This method could save you from injury — in serious situations, it could save your life. You will watch the demonstration and then we will practise.'

A world away. A lifetime away. Twenty-six young nurses dressed in white and pink tunics watching and listening.

'Up close and strike with your fist into the lower back so that the body will arch. This will give you a better hold. Thrust out your arm, bring it around the throat, so. The crook of your elbow should now be against the trachea. Bring up the other arm so that your elbow is against his opposite shoulder, and using your dominant hand, grasp your opposite upper arm.

'You now have a hard, firm hold. Reach with your other hand, grab the back of his head, forcing it down into your arm. Flex the forearm and the bicep of your dominant arm so that you're squeezing the sides of your opponent's neck and keep your grip. If this is correctly achieved the patient will pass out in less than a minute, allowing the nurse to utilise conventional strategies of restraint. I repeat, this method must never be used lightly and the hold never maintained past the initial point of unconsciousness.'

Twenty-six young nurses dressed in pink and white tunics watching and listening.

'Why does it work? Who can tell me? Yes, that is correct. When you squeeze your arm in this way you are cutting off the flow of blood to the brain by clamping down on the carotid arteries. If this hold is managed correctly, even a small woman may overpower a very large male. But with this technique there can be no hesitation. Speed is essential.'

He's coming. He's after you, he's behind you. Hurry. Hurry. But you have to make sure that you don't fall, you need to reach forward with your foot to test the place in front of you.

Probably near the middle now; the river's deeper, moving more rapidly. Kai's not crying any more though she senses he's still awake. He snuffles a little and she feels the rigidity in his little body.

He knows. He knows and he's frightened

She slips and regains her balance. Not so fast. But he's after you. He's coming.

If this hold is managed correctly, even a small woman may over-power a very large male. But with this technique there can be no hesitation. Speed is essential.

Move. Move. She has only seconds. A world away and a lifetime, yet her body is moving powerfully and intuitively into the sequence, her fist driving into his lower back, her right arm hooking his throat, her left rising, her elbow against his shoulder, she grasps for her opposite arm and she has it and now she is reaching upwards and grabbing the hair on the back of his head. Grip and force downwards. He is bucking, twisting, can she hold him? Lynnie has her own arms clamped around his body trying to stop his arms from flailing out.

The strength of him, the great, brutish strength of this man, this man who smells of meat and sweat, who has used his strength against children. Hate is forcing her onwards, the hard black hate in her belly is forcing her to keep her grip, to tighten, tighten, tighten with her forearm and he is kicking out, how can she hold him any longer, how can she keep this hold, he is bellowing, a strangled bellow of rage.

Tighten. Tighten. Tighten. It takes all her strength to hold him. The patient will pass out in less than a minute, less than a minute, less than a minute and now, now at last he is stilling, stilling, collapsing and sinking, down, slumping down and she is down with him, her arm crooked still around his neck.

'Go', she says to Lynnie. 'Go and get them back.'

'But what about you?' Lynnie's face is grey, her voice ragged with fear.

'Go.'

The baby. Where is the baby?

When you squeeze your arm in this way you are cutting off the flow of blood to the brain by clamping down on the carotid arteries.

When you squeeze your arm in this way you are cutting off the flow of blood to the brain by clamping down on the carotid arteries.

The hold must never be maintained past the initial point of unconsciousness.

She slips. Regains her balance. Slips again. The water is up around her thighs. She can feel the surge of it, the power. It's too deep. She can't keep going. It's too dark to make out the opposite bank. She could step forward and be up to her neck in water. There are deep pools all through the river, she knows that. Kai whimpers and she holds him closer. She feels his mouth searching her skin. It's time for his night feed.

Kai. She's tried to look after him properly. She's tried so hard. She wanted him to feel safe and loved, never wanted him to feel scared. Not ever.

But she couldn't stop it. He's only a little baby, and already he's been frightened; the shouting, the shoving and the hitting. No one's going to believe some story two dirty sluts've come up with about where that little bastard's come from.

They'll take Kai away. She can't stop that but neither can she bear it. Not for herself, not for him. Because who would look after him? Who could love him properly the way a little baby needs? Who could keep him safe from people looking at him and talking to him like he was nothing? That little bastard. Who would be there to tell him it didn't matter when other kids called him names and left him out? Who would keep the eyes and the voices and the hands away?

It's nice here, standing in the water. It was freezing at first, but now her body's got used to it, she feels quite warm. There's nice sounds too; the crackle of scrub as the wind catches it and the river rushing along and the stars are out in little glints and dazzles.

She has done it. She has killed this man. She has gripped his neck until his body has shuddered and his feet have drummed against the floor. She has smelled the stink as his bowels have failed; she has heard the rattle in his throat.

'Up above the world so high, like a diamond in the sky.' She has the book with the song in it. There's a big shiny star at the end with little kids looking up at it out of the window of their bedroom. Miss bought it for Kai. Miss said it's never too early to read to children. She always sings it. She sings to Kai a lot. She knows he likes to hear her sing.

She sings it softly to him now. 'Twinkle, twinkle little star.' He's quiet. Maybe he's given up on the feed and gone to sleep. She settles him higher on her shoulder. She wonders if babies remember things. Like, if they took him away, would Kai remember her? Would he remember Oma and Miss and Lynnie and Anja? Would he remember how warm and happy and safe he was then and how much they all loved him?

The thought comes to her. It's like when she's really tired and feels herself falling into sleep and she's glad to let it take her. Upriver, further up beyond the bridge, she can hear the gush and heave of water. She could step out and follow the river with Kai sleeping in her arms. He wouldn't know anything. Drowning's a nice way to die. She read that somewhere. Somewhere. She sways slightly on her feet.

She is tired. So tired.

She kneels there staring down at him. Yes, it is done, she has done this and she will take the consequences. First she will tell Ilse why she had to do it. She owes her daughter this explanation and then Ilse will phone for the police and ask them to come.

She will tell Ilse of her brother. In all these years she has not spoken of him although she has thought of him every day. She has seen him as a ghost child behind, beside, skittering around her Ilse.

The little one who reaches high for his sister's hand; and there now he is up to her waist and now at her shoulder and here he is, a young man, his head higher than hers.

She will tell how, when the Wall came down, she searched the faces on the television screen looking for a boy who looked as she knew he would look. She will tell how although a mind will analyse and reject, the body will remember and yearn.

She will tell Ilse that in all these years she has held the blackness within her of bitterness and hatred, that she has been woken in the nights by this and by a compulsion to track down and punish the people who did this to them. She will tell how this man is not only the policeman who has used his power for his own purpose, but all of them: those who told, those who lied, those who wrenched the baby from her body, he is all of them.

She is not sorry. This man did not deserve life. She stands and covers his body with a sheet she takes from the washing basket. They should not have to look at him. She sits on the sofa, draws up her feet and stretches out with her head on the cushion and closes her eyes. She is not sorry. She will never be sorry. She will be imprisoned but the girl and her boy will have their chance.

11

Ilse senses trouble, feeling it like the edge of something sharp grinding into her gut, even before she turns into the street. There is a car parked outside the house. Not a police car. It is not a police car. But there is a car and the house is in darkness. She drives in off the street and as she runs, Anja behind her, she sees the front door gaping open, she hears the silence.

She slams the door behind her. Why are the lights turned off? Where is everyone? What is that smell? 'Mutti. Mutti!'

Gerda is on the sofa, her eyes tight shut, as they come into the room and Ilse kneels beside her and takes her hands. 'Mutti? Are you all right? What has happened? Where are Serena and Kai?'

Gerda sits up. 'Lynnie has gone after them. This man —.' She points to the covered body beside the door. 'This man came into the house.'

Anja switches on the light, goes to the body, pulls back the sheet and places her fingers on his neck. She stares back at them, her face pale and frightened.

'Ilse,' Gerda says, 'first I must talk to you and then you will phone for the police.'

Ilse shakes her head. 'I don't understand. What has happened?'

Schlaf, Kindlein, schlaf. Schlaf, Kindlein, schlaf.

Up above the world so high. Up above the world so high.

Oma singing to Kai. Oma. Oma.

'Serena!' Someone is calling for her.

She must go back to Oma.

'Serena! Please. It's okay. Please, Serena. Where are you?'

She must go back to Oma.

There is a shrill on the doorbell and Ilse moves swiftly to her feet, her face alarmed.

'It will be Lynnie,' Gerda says calmly. 'Serena ran off with Kai and I sent her after them.'

And now they are all together in the living room.

'He is dead,' Ilse says. She cannot quite believe the words she is now saying.

'Fucking good riddance,' Lynnie says. She is closest to the body and she stares down at it.

'Dead?' Serena holds Kai sleeping against her shoulder. 'How can he be dead?'

'I have killed him,' Gerda says.

'No, Mutti. You could not have done this,' Ilse says. 'You are not strong enough.'

'Even so, I killed him. He hit Lynnie and he made threats. He was going to take Serena and Kai. I could not allow this to happen.'

'You should've seen her,' Lynnie says. 'She came up behind him and next thing he's on the floor.'

'And so,' Gerda cuts in, 'first I must talk with Ilse and then you must call for the police to come. I have broken the law and I will now pay the penalty.'

'But Tante Gerda,' Anje says, 'it was self-defence.'

'This was not self-defence, Anja. You are very kind but that is not the way it was. The police must come. They will take me away but that is how it must be.'

'You're not going anywhere, Oma.' Serena's voice is raised and fierce. 'We won't let you.'

They huddle around her, holding her, stroking her arms, touching her face. You will not go, no, you will not. And then it comes. Shrill, jangling guitars. From the body. This shoddy, tinny, absurd and terrifying sound coming from the body. Repeating over and over. From the body. It rings off abruptly. Begins again.

'Jesus fucking Christ,' Lynnie breathes, 'Jesus fucking Christ, what do we do now?'

'Turn it off,' Serena says. 'Turn it off!'

'No,' Ilse says, 'If we turn it off they might suspect there is something wrong.'

It stops. Now comes the sound of three sharp beeps.

'I'm going to look at the message,' Lynnie says. She bends down, reaches under the sheet, fumbles in the pockets and takes out a phone. She presses buttons, frowning. 'Voicemail,' she says. 'Okay, we're going to listen, right?'

It is a woman's voice. Sharp, cross-sounding. 'I'm at the barbecue. So where the hell are you?'

'This woman,' Gerda says suddenly. 'I have killed her husband.'

'Forget it,' Lynnie says. 'You've done her a favour. She's better off without that bastard. So what do we do?'

'Answer the message,' Ilse says. 'Send a text. Say that something has happened.'

Lynnie is clicking on the phone. 'I need to check first. See what he sends. Okay, here's one, he uses "n" for "ing" and he cuts out words. I'm saying, "can't make, somethn up".'

'Say he'll be late home,' Serena says.

'Late. Okay, got it.'

'What if she gets worried about what's happening and calls someone?' Serena says.

'Let's hope,' Lynnie says, 'she gets totally pissed at this barbecue and goes home and snores her fucking head off.'

'But what are we to do with him?' Anja says.

'One's thing for sure,' Lynnie says. 'They'll be looking for him in the morning.'

'Can't they tell where someone's been from their phone?' Serena's voice is shrill with fear. 'They might be tracking him right now.'

'I think only the vicinity can be traced,' Anja says.

'All the lights are on next door,' Serena says. 'I saw them when we went past. They'll tell about the car being here and then they'll start looking. We can't —. There's nowhere to hide him. They'll take Oma. And they'll take away Kai.'

269

'Stop it,' Lynnie says sharply. 'Nobody's taking anyone anywhere.' She puts her arms around Serena. 'We'll work it out. It'll be okay.'

Gerda stands. 'It cannot be okay. We cannot stop them. I will phone the police now and put an end to it.'

'Mutti, please. Please sit down. What you did was necessary to protect Serena and Kai and Lynnie,' Ilse says. 'And perhaps the court would see it that way but I will not have you endure all that. We have to be calm and we have to do what is needed. We must, what we must have is time.'

12

It is close to lunchtime when they knock on the door. She has seen the cars, seen the men disappearing up the paths, reconvening and talking out in the street. Now it is their turn. It is a hot day, one of the hottest of this summer, and the men who knock are flushed and sweating. 'Yes?' she says. 'Can I help you?'

It is the large man with the fair hair cut almost to his scalp who speaks, 'I understand that you are —.' He looks at his notes. 'Ilse Klein?'

'Yes.'

He holds out his hand. 'I'm Constable Bob Allan and this is Senior Constable Murray Cunningham. A police officer, Sergeant Withers, is missing and we're making enquiries. We understand he was in the area last night.'

'Ah,' she says. 'Yes. This police officer called at our house.'

'And why was that?' It is still the policeman with the fair hair who asks as the older one with the dark, shrewd eyes watches. Do not hesitate. Simply tell the truth. Anything which is not the truth can be discovered.

'He wished to know whether a schoolgirl, a student in my class, had made contact with us. He had asked already once before when she first was missed.'

He writes in his notebook. 'What did you tell him?'

'I said I had not seen this girl.'

'Your neighbours told us there was a car outside your house for some time.'

'Yes?'

'It was Sergeant Withers' car?'

She frowns slightly. 'It may have been. I did not see a police car.'

271

'How long was he here for?'

She makes a pretence of thinking. 'I am not sure. I was in Wanaka with my cousin and when we returned he was already here speaking with my mother.'

'Inside your house, you mean?'

'Of course, yes, and when I arrived he remained to ask his questions.'

'Questions?' the other man, Murray Cunningham asks, his eyes inquisitive, searching.

'Questions about this girl,' Ilse says, shrugging. 'If I had heard anything about her.'

'You said he had already been here. Why did he come back?'

'He said he was passing by the house.' She shrugs again. 'And that this was a routine visit.'

'Do you mind if we take a look round?'

'I do not mind.'

She opens the door into the hallway and stands behind them as they peer into first Ilse's bedroom and then Gerda's. The door to Serena's room is closed.

'What's in this one?'

'I will open it for you,' Ilse says.

She turns the doorknob. The curtains are drawn and the room is silent and dark. They step inside. The dark man's eyes are moving around the corners, taking in the crib, the sleeping baby. 'Whose kid?'

'Please.' Ilse raises her finger to her lips. 'My cousin's child. He is sleeping at last.'

Gerda and Anja are in the living room. Both have sandwiches on plates and mugs of coffee on the coffee table in front of them. Gerda looks up from the newspaper she is holding.

'As you can see,' Ilse says, 'this is my mother Gerda Klein and my cousin, Anja. Have you now seen enough?'

'We'd like to ask a few more questions.'

Gerda stands. 'Sit down,' she says. 'Please, sit down. Would you like coffee?'

'No. No, thanks, we're fine.' Again it is Bob Allan who speaks. He looks awkward, out of place as he perches his bulk at the edge of the sofa. 'Thing is.' He clears his throat. 'Thing is we've had reports there were noises coming from this house last night.'

'Noises?' Ilse looks puzzled. 'What are these noises?'

'Well. The reports say —.' He looks again at his notes. 'Banging and shouting.'

'Banging and shouting?' Ilse smiles. 'It was warm last night. The windows were open, the television was on.'

'This is my fault,' Gerda says. 'Ilse tells me it is too loud but my hearing . . . I hope I have not caused nuisance to anyone.'

Murray Cunningham, this time. He, Ilse thinks, is the one to watch. He leans forward, his eyes narrowed. 'There's been a report of someone coming out of the house and running up the road carrying something.'

'Carrying something?' Ilse says, frowning. 'What is this something?'

'A bundle.'

Ilse laughs. 'I thought you were next telling me we are running up the street carrying this, this policeman.'

Bob Allan grins a little. 'Only a small bundle.'

'Ah, yes,' Gerda says. 'This was Anja. The baby was disturbed so she walked with him.'

'We were told she was running.' Murray Cunningham turns to Anja, his voice severe. 'Is this right? You took the baby up the street for a walk in the dark?'

Anja looks at Ilse.

'Did you see the officer who was here last night?' He is eyeballing her and scowling. Anja puts her hands out palms upwards, shakes her head.

'She has only a little English,' Gerda says. 'It was not so dark. She thought the motion and the cooler air may soothe the child. He was hot after travelling in the car.'

'Uh,' the notes again, 'the reports also say there were noises of cars coming and going.'

'Cars coming and going?' Ilse says incredulously. 'This police officer's car arrived and left. We arrived home in my car. This is not so much coming and going.'

Bob Allan raises his eyes from his notes and looks at the three women. 'But we have reports of noise and cars and someone running from the house and now we seem to also have a missing police officer. You can understand our concern.'

'It is these neighbours who tell you these stories?' Ilse points in the direction of the Taylors' house.

'We cannot divulge that information.'

'Even so,' Ilse says, 'we understand each other. Please. My mother and I live here together and now we have Anja visiting with us. We are quiet and we do not make trouble for anyone and yet, always these neighbours are watching us. These people have said things to me and to my mother. Upsetting things about our nationality. This Mr Taylor, he has told my mother that his father fought the Germans in the war and they do not want our kind here. Each time, if he is in the garden, when my mother and I walk into the drive he spits upon the ground.'

The fair police officer looks embarrassed. 'Would you like me to have a word with him, Miss?'

Gerda raises her hands. 'No, no. We do not want bad feelings.'

'My family left East Germany because of the hardships there,' Ilse says. 'My mother finds any trouble upsetting.'

There is a blare from a phone. Murray Cunningham takes it from his pocket and moves to the back of the room as he raises it to his ear and listens. He puts it back into his pocket and raises his eyebrows at Bob Allan who gets up. 'Well, that's about it,' he says. 'Thanks for your time. We can take a look around the section on the way out.'

They stand and Ilse takes them through the kitchen to the back door. They walk through the garden at the back of the house. 'Good lot of vegetables,' Bob Allan says.

'My father started this, and we like to keep it up.'

'That was Horst Klein, wasn't it?' Bob says. 'My Dad worked with him. He was a good man.'

'A very good man,' Ilse says. She opens the garden gate and leads them out into the driveway.

'This yours?' Murray Cunningham is beside the car. He touches the cover which tightly swaddles it.

'This is my car. Yes.'

'You obviously like to keep it clean?' Bob Allan says.

'The birds and the rust,' she says. 'I try to keep my car untarnished.'

'Untarnished, eh?' He's grinning and she smiles back.

'These spinster schoolteachers,' she says. 'So picky about such things.'

They're beside the gate. They shake her hand.

13

First, they remove the covering from the car and then Ilse gets into the driver's seat, releases the handbrake and slips backwards down the drive and glides down the sloping street into the main road. She switches on the lights and the engine and drives slowly, cautiously. What they have banked on is that the streets will be empty at this time but she knows that this is the most dangerous part: if they are seen they will be done for.

You must do everything correctly, you cannot be noticed, you must not be pulled over. The back streets, avoid the main road, almost there, almost out of town. She relaxes as she passes over the bridge, slows to turn from the highway onto Earnscleugh Road, switches on the indicator lights and cries out as the windscreen wipers suddenly and crazily begin to slide and whirr across the glass in front of her. It's the opposite side, oh God the opposite side. As she turns them off, reaches for the switch on the other side and begins her turn, a truck bearing a huge, swinging trailer of logs careers down from the top of the hill, lights beaming and the horn blaring. She brakes hard, checks the road and turns. She feels the sweat under her arms and on her forehead.

'Ilse?' Anja says, 'Are you all right?'

'It will be fine.'

It will be fine. Alles wird gut. It will be fine. Alles wird gut.

She stops further up the road and Anja unfastens her safety belt.

'You've got the keys?'

'I have the keys and I can drive this car. I will turn off the lights once I am in the street. I know what I must do.' Anja quickly kisses her cheek. 'Keine Sorge, meine Liebe.'

'Miss, I could do that part. I can drive.'

'You do not have your licence, Serena, and if you were stopped —. We cannot take that risk.'

'I can drive.'

They all look at Anja. 'I have my international licence.'

'But the driving here is on the left-hand side, Anja. I will do it.'

She watches as Anja slips behind the trees, listens as the engine groans a little. She cannot stay here but she drives slowly until she sees in the rear-view mirror as the lights move slowly onto the road, head in the opposite direction.

'Keine Sorge, meine Liebe.' Do not worry, my love.

She follows the road as it begins to rise and twist. And now there are two cars following. Her body is rigid with tension, her breathing is shallow and she is sweating so much that her back and hands are wet.

Keep driving, steadily and smoothly, you must drive in a normal way as if you have merely been out late and are now returning home. You must drive slowly but not so slowly as to draw attention to yourself.

'Miss, whatever you do don't drive too slowly. Darryl says it's a dead giveaway. If the cops see anyone driving slowly at night they know they're driving pissed.'

Sixty-five, seventy, is this a sensible speed to travel on a winding road in the night, or is this too slow? She does not know but she continues on. It is darker now that she has passed into the country, into Earnscleugh itself, which is unlit other than for the few glimmering lights from the houses on the orchards she is passing. She switches the lights to full beam, dips them as a car approaches on the other side. Do everything correctly, everything must be done correctly.

She glances up at the car following behind her. It is a large car and it is up close behind, the full power of its lights flooding the inside of her car and she is shaking so much she can hardly keep her hands steady on the steering wheel.

Perhaps they did not believe her story yesterday. Perhaps their nice talk of gardens and the care of cars and the goodness of her father was only meant to reassure her while all the time they were watching, waiting.

Stop this now. Stop it.

Alles wird gut. Keine Sorge, meine Liebe. It will be fine. Do not worry, my love. It will be fine. Do not worry.

Sweat trickles down her face, slips down her spine, slimy on her hands, her hands are so slippery. It will be fine. Do not worry, my love. It will be fine. Do not worry. The words. Around and around and around. And now this powerful car races forward, almost touching, and a horn blasts, lights beaming in as it careers past, stones pinging up from the road. She hears the booma-booma-booma of the stereo, sees the boys crowded together. One of them throws a can from the window and she swerves to avoid it, nearly veers off the road.

But the car has gone, thundering off into the distance and down a side road. She is shaking. And now the other car approaches, flicks its lights.

'It'll need three of us.'

'But Anja will be picking up Ilse's car.'

'Let me come, Miss.'

'Yeah, Serena should go with us.'

'We can't take the risk. What if someone recognised her?'

'She can come with me. Anyone asks, I'll say she just turned up. Anyway, who's going to see her in the dark?'

The car flicks its lights. She looks up into the mirror, sees their faces. Serena waves her hand.

They're at the turn-off.

'No one goes down that road. Not at night so someone may notice the lights.'

'Who would notice? Only people who'd see you would be heading up the motorway. Only trucks at that time of night.'

'Even so. Two cars driving closely together could look suspicious.'

'Only the front car needs lights and keep them low. Or you could just use the parking lights.'

Ilse wants to speed up, to recklessly speed up and have it all over with but she must move at a snail's pace. The road narrows and she turns down onto the track leading down towards the lake, the car jolting over stones and undergrowth. She hears the car behind her start to rev. The track is only a fine layer of gravel over earth, what if we got stuck here, how would we manage if we got stuck? But it jerks slowly forwards and they're moving again. The further they go, the safer it will be.

She's there now and parks at the edge of a bank of rocks rising above the lake. Serena and Lynnie walk towards her. 'We parked back a bit,' Lynnie says. 'Easier to turn around after.'

'Everything's okay,' Serena says. 'We didn't see anyone.'

'Just those dicks on the road back there,' Lynnie says.

'So.'

They all turn to look at the car. 'What if we just pushed it in,' Serena says. 'No one's going to find it.'

'We've already talked about this,' Ilse says. 'We have made an agreement. We cannot change our plans.'

'It's —.'

'I know,' Ilse says. 'I know.'

'If we are to move this man we must do it immediately.'

'I cannot allow you to take these risks.'

'Sit down, Mutti. You're not going anywhere. We're all in this together.'

'She's right. We have to move him and we have to move the car. We have to hide them both. Now. Tonight.'

'He must be moved before the onset of rigor mortis. If he is to be moved again, it will be forty-eight hours before this can happen.'

'He's big. It'll need three of us.'

Ilse moves forward, inserts the key and opens the boot.

14

He'd been in there three days and two nights in temperatures getting up near the thirties. They hadn't been able to do anything about that but now they had to deal with it.

The stench which rose up and enveloped them, sealing off the air, was like nothing she could have imagined; it was like nothing else in this world, this smell so rank yet tinged with an unbearable sweetness, as if a joint of rotting meat had been sprinkled with cheap perfume. This she will never forget. Nor the sight of the crooked body, bent and twisted to fit inside the boot of the car with the maggots crawling across the green-tinted bloated flesh.

They reeled back from the car. Serena lurched away into the dark and they heard the splatter of her vomit, the sounds of her retching. She came back to them. 'I can't do it,' she said. 'I can't.'

Ilse brushed Serena's hair back from her face, laid her hand against her cheek. 'This has to be done and we need your help, so let us get this over with, hey?'

She handed them the rubber gloves she had brought with her and snapped on her own.

'Okay, let's go. You take the legs, See, and we'll take the top half. Now. Hold and lift. Lift and —. Right. Put him down. We have to straighten him out. Open the car door, Serena. We're going to lift him again. I'll take his shoulders. You got him? You got him. Nearly there. We're nearly there. Just hold on.'

They worked together, breathing in brief bursts through their mouths — the slippery, rubbery flesh, the feel of it sliding beneath your hands hard to get a grip the stink, the maggots clinging — shoving, heaving until he was in through the car door and onto the seat. They stepped back, panting, surveying the car. He was propped behind the steering wheel.

'We should open the boot,' Lynnie said. 'That way it'll sink faster.'

'If the car is discovered with the boot open it could look suspicious,' Ilse said. 'We'll open the front windows. That should be enough.'

'And the seatbelt. He should be wearing the seatbelt,' Serena said.

'I'll do it.' Ilse took a deep, shuddering breath, opened the door, switched on the engine and pushed the lever that wound the windows down. She took the clasp of the seatbelt in her hand and reached across. Across the white, bulging eyes, the swelling, protruding tongue, the stink, the stink.

She clipped the catch on the seatbelt, released the handbrake and shut the door. It was done. She stood back, anxiously scanning the car. Was there anything they had missed? Anything they could have forgotten?

'But they will know we have moved him.'

'Not after he has been in the water.'

That is what they must hope for. Days, hopefully weeks, in the water. Perhaps the car would never be discovered.

'Okay?' She turned to Serena and Lynnie. They lined up against the back of the car, their hands on the boot.

'Go,' Lynnie said. They pushed with all their strength and the car shifted forwards, slowly at first and then gathering speed as it began to move downhill, faster, faster, until in the end they were running as it is catapulted downwards towards the bank above the lake.

'Let it go,' said Lynnie, 'or we'll be over as well.'

They stood breathing hard as it plummeted down the bank, the sound of it scraping, grinding over the stones and undergrowth. Will it go in? Will it make it into the water?

'Come on. Come on, you fucker,' Lynnie breathed.

The sound was colossal as it smacked into the water. And hung there, floating. Serena gave a small cry and moved towards the bank.

Ilse gripped her wrist. 'Wait. It'll be all right. I'm sure —.'

They watched as it hovered, suspended on the surface of the water.

They hadn't thought, not for a moment had they thought about the possibility that it might not sink. 'If we get it in somewhere deep enough, chances are it'll get wedged way down in the silt.'

'Jeez,' Lynnie said. 'Oh, jeez, oh fuck, oh —.'

But now, at last it was sinking, slowly sinking, sending out circles of ripples that languidly spread and drifted across the lake.

'Let's get back.'

Lynnie left them at the end of the street. She got out of the car and hugged them hard. Tomorrow she would drive to Dunedin leaving the rental car at the airport before she flew back. 'I'll see you soon,' she whispered to Serena.

Ilse's car was back in the drive swaddled within the car cover. Triple layer car cover, fabric provides maximum water-repellence and resistance.

The words turned around and around in her head, blocking out the images, the fear, the stink, the exhaustion.

Maximum water-repellence and resistance.

Maximum water-repellence and resistance.

Mutti and Anja were waiting in the living room. They both stood up. Ilse saw their faces trying to read her own and Serena's. She tried to smile. 'We did it, it is fine. We need to shower and to sleep.'

Serena began to cry. Gerda enfolded her in her arms. 'Hush now. It is over.'

15

Even now, almost a whole year later, Ilse is sometimes woken by the cry she has uttered in her sleep. She wakes with her body again slippery with sweat and that rank stink is there in her nostrils and in her mouth.

The stink. The bulging eyes. The stink.

That night she stripped off all her clothes, walked naked out into the night and dropped them into the garden incinerator. She took her wrap from the bedroom.

The shudder of the bridge as she crossed it. The familiar feel of the planks of wood beneath her bare feet. The cold of the river as she plunged in, moving into the deepest water she could find, scrubbing with her hands at her hair and her body; she kept her eyes wide open, opened up her mouth letting the water fill her mouth.

The stink and the eyes.

The stink.

'Our son. Your brother, Ilse. He was taken from us. There was no proof but I know this. I knew it then and I know it now. Our son. Your brother.

'When I held my hands to that man's throat, Ilse, it was to protect them. It was the only way I could keep him from hurting them.'

'But then.'

The eyes, the slippery rubbery flesh. The flies. The stink.

'But then. I could have removed my hands from his throat. I knew he was unconscious. I knew he was powerless. I wanted him dead. With all my body and my soul I hated that man and I wanted him dead.'

'I wanted him dead.'

Now it is a year in the past, that summer of Serena and Kai and

Lynnie and Anja. What to make of it all? I wanted him dead. When she thinks of her mother's words, this woman so sweet and kind and loving, yet capable also of hatred and, yes, murder, she must think also of the camps and the monsters, of the soldiers who raped and murdered and destroyed. What are we capable of? What hope can there be for us?

And yet she cannot put aside the many acts of generosity and love. The woman who grips the man's throat, who holds on through the throes of his dying, is the woman whose face is radiant with love as she looks down at the child she holds in her arms.

This city is new for Ilse. New and old as well. She has found the building in which the Kleins once lived and stood below staring up into the top floor. Nobody lives in this apartment block any more, although she has been told that there are plans to refurbish the workers' residences once built by the Soviets. She has been astounded by the opulence of the refurbished railway station, the Leipzig Hauptbahnhof, and by transformed buildings. She is no longer recognised as belonging. Yesterday a woman complimented her on her German: 'Where are you from? You barely have an accent.'

Last year she swam in a New Zealand river but this year she walks along icy streets in her boots wearing a hat and gloves and a down-filled coat. On the other side of the world Mutti and Serena and Kai will be waking in the small apartment in Wellington Mutti has purchased with proceeds from the house. Their news flows regularly through email: 'We are to have a picnic for Christmas. Lynnie and Sean will join us at the beach. I have a ride-on tractor for Kai for his Christmas present, almost he is walking now.'

There are photographs. The apartment. Lyall Bay, where they like to walk. Serena and Lynnie. Serena holding Kai laughing in her arms.

'Serena has completed her exams. She has worked so hard, Ilse, she will do well. I am learning to drive now. Next year I also will be a student. I have made enquiries. I can return to nursing if I complete a two-year course. I said, surely I am too old for this. The woman at the reception, she said poof, you are only fifty-seven, plenty of time for you.'

Gerda also smiles out into the camera. 'Serena will in time make her own life with Kai. I must make my own life as well. Ilse, I am no longer afraid.'

On the other side of the world Kai and Serena and Gerda will be waking, but here the candles glimmer. Children are tucked against their parents, their eyes bright and watchful. Ilse looks up at the windows as snow begins to drift against the glass.

She has walked past Bach's statue outside the church where he stands on the pedestal, lofty and stern and eternal, grasping his sheaf of music. The voices of the choir soar upwards filling the shadows of this great, dark place with aching sweetness.

'Jauchzet, frohlocket, auf, preiset die Tage.'

'Rejoice, rejoice to praise that day.'

Such hope and promise in the celebration of the birth of the Christ child yet the dark rolling sounds of the organ warn of the anguish that inevitably must come. Anja turns her face towards her and they both smile as they see the tears in each other's eyes.

Soon they will go out into the snow. They will walk, holding hands, across the cobbles through the main square, passing windows brightly lit for the festivities ahead.

They will walk, holding hands, across the cobbles. There will be the silence created by the snow now muffling the streets, the snow that dives and soars in pale gusts and flurries, snowflakes flaring in the light, silvering the dark. They will go out into the snow and the bells of the clock tower will peal for the joy and the sadness which lie behind and beyond.

Acknowledgments

The following books, stories and films have been helpful in the writing of *Swimming in the Dark*:

Hans Christian Andersen, 'The Snow Queen' from *Ten Tales*, Horace Elisha Scudder, USA.

V. R. Berghahn, *Modern Germany: Society, Economy and Politics in the Twentieth Century*, Cambridge University Press.

Harald Fritzcsh, *Escape from Leipzig*, University of Hamburg, Germany.

Anna Funder, *Stasiland*, Granta Books, London.

Jana Hensell, *After the Wall*, Rowohlt Verlag, Hamburg, Germany.

Thomas A. Kohut, *A German Generation*, University of Yale Press, USA.

Peter Schneider, *The Wall Jumper*, The University of Chicago Press, USA.

Christa Woolf, *Patterns of Childhood*, Aufbau-Verlag, Germany.

The Lives of Others (2006), directed by Florian Donnersmarck.

Barbara (2012), directed by Christian Petz.

The inspiration for *Swimming in the Dark* came from my attendance at the Leipzig Book Fair in 2012 and I would like to express my gratitude for this opportunity to the Publishers Association of New Zealand.

Thanks to Kevin Chapman for his enthusiasm for this novel from the initial drafts and congratulations to him and also to the team at Upstart for the creation of a new publishing business — it's very exciting to be a part of that. I'm grateful to have again had

Stephen Stratford as my editor; his comments and suggestions were, as always, invaluable.

Thanks to Jim for his calm endorsement of my compulsion to write and for sharing the wonders of Leipzig with me, and thanks, also, to my family and friends for their continued encouragement, support and interest in my writing.

And, finally, many, many thanks to Carmen Ramirez, my German friend, who so generously gave her time to my novel. Her reading of the manuscript was meticulous as was the further research she undertook, and the suggestions she made and insights she offered have given this book an authenticity which would not have happened without her help.

About the Author

Paddy Richardson is the author of six novels and two short story collections. Her fiction has been a finalist for the Ngaio Marsh Award for Best Crime Novel and short-listed for the BNZ Katherine Mansfield Awards. She has been the recipient of the University of Otago Burns Fellowship, the Beatson Fellowship, and the James Wallace Arts Trust Residency Award. Four of her novels have been translated and published in Germany. Paddy has lectured and tutored English Literature at university level and taught on many creative writing courses. She lives on the Otago Peninsula in New Zealand.